Edgar Fawcett

**Purple and Fine Linen**

A Novel

Edgar Fawcett

**Purple and Fine Linen**
*A Novel*

ISBN/EAN: 9783337002268

Printed in Europe, USA, Canada, Australia, Japan

Cover: Foto ©Andreas Hilbeck / pixelio.de

More available books at **www.hansebooks.com**

# FINE LINEN.

## A NOVEL.

BY

## EDGAR FAWCETT.

*Faithfully Yours,*
*Edgar Fawcett.*

*London —*
*Aug. — 1900.*

AND

# FINE LINEN.

## A NOVEL.

BY

## EDGAR FAWCETT.

Quiconque aima jamais porte une cicatrice ;
Chacun l'a dans le sein, toujours prête à s'ouvrir ;
Chacun la garde en soi, cher et secret supplice,
Et mieux il est frappé, moins il en veut guérir.

ALFRED DE MUSSET.

NEW YORK:

G. W. Carleton & Co., Publishers.

LONDON: S. LOW, SON & CO.

M.DCCC.LXXIII.

Stereotyped at the
WOMEN'S PRINTING HOUSE,
56, 58 and 60 Park Street,
New York.

# PURPLE AND FINE LINEN.

## CHAPTER I.

**S**EPT. 21.—I wonder why mamma always crowds Pineside with people the first week in October. I think that she does so partly because we are pretty sure to have divine days at that period, and partly because if ever people are obtainable as country-visitors it is just then,—at least the sort which mamma likes to have about her.

Now that October is on the verge of appearing again, it seems very natural that certain preparations should be made among the "many-corridored complexities" of Pineside; preparations which I have observed speechlessly. For that matter, I usually observe all the features of mamma's domestic management with silence enough to quite charm a sphynx. It is very possible that if I should discover combustible indications among halls and pantries, some morning, of an intent on mamma's part to burn the house down, my objections to such a procedure would merely take the placid form of rushing for personal valuables. Mrs. Jeffreys is a despot in her own household; and I, the despot's only child, am certainly not her grand vizier.   Indeed, if I hold any portfolio at all in our little principality, it must be represented by such a sinecure that I am only required to mind my own affairs in fulfilling the duties of office.

Throughout the week previous to our siege of autumn visitors, I hope to pass a very agreeable time ; and even if there should be nobody among the arrivals next week whom it isn't the dual burden of a bore and a falsehood for one to say that one is glad to see, I shall still have my little box of memorial ointment, perhaps, in the shape of last week's remembered occurrences.

Not since mamma and I got back from Newport on the final day of August, have I known much positive enjoyment.   True, girls and men have been up from town to see me all through September ; and among the latter were those whom I really like, too, as well as those for whom my feelings run the emotional gamut the whole way from indifference to disgust.   But until last week I have always been attacked with violent incidental yearnings that he or he or he would go away and not render it a necessity for me to eat my breakfast with unrebukable hair and a blameless morning-dress.   If mamma would only not make mankind such a rigid weekly requirement at Pineside, perhaps I should never fall a victim to these painfully unfeminine feelings.   If she would only let a Sunday come, now and then, without the irreversible male visitor, there is much likelihood that I should learn to see the awful social vacuum thus made as it deserves to be seen.   I suppose mamma's system will terminate with my marriage, and with nothing else.   And looking at the case from this matrimonial stand-point, I should call it a system without much chance of prompt termination.

Day after to-morrow, two men with either of whom I usually manage to obtain a creditable amount of amusement, intend beginning a week's visit at Pineside. Of course my fixed certainty that Melville Delano is the special abomination of Fuller Dobell, and that Fuller Dobell occupies back attic apartments in the affections of Melville Delano, would have prevented me from putting, of my own accord, two such nicely harmonious souls under one and the same roof. Fate, and not I, must bear the blame of this unlucky combination. Each of them had promised me a week at some time during the summer. Melville Delano, when I had last seen him in town, was vague on the subject of when his vacation from business would take place—poor hardworking fellow that he is, with three pretentious sisters to keep dragging him down forever, always failing to get married, and dancing about in his earnings with such a matter-of-course kind of cruelty! Anyhow, he was anxious to spend a half of his fortnight at Pineside whenever he found himself able to get away from town ; and it had been arranged that he should drop me a note just before the opportunity offered itself.

This note came yesterday by the same mail as Fuller Dobell's. I mean Mr. Dobell's. I don't know him well enough to call him Fuller, even in the presence of this little double-extra-confidential morocco-bound second self, my diary. Mamma had given orders at Newport that Mr. Dobell was to be invited here before we left, and that a week was to be offered him, with suggestions to take it whenever he wished. This great sugar-plum of civility was of course presented just as it had come forth from the confectionery of maternal courtesy. But what Mr. Dobell probably found quite toothsome and savory, was to me rather bitter and unpalatable. He is a man to whom I should never, of my own accord, extend any exorbitant civility—not, indeed, without knowing him much better than I know him now, and having gotten rid (were such a thing possible) of an occasional gnawing suspicion that he considers mamma a sort of ponderous snob and myself unlikely at any future period to perpetrate the smallest incendiary act upon the Hudson. However, mamma had said ; and it was for me to obey.

Mr. Dobell agreed to do very much as Melville Delano had agreed to do, with the exception that what leisure one might be able to snatch from the pressing requirements of business, the other had only to snatch from those of personal enjoyment. I suppose, on the whole, that this latter gentleman has reduced pleasure to about as thorough a business as it is capable of being made. By the way, I believe that an account of these invitations has been given pages ago, Diary. But you don't care for that, do you, pearl of confidants ? I can tell you a thing twenty times over and never bore you a bit, sweet morocco model of patience and self-control !

Both notes were very nice reading. Both regretted having been delayed the pleasure of seeing Pineside until so late in the season. Both informed me that their writers had made efforts to come at an earlier date. Both furthermore stated that their writers would be happy to take the five o'clock train on Saturday afternoon, provided such an arrangement suited.

I brought the notes to mamma, who laid down her novel graciously on hearing the writers' names. I am not sure that mamma omitted polishing her gold eyeglasses as a serene token of respect toward these noticeable documents. She is not one to approach even the handwriting of important people without a little gentle ceremoniousness, and the present epistolary collision was of enough consequence not to be surveyed through an eye-glass dimly.

"It's a little awkward, you know," I began to ramble whilst she read. "Neither of the men like each other, I'm sure. Mr. Dobell has certainly procrastinated as though he hadn't a remote suspicion what the thief of time is. Positively, I think he deserves to be snubbed a trifle, with nothing on earth to prevent him from coming earlier except his languid caprices. There isn't a doubt that the engagements he speaks of have been made since I asked him here. It's so different with Melville Delano. Everybody understands how hard he has to work, and—"

Mamma's frown stopped me. It was one of her most august successes in the imperial way, that frown mamma was frowning. It said with curious coherence that I was to hold my tongue, and stop running down a person whom I might much better praise. She had finished Melville Delano's note by this time, and was occupied with Mr. Dobell's. Not until in the act of restoring that to its envelope did the enunciation of her orders commence.

"Let Melville Delano come, if you wish him. I cannot see why a visit from Fuller Dobell should keep him away. It is very kind of Fuller Dobell to remember your invitation—very kind." Mamma showed how kind she considered it by a little dreamy self-absorbed smile, quite ignoring my presence, and giving one of the candlesticks on the opposite mantel every reason to believe itself her bosom-friend. Suddenly the smile vanished, and the candlestick lost favor, and mamma turned toward me. "You ought to esteem it an honor, Helen, to have a man like Mr. Dobell pay you attention."

1*

"If it is paying me attention," I dared, "to post-
pone until the last possible moment the acceptance of an
invitation given weeks previously, then I shall much
prefer the man's rudeness to his civility."

"Tush!" asserted mamma, lending force to her ireful monosyllable by rapping rather sharply on the table
at her side. "I won't argue the matter. You understand my meaning clearly enough. Fuller Dobell is
more to me than many Melville Delanos. I wish he were
to you. Now go and answer both letters; one in as
cordial terms of acquiescence as you and Noah Webster
can manage between you, and the other—" mamma
made her shoulders inform me that it was quite immate-
rial what answer I gave the other. And in reply to
such negative sort of permission as the shoulders had
bestowed,

"There had better be some girl," I recommended:
"if those two men, disliking each other, are both here
at once, I shall probably have my hands full, in a social
sense."

"You forget me," bristled mamma, feeling one of
her large gray front-puffs with majesty. "Mr. Dobell
and I are excellent friends. However, have Selina
Matthers up if you still cling to Melville Delano. Poor
Selina will be delighted to come."

"I don't doubt it at all. You are not making any
mistake? Selina is the one with the Mouth and Teeth."

"And Rachel is the pretty one. But I mean Selina.
Mrs. Matthers will be charmed at my kindness."

"Which is more than our two other guests will be.
The girl is so ugly that she awes me, at times. I doubt
if she comes."

But I wrote for her. And whilst engaged upon this
note and the two others, I could ill keep my mind from

asking itself whether mamma was really bent upon trying to make anything of an important character result from this meditated visit of Mr. Fuller Dobell.

Has she advised (the word has keen irony when used with reference to one of mamma's fiats) that Selina Matthers be made my companion next week, simply because Selina Matthers, ugly enough to sit for a graveyard ghoul, may bring out physical contrast with superb effect? Such a manœuvre is unworthy of mamma's tact and common-sense. Mr. Fuller Dobell will be much more likely to invest me with an atmosphere of the grotesquely horrible than anything else. Poor Selina! I was reading somewhere, the other day, about "the moral uses of dark things." Assuredly your countenance and frame are dark things enough to deserve a more moral use than mamma is going to put them to!

Don't you feel like shuddering, Diary, whilst I write in you that mamma is morbidly anxious to have me marry a certain person? The idea gripped her with an iron grip whilst we were at Newport. She shows it to me in hundreds of unexplainable ways. It possesses her. She talks it, walks it, eats it, and for all I know, sleeps it.

Nearly everybody says he has lost all his money. Some people say that there seems no end to his wild oats. I remember hinting this last fact to mamma one day at Newport, whilst he was being nice to me; and mamma laughed very scornful denial. *Could* she have done so with a purpose?

I don't believe she knows what color his eyes are, for all that they are the loveliest deep deep blue realizable. I am sure she would shrink from anything like an affidavit concerning the shade of his hair. And his suave rythmic sort of voice—I'm certain she has never given that a moment's regard. No, no; it is not the man himself, with mamma. It is neither his virtues nor his vices, his beauty nor his ugliness, his fortune nor his lack of fortune. It is something less palpable than all these, yet in one sense more palpable. I daresay mamma considers that it outweighs them all. It is his name.

Dobell—Fuller Dobell. Mamma worships those two little dissyllables. She laughs at the chances and changes of New York society; she sneers mild sneers at So-and-so presuming to assert a social supremacy over Thus-and-thus; she makes the rustle of her corded silks drown all cavilling murmurs when she moves among the prosperous; she may be applied to at nearly any hour for a superb stare upon whomsoever shall vaguely hint at papa having once been at all connected with Soap; you would be slow at saying that her coupé or her cachemire were the burdens of honors unto which she was not born; and if you were to say so, there is likelihood of her convincing you that the Gorgons possessed an ocular eccentricity capable of modern imitation. Ah, no; nothing about mamma hints that she reveres the shadow called birth, and yet I am sure that all her innermost thoughts make a right devout genuflection before it. One will crave the saccharine dainties after one's appetite has been sated upon the substantials. Success is an endless stairway. Mamma has money and the social power which money, skillfully managed, is apt to gain in New York; but now that she has sent away so many proud hopes ticketed *nil ultra*, there yet remains a last one to torment her with its unbadged coyness.

That is the hope of having my name turn from Helen Jeffreys to Helen Dobell. "My daughter, Mrs. Dobell," is the one boast she cannot make. I wonder if her ambition is going to o'erleap itself. Though denied much voice in the matter, I should think yes.

I don't believe he was very greatly attracted at Newport. I fancy he only came because others came, and with a view to eclipsing everybody else.

Heavens! how late it is! I shouldn't like to shock you by stating the hour, Diary dear, or flatter you, either. I ought to get in the habit of writing you by daylight, and not make myself your accomplice in the destruction of all this midnight oil. It makes me shiver to think of how much beauty-sleep you've stolen from me, and those men coming day after to-morrow!

# CHAPTER II.

SEPT. 22.—To-day has been a void of eventless-ness; or nearly so. It has rained preposter-ously and blown lugubriously since my earliest acquaintance with it. Singular to relate, mamma and I met at breakfast this morning, and drank coffee to-gether. We didn't behave specially charmed to see one another. I don't think that after a polite mutual agree-ment as to its being the equinox, we broke the coffee-sips and the fork-tinkles at all with human speech. I saw promptly that mamma was in one of her ignoring moods, and preferred holding my tongue to talking and being treated like a piece of furniture whilst I did so.

Between ourselves, Diary, she's worried. I don't state it for a firm fact, but I have my doubts as to whether some potentate hasn't been asked to Pineside, whose reply has not yet made an appearance. Mamma has climbed high, but is she yet quite unassailable? Are there not some people who call her crown paste-board, and her insignia shreds and patches, social queen though she has made herself? I haven't forgotten that affair of hers with Mrs. Wallingford Ashburne at the Races, June before last—how the vulgar little self-styled aristocrat measured us both insolently from head to foot, when we went up to speak with her there on the Grand

Stand, and how, though mamma swept away so magnificently with a protective arm in mine, I knew for days
afterward, by certain indubitable signs, that the iron
had entered her soul.  She has had her supreme
triumphs, but she has had her stinging failures likewise;
and though such failures are now things of yesterday;
though she can afford to brush away future impertinences like mosquitoes, or hand them back to the owners
with a smile, as the courteously satanic gentlemen in
the plays or the stories have a habit of treating the
bullets directed against them, yet, for all this, memories
are memories, the oldest veterans make the most cautious soldiers, and a black ugly past can throw a very
black and very ugly shadow.

Pineside is lovely, this saturnine weather, if one only
knows how to take it.  I mean, too, even when one is
all alone, as I have been to-day.  Immediately after
breakfast I went into the library and remained there all
day, lunch and dinner-time excepted.  Our nonpareil
of libraries !  Human taste has never made a more perfect harmony of combination than those lordly bookcases, that grotesquely-carven ceiling which looks like
a little Gothic remnant left over from the making of
Notre Dame or some such mediæval somewhere, the
marble heads of Dante and Milton, and Heaven knows
who else, jutting out of the dark wall, a yard or two
above the great deep wainscoting, and then, most
prominent charm of all, the blooming stained-glass window that is a very riot of glad color at end of the
delicious solemnity.

This morning I lit the fire which waited to be lit in
the huge cavernous chimney-place, and presently two
large logs were wrapped in flames, and the room had
gotten the one only thing this harsh day made it want.

I spent the day here reading, enjoying an open-eyed nap, and reading again. Among other things I read *The Eve of St. Agnes*, and tried to persuade myself, with the help of mediæval surroundings, that I was Madeline. Unfortunately there was a stained-glass window and a quaint-carven ceiling, but no Porphyro. Perhaps if I had had a Porphyro the illusion would have been perfect.

I said the day had been eventless. I suppose, however, that a telegram which reached us from Mrs. Matthers, this evening, to the effect that she "will be very happy to send Selina in train specified," possesses the dignity of an event. I have been filled with pensive dread ever since learning that her arrival to-morrow is a certainty, lest she may possibly be a coward about sleeping alone. I can only hope with silent fervor that I shall not be compelled to lie down in bed beside that Mouth, those Teeth, that general hideousness. It would be like recklessly tempting nightmare.

*Sept.* 23.—The limit of my wakeful recollections last night was something like a hoot from the wind and a crash of rain against my window ; but on opening my eyes this morning, I made the exhilarating discovery that it was a vigorous rigorous autumn day, with a sky like a mighty hollowed turquoise for blueness and cloudlessness, and the air delicious enough to make one wish one might cask stores of it for future use.

I went to the dépôt in time for the five o'clock train, and brought them all home in one of the close carriages. I didn't need to be precisely a clairvoyante for the purpose of discovering that each gentleman was a bombshell to the other. All through the drive home, Melville Delano wore a look of grieved amazement, as though he had recently made some depressing discovery to the

effect that the world was a hollow fraud, but had resolved to suffer and be strong in spite of this recent har-
rowing knowledge. He talked and laughed a little more,
perhaps, than seemed consistent with such evident inward melancholy; but there was perceptible in both
words and laugh, I fancied, a ring of resignation.

Mr. Dobell's surprise wore off very rapidly, I think.
But then there is very little that would cut through that
hard rind of placidity he possesses. Besides, he is an
indolent fellow, to whom it doesn't much matter whether
this week at Pineside is passed pleasurably or no; it
isn't a piece of his precious vacation from commercial
drudgeries, as in Melville Delano's case. I was not at
all astonished, on my own part, to see the two men
treat each other with rather glaring geniality. Not
astonished, Diary dear, because I am getting old enough
to understand that if any facial artist wants to paint a
little loving-kindness, he can probably get his most
valuable practical hints from observing two well-bred
enemies when they meet.

I wonder, by the way, why these men are enemies.
Do they hate each other badly enough to wait at dark
corners for each other with daggers and things, if New
York were Mantua or some such place? One would
certainly never think so, to watch them. Wasn't it
Kate Plaisted who told me that she heard they were
once on the verge of a horrid quarrel about something
which Fuller Dobell had done to Delano's sister?
Some rudeness at a party, wasn't it? I daresay this
was mere gossip. I shouldn't be surprised to hear that
the dislike was a sort of mutual Doctor-Fellism. Anyhow, whatever barnacles of idle report may have clus-
tered round it, the fact of their enmity remains. Everyone knows they are not friends; possibly because they

are both prominent members of one set, and that the leading set of New York society.

Poor Selina Matthers seemed charmed with everything as we drove her to Pineside. She tittered profusely, and in doing so, revealed her two colossal front teeth, not to speak of their many gigantic dental satellites. There is no forgetting the sepulchral suggestions which that mouth of hers offers ; and if one of those front teeth, in its slab-shapen purity, had a *Requiescat* or an *Our Tommy* neatly inscribed thereon, the illusion would be thorough.

The men didn't seem to mind her much, even though she was new to them. Perhaps their breeding prevented the least outward sign from showing itself of how appalled they were. Selina talked as well as tittered. My limited acquaintance with her has until now precluded the discovery that what she says is almost never worth listening to. It is twaddle ; and twaddle of an indistinct articulation, owing to the teeth. Nearly her first remark after entering the carriage was something to the effect that next winter she would come out, and it was so jolly to think of coming out, as she had been envying sister Rachel for over two years.

"Good gracious!" I thought, staring through the carriage-window to avoid both pairs of masculine eyes, "she is going to be garrulous."

I was right. It seems to her quite natural, one would say, that either Mr. Dobell or Mr. Delano should occupy themselves with keen pleasure in talking to her and hearing her talk to them. She is as self-confident as if there were no such things as looking-glasses. One cannot snub her, even were it admissible in one's own house ; the combination of silliness and ugliness is too pathetic for that.

If mamma has wanted to have a great chasm of contrast between me and some other girl during Mr. Dobell's visit, she has veritably succeeded in obtaining her desire. And I tried to tell her so with a glance, this evening, as she met us at the door. Her copious courtesy toward Selina doubtless delighted its recipient. "I'd no idea your mother would be so glad to see me," gushed the young lady, whilst I was going upstairs with her. "Nor I," was my own mental response.

This being Melville Delano's second visit to Pineside, he seemed to accept its grandeurs in a rather matter-of-course way; but I saw plainly that Mr. Dobell felt, in spite of that unimpressionable style he wears, the usual quiet awe of our new-comers. First the august gateway wrung from him a little gentle deference as we drove through it; then the noble amplitudes of fluctuant lawn, with their superb pines and their lake, keen-silver in the early autumn dark; then the solemn ivied dignity of the house itself; then the well-trained servants in readiness; then the wide long hall, with its sombre rich beauty of detail; then the sitting-room, that precious medley of bronzes and marbles and paintings against a deep-blue back-ground; and lastly, perhaps, mamma, imperial in black silk and guipure trimmings, with her peach-colored skin, and her radiant dark eyes, and her two great puffs of placid gray hair at either temple.

I could discover no difference between her ways of welcoming the gentlemen. Mamma had no intention, I suppose, to let any difference be perceptible. I am afraid I watched Mr. Dobell a trifle too steadily during those few moments in the sitting-room, immediately after our return from the dépôt. I don't believe he noticed the scrutiny, but I couldn't have helped it if he had. I remembered that old feeling of mine—the feeling which his presence would rouse sometimes at Newport, even when he was being most civil and attentive to me—the strange conviction, strong in spite of seeming so causeless, that a sort of dormant contempt for us, and for all people like us, was smiling a languid invisible smile somewhere under that polite exterior of his. Just, indeed, as if little voices were vaguely murmuring all around him, to the effect that he was a Dobell and my better, and that once upon a time—quite long ago, perhaps—"a certain honest sort of person, you know, got terribly rich out of Soap, or something of that description." This evening I watched his face with a childish eagerness that I hope was in a measure concealed. I wanted the majesty of Pineside to strike him to the marrow. I wanted him to see what a power wealth is, in hands which know how to use it. I sat near him, hoping that every bronze, every art-gem, every tasteful touch that the room contained, would help to impress him with a sense of mingled splendor and refinement. I was glad that mamma looked her queenly best. I was glad that there had been two alert liveried servants in the hall as we entered it, ready for the wraps and traps, instead of only one. For the time I felt myself to be mamma's accomplice and co-adjutor in *almost* whatever plan she meditated.

Wealth is a superb fact. The plebeian can appall the prince with it. Whatever Fuller Dobell had said or acted 'or hinted when we were last together, must be answered now. Pineside should revenge Newport.

Mamma gave us a flawless dinner that evening, by which I knew, of course, that there was to be a sisterhood of flawless dinners until the end of the visit. I saw plainly, after the third course or so, that Pierre had been put on his mettle. We shall probably have nothing so sumptuous whilst the multitude are here next week ; and we cannot, by reason of there being a multitude, have anything half so exquisite.

Selina Matthers led me to believe during dinner that all our magnificence had awed her into a permanent silence. A little while after we ladies had left the table, however, her bountiful babblings re-commenced. When the men joined us, she was evidently, according to her own belief, in splendid conversational condition for one of them. We had gone into the sitting-room. Mamma was showing Selina some photographs of cosmopolitan notables when they entered. I had seated myself at the piano, and was doing some tender little pianissimos there. I knew that mamma intended to arrange matters according to her own satisfaction. For myself, I determined to be passive, just then. It was rather interesting to watch how she would manage.

Mamma was seated near the doorway, with Selina at her side. I was at some distance from them. Melville Delano entered first. I knew that he was yearning for a talk with me, poor Melville : I knew that he took in the situation with a rapid efficient eye. If mamma and Selina were to be passed, it was only under cover of as beaming a smile as possible. Poor Melville had commenced to beam, his steps being bent in my direction though his head turned propitiatingly in another, when mamma's voice, polite with a great politeness, ruined everything.

" Don't you want to see the likenesses of some famous people, Mr. Delano ? "

Of course he was obliged at least to appear to want to see the likenesses of some famous people very much indeed. But he couldn't help throwing a bereaved look toward me whilst seating himself in the vacant place mamma indicated, at Selina's side. I, for my part, answered the bereaved look with as sympathetic a little pianissimo as I could command. And by this time Mr. Dobell, whom mamma had *not* detained on his way toward me, was only a few yards off.

He had a rather excited look as he leant over the piano and began talking with me. I think he had been drinking more than was right. Perhaps he had felt himself forced to drink, in order that relations of the proper self-controlled sort might be preserved toward Melville Delano during the consumption of the vital after-dinner cigar. If this is the fact, then he is a man whom wine makes handsomer, putting dark fire in his eyes and a rich flush in his fair-skinned Saxon face.

But does it sharpen his wits? I am not sure. It certainly makes him say bold odd things and act with a kind of devotedness that seems to go swaggering perilously along the very verge of impertinence.

But pshaw! perhaps I only fancy, after all. I shouldn't wonder if I were wrong about the wine, too. Why is it that this man, of all others, should fill me with queer doubts and suspicions concerning nearly everything he does? Now I am imagining this about him, now that. I daresay the belief that he ever puts on those elusive undefinable airs, in spite of having bothered me so much, springs also from an imaginative source.

There is no doubt of one thing: I enjoyed the evening superlatively. From whatever cause Mr. Dobell seemed different I will admit to be a mystery; but he did seem so. The Newport man was a sort of shell from which had emerged the Pineside man. He talked more. He smiled more. He somehow put his face nearer to mine whilst he talked and smiled. He seemed to be having a superexcellent time and also to be acutely desirous that I should have a superexcellent time as well. And I did. And I do not believe, on second thought, that the wine is in any manner answerable for what must be called his social amelioration. Wine wears off, after a while, and his nice manner (bold and roguish, but nice) was too prolonged and regular to have had vinous origin. No ; he must be in better spirits now than when we first met—met, I mean, to know each other at all intimately.

And yet, Diary, to you, most indulgent of listeners as I feel sure you are, I must confide one more suspicion. In spite of the man's brightened eyes and color, his livelier deportment, and everything else which would point toward mental buoyancy, I fancied, once or twice this evening, that he bore the outward stamp of some inward worriment, and—

He is not worth all this flattering dissection on my part. What are we to each other that I should lavish nice white paper upon him to such an exorbitant extent ? We talked together unmolestedly for about three hours after he joined me at the piano. There is the unvarnished fact, my dear Diary ; all that you cared to hear, doubtless, and all that it was really necessary to supply you with.

At least two of those hours, I suppose, were purgatorial to Melville Delano ; for mamma arose and went away when the photographic salt had lost its savor and the notable personages had been shut up and replaced upon the sitting-room table. I think he wanted me to believe that Selina was endurable, after they were alone together ; for there was a kind of obstinate made-to-order smile on his lips, as I discovered by occasional glances in his direction, and the persistence with which his eyes refused to wander pianoward would have been a shining example for Lot's wife.

He tried, when we separated, to look as if Selina had been a mere trifle and he hadn't minded her a bit. In this attempt I cannot say that he met with absolute success. When I shook hands for good-night with him (Selina standing by and smiling that horribly dental smile of hers, which is enough to paralyze the most energetic clock conceivable) I endeavored to make my hand say pleasant things about to-morrow. I mean to keep the manual promise, too, though perhaps he did not understand it as such.

To my deep relief it has been discovered that Selina is not at all nervous in the matter of sleeping alone. In truth, she prefers it. I am of course grateful for the circumstance; but then it is a fact that the more one becomes used to her the less dread one has of being left alone with her in the dark.

Yes, I am going to be very civil to Melville Delano to-morrow morning. That is, if mamma permits.

## CHAPTER III.

SEPT. 24.—But mamma hasn't permitted yet, and it is now "to-morrow" at bed-time; and every word which I write in you, by the way, dear Diary, is a scandalous violation of my duty as a keeper of respectable hours.

Wherefore I shall go through the day's events at a mild gallop, if you don't object. In the morning, between breakfast and church, I made an attempt to enjoy a little of Melville Delano's unadulterated companionship on the hall-lounge. I began conversation with a reference to his pitiable captivity of last night. "No doubt you found Miss Matthers the pinnacle of bores," I went on; "but unfortunately, you know, the poor girl must be entertained whilst she is here. I was very sorry. You and Mr. Dobell will have to alternate in the casting of your pearls before—I won't say what—from day to day. That will be only fair, will it not?" And as I laughed he laughed too, his face gaining all the pleasant characteristic light which I had fancied that it had lacked during breakfast. After that we fell to talking together in the old easeful intimate way, and were just beginning to get on charmingly when mamma, emergent from I cannot say precisely where, made the statement that it was time to dress for church.

2

It was not time, and I knew it, and moreover I knew that mamma knew it. But one could guess without difficulty from mamma's " Find Selina, my dear, and take her upstairs with you," that Mr. Dobell was somewhere in Selina's clutches.

She had made a harpylike pounce, probably, as we left the breakfast-room, for I found herself and victim in its immediate neighborhood. It was not hard work to part them : no tearing asunder was necessary. I fancy she has already formed a rapid preference in favor of Melville. It would seem as if Fate smiled upon mamma's dark designs.

During the drive to church (mamma did not go, by the way, because of there being a carriage-load without her), I made the alarming discovery that Selina could babble much more copiously than we had yet heard her, and during the return-drive matters had even become worse. This girl is an irrefutable nuisance. She seems to have fallen quite in love with poor Melville, who bears his misfortune with the dignity of a thorough gentleman.

After our return, mamma secured Melville until it was certain that Mr. Dobell had permanently attached himself to me : then she treacherously retired in favor of Selina. Melville's visit is being ruined ; I don't believe he will stand a week of this sort of thing. He would be insane to do so, I should fancy.

Mr. Dobell and I have been almost uninterruptedly together throughout the whole day. There is no use of my trying to put down what I think. I don't know, indeed, whether I think anything. I am very confused —very surprised. If Newport was a flirtation, what is Pineside ?

Mamma met me at the door of her room to-night, as

I passed it after having disposed of Selina until to-morrow morning. She made me a sign that I was to go in and be talked to for a few minutes. I immediately took a kind of memorial scamper across the day's proceedings, and by the time that I was in flesh crossing the maternal threshold, in spirit I was using the breakfast-table as a post whence to sweep swift intelligent birds'-eyes over all which had occurred since morning. The result of this brisk mental proceeding was satisfactory enough. No spire of misconduct lifted itself from the level of obedience which met my gaze. No; it could not be possible that mamma was going to scold.

As she turned and faced me, after closing the door, her demeanor justified me in feeling convinced that she was not going to scold. And her words, when she spoke, were veritably not of a scolding character.

"I think the two enemies get along very well together ; don't you, Helen ?"

"They are not a great deal together," I objected, with much meekness. "I think they are kept apart rather successfully, if you mean that, mamma."

"We won't split hairs," she smiled, instead of frowning it, as I had half-expected her to do. "*Your* conduct, my daughter, has been in every manner satisfactory."

Doubtless I ought to have tingled to the finger-nails, as most good and faithful serv—I mean daughters, would have done under similar circumstances. But I didn't tingle, somehow. "You mean about Mr. Dobell, mamma ?"

"Yes, my dear." She came very close to me then, and took my hand. The touch of her own hand was like what her words were—a mixture of softness and firmness. Her penetrant eyes searched my face. I wanted to get away. I only remember her having once before secured me in these manual and ocular manners both together : it was a long time ago, and I was a mere child. But a mere child then that wanted to get away, just as I was a big creature and wanted to get away to-night.

"You are a quick bright girl at most things, Helen. You must have noticed what I have desired you to notice —and act upon. But the acting upon it, of course, would necessitate your being an obedient girl as well." Her disengaged hand had stolen up into my hair, now, and was pushing it back from my forehead.

"I hope I am obedient, mamma," was the effort which I made, presently, to fill what had grown a keenly awkward silence.

"So do I." By this time her arm was about my neck. The action was tender indisputably—and mamma performed it. I should be much amazed to encounter in some Austrian history the fact of Maria Theresa having caused, during a moment of mental alienation, the throne of the Hapsburgs to tremble beneath a pigeon's-wing ; still, events can be imagined which would surprise me more ; and at least until this evening one of these events was anything resembling a show of tenderness on mamma's part. "But there are such things as knights with bloodless swords and virgin shields," she loitered on, murmurously. "I don't think, dear, your full powers of obedience have ever been proven yet. Have they ?"

I gave a kind of nervous laugh at this : it was because those dark unvarying eyes of hers fluttered me, I suppose. "Gracious, you're very allegoric, I should say. I don't know, surely." After that I plucked up a little courage : it seems so inane for a great girl like me *always* to stand in such awe of a mother. "If you'll allow honest candor, mamma, I think we may as well use it toward one another."

"Right." The little word rang clearly through the still room, as she dropped my hand and left off being affectionate in the region of my neck and shoulders. "Let it be simple A, B, C between us, Helen. I want you to marry Fuller Dobell. There are no men in New York (except one or two, perhaps; and those are unreachable) whom I more greatly want you to marry. You have heard idle stories about him; believe them or not, just as you please, but don't let them prejudice you against the man, howsoever slightly. It is of no importance what a man's life has been *before* marriage. Very often the married reprobate will make the model husband—if it were a question with you of model husbands or their opposites; which it is not. You marry in a world where the connubial chain isn't always worn precisely like a fetter;"—a light low laugh ending this sentence. "We needn't inquire, either, whether Fuller Dobell has lost his money or no. You have nothing, it is true, but I have much; and out of that plenitude there shall be spared to you all you need until some day when you shall possess it in entirety, no doubt; so that even if poor himself, he should have no moneyless woman for his bride when he married you."

"And you think he is going to marry me, mamma?"

"He is going, if I can make him."

"What do you mean?" My words came sharp and harsh. Years of allegiance and obeisance were forgotten in them. For the moment it was somehow no longer the woman of whom I have stood in perpetual fear and reverence, no longer mamma the august and formidable, but rather some voice that had spoken forth a stinging prophecy of my own future humiliation. This thought had flashed through my mind with only a thought's fleetness :—*There is to be some bold horrible attempt made, which shall more than cheapen you in Fuller Dobell's eyes.* And I had answered what impulse had commanded, forgetting the potentate whom I addressed : just as though some lady-in-waiting, taken by surprise with a monarchical box on the ear, should let the aural twinge corrupt her loyalty to the extent of an impetuous tit-for-tat. But a few seconds after the words were spoken I was trembling with the thought of their audacity.

Mamma looked thunderstruck, at first ; then her eyebrows were haughtily lifted as I have seen them more than once. I expected something blood-curdling in the way of a rebuke, and stood waiting for it. But only this came :

" Do you believe me capable of disgracing you in the matter, Helen ? It is easy to guess your thought behind your question."

The eye-brows had lowered themselves. I saw to my amazement that her face bore no traces of anger. Some spiritual zephyr of the balmiest character conceivable had blown away every tempestuous sign. Had it sprung from amiability or from policy, this genial annihilator? From the latter, I am disposed to suspect. People do not act at a moment's notice contrary to their most prominent personal traits without some decisive reason therefor.

My amazement did not prevent me from murmuring a prompt apology. " Pray excuse me, mamma. Of course you must understand that the idea of his learning what you desire would be painfully mortifying to me." Then I acted as if making the carpet a very important confidence. "It is true—that is, there doesn't seem to be any doubt just now in my own mind," I floundered, "as to whether I would refuse him, you know. There's nobody whom I have ever liked better, so far."

Mamma's face lit up with its most brilliant smile, then. By the way, how handsome a smile makes her! "Helen, you are certain of success, in that case. I have reason to feel sure that he will offer himself in a day or two."

"Has he said anything to you about it?" I flashed, eagerly.

"No." The negative was quickly given, and then came a little pause. "But there are means of judging to one who knows the world as I know it." She came close to me now, and kissed me in her usual business-like way. "Good-night, my dear; you had better go to bed at once. I have probably done wrong in exciting you at such an hour."

"You haven't excited me," I softly contradicted. Fixing my eyes upon her face, I went on: "Promise me, mamma, that under no circumstances will you drop the slightest hint to Fuller Dobell—"

Her hand, raised imperiously, made me pause there. And her face had darkened irefully indeed, now; looking beyond the power of any sudden facial summer to thaw its frigidity. "I hold it to be an impertinence that you should again touch upon such a subject. Whilst our interests are common interests, I should at least be trusted with the guardianship of your respectability."

"But, mamma, I—"

Up went the imperious hand, as if ascending with little jerky steps a little airy stairway.

"Leave the room, please."

I left.

Well, for once it has paid to have mamma treat me with the same demolishing lack of ceremony usually received by a caterpillar which goes where it oughtn't to go. I have made sure that her desire to bring about a certain event will not result in anything that I should think of with a shudder of mortification ; unless, indeed, her indignation was a sort of mask, and I am inclined to think no on this point. Mamma is zealous enough, but her zeal will never carry her beyond the bounds of a certain politic propriety.

Her worldly wishes regarding the man make her more hopeful than my unworldly wishes make me. If he offered himself to-morrow, I should marvel besides rejoicing. She would rejoice and not marvel greatly, I rather fancy.

Whence springs her apparent confidence in my success ? (Bold, scheming thing that I seem like,·to use the horrid Becky-Sharpish word !) Does it spring from any hidden reserve-power ? But what hidden reserve-power could she possibly have ?

Yes, what they call a downright offer would surprise me hugely. And yet how many girls in my situation would have triple my hopefulness ! But then veteran flirts are such eels in the way of reliability. I have not forgotten John · Driscoll and those first three months after I went into society, though mamma warned me there, and it was a little game in the playing of which I had consequently a cool clear head. Then, too, there was after all no great need to warn. John Driscoll is a charming man, but I doubt whether he would not under any circumstances have left me as he found me—heart-whole. Now, however, mamma encourages, pushes on, and now her encouragement is as little needed as was her warning of other days.

Why?

I'd write the answer in invisible ink, Diary, if only I possessed some of that phantasmal commodity. What a pretty way of telling you a real secret, by the bye— one which any mischievous character might not, after addressing my desk in the persuasive terms of a skeleton key, presumptuously read. But pshaw! you have heard my stumbling admission to mamma. A diary of your intelligence can readily imagine how florid, not to say torrid, those unseen sentences would prove. A word to the wise, you know.

2*

## CHAPTER IV.

EPT. 25.—To-day was rainy again. I have spent nearly the whole day with Fuller Dobell in the library. Melville Delano has made up his mind to leave to-morrow afternoon. He broke this piece of news to me during a few words which we held together after dinner. He assures me that his departure is a necessity; but I doubt the truth of this. How can one blame him for running away from Selina?

I like Melville Delano with all my heart. I know that he detests Fuller Dobell; I know that he feels himself grossly maltreated; I know that he is fond of me; and yet not one word of bitterness left the man's lips whilst we spoke together. Perhaps he believes that my apparent preference is all the result of maternal command, and that I am in truth more deserving of pity than he is. It would be much better if he really had some such opinion of the matter, poor fellow! And it wouldn't be wholly a wrong opinion, either. Mamma *does* make me behave as I am behaving—only I find it very agreeable indeed to obey her. There would be fell hypocrisy in my making mouths over currant-jelly, and treating it like castor-oil, even though it is administered in medicinal form.

I appreciate Melville Delano's disappointment profoundly. He had no doubt been promising himself vast enjoyment during this visit, all through the summer. When we last saw each other in town, I had hardly spoken twenty words to Fuller Dobell in all my lifetime ; now Melville comes to Pineside, and finds me on intimate terms with his pet aversion, and must watch me disappear into retired nooks and corners, leaving him for consolation a chatterer with astonishing teeth. It is very hard.

When I recall, however, the gloomy manners which he wore on Saturday evening and on Sunday morning, the conviction forces itself upon me that only one kind of salve has healed his wound with such unexampled rapidity—the salve of conceit. Yes, he is confident that I act merely from motives of blind obedience to mamma's will. And how mamma must be anathematized in his private thoughts, by the way !

I have not yet told her that Melville is going to-morrow. No doubt she will insist upon his remaining, on Selina's account. I wonder whether Melville would go at the risk of offending her ? I should fancy yes; Melville Delano has nothing of the time-server about him, notwithstanding his commercial struggles and those three dragging sisters. And this reminds me of how he has begun to treat Fuller Dobell ; there is no more smoking together after we leave the dinner-table. " I shall not smoke, thanks," Melville announced this evening, passing from the room when mamma and Selina and I retired from it, and leaving Fuller Dobell to make the dining-room nebulous in tobacconalian solitude. Don't men usually prefer the cigar of certain moments to almost anything else of things terrestrial ? And isn't there something truly horrible in the fact of one man hating another, so to phrase it, a whole after-dinner cigar's worth? Perhaps if I knew more about smoking—had ever gone into clandestine cigarettes, like some girls, for instance—I might confidently answer these questions.

Mamma has given me incidentally applausive looks whenever we have met throughout the day. I don't see, for my part, why I deserve to be treated as if I were going the way of all duteous daughters. Even viewing the matter from mamma's standpoint, my obedience consists in nothing except sitting still and being talked deliciously to.

He does talk deliciously. One might define his conversation as a mellifluous stream of nothing remarkable. He isn't clever. I said so at Newport, and I repeat it now. He isn't fit to tie the latchet of John Driscoll's intellectual shoes—or of Melville Delano's either. I always believed that I should fall in love with a very clever man. How odd that I haven't, after all!

But then he is never stupid. In fact, I do not think that with his deep rich-colored eyes upon me, and with his tuneful mellow voice near me, chimpanzees or even hippopotami would seem at all like undesirable topics. Everything that he says is of interest, somehow, not (as I don't hesitate a single moment to confess) because there is really much in it, but because—

Oh, gracious! because he is charming. It is sometimes a colossal bore to be logical, Diary dear.

# CHAPTER V.

SEPT. 26.—How much of the odd and unlooked-for has happened to-day !

This morning was a return of the perfect autumn weather. Everybody seemed in sparkling spirits when we met at breakfast; even mamma's grave stateliness was touched with mirth, now and then, like bright broidery about the edges of some sombre robe. Melville Delano, who had the least excuse of anybody for being merry, turned more than once toward the prattling Selina and looked her bravely in the teeth, and smiled, and was strong.

After breakfast I proposed croquêt. Acquiescence was universal, and we sought the lawn. Mr. Dobell asked me rather loudly, so that all heard him, to be his partner, just as we reached the ground. " Certainly," I assented; and so the division was made of Mr. Dobell and me against Melville and Selina.

My partner and I succeeded nicely, both of us playing very much after the same theory. Occasionally his ideas were at fault, but he isn't vainglorious as regards his game, nor adamantine in the matter of following suggestions. It is not necessary, on the one hand, to delay the game with polite pleading or argument when you play with him, or yet on the other, with laborious

explanations of what you feel certain is the proper shot.
Altogether, I think we may be called sweetly harmoni-
. ous in croquêt. If, however, there is a shade of superiority possessed by either, I am the fortunate owner. I
think also that he understands this, and suggests my
superiority in a nice, delicate way, by no means cum-
bersomely reverential.

But Melville eclipses us both. His eye is straighter,
his hand is steadier, his shots are surer. He is infallible, too, on the subject of who plays next and who does
not play next. If he had had an ordinary partner, let
us say, the game might have been fine fun. His partner, on the contrary, was very extraordinary indeed.
She garrulously preluded her first shot by more than a
single statement to the effect that she was a beginner
and "deserved to have loads of allowances made, you
know." We were all willing, and expressed our willingness, to strew her path with the roses of extreme in-
dulgence in the matter of making such allowances.
Our offers were appreciatively answered by a nervous
giggle; and with her body bent in painful curvature
and both hands grasping her mallet-handle as though
it were the proverbial straw beloved of the proverbial
drowning man, Miss Matthers, after what appeared
supreme physical effort, faintly tapped her ball and
made it roll perhaps ten inches. She was cordially
asked to try over again, as soon as our surprise at the
mountain's immense groan and the poor wee mouse of
which it had been delivered, made speech possible.
The second attempt was the merest phantom of an improvement on the first. We might have pitied her,
but bared by a broad self-satisfied grin the teeth
gleamed defiance at all commiseration. Throughout
the remainder of the game, she was just a ponderous stone

round poor Melville's neck, although to her own thinking she was doubtless no more than would have been a
rose in his button-hole.  All his exquisite skill at assistance was thrown away upon her headlong blunder-
ing.  If he put her ball so that a breath would almost
send it through its wicket, and the judgment of a
chicken might settle upon the force required for its pro-
pulsion, the result was sure to be something about as
violently zigzag as human power can attain.  Considering Melville's love for croquêt, his gentle patience
under such an exasperating drawback gave to his game
a flavor of real old fifteenth-century martyrdom.  We
beat Selina by many wickets—him by only one.

It was on the end of my tongue, when this game was
finished, to suggest that Melville and I should now play
against Mr. Dobell and Selina; but somehow I didn't
make the proposition.  "Shall we have another?"
noised Miss Matthers, brazenly.  "I like it so much!
I'd no idea that it was so nice.  I must always before
have played with bad players, and never really gotten
into the spirit of it, you see."

"I, for one, admit to being wearied a little," Melville Delano announced, meditatively injuring our
trim-shaven lawn with his mallet—which, by the bye,
ought to have brought forth buds and bloomed blos-
soms, like Aaron's rod, as a sign that the tutelar genius
of croquêt had seen and pitied its wielder's patience and
long-suffering.

Selina pouted repulsively whilst I was turning to see
what Andrew wanted, that domestic having just made
his appearance on the croquêt-ground.  Andrew wanted
to give Mr. Dobell a letter which somebody had recently brought over from the hotel.  Mr. Dobell was
standing at my right, and Andrew stood at my left; it

was consequently quite natural for me to receive the letter and pass it to the owner; quite natural was it, also, for me to sweep my eye over the superscription, whilst acting as this sort of postal medium between Andrew and my guest: curious if you please, Diary, but not unwarrantably so. Andrew had stated that the letter was for Mr. Dobell, but handwriting is handwriting, and the scholarship of Andrews in general is not unassailable, as everybody knows.

This handwriting shaped the name of Fuller Dobell, in lines of lovely flowing gracefulness: my swift eyesweep told me thus much. "Indisputably a woman's hand," I had decided to myself, before that which was Cæsar's had been rendered unto Cæsar. He took it rather wonderingly, stared at it rather surprisedly, and glanced up at me with courteous appeal. "Have I your permission to open?"

Being permitted, he opened. Of course, I looked away—walking away also. Of course, too, I was wondering from whom at the hotel the note had come. Lots of people are there during the summer—a veritable social hodge-podge, in fact, of somebodies or worse than nobodies; but now, at this late September day, I had imagined that nearly everybody was gone, the fickle multitude being usually known to depart at the first cold dewfall or so, and long before Autumn has begun her operations among the leaves with that "fiery finger" that Tennyson tells us about.

He began speaking, presently, and then I looked round again. "Is it settled that we are not to play any more, Miss Helen?" He was re-wedding the sundered envelope and paper, by this time. "I feel quite ready for another game."

"You heard Mr. Delano, did you not?" I shoulder-shrugged, rather coolly. Sharing the common feminine doom of being one of Eve's distant relations, it wasn't out-and-out bliss for me to see him put the envelope into his pocket and so dismiss all further thought, apparently, of from whom it had come. But, of course, I was just an idiot to show my disappointment.

"I will play to oblige you, Miss Helen," Melville hastened to state, and so pointedly that I saw Mr. Dobell's brown moustache abruptly lapse over his lower lip, as though something was biting something else in the convenient ambuscade thus formed. After a second of silence the same speaker went on: "You know I leave to-day. Would it matter at all if I were to take the half-past twelve, by the bye, instead of the two o'clock, as I suggested last night?"

"Oh, no, not at all!" and I fixed my eyes very steadily on Melville Delano's face, after saying this, and tried to make them tell him that his going was a miserable shame. Then, aloud: "I will order you an earlier lunch, if your plans are changed."

"Thanks very much." We had gotten together, by this time, and he spoke in lowered tones. "But I shan't need any lunch. I shall reach town a little after two, you know."

"I haven't told mamma that you are going yet," I hesitated, annihilating a leaf, nervously. "I'm afraid she will be quite averse to your departure."

"I don't doubt it: on Miss Matthers' account, possibly," he muttered, neither a smile nor a sneer gaining exactly the mastery on his face, but both manifestly contending there. "I am going into the house now. Shall I find her, and break the momentous tidings?"

"*Must* he go to-day?" whined Selina indelicately, approaching me almost before he had left the ground.

Her pout was now among things forgotten.  " *Do* persuade him to stay."

"Perhaps you could perform that task with better
success than anybody else," I lied, amiably.  Conscience
must shrivel before hostess-ship, as every one is aware.

Selina grinned a bashful grin, the awful dental disclo-
sures of which I can compare to nothing except the sea
giving up its dead.  "Pshaw! you horrible girl! I
don't believe it a bit!"  Then I was smitten on the
shoulder with tender violence, as a punishment, doubtless, for being so horrible and so unworthy of credence.

We strolled toward the house, presently, Selina tripping buoyantly along at quite a distance from Mr. Dobell and me, still under the happy spell, probably, of
my recent mendacious compliment.

"Shall you object to having me leave you for a little
while this afternoon?" my companion abruptly questioned, as we walked along.  "That is, do you mind
lending me a horse and wagon, and letting me do what
I want with them, say from about two until dinner-
time?"

"Certainly not," I laughed.  Mother Eve may have
been my progenitress, but I chose to remember just
then that she was a remote one, and disclose not an iota
of curiosity.  If he cared to reveal the whither of his
proposed journey, which had much to do, of course,
with the envelope Andrew had recently brought, why,
let him do so.  Anyhow, there was the comfortable
certainty behind my dignified reticence that mamma
would want to hear where he was going, and most
probably succeed in finding out.

But his next words dizzied me with surprise: "Would
it be asking too much if I asked you not to mention
anything about my proposition to your mother?  I

heard her say at breakfast this morning that she was
going to drive twelve miles across country in the afternoon, to Mrs. ——, Mrs. —— Somebody's house."

"Landesdowne." I supplied the name mechanically,
as it were. "You don't want me to tell mamma, Mr.
Dobell! Do you mind my saying that there is something quite glaring about the oddity of your request?"

He gave his moustache one or two energetic tugs.
"Perhaps when the novelty has worn off you'll not
find it so difficult to grant. By the way, I put it to you
in the form of a very earnest request. You know what
a universe of coaxing a child's 'ah, please' is supposed
to contain: pray imagine me very juvenile, and consider
that you have been 'ah-pleased' a great many times."

I knew him well enough to see depths of sincerest
urgency under these trivial phrases. If his eyes were
emphatically *not* "each about to have a tear," his forehead was something a little more than merely prophetic
of a frown : he walked at my side, too, with head path-
ward, and eyes roaming somehow restlessly anywhere
except in the direction of my face.

"Of course," I assented, rather frigidly, "you are
welcome to the horse and wagon. I shall say nothing
to mamma, since you desire that I should not. And
am I authorized to explain your absence in the hearing
of anybody else, by the bye, or must it remain a secret
between you, me, and the coachman?"

Instantly his face took a full rich smile. "Can't you
do me a kindness without saying something sharp as a
sort of counterpoise, Miss Helen? For I see that you
have consented : and since, consent being given, you
have actually put the question, please *do* let the matter
of my disappearance remain the sort of secret you have
described ; at least as near as possible."

" You may rely upon me. But—" Then I paused.

" But ?" he queried.

" Is thy servant an angel, that she should do this thing and have no curiosity to learn wherefore she does it ? "

" Wherefore, Miss Helen ? "

" As Mr. Booth remarks in Hamlet : ' Ay, 'twas my word.' "

He became abruptly interested, at this, in the picking up of a fallen maple-leaf that lay just in our path ; a scrap of gold and scarlet brilliance, like the lovely little leaving from some over-opulent tropic sunset. " I am afraid you have veritably put a beggar on horseback," he murmured. " Finish the good work thoroughly, and don't ask wherefore."

" But Selina Matthers will ask."

He was silent for a little while, and then : " On the whole, I really don't care very much if she does."

" But mamma will undoubtedly hear of your absence through *her*, unless she is made an accomplice in our mysterious little plot."

He laughed a soft unconcerned laugh. " She may not divulge ; let us hope for the best. It isn't a plot ; pray think that it isn't. You are doing me a pleasant little favor ; that is all."

As we entered the hall, mamma and Melville became visible in conversation together, at one end of it. " I have persuaded Mr. Delano to remain at least a day longer," she presently announced, coming forward ; whilst Melville, not looking altogether like a confirmation of this statement, staid in the background.

" Oh, I'm real glad ! " gushed Selina, bringing both hands together with exuberant girlish rapture, and expressing eloquently with teeth the joy to which words seemed unequal.

Mamma started for the Landesdownes' some time before the lunch-hour. "It is decided that Mr. Delano will not leave to-day," she had augustly proclaimed, addressing nobody in particular—not even Melville himself—a little while before starting. I wondered what potent spell she had used to detain him. I suppose it was as much as anything else the thought of having been persuaded by one who persuades so rarely, that prevented him from going. Melville is not a time-server, it is true, nor a toady, nor a snob; but when a woman like mamma graciously stoops from her pedestal, people whose power isn't her power and who stand a grade or two lower than she does, are apt to feel a few reverential tinglings among the dorsal muscles furnished by an all-provident nature for us to make salaams with.

It occurred to me as soon as mamma was gone, that now a golden opportunity offered itself for wiping out, as far as lay in my power, the sins of omission committed upon Melville since Saturday last. And so, during a temporary absence of Mr. Dobell, and whilst Selina had disappeared for the possible purpose of a short discussion with her mirror, I stationed myself syrenwise in the bay-window and easily lured him to my side. After a little while we both concluded that the privacy of our pleasant retreat would perhaps be violated, and by mutual consent the curtains were loosened, shutting us in a lovely wee hermitage of blue silk and window-panes :

"You must think me a rather weak specimen of manhood," murmured my fellow-recluse, presently.

"Because you changed your mind about going to town ? Not I. But I admit to having felt a trifle annoyed that you should have been such marble to my persuasions, though such clay to mamma's."

I saw the crimson color steal slowly into his swart olive face. "There is such a thing as being perverse for mere perversity, you know. Perhaps, too, a remnant of my bitter feelings existed this morning. You probably are not aware of those feelings."

"Certainly not," I returned, wide-eyed. "Had I done anything to offend?"

"I fancied you had." His dark full eyes were fixed glowingly on my face. "But it was all fancy, I am sure. *You* have not been to blame."

("O vanity of man," was my mute comment. "How is your own personality precious beyond rubies in your own sight!") But aloud:

"I think that I guess what you mean." Then I laughed a low little conciliatory laugh. You mustn't believe anybody to blame. Mr. Dobell was a stranger at Pineside and not an old acquaintance, either. You, on the other hand—"

"Pshaw!" he broke in, brusquely; "if I am a friend of long standing, as doubtless you were going to say, then I don't deserve being treated with any paltry disguises. . Either you do or you do not prefer Fuller Dobell's society to mine: I am inclined to believe that the latter is most likely a fact. But I suppose that your excuse for inconsistent behavior, provided my theory be correct, is the soldierly one of having been forced to obey orders."

I am sure that my cheeks had each gotten a rose of angriest crimson, and that my eyes were dancing very briskly as I snapped out in answer:

"You've made a ridiculous mistake, and you're a mountain of conceit."

"He caught my arm with a quick hard hand. You don't mean, Helen Jeffreys, that all your avoid-

ance has been a matter of free will—that you yourself
have *chosen* to show this preference for—"

" Helen," bleated Selina, peevishly, from the adjoining sitting-room. "Hel—en, where are you, dear?"

His hand fell forceless at his side. I saw that he had
grown quite pale in these few moments. I had turned
toward him with haughty words on my lips—words
demanding his reason for that rude grasp of my arm :
but such words went back again to the mental arsenal
from whence they had come, to be re-stored, I suppose,
as ammunition for future quarrels. A great melancholy change possessed his eyes. I saw, and understood, and wondered, whilst wonderment sent my
anger vanishing like a pricked bubble.

"It isn't surely a matter of such importance to
you?" I faltered. " Mr. Dobell and I have come to
know each other very well of late. You mustn't jump
to the conclusion that his society is preferable to yours :
indeed, I haven't said so. The vanity in your explanation rather piqued me, I'll admit."

There was a bitter smile under his scant dark moustache.
"I think I understand you very clearly, now. My explanation *was* vain, perhaps. Pride, you know, goeth
before a fall," he ended, the bitter smile becoming a
light bitter laugh.

"Helen," lamented Selina, from the distant hall,
"aren't you anywhere, my dear?"

I rose. "We shall see each other after lunch," I
prophesied, meaningly.

"Just as you please."

" You shall take me driving, if you want."

He looked amazed ; or was it satirical for amazement ?
"What sop shall be given to your Cerberus in the meanwhile ?"

"You don't mean Selina Matthers? She frightens people with her teeth, and so did Cerberus, I believe."

"No; I mean Mr. Fuller Dobell."

In spite of myself the color would break dykes a little; if not an inundation there was certainly a heavy leakage made evident, as I rattled off with rather bunglingly-feigned indifference: "Oh, he is going somewhere, I think. Anyhow, whether he goes or not, it will be all the same. On second thought, *I* had better take *you* driving, in the basket-wagon. I trust Selina can be persuaded that we're not treating her with precisely heinous rudeness."

Mr. Dobell left at about two o'clock that afternoon. Selina and I had gone upstairs for a nap on the same bed. I had given orders at what time his carriage should be brought round, and whilst lying on the bed I could now hear the tell-tale wheels come crushingly up along the gravel to the door; then in a little while their locomotion commenced again, and I knew that they were being drawn hotelward on that mysterious journey.

"Selina," I began, "Mr. Dobell has gone away on a little business of his own; driving, you know; I can't precisely say where."

"That's nothing to me, Helen dear," yawned my bed-fellow, taking the home route from dreamland by easy stages.

Determined to get the ice broken and done with, I went on, with voice "like the waters of Shiloah that go softly." "No, of course not. But I was wondering whether you wouldn't find it rather disgusting to be left all alone this afternoon; and so when it was proposed that Melville Delano should take me driving I rather hesitated to adopt such a plan." Then followed a gentle gush of entreaty. "You won't mind, dear, will you ? We'll promise not to stay very long, and I'll lend you ' *Why Did She Desert Her Husband ?* ' It's charming ; even better than ' *Leaves from the Life of a Fast Man,*' by the same author, which I am sure you must have read ; nearly everybody has." Thus far I had felt considerable doubt as to the result of my supplications : but now a smile, hideous with good-nature, reassured me. Much emboldened, I went on, after that, with " *Will* you think it rude, my dear ? *Had* I better not go ?" et cetera for some distance. There was something quite queer in the sudden self-searching character of these remarks ; a change which took place, oddly enough, after I had made sure that Selina was likely to detect no rudeness in my proposed desertion of her.

It must have been about an hour later when Melville and I drove off in the basket-wagon.

He was not at all in good spirits, I noticed, at the outset of our ride. Indeed he had been in the antipodes of good spirits ever since our dialogue behind the curtain. The afternoon was so delicious that anything but genial companionship seemed a right troublesome discord. Breadth after breadth of beautiful candid color, the frosted woods rose at either side ; long jungles of ruby-red sumach tossed their brilliant wee wyverns in the brisk bracing air ; whole meadowfuls of goldenrods, battalion by nodding battalion, lapsed away like new golcondas under the clear-blue afternoon sky ; the wild asters lavished their opulent purple plumes along lane and pasture, in loveliest largesse. O these exquisite autumn days, with their gladness and their sadness braided together, like a tress of gray hair with a child's bright young curl ! O hours wherein summer, like a dying queen, bequeaths to all her constant patient subjects what the unleal and faithless left behind them

3 .

as they fled, clothing her loyal foliage in all her lost flowers' abandoned beauties !

Matters had reached a condition of dead silence between us, when Flirt unconsciously supplied a topic by shying rather badly at a stump.

"She's pretty gamesome to-day," I announced, straightening myself in a responsible style, as though one had to be a sort of trustworthy character in order to drive her properly. "I almost wish, though, that she'd shied worse, if that would have waked you up at all."

He started. "Do you? One can ill talk of gnats when one is thinking of lions." He gave a short harsh laugh. "You might better have driven Miss Matthers out, I fancy ; she would have been nicer company than I am, surely."

"Dear me," I commented, reining in Flirt, who had gotten going a little too impetuously, "it's a shame that your visit should turn out the failure it's doing. You expected to have a jolly time, I know."

Silence. Presently:

"You are quite wrong. I never have a jolly time where you are ; I don't know why I ever go near you. Even when you are most charming to me you make me most miserable."

I knew that his eyes (with something so Spanish about the blackness of their darkness) were fixed upon my face ; but I kept my own eyes riveted on an imaginary point precisely between Flirt's alert ears. "That's too bad," I criticised, with horrible lack of appropriateness and much embarrassment. After which, becoming more self-possessed, I gave birth to the following platitude : "It is very unpleasant to feel one's self the means of making another miserable."

His voice was softer—much softer, then. "I believe

you think so. But it is not your fault, certainly, that
you are coveted and yet unreachable; you've the consolation of knowing that fate made you rich and a great
match, and guarded you for the one fortunate suitor,
whoever he may be, with a very awful sentinelship.
Don't think me impertinent by this; but I mean your
mother's ambition."

"I *do* think you impertinent," with sharp voice I
made answer, turning my eyes away from Flirt that they
might flash their most irate lightnings upon him.
"What right have you to question either mamma's
ambition or her humility?"

The odd-sounding laugh again. "No right, of course.
No right to love you and long for you, either. I don't
suppose it is anything new to you, this hearing that I
have loved you, by the way. You must have guessed
it long ago."

"I prefer talking of pleasanter subjects," I frowned,
my anger cooling. "You rightly call me unreachable,
though for more reasons than one, am I beyond your
reach. I do not love you."

I saw pain drag down the corners of his mouth for
a second; saw it quiver in his thin thorough-bred
nostril; saw it leap up glitteringly in one swift sweep
of his eyes across my face. After that came a little silence, which he at length broke, with his voice set in a
dull hard monotone: "Strange. Very strange indeed."

"What is strange?" I questioned, shortly. "That
I shouldn't love you? Or is it that you're only trying
to be oracular?"

"No, no," he hurried along, with sorrowful sternness.
"I was thinking that before you met Dobell, there was
possibly no man among all your friends whom you
would rather have married than myself—at least as far

as personal and not worldly feelings went. Now it is wholly changed. You have met that man whom I prefer less for a rival than almost any one I know, and even the poor chances once held by me of winning a place in your heart, are swept completely away. I was a fool not to have seen this yesterday. A man's vanity makes him play at blindman's-buff with the truth, sometimes."

His tones had become miserably desolate. I like him so well that I could not help pitying him passionately. I know there were tears in the eyes which I turned toward him. I know that sympathy made my voice tremulous, not to speak of my lower lip.

"You have no business at all to connect my name with Mr. Dobell's," I didn't by any means say harshly. "You've no business to infer that I am in love with him."

He must have taken my words to mean more, a great deal more, than I had intended them to mean ; for they were scarcely spoken before I felt his yellow dog-skin hand making intimate acquaintance with my driving-gauntlet, just in the region of the wrist. "Helen, Helen," he was murmuring close at my ear, the next instant, "am I wrong, then, after all? Have I a dim hope of winning you in the future? If you have the courage to stand out against persuasions, perhaps tyrannies, I have the strength and resolution—"

"No, no, no," I opposed, with decision, when he had gotten thus far. "It isn't that at all. I could never marry you in any case. With me there just *must* be love of a certain sort—that is, I suppose so—and I don't think—indeed I'm sure that you and I— Well for Heaven's sake drop the subject," I perorated, red and wretched because he had so misunderstood me.

He released my wrist with a heavy frown. There fol-

lowed quite a long period of silence, after that, during
which I felt him to be angry, and made many mute
mental statements to the effect that he had no right to
be angry. By and by I reached the conclusion that
since there was no other way out of our tiresome silence
we had better get up a quarrel together. Quarrelling
usually makes conversation at first, however murderous
an effect the result may produce upon it.

Of course it was for me to fire the first gun. I remember that I had such a gun all ready—liberally loaded
to the muzzle, in fact, and that, to continue the bellicose
metaphor, my finger was on its trigger. No matter
what I was going to say: we all know that there have
been many great sayings which never had the good fortune to slip past the door-keeper of history. This of
mine was never uttered, much as it may have deserved
the applause of posterity. And Flirt is to blame; Flirt,
who shied furiously just as the valuable remark occupied
my tongue's extremest tip.

I suppose that an organ-grinder was her present
excuse for leaving it to fickle fortune whether the
basket-wagon should end its days prematurely against
a tree-trunk or not, and then galloping like a stag out
over the road again; for just as we bounced past the
spot which seemed so to disgust her vixenship, I caught
a glimpse of a gentleman whose huge green-baize burden
indicated his profession as plainly as dark complexion,
ear-rings, and a general suggestion of much filth pointed
toward a recent residence in the sunny South. Melville
Delano's hands were heavy on the reins before Flirt's
third gallop, making baby-play on the instant of my
own tugging hold. Now it is usually an article of faith
among men, as everybody knows, that when one of them
is driving and another unsolicited makes a grab at the

reins, *damn you* at once takes rank among the worn-out extravagant politenesses of the old-school in comparison with the thing which it forthwith becomes right and admissible and even necessary to say. Every man likes to have his neighbor's hands kept at respectful distance from his pocket, his wife, and the reins of the horse he happens to be driving; and altogether I think such preferences completely proper.

But how about every woman in this last equine particular? Well, I suppose that nearly every woman would expect, under similar circumstances, to receive the same courteously protective treatment which I received. But all women are neither cowards nor bad drivers, despite the amazing majority which is both. I am not at all a coward about horses, for instance; and I don't want any one to waste breath by telling me that I drive astonishingly well.

Wherefore (and also because of past quarrelsome intentions, doubtless) I chose to be wroth exceedingly at Melville Delano's interference. "Let go of the reins," I snapped. "I'm quite able to govern her myself, if you please."

He turned toward me with amazed eyes, whilst Flirt was bounding on. "Do you really mean it."

"Of course I mean it," shouted I, fierily.

A second after that I found myself driving again. Flirt pulls ferociously when she chooses, and she was choosing then. "I don't suppose one could call it a runaway, could one?" was the dismal mental question I began to put myself. She has always been renowned for her incidental gymnastics, has Flirt, but I couldn't recollect any occasion except the present one, when a little brisk pulling hadn't tamed her down. The only exhaustive effect, however, which the pulling seemed to have, was produced upon my wrists and elbow-joints. She *wouldn't* stop galloping; indeed, every fresh stride that she took seemed to carry me nearer the conviction that she was running away. Her head, bent ground-ward, had in its pose all the defiance of rankest rebellion. It appeared to announce, as no spoken sentence could announce clearlier, " I won't listen to reason any more; I've got my head and I mean to keep it till something is broken or somebody killed."

As we bowled on, I began to creep from crown to sole with an awful dread. What if feminine strength indeed proved of no avail, and the man at my side still chose to sit passive? Well, it would be my own fault; I had flown into a passion when he ventured to grasp the reins, and now he preferred maintaining a gentle-manly silence whilst we both were being scampered with straight to destruction. I couldn't reproach him; no, not even if the consequences reduced me to a stump which would have to be wheeled round in a carriage all the rest of its days.

Presently I was having severe spinal chills. Something laconic but heart-rending in the way of an appeal was trembling on my lips; but instead of making it I merely screeched to Flirt as commandingly as I was able. Alas! I might as well have told a streak of light-ning to behave itself, or have offered suggestions about blowing to the wind that " bloweth where it listeth."

Matters were becoming horribly serious. I don't think I'm a bit of a coward, or I should have been less of a mule in the matter of calling upon Melville for assistance. There is something sublime, to my think-ing, about mulishness that would rather break its neck than be concession. I can't say that mine is ever of this superb sort. Usually it just misses the heroic laurel.

I have known important occasions upon which I would cheerfully meet with a serious *injury* of the neck in preference to yielding my point; but as for a full breakage—well, I'm neither Joan of Arc nor the Maid of Saragossa.

Flirt had given a terrific straight-ahead bolt that made me cold all over, and somehow caused my tense-strained arms and hands to feel as if they were somebody's else, stuck stiffly forward with a rein in each, when I turned a despairing sheep's-eye toward my companion. His face had a gray stone-cut look which I had never before seen it wear. He was evidently quite willing to be dashed in fragments.

On shot Flirt. My obstinacy was in its death-struggle by this time. Just before its final decease, I remember thinking whether I couldn't compromise matters by making believe swoon away on Melville's shoulder: but as common-sense urged that an abandonment of the reins would be inseparable from any such graceful proceeding, I dismissed the idea as more pathetic than discreet.

"Don't you see that my arms are being torn off?" I suddenly shrieked, very much as though I had been making all sorts of futile appeals for the past half-hour, and he were the most craven-hearted caitiff who ever sneered in scorn at suffering womanhood.

My words acted as flame acts upon powder. Instantly he bent forward and caught the reins. I suppose he caught them just in the nick of time. People who save other people from violent deaths of any sort whatever usually do so, I have noticed, just in the nick of time— at a period, in fact, calculated with such providential nicety that the billionth part of a second would have made a dolorous difference in results. Flirt seemed to feel very sensibly, at first, the new fresh power tugging at her insubordinate mouth. Indeed, I was beginning to have strong hopes that she had found her match, when Melville Delano muttered, in a voice low enough to be called abdominal :

" This sort of thing must stop, if possible."

It did stop, presently, with a shock that wasn't Titanic enough to overturn our little stout low wagon, or to cause an eruption of either Melville or myself, but a shock, nevertheless, which narrowly escaped unseating me, and as it was flung me against my companion in a fashion that proved how little regard for maiden modesty is possessed by what we generally term the force of circumstances. Melville had managed, somehow, to turn Flirt's head in amidst a very impassable-looking coppice of brambles and brushwood, and whilst she made several spiteful plunges that were in reality the epilogue of her evil behavior, I sprang out with grateful agility. Presently Melville was out of the wagon also, and had caught her by the bridle.

"Wasn't it awful?" I whispered, with much bad taste. " I'm so glad the wagon isn't broken."

" Excuse contradiction," he made answer, quietly, patting Flirt, whose lustrous auburn body shook as though it was allowed by nature for mares to have hysteria ; " but don't you see that the shaft is nearly split in two ? We must have a little help here. Whose is the white house yonder ? "

I hadn't noticed any white house as yet, for the powerful reason that my mind had not begun to occupy itself with the geography of our encompassing brambles and brushwood. A glance at the large white building to which Melville alluded was enough for me, however. " Oh, that's the hotel. I didn't think we'd gone so far."

3*

"The latter part of the drive was rather deceptive in its rate of progress," criticised Melville, dryly. "I suppose there is somebody there," he went on, "who could be of assistance in tying this shaft up?"

"Oh, yes. Mamma knows Mr. Collins, the present proprietor, quite well. He is indebted to her for several boarders during this summer and summers past, and will treat our shaft, I feel sure, as though it were personal property. Shall I go and pay him a visit?"

"Hadn't you better let me go?" he proposed, courteously. Melville is nearly always courteous except when offering himself in marriage to people, I have thus far found. "The mare is quite quiet now, and I will fasten her to the tree yonder."

"In that case we might walk up to the hotel together," I suggested, good-humoredly. "It will look as if we were more experienced in runaways, you know, and rather superior to them."

He laughed that pleasant laugh of his; and shortly afterward we were crossing the hotel-grounds side by side.

The monstrous vacant piazza looked dreary beyond language; all the building's multitudinous windows were shuttered solemnly; "life and thought have gone away," appositely murmured itself through my mind, as I recollected the style which children have of making hotel-piazzas hideous whilst the dog-star rages, and how fashion and folly and gossip meet there like the three Macbeth witches, to hob-and-nob, cheek by jowl.

"Can I see Mr. Collins?" I asked of the servant who appeared at the front door, after we had rung several resultless peals thereat.

Mr. Collins was away; would Mrs. Collins do?

We concluded, after a mutual glance, that Mrs. Collins would do.

Would we care to step into the parlor and wait ?

A second mutual glance decided us in favor of stepping into the parlor and waiting.

The parlor was a huge many-windowed curtainless barn of a place, with cohorts of cheap cheerless chairs and a pompous carpet, all dizzying flourishes. I seated myself at a window which looked out upon the piazza. Melville did the same.

I had given my name to the servant, and now regretted having given it. " Mrs. Collins is a dashing pretentious little body, who will probably put on her very smartest gear to receive us in," I informed Melville, "and flutter innocently downstairs after prinking twenty minutes."

The last word had not left my lips when a sound of steps on the piazza outside caused me to turn curious eyes in that direction.

A man and a woman came slowly toward me ; slowly enough for me to observe them both with the utmost distinctness of scrutiny.

The woman was tall beyond the ordinary height of her sex. She wore a black-silk walking-suit which was just perfection in every way, and which looked as if nothing except the dainty deftness of Parisian fingers could ever have made it so lovely and of such admirable style. Her figure, full of nobly symmetric lines, blended grace of motion with its rich rounded fulness : instantly I thought of a certain scrap which John Driscoll had marked in the Browning he lent me last year :

" And the breast's superb abundance where a man might base his head."

I have no business, I suppose, to dare describe her face. It was patrician ; it was languorous ; it was soulful ; it was saintly. Large light-lashed eyes lit it ; from firm fair throat to tender temple one soft peachy color prevailed over it ; a deep tiny chin-dimple gave it piquancy ; a straight Greek nose, delicate-nostrilled and clear-cut, refined it ; a small mouth, ripe and red-lipped, sweetened it : and of all this the sum and substance was beauty such as one meets not many times whilst one lives and observes.  It was only when she had come directly opposite me that I saw to thorough advantage her massive knotted hair ; for until then her black round-hat had left only one little fragment of it to gleam above either shell-pink ear.  In speaking of that hair I use the possessive pronoun with a fearless sense of correctness.  I don't believe that any hair-dresser ever had anything just like it in his life.  I doubt if he could find any customer for it, were such the case, though possibly some actress, mad to look bizarre, might have rioted with it through a semi-nude can-can.  And as for its being stained hair, the idea isn't worth thinking about ; for though red, brilliantly, sensationally red, there yet played along its pliant silken curves " a light that never was " in dye or wash, to mutilate an old quotation.  No " golden-fluid " ever accomplished the lustre of that beautiful glimmering luminousness.  It was the kind of hair that some people would have turned from in dismay, if not disgust, hating its keen fierce unconventional tinge ; but just, I  suppose, as olives and truffles and anchovy paste require cultured palates in their consumption, so did these odd gaudy tresses require a taste quite unmanacled by any cumbersome prejudice in order that they might be properly admired.

This ponderous descriptive passage of mine compares strangely enough with the short little chain of glimpses from which it has resulted.  So much for the woman who strolled past me, tossing in one of her shapely ungloved hands a vivid spray of golden-rod, and murmuring, with exquisite sidelong head, some low slow words to her companion.

I have said, I believe, that her companion was a man. I have not said, however, that this man was Fuller Dobell.

Yes, Fuller Dobell, in all the tangible reality possessed by flesh and blood, not to speak of broadcloth. There he moved, leisurely, well-favored, high-bred looking, irrefutably himself: and the mystery of that solitary departure from Pineside was no longer a matter of Cimmerian darkness. He had come here to " piazza " the afternoon away in this houri's company, whoever she was.

I drew back fully two yards from the window the instant that I recognized him. I will confess to you, Diary, that the woman's rare and radiant beauty struck me a hard miserable blow. One little moment will tell us so much, sometimes ! That little moment told me how Fuller Dobell had power to sicken me with bitterest jealousy.

They were no longer visible to me, and I stood very close up against the window, now, having followed them with my eyes as far as such pursuit was possible, when Melville Delano's hand fell upon my shoulder, and fell there by no means lightly.

As I turned to meet his face it struck me that he was in what we usually term a quiet rage. " Miss Helen," he began, bright-eyed and harsh-voiced, " I must insist upon your leaving this house at once. Pray don't ask any questions ; and pray come."

" What can you mean ? " I wondered. " Shan't we wait for Mrs. Collins ? "

" For no one. You will thank me, perhaps, at some future time for taking you away." By this he had reached the door of the parlor, and stood with a hand on the knob. There was the sharpness of irritation in his tones, now : " Don't you intend coming ? "

" Yes," I made answer, walking toward him with brisk steps, more than a merely vague idea of the actual truth having begun to dawn upon me.

Precisely at this moment enter Mrs. Collins by the very door whose knob Melville was holding : I had proved a false prophetess with regard to the smart toilette and the twenty minutes of expectancy. Mrs. Collins' vast smile as she bustled forward to welcome me was quite out of proportion with her little active anatomy of a body.

" I'm *so* delighted, my dear Miss Jeffreys ! How's mamma ? *Very* well, I trust. It's *such* an age since—"

Melville cruelly dammed the poor mite's further current of civilities by rapidly and with crushing conciseness telling her the object of our visit. " Could you spare us a man and a bit of stout rope ? " he finished, mercilessly careless of how polite amazement and polite sympathy were going far toward making the little lady entirely mute in the matter of a reply. " If so, Miss Jeffreys and I will at once go down to the wagon and wait there : the mare is not very securely tied."

" Of course," cooed Mrs. Collins in a dazed style ; silently wondering, I am confident, why my mother's daughter should allow herself to be run away with in the company of such a rude young man.

After that Melville indicated with a few hurried words the exact spot of the accident, leaving the parlor as he did so and drawing near the hall-door, whilst I

followed obediently enough. I remember that in his
excitement he did not overlook courtesy, but on opening the hall-door drew back for me to pass out first. I
should have done so at once, if directly in my path,
standing opposite the threshold I was about to cross and
evidently in act to ring for admission, I had not lifted
my eyes to behold Mr. Fuller Dobell and his beautiful
fellow-pedestrian. As it was, I just stood and stared.

Fuller Dobell, for the first time in all my cutaneous
acquaintance with him, blushed peony-red to his hat-
rim. His companion raised her straight amber-colored
eyebrows and heightened her bewitching chin a trifle, in
lovely serene surprise ; but that even peach-bloom of her
flawless oval face waxed not nor waned, howsoever faintly.

" Upon my word," Fuller Dobell broke silence, very
stammeringly indeed, "this is so unexpected that
really—"

" That you will oblige me by not even expressing the
surprise it causes you," rang forth Melville's voice from
behind me, sharp and trenchant as a scythe-stroke.

Fuller Dobell seemed to draw in óne short hard
breath which made his shoulders squarer and his breast
broader. "Pray what right have you, sir," he sneered,
" to mark out lines of conduct for my following ? " His
tones fairly rumbled with smothered rage. It was the
low-voiced fury of a man who would rather strike than
speak, as I plainly saw, who now saw him angry for the
first time.

" Only the right of having this young lady under my
present protection," sped Melville's defiant answer.
" I forbid you from addressing a word to her here and
now : you cannot do so, and you well know it, without
insult."

I daresay that I shouldn't have seen the arm which he

offered me, if it hadn't been thrust before my eyes in so prominent a curvature; for the beautiful cold angerless disdain which had suddenly asserted itself on that woman's face, and of which I seemed no less the object than Melville Delano, enticed me far more than if I had met with its striking effect midmost the four golden boundaries of some elegant picture-frame, with a tiny link of ugly letters in one corner, meaning Toulmouche or De Jonghe, or somebody of that gifted sort. As it was, I had to see the arm which Melville put forward: but being seen by no means necessitated for the arm that it should be taken.

Nor do I think that I would have taken it, had there not seemed something guiltily red, and not confusedly, about the flush that still fired Fuller Dobell's face. Everything else was in his favor, except Melville Delano's eager shocked expedition in the matter of trying to get me away; that looked like honest gentlemanly zeal.

Everything else?

On second thought I must admit those words to be rather strong generalizing, since I only have reference to the black-silk walking-suit and certain lesser accompaniments, worn by Fuller Dobell's lady-friend. I have lain to my soul for at least two years past, the flattering unction that the power is a new sense with me, of detecting dim differences between what is called bad style and good style. In things relative to the proprieties of a woman's wardrobe, there is no necessity whatever for the wind to be southerly in order that I may detect a hawk from a hernshaw. No woman could impose upon me by means of a generally correct style and minor details that were flagrant abominations. And when a woman has passed, blamelessly dressed, across my field of vision, the citadel of my good-will is already three-quarters won. I should very much prefer the society of a wicked sister whose misdeeds have nothing in common with her bonnet-trimmings, to that of a wicked sister who has trodden her evil path in vulgar-looking boots.

To state the case with brevity, Melville Delano had given me pointedly to understand, that my lungs were doing duty in a very contaminating atmosphere: I should have been the most tiresome sort of an ignoramus not to have guessed some such thing as this. Eloquently in refutation of his implied charge spake forth the black-silk walking-suit, that looked as if it wouldn't listen for a moment to being worn by any one but an absolute lady, the unimpeachable little round hat with its one broad burnished feather full of soft rainbow lights, the small embroidered linen collar, the pretty jabot in place of brooch, the glimmer of oblong ear-rings, (it is so easy to be bad style in ear-rings) and lastly the thorough-bred pose and movement that is about as difficult to catch and copy as to make some spurious coin ring "like a piece of gold thrown down."

There stood that woman, with "lady" in every fold of her faultless garments, every curve of her perfect figure, brilliant in her haughty beauty, a silent contemptuous refutation of Melville's hard innuendo. But on Fuller Dobell's cheek that guilty blush was burning, and through my mind stole sternly the remembrance of how he had cloaked about with all available secrecy his departure from Pineside. At least there was the doubt to be met, the risk to be run. All proper (or professedly proper) females are cowards when placed as I was placed. I neither dared meet the doubt nor run the risk. Melville's arm waited: I dropt my eyes, after the manner of the "virtuous gentlewoman deeply wronged," and hurried with him across the hotel-lawn, no more presuming to look behind me than if saline consequences of a most disastrous nature were sure to result from such an action.

We didn't speak a word to each other during that little journey wagonward.   Flirt was found to be in unmolested duress when we reached her.   I watched Melville potter with the damaged shaft for a little while, and then strolled deeper among the brambles, meditatively tearing my clothes upon them and picking beautiful red sumach-leaves which I didn't at all want. Once or twice I stole a glance at Melville's face : it wore severe drear solemnity, as if he felt thoroughly satisfied with his late line of conduct.   It was no doubt quite criminal of me, but I had an unamiable desire to commence walking home alone, and leave him to follow in the wagon as soon as its resuscitated shaft would permit.   Temporarily, I disliked Melville very much indeed ; a dislike engendered, quite possibly, by the reflection that in case certain suspicions were well founded, I ought to feel the roots of my being moved toward him in grateful respect.   Such anomalies of ingratitude are now and then to be encountered in human nature.

Presently a man appeared with the desired ligatures ; upon seeing whom I strolled farther away from the wagon, trying to absorb myself in outward things—such, for instance, as the sun, westering superbly along pale greenish heaven ; the lissom grace of a huge purple-beaded elder-bush ; a journeying company of dark birds, distant yet distinct in that pure clear autumn air, and looking because of their single-filed flight like some great rosary falling earthward, as if dropped by some

dozing saint from where "saints in glory dwell," incessant glory being conducive to drowsiness, as nearly
everybody will admit. I hated to let my thoughts turn
upon other things than these. The time to canvass
Fuller Dobell's doings had not arrived yet : there was
more than a ghostly chance that Melville Delano's com-
mendable rescue had flavored the least trifle of Quixot-
ism. The bad passions are always lightsleepers enough ;
anger will start from her bed at the suspicion of a sound,
and her own grim dreams will often rouse up jealousy.
For once at least let my bad passions wake to no false
alarm. Let the wheelwork of my thoughts stand idle
till fed with the proper mental grist. Time enough to
fume and storm when the real truth should unveil its
naked ugliness.

The joining together of what Flirt had broken asunder
didn't occupy at all a long time. Melville called to me
much sooner than I had expected to be summoned, and
received no answer until he had repeated my name for
the third time : of course this affected deafness was
nothing except scurrilous of me, though I truly don't
believe that he had the remotest suspicion about it.

I usually recollect conversations with infallible distinctness, memory with me photographing sentence after
sentence as though her camera possessed an infinity of
plates ; but during that ride home I remember no one
of the trivial nothings which left mine and Melville Delano's lips " on wings of articulate words." We talked
to each other ; and that is about all. Our speech was
but a flimsy disguise for the disturbed mood of either,
and evidenced what lay beneath it no less clearly than
the thin trembling earth-crust of equatorial regions will
evidence how that colossal unhatched vulture, Earthquake, prepares to peck his terrene shell, and thrust,

perhaps, the horror of his ruinous beak cracklingly up through the heart of some proud populous city. To continue my rather ponderous parallel, smelling, Diary, so strongly of hyperbole, nothing of a volcanic sort broke the crust of Melville's and my own common-places during all that ride home. Selina met us in the hall, as we entered it, with a remark to the effect that she had begun to feel very lonely, her sentence being neatly divided during its delivery by an impulsive gig-gle. We learned furthermore that mamma had returned only a short while before ourselves ; Mrs. Landesdowne, Selina said, had not been at home, she believed ; any-how, mamma had spoken of getting back a good hour earlier than she had expected to do.

" Was she very much horrified to learn that we had deserted you ? " I asked, absently, hardly hearing Se-lina's responsive " Of course not," when she had the politeness to titter it. I was asking myself, just then, whether it would be the wiser plan to tell mamma all that had recently occurred—runaway, application for succor, strange encounter, and the whole engaging little chapter of what the advertisements of novels term " cu-rious developments ; " or whether an entirety of silence on these points would form the better plan, at least until I learned what course Melville meant to adopt. Some-thing told me (I suppose that something was his som-brely set face, his chilled hardened pair of eyes) that he meant to adopt a course of Draconian sternness. If it were true that he was merely tilting at a windmill, then he intended to tilt with all his might.

" This way and that dividing the swift mind " resulted in a decision not to go near mamma until dinner-time ; and until dinner-time we did not meet. About ten minutes before our dining-hour, and whilst Blanche was exerting all her Gallic skill upstairs in my room upon the proper moulding of my sash-bow, I heard a sound of wheels outside which didn't leave me in much doubt as to whose wagon was making it.

He must have gone upstairs to dress for dinner immediately upon arriving. When I came down into the lower hall it was quite vacant. Entering the sitting-room I found Selina there, with lugubrious eyes turned fireward and with evidently no curiosity, to judge from the closed book in her lap, regarding the question of " Why Did She Desert Her Husband ?."

" Mr. Delano has taken your mother into the library for a private conversation, I think," she made haste to inform me.

" It's almost dinner-time," I tried to say carelessly, giving the clock a fleet glance. " Mr. Dobell isn't down yet ? "

" No ; I believe not."

Whilst Selina was answering my question I left the sitting-room again. Even in these pages I should prefer surrounding with some slight haze of uncertainty the fact of whether I had any positive intent to play eavesdropper or no, as I approached the library door. Look on the bright side of things, Diary, and don't even suspect me of the vileness.

Indeed, I didn't listen. We have all heard the rather sneering elucidation of why Jack preferred a stomachic vacuum instead of his supper. And yet I don't want to sow, by means of this assertion, the tiniest seed of a belief that I would have listened if I could. Idle dreamers may concern themselves with what might have happened ; what did happen was this:

Just as I reached the library door it became evident from the steadily increasing loudness with which some

sentences of mamma's made themselves heard, that the
conversation between her and Melville was nearing its
end and that the library was about being vacated.
" Rest confident, Mr. Delano," I heard mamma enun-
ciate in her superbest manner, "that you have acted
with praiseworthy promptness and wisdom.  I like the
rough candor with which you have put me on my
guard against further insult.  Pray accept my warmest
thanks."

Almost immediately afterward the library door was
opened and forth swept mamma with unwonted majesty,
followed by Melville.  I contrived to give my nearness
to both people a purely accidental look, and was just
feeling convinced that I had succeeded when mamma
glided rapidly up to where I was standing, wreathed my
neck impetuously with one of her black-silk lace-
trimmed arms, dropped her stately head on my shoulder, and moaned out with a splendid combination of
plaintiveness and dignity :

"My poor poor Helen !  We have  both  been
shamefully deceived."  At this I felt myself patted
flutteringly on the back.  " But you don't understand,
my dear ; of course you don't understand.  I was
wrong to say anything about it."  Then mamma dis-
continued her statuesque droop against my shoulder,
and made something very like a silent appeal for sympathy to Melville Delano.

It was an absurd position, this standing there and being represented such an out-and-out dove of purity ;
and a remark to the effect that I had understood only
too well was naturally desirous of labial exit ; but I
drove the remark back, and instead wondered audibly
whether dinner wasn't ready.

We were all seated at the table when Fuller Dobell

appeared below stairs. He looked a jot paler than usual, I fancied, on letting my eyes just sweep his face swiftly as he entered the dining-room; but perhaps mere fancy had indeed all to do with this conclusion. Selina bowed to him with vigorous sociability. I am quite sure that mamma averted her eyes from him. Amid entire silence he took his seat.

There was something solemnly august about that silence, to my thinking. It had a grandeur of repri-mand much more effective than our entrance into the dining-room without our guest had exhibited. I am sure it would have awed Fuller Dobell completely if Selina hadn't broken its sombre spell by prattling some pueril-ities to Melville. The culprit promptly, at this, felt himself freed from Coventry.

"I must apologize, Mrs. Jeffreys," he broke forth courteously, "for being such a straggler at the dinner-table. The quality of your soup heaps coals of fire on my tardy head; you ought to tear it away from me as a punishment."

Mamma smiled an arctic smile. "We tread on dan-gerous ground, Mr. Dobell, when we begin to suggest punishments for our own misdemeanors."

His eyes dropt soupward and staid so, his next spoon-ful or two being taken with rather nervous haste. Something like the same guilty red that had besieged his face on the hotel-piazza I saw it wear now. My last doubt took wing forthwith; he must be culpable; what was more, he knew that mamma knew. My wrath, kept in leash heretofore, felt its bonds suddenly cut. He had tried to make me his tool in the perpetra-tion of a gross insult to our house. All those past im-pressions of his latent contempt for us were remembered, and grew deeper as I recalled them. I was on mamma's side, no matter how severe was the course she might take. His very presence at our table was like a sting-ing jeer to me ; more than once during dinner I shivered as though that presence had literally cast " a chill across the table-cloth."

Everybody kept unviolated silence except Selina, for a little while : presently Melville and I were delivered of occasional commonplaces. But as for mamma and our interesting delinquent, each remained worldless through-out the rest of dinner.

When, however, we ladies and Melville rose from the table, mamma turned toward Mr. Dobell. Her voice, as she spoke, had the "icily regular" sound made by measured syllables and a metallic tone. "With your permission, Mr. Dobell, I shall see you in the library some time this evening. Say in about fifteen minutes?"

The thorough easeful suavity of his reply was super-fine affectation, if affectation indeed. " I shall be most happy to meet you there. You don't mind my smok-ing first, by the bye ? Thanks."

After leaving the dining-room I went straight up-stairs to my own, and locked myself in and cried. It wasn't a good candid cry, but rather a little weak mix-ture of timidity and lamentation very much like a pro-tracted whimper. If such a thing had been possible as for any one to ask me, just then, what I was crying for, no doubt I should have indignantly denied that my con-dition had anything at all lachrymose about it, and de-clared myself quite too angry for tears.

After perhaps ten minutes of this mildly tragic em-ployment I went down-stairs again, meeting Melville in the hall.

" I was looking for you," he stated, a certain abrupt-ness in manner and voice. " It had occurred to me,

I can scarcely tell why, that I have in some way offended you."

"Did I show you that I thought so?" was my questioned answer. "I meant to conceal my annoyance. Has the wrong-doer met his judge yet, by the bye?" pointing libraryward as I spoke.

"Yes—your mother and Mr. Dobell are together, if you mean this. But pray state in what way I have offended."

I tossed my head. "Pshaw! your rushing to mamma in that tell-tale style was a shallow performance, take it all in all. I am neither a prude on the one hand nor a baby on the other: you might have consulted me first as to what course you should take."

He was scanning my face narrowly. "I don't believe that in your heart of hearts you object to that course."

"How am I able to pass reliable judgment upon it?" was my ready retort. "I don't even know what provocation you have received, except in so far as my woman's wit has helped me to imagine. You have left me to guess everything. I will admit that my imagination may not have gone a hair's-breadth from the truth. But anyhow, you have treated me like an utter infant." All this I pronounced with caustic snappishness, and passed him, not waiting for his answer, and feeling myself a wretch for condemning where really there was no valid reason to condemn. My conduct was modelled on the same perverse plan, I suppose, as it had been that afternoon, when he called my name twice before receiving an answer from me; that is, I committed an injustice with the keenest sense of its being such. If the angels ever trouble themselves at all to weep over mundane sins, very certainly it is over

4

this open-eyed and cold-blooded sort that they are most emotional.

I suppose that mamma and Fuller Dobell were both closeted together for about an hour ; and it was an hour during which I felt more than once an eager yearning to go and glue my ear against the library key-hole and disgrace myself generally by the most flagrant kind of eavesdropping. Fortunately there was a preventive furnished against any such depraved inclinations now as in a previous case : Melville Delano, instead of choosing to occupy the sitting-room in Selina's and my society, sullenly lolled with a book upon one of the hall-lounges.

At last mamma glided into the sitting-room with a little dot of color on each cheek, but otherwise lacking none of her usual serenity. I wondered in what condition she had left the field whereon her battle had been waged. Doubtless the enemy was in woful case by this time.

Mamma seated herself and took out her gold eye-glasses and began to read with their assistance. Meanwhile I stole incidental glances across my book at her composed haughty face, and told myself with savage pride that she had won a complete victory over a certain presumptuous insolent.

Presently the dead silence became, under existing circumstances, intolerable to me. Selina seemed, at last, to have found the question of the fictional wife's desertion one worth considering in Melville's absence, and I felt too grateful toward the literary gentleman whose work had furnished me with this nice composing agent, to break its spell by any remark directed Selina-ward. Mamma was the only one left for me to address, and I accordingly addressed her to this effect :

" Where has Mr. Dobell gone, mamma ? "

She shot a keen glance at me from over the gleaming eye-glasses. "I cannot answer that question, Helen. He has probably gone to his room, and will not make another appearance this evening. I would not, if I were he."

The cold austerity of mamma's tones thoroughly roused Selina, who levelled looks of the most searching inquiry at both of us in turn. "She is going to be inquisitive," I thought, "and I had better get away and leave mamma to deal with her." And I did get away, but not because of her dreaded inquisitiveness. Oh, no! rather because there was a knot in my throat, setting aside two little armies of tears that were laying silent siege to either eye; because I felt that whatever magnificent answer mamma may have given to the contemptuous blow hurled at us, no answer, how magnificent soever, could lighten my bitter load of disappointment, or lesson my mordant sense of having been right shamelessly trifled with.

I have been up here in my own room ever since then, giving my scribbling propensities the most untrammelled license, and stopping every once in a while to sigh a colossal sigh.

No doubt he will go early to-morrow morning. I suppose it would be much nicer if he got away before breakfast. Of course mamma will not allow me to notice him when we meet each other out next winter, even if I wanted to do so.

But I don't want; indeed, indeed no! When I think of how he tried to make me his accomplice in that secret departure from Pineside, I feel like walking the floor, not to mention grinding my teeth.

That person must be an awful character. I should not be a bit surprised if mamma, who knows such lots, had heard about her before Melville told his tale. What a beauty she was! I wonder how well they knew each other. She is probably educated and all that—one of the sorts of women whom it makes only lovelier in *some* men's eyes to be very bad. I judge of her education by her handwriting—provided she wrote the superscription on that envelope; which it is fair to suppose that she did.

Perhaps they are very intimate and he only came to Pineside for the purpose of being near her. If I thought this, I should go on my knees to mamma concerning the matter of making him pack his portemanteau instantly. At present, as there is no such damning evidence in my possession, I had better adopt the meeker course of getting myself in bed.

# CHAPTER VI.

EPT. 27.—It is marvellous, the mighty changes one little day can make in our thoughts, our hopes, our creeds, and all which is portion and parcel of what we name life. I don't mean to hurl a sermon at you, Diary; I'm too happy to moralize. But it really seems very hard to identify myself with the same miserable biped who wrote your previous page not many hours ago. I almost feel like saying with the man in *Maud*, after he has killed Maud's brother, " it is this guilty hand."

Yes, this guilty hand that wrote such mean suspicions in you last night : they *were* mean, as sure as you are morocco.

I overslept myself this morning, as a natural consequence of lashing my mattress like a whale and kneading my pillow like putty, for certainly three hours after going to bed last night. That is, I incoherently snubbed Blanche when she came in to dress me for breakfast, and didn't get up till long after breakfast was finished.

Having drunk my coffee in solitude, I went to find the people. Nobody seemed to be anywhere. Going from room to room, I finally reached the library and pounced into it, notwithstanding the closed door, vacancy of rooms had begun to seem the order of the morning, and the idea of finding this occupied hadn't occurred to me.

But it was occupied. Mamma and Fuller Dobell were there. They were seated on a sofa, quite close to each other. Of course there was an ocular fusillade directed upon me in a surprised way, as soon as my pounce was accomplished.

"Excuse me," I apologized, rather awkwardly, with a gradual backward locomotion. "I was looking for Selina and Mr. Delano."

"They are playing croquêt," mamma hastened; "I heard Selina ask him for a game just after breakfast."

"Oh, thanks." I commenced noddingly to close the door, and had in truth nearly closed it, when mamma's voice stopped me.

"I've a few words for you, Helen, in a few moments. Just go upstairs, please, to my room and wait there till I join you; which will be immediately."

I searched mamma's face with swift scrutiny : there was no vaguest sign of anger upon it. As for Mr. Dobell, the seal-ring on his little finger appeared suddenly to have commanded his whole attention; for which reason his blond locks and a segment of forehead were all the facial view I could just then obtain of him. Answering "certainly, mamma," I closed the library door behind as graceful an exit as I knew how to make, and went upstairs in deepest thought, at the pace of a lame snail.

What could it all mean ? Had there been an explanation, an exculpation ? On reaching mamma's room, I interred myself in one of her cavernous cretonne easy-chairs, and folded my arms meditatively and wondered what was going to happen. I had not long to wonder.

Presently mamma entered, closing the door behind her.

" Helen."

" Well, mamma."

" You found me talking with Mr. Dobell." She was standing before her dressing-table, seeing that all was well with her gray puffs. " The interview, my dear, was of his own making. I should have been quite willing for him to leave breakfastless, if he had chosen to do so."

I had excavated myself from the easy-chair by this time, sitting bolt-upright therein. " But instead of that, mamma, he offered you some apology, I suppose. It must have been a rather flimsy one, if there was really good cause last night for your own and Melville Delano's indignation."

She faced me, at this, looking determined and absolute. " There was not good cause. Melville Delano was right enough, I suppose, only he went too far. That visit to the hotel was, after all, only an imprudence. Of course the woman's character is abominable, and of course it was an insolent act for him to meet her. But we must remember one thing: had it not been for your accident, you would have gone home without a suspicion of Fuller Dobell's bad behavior."

I bit my lips for a second, so as to answer with self-control. " Is that his apology? In my opinion, it looks much more like a sneer."

" But it was not his apology: it is only my sober afterthought. The man himself sees his fault clearly and repents it stingingly. He offers no special excuse except his deep regret, if this may be called one. I can't blame you for having condemned with heat and haste, since I myself did the same. But listen for a moment to what cooler judgment ought to tell both you and me. Helen, it ought to tell us that we have both been far too severe. A man in Fuller Dobell's sphere of life, and with Fuller Dobell's advantages, would have to be a miracle of continence and modesty if he had met all his temptations without flinching. It is certainly presumptuous to believe him a sort of white crow as regards these matters ; let us rather choose the sensible opinion that he is no whit better, no whit worse, than the majority of publicans and sinners who make up society. Allowing this, allow that the person who sent for him yesterday morning had some slight acquaintance with the man whereby to justify in her own eyes, doubtless, the brazen course she adopted ; and that he, though conscious of committing a gross discourtesy towards us in noticing her communication—"

" Stop there, please," I broke in, with face aglow and eyes aglitter. " Is all this anything more than a supposition on your part, mamma ? Do you suppose or do you *know* that their acquaintance is slight ? that Fuller Dobell had no foreknowledge of this woman's presence at the hotel, and that the whole meeting was partially the result of accident, partially of careless daring on the woman's side ? "

I felt that as I spoke the last word of this question my stretched-out neck and anxiously-creased forehead told with what eagerness I craved the answer. But mamma's face had grown hard and harsh by this time. " I cannot see, Helen, how these details can be of any consequence to you."

" But they are of supreme consequence ! " with passionate voice I made answer. " If he went there only for the reasons you have hinted at, then I can't help feeling the force of his insult to me personally (me whom he wanted to make his abettor in the payment of that secret visit) weakened and diminished ever so much. I could pardon more easily than you, perhaps, if only I knew what you know."

Mamma's answer didn't come as promptly as I might have wished it to come. Indeed, I fancied that an odd undecided look held her face for a moment or two, and that her few first words lacked their speaker's usual direct pertinence and point. Her manner and voice, however, were both softened. "It was really quite cruel of me, Helen, not to understand more readily that special facts regarding this affair are much dearer to you than any—any charitable generalities, my child. And after all," mamma progressed, with a moderate little laugh, "very possibly I myself have been more influenced by these than by those. I have learned that Fuller Dobell's objectionable rendezvous was precisely as you have well expressed it—partially the result of accident, partially of careless daring on the woman's side. All in all, my dear, an imprudence, an impertinence; yet with none of that unpardonable element which would have resulted from some gross arrangement like an assignation between them, or in fact any understanding whatever, based upon close previous intimacy. But, Helen, dear, what are you crying about?"

"Never mind," I gurgled, having risen and begun to walk the floor. "I know I'm idiotic to cry." Then I stopped in front of where mamma stood, and looked at her with swimming eyes over a parapet of handkerchief. "You're *sure* of this, mamma?"

"Quite certain," she smiled, her fingers glancing among some flowers on a little ebony table.

"And he isn't gone, is he?" I grievously questioned.

4*

"Oh, no. He intends remaining, of course. I think he would like to see you very much, Helen. Why not go downstairs at once, and stop your crying before you have red eyes?"

I did not go down until some time afterward, when wholly sure that my eyes were above all suspicion. Selina and Melville were just entering the house as I appeared in the hall.

"Oh, Helen!" clattered Miss Matthers, on seeing me; "I've been beaten two games so awfully! You just never! Mr. Delano wouldn't be induced to play another. He says it's because he intends going very soon."

I looked at Melville frigidly. "You're going in the half-past twelve?"

"Yes." He was giving my face, meanwhile, a steadfast ransacking stare.

I turned toward Selina. "Have you seen Mr. Dobell?"

Selina had not seen him. "I wonder where he can be, I murmured, saying the words in an absorbed way, and managing to discover with the corners of my eyes that Melville was doing his best not to scowl. Then I walked away, presently reaching the library door. It was open. I entered the library.

A fire was dancing in the great hearth-place with ruddiest vivacity, making mobile mosaics of shade and shine along wainscoting and bookcase. In a great chair wheeled close to the fire, with the shifting light on his blond head and a ponderous book open in his lap, sat Mr. Fuller Dobell.

Whilst I came boldly forward, he rose with a great deal of awkwardness, injuriously holding the vast volume by one of its covers.

"You had quite a scholarly look," I laughed, addressing the fire. "It's a pity to disturb you, as I have evidently done."

"Anything but that. I was just beginning to get very tired of my solitude. Will you not sit in the chair there at your side ? It opens its arms longingly for you."

Presently we had both seated ourselves. The ponderous volume was lying at his feet, now. "What is the name of your mighty tome ? " I questioned, merely to make words.

He accomplished a hasty dive toward it. "I really can't say. I just took it up, you know, and opened it, and then got thinking of something else. By Jove ! it's a Greek lexicon." After that his deep deep and blue blue eyes behaved their very tenderest toward mine. "You see, I must have been at mental sixes and sevens. It's always darkest before dawn, say the old proverbial authorities, and how little I dreamed that you were coming in to terminate my perplexity with that pleasant face ! I thought, you know, that your wrath against me was something truly awful."

"Well," I just articulated and no more, "you see that you were wrong." Then a little louder : "Suppose we don't say another word about that, if you please."

"About what ? Your imagined wrath ? I'd much rather, though." And now his huge chair was pushed appreciably nearer my own : I never knew that those library chairs of ours, by the bye, had such eminently easy rollers. "It's a great shock to me to find you so nice, when I anticipated dozens of cold shoulders."

"A great shock ? "

"Of pleasure." At this there came a tiny treble sound from the neighborhood of his chair-rollers, and presently something touched my elbow. I didn't draw my elbow away. "Do you know," he very softly went on, "that I was thinking about going to you with a formal good-by, just as you entered this room? It would have been formal even to stiff-neckedness, I assure you; I am a very bad hand at apologies and other recipes for humble pie."

"Well, well, there's no need of an apology," I hurried. "To change the subject, Mr. Delano is going to-day in the half-past twelve train. Selina Matthers is to be left wholly cavalierless, unless you take pity upon her. I hope you'll occasionally be nice."

"I'm afraid you're asking too much," he hesitated, with a droll grimace.

"Pshaw! you must practise a little fortitude; it's a lovely virtue. One shouldn't shirk every burden. Life has its Selina Matthers', you know, as well as its—its—"

"Helen Jeffreys'," he finished, with lips so near my cheek that his breath warmly touched it.

"Agreeable, but angled for," I laughed, coloring a little.

"I always snap at tempting baits. However, I didn't mean to say anything specially hard against your guest. If she *hadn't* those abnormal teeth and *didn't* gush so and *was* pretty, and all that—"

"Well?"

"Why, it would make no fragment of difference in my manner toward her, I assure you."

"I don't understand, Mr. Dobell."

"No? Let me explain." (I wonder how many inches, or rather how few, his face was from mine, just then.) "I mean that I have eyes and ears for only one person at Pineside, and that person is near me now, with the firelight playing over her silky brown hair, and making the rings flash brightly on her dim little, slim little

hands.   By the bye, isn't there room for one more ring
on a certain finger I see ?   A ring of my giving, Helen.
A ring that would tell you, whenever you glanced down
at it, of how Fuller Dobell had asked you to marry him,
and of how you had consented with sweet willingness.
In the name of roses and peonies and everything else
that is red, what makes you blush so prodigiously ?
One would think I had already taken the kiss that I'm
going to take now."

After that his lips made a wholly unprovoked assault
upon my cheek, and staid there lingeringly, clingingly,
for one quick blissful second.

I ought to put little stars after that paragraph, Diary,
as they sometimes do in books, so as to make the situation more effective.   Besides, it is wrong that you
should create such complete havoc with my most sacred
secrets.   I literally find a diary rushing in where an
angel might fear to tread.

But after all, what matters it whether I put stars or
no ?   It is true that he who runs may read this neat
handwriting of mine, but as long as Heaven spares my
thumb and my first finger I can place a locked writing-
desk in the way of any.such probability.   And if I die
so abruptly as to preclude, among other luxuries of the
moribund, all giving of farewell injunctions, then I
flatter myself that whatever violating peep may be
taken into these journalistic mysteries, the peeper must
smile whilst he frowns, must admire whilst he condemns,
and speak of me thenceforth as one who scribbled—not
wisely but too well.   And I, in truth, being numbered
among those of whom Swinburne says, with such de-
solately beautiful melody, that

> "They know not, neither can remember,
> The old years and flowers they used to know "—

in what manner shall it irk my slumber and my silence, if shocked eyes read this posthumous record of a certain delicious hour in the library of Pineside, at a time when this tell-tale hand shall be neither more nor less than the ashes of the embers of the hearth-logs which once laughed their noiseless yellow laughter a yard or so from our quiet beatitude of love-making ?

No, I shan't put stars. Let me rather go on to say, that we billed and cooed for a good hour, after that, in a manner which should have made all the turtle-doves feel like coming to school to us. He bills and coos irreproachably. He says that he has liked me ever since we first met at Newport, this summer. It was at Mrs. Crushington's ball, and I wore my lavender tulle with the trimmings of pansies ; and to think of his remembering the dress and going over all its prominent points with glibness enough to have surprised a man-milliner ! If a straw will indicate how the wind is deporting itself, surely by such evidences as these one may judge the fervor of one's lover.

Thrilling with delight as I was all the time we sat there, I yet remembered, every few moments or so, how suddenly the whole matter had come about, and how three days ago my eyes, had any one prophesied or even hinted at such a thing, would have rivalled saucers, not to speak of soup-plates. Here was the hand whose softness and smoothness until now had paid mine those brief formal little visits of etiquette which meant so absolutely nothing whatever, on a sudden enjoying with it terms of the tenderest intimacy. And that blond moustache, too, of which I had often caught some very near glimpses indeed, but which had seemed to wear, for all this, a kind of inviolable dignity—how odd to feel its satin-smooth luxuriance meet my close-shut

lips, or sweep, leaving kisses in its path, along my tingling cheek.

I wonder what sort of a joy it is that a man feels,
when his arms gird for the first time the woman he
adores. I suppose it is a sort of joy different from what
the woman feels—provided she adores in return. The
one is a joy of possessing, doubtless; the other is a joy
of being possessed. And what a strange new intoxi-
cating joy have I found this last!

I shan't ever forget, if I live to be an octogenarian,
the rapture I felt after he had once gotten me firmly in
his arms and had laid his lips to mine. If, in hours
previous, the possibility of any such fleshly union
occurring at any future time has ever vaguely flitted
through my mind, an opinion has at once resulted, I
will admit, (correspondingly shadowy) to the effect that
I should like it very much indeed. But I never thought
then of what the real experience would resemble; of
how that extreme physical nearness to the man she loves
will mix a kind of silencing awe with a woman's delight,
whilst breath and heart-beat quicken, and her brain diz-
zies itself trying to realize the divine situation. Awe:
that little word is wonderfully apposite, right here.
Suddenly the beloved object is shorn of all intervening
distance; whether Mahomet goes to the mountain or
the mountain to Mahomet, they are together, notwithstanding. Awe is a natural result. I will not, of course,
speak for men, with their multivalve hearts, their manifold ways of loving; but I will jump upon the platform
of my own recent personal experience, and say for my
own sex that no member of it ever loved really and
thoroughly without feeling, when for the first time
brought very very near him who has been the inspirer
of such love, as if it would be right sweet to kneel be-

fore him and serve him reverentially.   A woman never loves what she believes weaker than herself; and when this power of manhood with which she has fallen in love takes her in its arms and purrs compliments in her ear, and makes a charming travesty on its own strength, like a sword garlanded with flowers, then, on the woman's side, every feminine impulse of spite and malice and contradiction assumes the form of a devoutest humility.

We might have sat there one hour and have made a huge hole in the next, if mamma hadn't entered the library.   I don't know what she suspected, but her entrance was benevolently heralded by several " Helen, my dear—s" before its accomplishment.   Fuller and I (he has been Mr. Dobell-ed to you for the last time, Diary) were posed very lukewarmly by the time that mamma laid eyes on us.

I wonder if she divined the truth instantaneously.   I suppose so.   What with love-making and the heat of the fire, I am afraid that my cheeks were giving such a high-colored account of recent proceedings as not even to tax the full powers of a dull-visioned physiognomist; which, by the bye, mamma verily isn't.

" I came to tell you that Mr. Melville is going, Helen," she began, carelessly calm in voice and manner. " He has had his early luncheon and is looking for you, to say good-by."

I rose and left the room without an instant's hesitation.   There waited Melville near the front door, over-coated and with hat in hand, being babbled to by Selina.   Somehow a pang of pity shot through my heart, then.   Doubtless it was because of my own supreme happiness.   Misery is a lover of company, but joy likewise loves it passing well.

" You must pardon my disappearance," I smiled,

drawing near him. "I half trusted, though, that mamma's persuasions might prove no less effective to-day than yesterday.".

He met my smile with grave eyes, grave mouth. "Well, you see they haven't. Is that the reason you wear so pleased a look, by the bye?"

Selina coughed a sickly effete cough, and strolled away. Just then wheels sounded on the drive outside, and just then, also, mamma appeared, advancing from the library.

"We might as well part good-humoredly," I suggested, putting out my hand.

He smiled, at this, a sort of dull solemn smile. "'Take hands and part with laughter,' as your favorite Swinburne advises. Of course you recollect the next line about 'touching lips and parting with tears'? You look in no mood for tears, however: and yet I will not be sure that you haven't been touching lips with any-one."

I scarcely blushed, shrugging my shoulders and speaking with hurt dignity. "That is nothing except *coarse*. I didn't think you would use such a weapon—you who were once my friend, and who will be always, I hope, at least worthy of so ranking yourself."

How rapid a change in him those few words wrought! "Once your friend!" he iterated with reproachful voice. "Treat me like a friend, and you shall find me worthy of all trust." He spoke very quickly, after this, as though trying to get the words uttered before mamma should attain hearing-distance. "Tell me, for instance, whether you mean to marry Fuller Dobell."

My answer came with blunt frankness: "I do—if I can."

"And you are engaged now?"

" I suppose one might call it so."

And then mamma was upon us. Melville made his adieus with entire composure. If I had really dealt him a hard blow just then, he had steeled his sinews to meet it, poor fellow, and had in truth met it valorously.

For a good hour that afternoon, Fuller and I behaved nothing unless sacrificially toward Selina. Later, I blush to chronicle that we plotted a little plot, which resulted in our taking an immense Selinaless walk. I never knew before that the brisk walking necessitated by cool weather would admit of so much mutual lover-like deportment on the part of two pedestrians with differing sexes. I somehow wouldn't take his arm during the first mile or so, making believe that my draperies needed the complete manual attention of their owner. But when our steps had been turned homeward, and a conviction had possessed each of us to the effect that we would both be late for dinner, and I had stumbled once or twice because of the fleet pace at which we were faring ; and when also the descended sun had left all the sky one luminous eerie bluish afterglow, and the sharp-shapen silver of a crescent moon gleamed keen above lines of black far-away foliage, and a drowsy dreamy noise, as though twenty separate mæstro-katy-dids were giving the word of command to as many little leaf-muffled orchestras, filled the cool dark world in wood-land or meadow-land or marsh-land,—then "it so fell out" (to borrow a phrase from the coy simplicity of Mother Goose) that my right hand left off caring at all for the draperies, and crept confidingly into a little loop-hole of animated broadcloth nearly as far as its elbow.

"Don't you find this arrangement much nicer?"

Fuller wanted to know, after it was about two minutes old.

" It rests me a little," I admitted, with some delay.

" Lean a trifle harder," he coaxed ; " as if you had a flesh-and-blood arm, you know, and were rather more robust than a feather."

Whereupon I did lean a trifle harder, and immediately had that dizzy delicious feeling which I attempted to describe several lines back ; and presently he stooped down, whilst were trotting along, and astonished my cheek with a short little stolen kiss, and called me an obedient darling. That is the first time, by the bye, that he has ever called me any nice name, such as darling. Perhaps he fancies I don't like that sort of lackadaisical thing. If so, he is mightily mistaken ; I adore it—from him. He has such a manly way of being silly, and makes the contrast so charming between the words said and the manner of saying them, that I truly don't think I should do anything but smile indulgently if he were to address me as "tootsicum ;" which you will admit, Diary, to be the very land's-end of amorous nonsense.

It is now about eleven o'clock P.M., and Fuller and mamma are talking together on one of the hall-lounges in the most incoherent sort of undertone, and Selina is spell-bound, in the sitting-room, by the final fascinations of her novel, and I am trying, all alone by myself, to perform the unperformable : such happiness as mine can't be put into black and white.

I suppose mamma is doing her best to make the remaining days of my spinsterhood as few as possible. I wonder if he has said anything about money-matters to her. Of course he has been compelled to do so, if report tells truth and he has really lost everything of his own.   I hope he hasn't, by the bye.   People will say that he is marrying me for my money, then ; and it is just horrible even to think of idle slanderers having it in their power to make such a story seem plausible.

But pshaw ! even if they should seek to soil him like that, surely both he and I can bear it.   And should the least doubt ever cast the faintest shadow on my heart, may I only have to search his loving eyes for surety that

> " The noblest answer unto such
>    Is kindly silence when they brawl."

# CHAPTER VII.

EPT. 28.—I saw at breakfast, this morning, that mamma was yearning to level upon me her mightiest cannon of congratulation, and shortly after breakfast she effected her purpose with entire success. I don't know what befell me if I was not bombarded by approval. Mamma evidently considers a hecatomb of fatted calves nothing to speak of when viewed as my merited reward for duteous behavior. As a rule she rather disdains cant than otherwise ; but this morning I detected a marked inclination toward it : such, for example, as

"Rest sure, Helen, that your married life is to be charmingly untroubled, my dear. Providence would almost be without the right to inflict unhappiness upon a daughter who had followed motherly counsel as you have done."

Of course, the correctness or incorrectness of the motherly counsel referred to was superbly taken for granted. I bowed with wordless acquiescence on hearing this valuable little suggestion, as though sharing mamma's apparent conviction that Providence would do well to profit by it.

After having been shattered, so to phrase it, by ami-

ability and approbation, I took the liberty of re-collect-
ing my fragments and of re-existing to at least the extent of a question or two. "I must ask you, mamma,
about yours and Fuller's conversation of last night.
Was any decision made?—anything important, you
know? or did you merely give your consent, and all
that?"

Mamma perceptibly stiffened—the result of habit, I
suppose—and then perceptibly softened again. "Yes,
Helen, we decided one rather important matter. Your
wedding-day. What do you think of the first of November next?"

"Goodness gracious!"

She met my astonished face with supreme calmness.

"Rather an ambiguous opinion, my dear. Does it
mean that you approve the arrangement?"

"It means that I'm thunderstruck, mamma," I
blurted out, whiningly. "Hardly a month's engagement!"

But the dictum was unalterable. I could merely offer
suggestions, if I chose, giving what I believed to be
good advice with an outsider's humility, like the little
maid of Israel who waited on Naaman's wife. Fuller
wanted a short engagement, for one reason; mamma
infinitely preferred it, for another. In the matter of my
trousseau a little energetic haste would accomplish marvels. It was best that I should speedily reconcile myself
to the idea, provided any real unwillingness existed.
As this final suggestion left the maternal mouth, I
clearly saw how worse than useless rebellion would be.
Besides, the glaring novelty of the announcement had, so
to speak, worn off a trifle, and already I had begun to
think about it with a little catching of the breath, something similar to the sensation with which I had thought

about my initiatory ball, during the ultimate and penul-
timate weeks of social seclusion.  And so,

"It's idle to spend strength on stone walls," I at
length mumbled, with sweet resignation.  "And now
I've one more question, mamma.  It's about money,
you know—Fuller's money.  Some people say that he
has lost nearly everything.  I should like to know,
please, whether you referred to this matter last night."

Mamma's handsome grayish eyebrows were holding
an indignant meeting with each other on the neutral
ground directly above her impressive nose ; and over
their gloomy union deepened a gloomier frown.  "I
must say, Helen, that your curiosity amazes me."

Then I fired up.  "Surely I'm entitled to know
about the pecuniary affairs of the man I'm going to
marry."

"It would be better taste," came the sharp answer,
"if you left that to me.  I have already told you that
it is a matter of no real importance whether your means
of future prosperity are supplied by your husband or
myself."

"Very true, mamma.  But it is a matter of importance to me whether I have or have not a knowledge
of my husband's affairs previous to marriage."  Then I
gave myself as grim a mouth, as square a jaw, and as
generally repulsive a look as I know how to extempor-
ize.  "If you don't tell me, I shall ask Fuller."

I didn't look at her whilst these words were growled
out : I don't suppose that I dared.  The most leonine
courage has its limits.  It takes a good many patriots,
sometimes, to make one tyrant tremble.  A body can
be brave, Diary, without being brazen.  Sacred chronicles do not inform us that poor little David cast any
self-important stares giantward when he marched against

his doughty foe : I daresay, for my part, that he just shut both eyes very tight indeed and let go of his Scriptural pebble, making the whole affair one of purely blind luck.

Mamma began to speak, presently, and in tones nothing less than conciliatory, if the term isn't a desecration. Policy will turn granite into wax very often, and she evidently chose to consider that her present course was one in which a soft answer would be altogether politic. With slowly lessening amazement, I found myself a listener to :—

" After all, your claim is a just one, Helen : I must allow it. A part of Fuller Dobell's fortune yet remains to him, but only a part. During our conversation last night he spoke on these matters with mingled wisdom and self-respect. He wished that you should be made clearly aware of his recent losses, and in fact sought my permission to enlighten you ; permission, however, which was not granted."

Having received an inch of concession, I grabbed an ell. " Your refusal seems very odd to me, mamma. Indeed, I can't help wondering how Fuller ever came to ask permission at all."

" No ? " There was a tinge of the old placid austerity about this little questioned negative. " Is it strange that he should believe you had been brought up to place full dependence upon my guiding-powers ? I think not, Helen. However," reproached mamma, " I have no wish to cast ill-timed reproaches. Fuller (rely upon it) will say nothing to you concerning his present pecuniary status, so to speak. Am I asking too much of my daughter, if I ask that she will adopt a like reticence ? "

" Oh, of course not," I succumbed, as gracefully as circumstances would permit. " I'd marry him, you know, if he hadn't anything but a counterfeit greenback to bless himself withal ; and there certainly ought to be lots of pleasanter subjects than money open to discussion between him and me."

Ah, how deliciously nearly all the remainder of to-day has proven this truth ! We have no more talked money than we have talked hydrostatics. As for poor Selina, (who leaves to-morrow, by the bye) she has not so much as placed a straw in our beatific way. I think the surprise of hearing that Fuller and I are going to marry each other has thrown her into a sort of intellectual stupor ; her characteristic current of commonplaces appears frozen in its channel, and she principally employs herself in staring us out of countenance and simpering extravagant simpers. Who knows that she is not stifling under these, poor girl, the most tragic inclinations possible ? Perhaps we remind her sufferingly of the absent Melville and of what might have been. I devoutly hope that she isn't going to be susceptible all through her earthly career ; for if some well-to-do dentist, enthusiastic about his profession, should really offer her hand and heart, the Matthers are just aristocrats enough to incarcerate and bread-and-water her out of such a sad misalliance.

Yes, our course of true love, thus far at least, has run without a ripple. Now that I recollect, though, its entire serenity must be objected to. A garter-snake (Heaven forbid that I should say a serpent) stole into our Eden just before dinner-time. Fuller snubbed me. I wanted to know whether he considered himself on speaking-terms, at present, with Melville Delano, and he replied by manipulating his locket studiously and making some guttural statement about female inquisitiveness. Whereupon I jumped up from my seat with

5

the rapidity of a jack-in-the-box, gave my panier one or two haughty touches, made manual inquiry concerning my back-hair, posed my head sideways in a manner that was archducal, to say the least of it, heightened, narrowed and bent my shoulders forward, crossed both hands a little below the region of my sash-belt, and rambled elegantly from the room.

I hadn't more than cleared the threshold, however, when his arm strongly cinctured my waist. After that I found myself being talked to and kissed simultaneously. "Beg pardon, Helen." (Kiss.) "I was a complete brute." (Kiss.) "But the fact is" (kiss) "that I'd just as lief never have you say anything to me about Delano." (Kiss, kiss.)

I was propitiated, somehow. "Do you detest him so, Fuller?"

"I've never liked him. Since Wednesday we have *not* become attached friends, you know. How about that sonnet of Owen Meredith's you promised to read me? I must cultivate a decent liking for poetry before next November; mustn't I?"

It is very hard not to pout a trifle when one's lover pets one. I have never had the minutest patience with engaged girls who pout, but now I begin to understand the enormity of their temptation. I pouted then. "It wasn't a sonnet a bit, and it wasn't Owen Meredith's."

"Not a sonnet?" (Kiss; followed by deep investigation of turquoise ring on my third finger.)

"No; an idyl, sir. You've such a shocking memory." I—the sensible I, Diary!—actually shook myself during this observation, with a petulance worthy of bare legs and a pinafore, not to specify loops.

"Oh, yes, to be sure; an idyl." (Much familiar

fumbling with the two little short-hair curls at my left temple.)

"And not Owen Meredith's, either," I twittered, with peevishness nowhere tolerable outside a nursery. "Tennyson's."

"Certainly : Tennyson's. I'm truly benighted as regards these matters. But you're a going to work miracles in me, you know." (Kiss, without any cessation of the fumbling.)

And so we were quite at peace again. I suppose he means to cut Melville when next they meet. I should hate to have him not get my wedding-cards. But that concerns the future, and it is very foolish policy to borrow trouble.

# CHAPTER VIII.

CT. 1.—I shan't apologize, Diary, for having ignored you during two whole days. Your leaves might have been employed in 'binding a book, or lining a box, or serving to curl a maiden's locks' far better than in the very trivial task of recording my own and Fuller's amorous idiocy.

Indeed, there has happened nothing since Friday which is of a sufficiently salient nature for the historian to grasp at and hold. Selina's departure is surely not worth the wasting of many words upon it. I trust that in the sacred name of hostship my grateful feelings were properly concealed at the hour of farewell. Mamma accompanied her to the dépôt. She went away in excellent spirits, distance lending considerable enchantment to the glimmer of teeth amiably turned towards Fuller and myself, just as the carriage was disappearing on its journey gateward.

To-day (Monday) has brought nothing but arrivals. Grandee has trodden upon the heel of grandee. Our guests are all of the superincumbent middle-aged description, except John Driscoll and Fuller. The agreeable lack of congratulations from any source whatever convinced me, by the time we were all assembled at dinner (a solemnity of about three hours in length), that nobody had as yet heard a syllable concerning a certain most momentous event. When, however, we ladies had effected our graceful retreat before that social bayonet, the after-dinner cigar, and had "buzzed in knots of talk" for a little while among the drawing-room furniture, I became aware that mamma was permitting the secret quietly to peck its shell of secrecy, and to burst with gradual grandeur upon our marvelling guests. Dowager by dowager, they had all besieged me, after a while, with their saccharine felicitations. I couldn't help stealing a few glances at mamma whilst the flattering ceremony lasted. Her touch of heightened color may have meant the wine she had taken at dinner, or it may have owned origin a trifle more subtle than this. Was it not in truth with her as with one who has cloven asunder many a difficult obstructing door, and has reached at length the very inmost and sacredest chamber of success? There are victories and victories: was not this of hers a victory so absolute and entire that the enemy had saved neither standard nor musket in their ruinous rout? Fortune had emptied into her lap the final fruitage of its plentiful horn. She had nothing more to attain; the last crag had bruised her foot, the last brier wounded it. Henceforth her days were to be one calm firm barrierless level of accomplishment. And knowing what I know of her life and her nature, involuntarily my thought put to my thought a kind of prophetic question: Will not her spirit feed on triumph till it sickens thereof, and will she not find in success the bitterest of all failures? There are some spirits that languish miserably except when they breathe an atmosphere of struggle and strife. Effort is a very water of Meribah to them. There isn't much chance, I fancy, of mamma proving a very contented Alexander when

she has found herself with no more worlds to con
quer.

The male grandees strolled in one by one, before
long, most of them looking the rosier for their recent
convivialities, besides bearing pungent suggestions of
their having smoked the dining-room into a fog. John
Driscoll and Fuller were late in coming, and at last entered together. By the bye, I wonder how my name
ever escaped being added to the list of John Driscoll's
conquests. I never look at him nowadays without
feeling a pardonable pride that this should have been
thus. Grace and girth unite so admirably in his six
good feet of humanity : then, too, that patrician head
of his, with its delicate little ears, and its crisp short
curls dashed with gray, always had such charms for me,
not to mention his grave hazel eyes and his martial sort
of moustache, so thorough a match to the gray curls. I
daresay nobody ever believed that I wasn't demented
about him in the days when we saw so much of each
other ; but to you, Diary, who take so many of my
statements without the suspicion of a salt-grain, I can
offer this statement in a spirit of pleasant security.

Presently John Driscoll and I found ourselves popu-
lating a corner together, with Fuller nowhere visible.
" I suppose you've heard about it," were my first words,
pronounced with matter-of-course kind of languor.

" It ? "

" My engagement. You don't mean to say that
Fuller hasn't told you ? "

" No," he murmured gravely, his eyebrows composing themselves after a leap of amazement. " Not to
Fuller himself ? "

" Yes," I blushed, rather engagingly, " to Fuller,
and nobody else." Then the solemn, drawn-down look

about his forehead almost frightened me, and I laid my hand on his arm. " What is there in my piece of news that should displease you, Mr. Driscoll ?"

He seemed an atom or so flurried after that, and attempted something which looked like the eighth cousin of a smile. " Pray don't fancy that I'm displeased ; " and then he took my hand. " But I do not think that in all my thirty-five years of mortality I ever recollect being more amazed."

" That's very odd," I commented. " You're such an intimate friend of Fuller's. Didn't you believe that he cared about marrying ? "

" No ; I believed the precise opposite. But man proposes, maid disposes, quite often. You are staring very hard at me, Miss Helen."

" I know it. I don't like the corners of your mouth, somehow. Be candid in answering a question for me, won't you ? "

" Certainly." He dropped his eyes after a quick glance at my face.

" This morsel of news did something more than surprise you, did it not? I mean that it displeased you as well."

" No, no," he rattled off at fleetest speed, the briskness of tone being quite characteristic of the man. " You are very sadly mistaken—please believe so."

Just then ponderous male grandee number fourth came beamingly up to me, looking from sole to crown one grand anxiety to congratulate. When I saw the next meeting between John Driscoll and Fuller it was observed from something of a distance. Fuller's back was turned from my view. I saw John Driscoll take his hand and say a few words with what seemed the emphasis of earnest feeling.

*Oct.* 4.—Here is Thursday, and to-morrow the last of their highnesses will depart townward. Fuller left this morning with John Driscoll. There are to be three miserable days before we meet again, and then we shall very possibly take the first of our many many kisses of greeting among metropolitan surroundings. Mamma purposes leaving Pineside on Monday next. I wish this week was a kind of diurnal deformity, and didn't have any Friday, or Saturday, or Sunday. Fuller's absence is so desolating ! I miss him as much as if we had been outgrowing our hair and teeth together in wedded bliss at Pineside for the past seventy years. The day before he left I made him go to the village with me and be photographed. The operator was a young man with oily black curls and the patience of several seraphim ; but I nearly drove him mad, for all this, by my interminable fault-finding. The result of his countless efforts to gain my difficult favor is an entirely unpleasing tin-type. But it is supremely better than nothing. I treat it just as I would treat a phial of Belladonna, or any other portable medicine, keeping it in my pocket always, and touching my lips to it once every hour, by the watch. Sometimes I take overdoses, one every half-hour, and find that they don't specially disagree with me. Now and then I try to forget that it is tin, and talk to it. A little while ago I actually cried over it, and my emotion resulted in giving it a scandalous ·stain on the left cheek, besides a soiled shirt-bosom. This will never do ; Fuller's linen is always so flawless, and his complexion a seek-no-further. I must hold in check, hereafter, my " tears, idle tears," or at least let them drop on a handkerchief instead of desecrating that hallowed tin.          •

Of course I'm the perfection of a goose to feel like

this, apart from the depraved folly of writing so. And he is probably bearing our separation at the present moment (about ten and a half P.M.) with the kind of resignation that permits him to smoke and drink and play cards at the club, as though there wasn't any Pineside, any awful void made there by his absence, any poor lonely longing Me having a chronic tear in my eye of equal importance with the legendary Susannah's, though differing from that heroine of song in one memorable respect : I haven't the appetite for a rose-leaf, throwing a buckwheat cake totally out of the question.

To judge from the devoutness of Fuller's farewell promise, I should suppose that nothing except death or an earthquake will prevent him from posting a nice long letter to-night in time for it to reach me by the morning-mail. He will be sure to have *his* letter for breakfast : I had written it and sent it to the post-office three hours after his departure.

Dear, dear! I am debasing myself by the scripture of these weightless platitudes. I don't think I shall touch you again, Diary, till we are back in New York.

5*

## CHAPTER IX.

CT. 8.—And I haven't touched you. Mamma and I reached town this morning. Not two hours after our arrival who but Fuller's only sister, Mrs. Louis Walters, should call upon me? Of course I was at home to her, though Fuller's recent failure in the matter of meeting us at the dépôt, and his continued non-appearance, had put me in no very. angelic humor.

I have never liked Mrs. Walters, but I liked her temporarily at least, whilst she was holding both my hands in both her lavender-gloved own, and saying all sorts of pleasant musically-spoken things about the engagement. "Such a surprise, too, my dear," she finished, in her cooing kittenish way. "Fuller tells me that you fell in love with each other this summer at Newport."

"Yes," I assented, adding rather shyly : "I suppose I'm privileged to speak for both of us, by the bye."

"Of course." Then her ruddy mouth changed its chronic lazy smile into a broad beaming laugh, that showed how bright a white her teeth were. "The idea of Fuller married! It does seem so immensely queer. Are you going to make him settle down into a complete family-man, and read to you evenings and all that, you know? I do hope you will. I shall take such bliss in poking fun at him."

I tried to laugh in answer, not entirely succeeding, though. All the world understands how little married Cornelia Walters has ever been, averaging about one notorious flirtation every six months, and turning wife-hood, not to speak of motherhood, into the ghastliest kind of a burlesque. It worries me whenever I think of Fuller's fondness for this woman. It is my private be-lief, privately expressed, that she has about as much moral principle as a mouse. She is assuredly lucky in one particular: certain would-be Samaritans say that her husband sets her the devil-may-care example. As if such an assertion could exonerate her one tittle! I wish Fuller would realize what horrible style she is. He always laughs with a kind of cordial indolence whenever her name is mentioned. He seems to consider her a delicious inexhaustible joke; but to my thinking her capers carry a most sombre suggestion of tragedy. Fuller certainly owes society such a trivial compliment as to feel ashamed of her, since beyond any doubt she hasn't the slimmest idea of ever feeling ashamed of her-self.

Mamma came in, presently, and presently, I rejoice to state, my recreant swain also entered the room. I took the liberty of forgetting all about Mrs. Walters or mamma either, for a few seconds, and of interlarding my copious kisses with quite a number of thrilling rebukes. "Not at the dépôt!" I concluded, with a hand in his and an arm about his neck, " and not here when we got here! I didn't expect it of you, Fuller."

" But you knew I wasn't dead, or anything," he affirmed, with gentle nonchalance.

" I didn't know."

"Then you're a goosie."

"Fuller, I am waiting for some vague evidence on your part that we're acquainted," reproached his sister, with an immense deal of melancholy. "Mrs. Jeffreys, if I mistake not, is showing a similar patience."

She staid to lunch, as I was sure that she had intended to do from the first. Somehow I felt all the while she was there, as if Fuller and I had somebody standing between us and quietly pushing us apart. She takes liberties with him that I would not dare to take. She says her mocking clever extravagant things about his deeds and misdeeds generally, and he joins in her laughter with the saintliest sort of good-humor. "Everybody I've met for the past three days," she informed him, as little awed by mamma's presence as though a crone of eighty were presiding at table, "is rabidly anxious to see you. I don't think you would have surprised people one whit more if you'd committed suicide. You and Helen are to be just pelted with dinner-invitations—mark my words—although there is really nothing going on at present in the way of festivities. Society intends taking a good long stare at you through its most powerful eye-glass. Just now you're both supplying huge material for small-talk: I daresay that you rank, in this respect, second to nothing except the weather."

"And what is the prevailing opinion about our engagement?" I struck in, determined, if possible, to stop these rollicking personalities on the homœopathic principle that 'like cures like.' "Do they say that Fuller is in love with me, or that he's merely marrying for money?"

Dead silence followed. Mrs. Walters became wine-color. Fuller stared at me with knit brows. "Of course, you know, Helen is only joking," presently meandered mamma, at whom I had not dared to look.

"Oh, of course," giggled Mrs. Walters, with a nervousness not precisely characteristic. But I had killed her little pleasantness for the time, at least, clumsily crushing as the blow had been.

Fuller did not speak to me until nearly an hour afterward, when we were alone together. And then his opening remark must be called a complete growl. "I should like to ask your motive, Helen, for having made a certain speech. You know very well what I mean."

"Certainly." We were together in the little reception-room on the ground-floor. Being seated near the window, I delivered my reply with gaze Fifth Avenue-ward. "There goes Emily Lester. What compromising bonnets that girl wears."

"Do you refuse to answer my question?" rumbled Fuller, very sternly.

I faced him, at that. "Not at all. I said it to make your sister stop her flippant fun-poking." Then my voice began to quiver. "I know *she* thinks I struck a home-truth. She doesn't believe that you're in love with me one iota; I saw it in her eyes. She thinks you a mere mass of worldliness, like herself."

I had expected that the tears in my voice would be commandant to him as far as concerned a tender reply; but he only softened the least in the world. "You mustn't call Cornelia hard names; I can't hear them, you know, Helen. She has always been a good sister to me, and I am thoroughly fond of her."

I didn't care for his severe manner, now. I was burning to have him deny that my belief regarding his sister's opinion of our engagement had been anything except ill-founded. "The fact of your liking anybody would of course be enough to seal my lips against all detraction, Fuller—would be another reason, indeed, for me to try and change my own dislike into its opposite. But then you can't deny," I added, with illogical eagerness, "that what I believe about Cornelia Walters' opinion is quite correct."

"She is entitled to her own opinion." He took out a cigarette. "Your mother lets people smoke here, doesn't she?"

"But have you no wish to undeceive your sister?" I hurried. Then excitement made my voice almost give way, yet whilst he looked round at me with amazed eyes, I managed to continue: "Are you willing, Fuller, that any one you like should believe so contemptibly of you?"

Just as he had flushed to the roots of his hair on that hotel-piazza when I met him with that beautiful Atrocity, whoever she was, so to the roots of his hair did he flush now. But that was a guilty flush; at least I so set it down. As for this, I don't know wherefore I waste paper in stating that it meant only surprise at my unanticipated imperative question. What else could it possibly mean?

And yet somehow I began to tremble nervously. Before I actually knew what I was doing, the distance between us had lessened to a noteworthy extent, and I was stooping over him, with my cheek laid upon nothing else but the crown of his blond silky-haired head, and my arms girding his torso a trifle below the shoulders.

"Oh, Fuller," I began to bleat, "of course I'm nonsensical and everything, but please tell me you love me, and will never, never tire of loving me. I have grown to need your love so, all on a sudden! I can't help making a simpleton of myself whenever I think of this. You do adore me, don't you? If I were Miss Smith, with nothing a year except what I made out of my sewing-machine or even my wash-tub, and you knew me as well as you know me now, you'd marry me just the same, wouldn't you, Fuller?"

After that (to be strictly consistent with my new character of simpleton, I suppose) I got crying ridiculously. And whilst I cried I hugged him the tighter and the tighter, till presently, as if for proof that he was not being smothered, he found a tongue to this effect:

"Pray, Helen, believe in the sincerity of my professions for once and for all. Is your faith in me built upon so slight a foundation that the least chance breath can shake it?"

Now this, it must be owned, was severely stilted for Fuller, who usually adopts an off-hand haphazard style toward the most momentous matters; and consequently, for the very reason that he had chosen so uncharacteristic a method of answering me, I felt convinced of how much deep sincerity underlay his words. All women are terribly prone to use hyperbole when they speak of their lovers; and yet I can't help saying, that I seemed now to have caught a happy precious glimpse beyond the careless languid exterior Fuller straight into the Fuller that lay beyond—large-hearted, honorable, and unwaveringly constant.

There is no use in describing the halcyon result of this discovery. He left this afternoon but came again in the evening, and has finally parted from me on the most blissful of terms—not "all my lover, half my friend," but as much of one as of the other.

In the earlier part of the evening we had quite a flock of visitors; the majority of them, as I couldn't help snobbishly observing, represented men to whom mamma's social countenance was of rather precious import. All potentates must have their satellites and their underlings, I suppose ; lesser fishes swim in the wake of large ones.

Fuller and I treated the guests with a fair amount of exclusive indifference, and I am afraid that I received some of their pretty speeches concerning my engagement with a bored manner that just grazed discourtesy. Somehow I don't care a fig for society any more. I wish Fuller would live in the country after we are married, or else ransack all the obscurest ins and outs of Europe with me, and let all the nabobs in all the capitals of the world dine and dance, flirt and flatter, strut and stoop, in forgetfulness that we ever moved amid their profitless masquerade.

But even if Fuller should sanction any such post-matrimonial programme, mamma would veto it, denounce it, do battle against it. So for the present I had best hold my tongue—and wait.

# CHAPTER X.

OCT. 10.—Mrs. Walters has prophesied with the skill of a real sibyl. Fuller and I are being literally inundated with dinner-invitations. Mamma decides what ones we are to accept. I am happy to chronicle that she is going to let me occasionally dine at home. My wedding-day has been fixed for the first of November. I am to be married very publicly in white silk and point-lace. I wonder if I shall make a brave bride as I march into church on Louis Walters' arm, with mamma and Fuller following. I wish Fuller wasn't fatherless and brotherless. I somehow hate the idea of going to the altar on that sacredest loveliest most revered mission, with frivolous blond-whiskered Louis Walters, whose married life has always been such a monstrous mockery.

I am to have four bridemaids. They were all asked yesterday by mamma, and have all accepted, as I learned this morning. I couldn't and didn't restrain a smile of amusement when she gave me their names; they make such a four-square tower of social supremacy. First, Susie Montgomery; second, Belle Dillinger; third, Margie Cartwright; and fourth, Kate Effingham. It has also been decreed that we are to marry each other without the important assistance of groomsmen. So much for nuptial statistics.

We went to a great dinner this evening, at Mrs. Montgomery's. I was beamed upon and made much of all through its eternity of courses, but couldn't enjoy my sovereignty, in spite of a conscientious effort to do so. Last year I would have thrilled under this sort of thing : truly love works wonders, and " time turns the old days to derision." I managed to make Fuller go away with me a good half-hour earlier than the correct time for going. But we had scarcely attained the quiet and seclusion of the little reception-room at home, before he gave signs of deserting me. I was bitterly piqued, though I tried not to make my pique at all evident. Perhaps if I had done this, he would have staid. As it was, he went. No doubt he went to the club. I wish New York was a clubless city, though in that case very probably Satan would find some mischief still for idle men to do.

I forgot to mention that Melville Delano was at Mrs. Montgomery's this evening. Just before dinner was announced, he came up to me and said a few unimportant things. Fuller, glancing at us from an opposite sofa, seemed as unconcerned as if I had been associating with one of his bosom-friends. Considering that he detests the man and has proscribed his name from our conversation, it would have been only consistent for him to frown a trifle. I *shan't* believe that his serenity had anything to do with indifference.

Well, well, I am out of sorts, somehow. Do you like me in the rôle of a grumbler, Diary ? No ; I am sure not. Suppose I resolve not to touch you again till I can write pleasant things in you ?

*Oct.* 16.—More journalistic neglect. But then a girl

who is beset with dress-makers and milliners and other such troubles as haunt the last hours of spinsterhood, can't be expected to show herself much of a scribe into the bargain. There was not enough time, mamma thought, for my trousseau to be gotten up in Paris, and so we have patronized domestic tradesmanship; although, by the bye, this immensity of preparation is quite ridiculous. Mamma seems wholly to forget that I have not been altogether raimentless up to the present time. She is having coals carried to Newcastle at the rate of several tons per day. What a godsend the Mesdames That, This, and The Other must consider her!

Writing of mesdames, I am reminded that I received a congratulatory visit, this morning, from my old schoolmistress, Madame Langlois. It is like standing under a shower-bath of sugar-plums nearly all the time that she talks to me. Mademoiselle had lost nothing of her delightful brunette beauty; Mademoiselle still preserved her charming dimples; Mademoiselle's marvellous French accent had suffered not the least change through want of practice: and so, "trippingly on the tongue," through sentence after sentence. Madame's amiability attained a climax when I showed her my engagement-ring (a beautiful scintillant solitaire, by the bye). If it had been the Koh-i-noor her praises would have sounded extravagant.

Her school was never more prosperous, she told me; and then burst forth into eulogiums upon a certain boarding-pupil, a Miss Tremaine, age about fourteen, birth-place Baltimore, beauty angelic. No stranger ever saw this divine little creature without admitting that she ravished them. Would not she prove an inducement for me to honor her school with my presence, some day? Adèle was usually guarded from visitors through a fear on the part of her discreet instructress that vanity might steal into her charming nature ; but if Mademoiselle would confer upon the school the honor of a visit, an exception should certainly be made in her favor.

I don't know why this slight circumstance has seemed to me at all worthy of record. Possibly because I am such an admirer of human loveliness, and especially of female human loveliness, that Madame's florid encomiums have made me desirous to see this little charmer.

No sooner had Madame Langlois taken her departure than Cornelia Walters called for me to go out and walk with her. We had hardly left the house, it seemed, when she was joined by that insupportable Summerby, her present devotee. I have never been able to understand how he has managed to get among decent people at all ; but Cornelia manifestly considers him adorable. To my thinking he is stamped with the stamp of low origin and stupidity and vulgarity, though of course his face is handsome after a certain bold red-white-and-black type of beauty. I daresay Cornelia has picked him up at some watering-place and is forcing society to gulp him down, unpalatable as the dose is. I tried my best not to hear what they were saying to each other after she had made me acquainted with him, though Cornelia attempted more than once to include me in their conversation.

" I am going to take you and Mr. Summerby as far as Stewart's, Helen," was her final attempt, when we had reached the corner of Fifth Avenue and Fourteenth Street, " provided, that is, it will not bore you too much to go there and buy some gloves with me. I sent for some Bertins a century ago and they haven't come. Just think of having to give New York prices ! "

To Stewart's we went. Whilst Cornelia was selecting her gloves Mr. Summerby made one or two vain efforts to obtain nice treatment from me. Feeling that my hands were tied in the matter of snubbing him outright, I limited myself to placid monosyllables, and showed a deep interest in the multitude of surrounding customers. Whilst thus occupied I chanced to let my eyes rest upon a lady who was standing just at my elbow, engaged in purchasing gloves. The color flew to my face, then, though I don't believe that the maltreated Summerby noticed it. I had discovered myself to be within a very few inches of a brilliantly beautiful woman, last seen on the piazza of a certain hotel.

Except that a tiny tasteful bonnet replaced the round hat of yore and its iridescent feather, she was dressed almost the same as when we had previously seen each other. Her faultless profile, with its lovely lines of brow and cheek and throat, first struck my recognizing gaze, whilst she leaned above the counter in a posture of languorous reposeful grace. I daresay that if the Venus de Medici had been made animate, and dressed exquisitely, and sent to buy herself gloves at Stewart's, she would have performed the action with no whit more charming effect.

I think that I stared fixedly at her profile for about three seconds ; and then, as if conscious of my scrutiny, the profile changed itself into a full face and stared at me in return. Instantly I knew that she knew me. Those great bluish-gray golden-lashed eyes nearly veiled themselves in the superbest sort of scorn ; the fresh rich-red mouth wore a sudden sneer ; the well-poised little head was thrown a trifle backward.

I suppose that it was the beauty of all this contempt rather than the contempt proper, which prevented me from turning away immediately and letting it waste itself on my back. Sheer admiration, and nothing except that, kept my eyes riveted upon the woman, until Cornelia's voice sounded appealingly from an opposite direction.

"Helen, which shade of lavender *would* you get?"

"Take care, Miss Jeffreys, how you decide rashly," smirked Summerby, who had noticed nothing, and was trying to be funny. He was standing between Cornelia and myself. I ignored politeness to the extent of a quick push in front of him. When, under pretence of deciding the vital question of the lavenders, I had gotten my head close beside Mrs. Walters' and my lips at excellent whispering-nearness to her ear,

"Cornelia," I hurried, "look over my shoulder at the woman buying gloves just on our right, and tell me whether you've ever seen her before." Then aloud, and for the benefit of Summerby, I added: "Don't you think the light lavender is the nicer? I fancy I like it better."

By this time Cornelia had obeyed me. Our acquaintance cannot be called ancient, but it is old enough for me to have discovered that she very rarely suffers from the feeblest qualm of embarrassment. Just now she looked as if some one had suddenly given her usual pedestal of self-possession a rather ugly sort of shake.

"Yes," she began to stumble; "that is, you know, I've heard she wasn't proper; in fact, my dear, that she's perfectly horrible." By this time her cheeks had colored into a match of my own. "You think the light shade the prettier? So do I." (To the clerk.) "Three pairs of these, please, and charge them to Mrs. L. Walters."

"Do you know anything more about her?" was my persistent whisper. "Her name, I mean, or—"

Cornelia's hand caught mine, then, and her lips came very close to my ear. "Don't, Helen, or we shall be noticed."

"Pshaw! Do you know her name?"

"No."

"Or anything about her?"

"Of course not." Her eyes searched my face with a short penetrant glance, and then fell counterward. "I know nothing—absolutely nothing—except that she's awful. Now *are* you satisfied?"

I wasn't, but feigned to be so. The object of my curiosity stood with face averted from my look, when I next stole one in her direction. Her purchases were evidently not completed by the time Cornelia's package was delivered and we left the store.

"You ladies are not going directly up town, I hope," remarked Summerby, with a little bow and a big smile, when we were again in open air. "Haven't you any more business in Broadway, this jolly morning? I was hurrying down town at the time I had the happiness to meet you. Am I to lose your charming company for all the rest of the way?"

·These thrilling compliments seemed for the most part addressed to myself. I answered them with a few cool words to Cornelia: "It's nearly lunch time; I shan't be able to go down any farther." Then I drew away from Mrs. Walters and her friend, as if to signify how fixed my determination was. Cornelia lingered for a precious moment in Summerby's society, and at length joined me, just as he was elaborating a very effective farewell bow.

"You weren't very civil to my friend, Helen," she laughed, with no perceptible ill-humor. "Poor Joe doesn't get much polite treatment, by the bye. I wonder how people can take dislikes to him; but then his unpopularity never alters my feelings a jot, you know."

"It's quite good of one to show such disinterested friendship," I generalized. "And so that woman is horrible, Cornelia. I'm amazed to hear it. .Besides being lovely to look at, she's such perfect style."

My fellow-pedestrian bit her underlip unmistakably. Apart from this sign of perplexity I could observe no other, now. "Yes. Oh, she's a superb creature. I don't know anything more about her than what I've told you. In fact I can't even remember how I first learned about her at all. It was quite long ago that I heard somebody speak of it."

"Has she been in New York a long time?" I was narrowly watching Cornelia's face. Am I mistaken, or did the pink deepen on her cheeks to something appreciably warmer?

"Years, my dear—years."

We walked along for nearly a block, with silence on my side, and a somewhat unusual volubility on my companion's.

"Could you find out her name for me, Cornelia?" I presently struck in. "The name of that beautiful creature, I mean, whom we met at Stewart's. I'm somehow curious to learn it; and you, being married, have opportunities—"

"Of talking to men on such a low subject, I suppose!" The interruption was made with an almost fierce harshness, entirely uncharacteristic. "No, I thank you, Helen Jeffreys. You must find some other panderer to your (excuse me) immodest curiosity. I can't conceive what is your motive in seeking to know any more than you know already."

This unexpected snarl took me so unawares that I

forgot to feel angry at it, and indeed commenced a stammering apology. "Pray don't be offended, Cornelia. My request *was* rather queer, I admit; but I had no intention of wounding you with it."

"Of course not, Helen." All anger had vanished from her face and voice. "I spoke altogether too hastily, and you must let me ask pardon instead of asking it yourself. And now suppose we consign the whole subject among the unmentionables. Here comes Effie Williams; how that girl's beauty is galloping away from her!"

We went home to lunch, and a little while after lunch Cornelia departed. This afternoon I got into one of my reflective moods. There is no denying that Mrs. Walters' whole behavior, as far as regards the meeting with that woman in Stewart's, flavors puzzlingly of the mysterious. I cannot bring myself to believe that Cornelia, the antipodes of a prude in everything else, should have shown prominent prudery concerning this one affair. And I find it very hard to believe that she was ignorant of a certain name. Yet if in reality not ignorant, why should she have attempted any concealment?"

I thought and thought and thought about these matters this afternoon, till I found myself on the limiting-line between good health and a nervous headache. And now, Diary, my pencil has been disfiguring the margin of your page with several shamefully-drawn inhuman profiles, just because the scripture of the above paragraph set me thinking and thinking and thinking once more.

Am I nothing but a suspicious whimsical fancy-ridden goose? Was there no acting in what Cornelia Walters did and said this morning?

G

Ah, what a devilish acrid loathsome poison suspicion is! How it can spread, with lightninglike fleetness of defilement, through the life of any earnest faith, clogging and palsying its brave strong heart-beats! Thank God that I warn myself in time against too deep a draught of it, and can dash the danger from my lips!

I am no fool, to let phantoms of my own summoning crowd in upon me. From to-night henceforward I shall make decisive end of all such purposeless self-torment. Somewhere in those manifold poetical wanderings of which my girlhood was so fond, I have met these lines. They did not seem more than a cluster of wayside wildflowers then, but I find that memory, like a faithful handmaid following behind her mistress, has gathered them and kept them till now :

> " Better confide and be deceived
> A thousand times by treacherous foes,
> Than once accuse the innocent,
> Or let suspicion mar repose."

Fuller dined with us this evening. He seemed in very pleasant spirits and staid until after eleven. By the bye, I suppose some people would say that I ought to cloister myself, after to-morrow, or else only take my airings inside carriage-walls ; for to-morrow mamma is to inform her friends, through the medium of numerous engraved messages, that " the honor of their company is requested at the marriage-ceremony of her daughter, Miss Helen Jeffreys, and Mr. Fuller Dobell."

Dear me ! I dread all the fuss and parade, and wish it was well over and done with.

## CHAPTER XI.

CT. 22.—"You haven't told me anything about whom I am to have for wedding-guests, mamma," I gently asserted at breakfast this morning. "Did you forget, or were you afraid that I should put forward any troublesome opinions on the subject?"

Mamma, who has been the soul of suavity and graciousness for days past, laughed melodiously whilst she stirred her coffee. "I fancied you rather indifferent as to who came, Helen." Then to Henry, standing behind her: "Find Marie and tell her to give you my writing-case."

The writing-case was presently brought, and presently I was in possession of mamma's visiting-book.

"You will find a tiny pencilled cross over against the names of those whom I didn't ask," she explained.

I ran my eye along the names, taking care to slight none of them. Having finished my inspection, I handed the book in silence to Henry, who handed it to mamma, who restored it to her writing-case.

Henry is the very Chesterfield of butlers. I have no fixed belief as to whether he listens at key-holes or not; but the possible possession of any such unfortunate habit surely does not interfere with his rapid percep-

tion of when his presence ceases to be desired. Whilst
mamma was replacing her list in the writing-case, he
glided soundlessly from the breakfast-room.

I at once broke silence. "You have asked the three
Delano girls, I see, but not Melville."

"No ; not Melville. Fuller and he are on such unpleasant terms, you know."

"But he has been an intimate friend of mine,
mamma." I made my voice calmly firm. "I prefer
that he should receive cards."

Mamma broke a piece of crisp toast very deliberately
before answering me. "Have you consulted with Fuller, Helen, on the subject of inviting him ?"

"No ; but I shall do so at once."

And I kept my word. Fuller dropped in at about
eight o'clock that evening. "You once said that you
didn't want me ever to speak with you about Melville
Delano," I boldly plunged, immediately after kissing
him.

His face darkened on the instant. "Yes, Helen ; I
said it."

"Very well. Prepare to be annoyed, please. I
want him asked to the wedding, and mamma objects.
She thinks that you should be consulted on the subject, and I agree with her perfectly. So now I request
of you that you will not decide against his having
cards."

Fuller's hand went moustacheward. "We are not
on speaking terms any longer."

"Nothing has taken place between you since—?"

He cut me short with a quick frown and the sharp
word : "Nothing."

"Not on speaking terms," I repeated, in a perplexed
way. "That makes the matter difficult ; although he

would be almost sure not to come—at least not to the reception, you know." Then an idea struck me, and I went on, after a second of silence : " Will you allow me to send him the cards, Fuller, and a little private note besides ?—a note merely showing that I understand how uncomfortably he and I are both situated as regards the affair ? "

Before the last word of this sentence had left my lips, I somehow had become confident that Fuller would fling forth an answer to it of the ugliest and most ill-humored sort imaginable. But he amazed me—I must add that he also piqued me—by nothing more savage than a very acquiescent nod of the head. " Do so if you choose, Helen," was the audible form presently taken by this access of sweet-temper. " I don't want to seem disagreeable. Manage matters precisely as you think proper ; only, manage them so that your friend and I are not placed in a position that would necessitate our shaking hands with each other ; for in that case I should feel quite dissatisfied with the whole undertaking."

My answer was something very amiable : I was resolved that he should not dream of how mortified his ready consent had made me. Esteem such mortification, if you will, Diary, the summit of frivolity and womanishness ; but I can't help feeling that since circumstances had put forward their imperative demand for a little decent jealousy on Fuller's part, his complete failure to meet so natural a liability was altogether trying. I must admit that it pricks me keenly to know his dislike of Melville based on personal reasons alone. Not that if Fuller were anything of an absolute Othello I shouldn't make the most insubordinate Desdemona realizable ; but then his placid willingness to have me sit down and write a note like that which I proposed writing, to the man who has assuredly paid me all sorts of serious attentions for months before my engagement, is very much at variance with the mode of behavior commonly recognized among lovers.

And yet, pshaw!   I thought I was a logical cant-hater. How should it concern me, this " mode of behavior," to quote my own nonsense ?   Other people are other people, and we are we.   What did I write about suspicion only a page or two back ? and here I find myself blaming Fuller for not being marred by it.   Perhaps if he had set a harsh veto upon my communicating at all with Melville, I should now be lamentational on the subject of his undeserved injustice.   Because he trusts me with a beautiful sincerity of trust, shall I not therefore believe myself blessed beyond the lot of most living women ?

This putting of one's feelings down upon paper is truly like holding a mirror up to one's faults, I find. You are somehow the broom, Diary, with which I sweep away many mental cobwebs.   Transcribe your follies in black and white, and you have, in nine cases out of ten, (provided the record be a faithful one) written with the act a recipe for their cure.

To-night, as soon as Fuller had gone, I went upstairs into mamma's room and found her just returned from a dinner at somebody's, (I have lately grown so indifferent to these matters as not to know precisely where) with Marie on the point of unsheathing her from a violet satin dress, whose lovely lustres glimmered mellowly in the shaded gas-light.

" We have decided to ask Melville Delano," I began, with a touch of triumph in my voice.   " Fuller offers no objections.   If you've a set of cards and a blank envelope I will address them to-night."

Mamma showed not a vestige of astonishment. " I will get them presently, Helen." Then in French to Marie : " You may bring me a dressing-sacque, and go away until I ring."

Whilst Marie was leaving the room mamma handed me the blank envelope containing the cards. " Was it necessary to persuade Fuller very much ? " she questioned, as I took them.

" Oh, no. He consented easily enough."

Mamma seated herself in a great tufted chair, closed her eyes wearily for a second, and screened with one white hand an undeniable gape, resultant, doubtless, from the fatigues of her recent dinner. " Fuller is so kind and yielding. It was charming of him not to refuse you."

I laughed, a trifle discordantly. " Does he deserve such very copious praise, mamma ? " Then, just as some words had reached the verge of my lips concerning a certain note which was to accompany the cards, I changed my mind and kept silent.

" He is acting generously," pronounced my parent, with at least a suspicion of starch in her manner, " and for that reason he deserves your praise. Isn't it rather early, by the bye, for you to begin depreciating him ? "

Whereupon I made expeditious answer : " Neither now nor at any future time, mamma, have I any wish to depreciate Fuller ; pray be certain of that. But I fail to perceive why he merits much patting on the back in the present instance. We should remember how this quarrel with Melville Delano originated ; for I suppose you have heard. I myself happened to be an eye-witness of the whole proceeding. Melville's behavior was just irreproachable ; no gentleman should have done less or more under like circumstances."

After that I moved doorward, having slight wish to take part in any dialogue, whether bellicose or friendly, at so late an hour. But just then a sharp cold laugh from mamma detained me. She does not employ that laugh often ; I do not think she would greatly relish the hearing of it by many pairs of ears except mine. Invariably she accompanies it with some words that well match its jeering icy pitilessness. I stood waiting for such words, and presently heard them :

" My dear child, it is high time you had gotten a grain or so more of worldly wisdom. Accept things as they are, and make the best of them—not as they should be, striving to make them conform with your fine standard. The right or the wrong in Melville Delano's behavior concerns you not at all. Fancy what social sixes and sevens would exist among humanity if some new law should suddenly make itself felt, by means of which everybody was rewarded or punished precisely according to his deserts. You and I have given Fuller all conceivable signs of pardon for what, when we first reflected on it, seemed a very grave sort of indiscretion. But in so pardoning him we are of necessity forced to stand as his defenders. Anything on our part in the least resembling sympathy with Melville flavors keenly of the ludicrous, now. His valiant championship at that country hotel, this autumn, should number itself among such good deeds as too often encounter the melancholy fate of being interred with their performers' bones. All which it remains our duty to remember is that he has quarrelled with Fuller, and that Fuller's quarrel should be our own. I confess that the plan of sending him your wedding-cards (though of course, by the bye, he will have the good taste to stay away from the wedding) strikes me as most advisable : no doubt Fuller, who is a man of the world, saw the matter in this politic light. It disarms, or ought to disarm, Melville Delano, were he at all inclined toward the employment of any awkward gossip : for this reason, Helen, I must express myself glad that you have carried your point."

By the time that mamma had finished, a sick bitter dejected feeling had crept about my heart; just as if with every breath of my nostrils I was breathing in a dreary doubt lest human life, looked upon as a kind of divine experiment, had proven a most monstrous and miserable failure. It is not the first time that one of these bloodlessly frigid harangues on mamma's part has affected me in much the same manner as now. For just a little moment, at such times as these, all that wholesome " hate of hate " and " love of love " which make up the thew and sinew of anything like a complete joy in living, will seem to crumble away with quick silent ruin. I remember that there have been men with wiser heads and larger hearts than mine, who have died denouncing their fellow-creatures as three parts wickedness to one of good. And at such times, too, all the bad people whom I have ever known (not by any means a meagre company) seem pushing themselves into my recollection at the expense of their superiors. " *Is* mamma right? " comes the desolate question. Is it not better, after all, to look upon humanity with her merciless and cynical eye? Are heart and faith and feeling indeed perilous guides ? Do they who make self their one dominant king and believe that self sways likewise the world with which they deal, gain in the end more by their callous creed than the most fervid-souled optimists who have ever spent years in humane services ? And since we can never see with these mortal eyes, hear with these earthly ears, any surety of

6*

evidence that death does not alike end fair deeds and
foul in one impartial silence and sleep and nothingness,
is it not wiser so to live that if life be in truth a mere
transient mockery of perishable brain and blood and
nerve, we shall have reaped from such a wretched evan-
escence whatever of gross personal profit may be found
there ?—revelling recklessly for one little night, before
the livid flare of dawn shall dim the palace-lamps and
we hurry to join, at the chilly portal, that graveward
march of tired-out masquers wherein, as Théophile
Gautier has pictured it so weirdly, so fearfully, so beau-
tifully—

> " *A chaque pas grossit la bande ;*
> *Le jeune au vieux donne la main ;*
> *L'irrésistible sarabande*
> *Met en branle le genre humain.*"

This attempt to paint my mood of mind at certain
hours (my mood of mind to-night until I had fought
against and overcome it) makes me marvel that a lifelong association with mamma should not have produced
in several ways more permanent results. But no ; she
has not quite stamped me with her stamp, as yet,
though perhaps if I had been made of less impression-
able stuff, I should always have heard unconcernedly
her world-wise counsels.

Thank Heaven! I am going to bed after all, though,
with a light heart. I think it must have been the recollection of Fuller's good-night kiss that has banished my
dismal humor. It was a trinity of kisses, by the bye—
three in one, and all such enormities ! the first loitering
into the second, and the second chirruping (I blush to
record) into the third. Ah, Fuller, your love is in truth
my amulet of safety ! It is a sweet fact that when the
dragons of dejection, of weariness—ay, even of indiges-

tion, reach out toward me their hideous paws, this is the charm which gives me speedy refuge !

Immediately after leaving mamma to-night I came up here to my own room and wrote Melville the following note :

MY DEAR MR. DELANO :—Please believe that in sending you the enclosed cards I am showing a mindfulness of our past friendship, and do not merely intend them as a piece of hollow courtesy ; although I feel sure —am indeed forced to hope—that when you have remembered a certain most unpleasant matter you will perceive, and perceive with a regret no keener than mine, the one negative course which it is so much better for you to take. If these words seem cruel, pray believe that they are meant only as kind. Not patronizingly kind, recollect, but kind with the friendliest fairest motive.

Is this whole note a blunder, by the bye? Since I could not send the cards without it, ought I to have sent neither ? Perhaps. Judge me, if you please ; only, I point to your knowledge of what I am, and in the name of that knowledge demand that you shall reflect well before you *mis·*judge me.

Just a word more : I am going to be stared at in church, a week from next Thursday, by hundreds of pairs of eyes that will regard me simply in the light of so much white satin, so much point-lace, so much nice jewelry. *Your* eyes, if you choose to mingle them with this ocular multitude, must of necessity scrutinize me from a less mercenary standpoint : and therefore it would please me to fancy that you were present, even if I have no certainty to this effect.

Very truly yours,

HELEN JEFFREYS.
—— FIFTH AVENUE, 22d Oct.

MR. DELANO.

This shall be sent to his club to-morrow morning. He will probably turn green with rage at first, but afterwards, on a second or a third reading, begin to wear a healthier complexion and look at the note with more rational eyes. Anyhow, it is wiser to select the pleasantest probability regarding his behavior.

# CHAPTER XII.

CT. 26.—All my bridemaids elect lunched with me to-day. It is certainly a very pretty assemblage of girls. There doesn't seem to be any striking dissimilarity of traits between its individual members. One might almost say of the group that they are four souls with but a single thought, four hearts that beat as one. I somehow feel all the time that I am presiding over this fair congress, wherein the flattering position of chairwoman has been with mute courtesy offered to me, that one or two downright unconventional inharmonious spirits would give a very pleasant break to the monotony. As it is, they all think alike and talk alike, and (in a general sense) dress alike. What elicits a "Dear me!" or a "Gracious goodness!" from number one is infallibly certain to elicit corresponding comment from number four. That is a very worn-out simile, I am well aware, which likens the demands of fashion and folly and vanity to the bed of Procrustes ; but I couldn't help thinking to-day, as I surveyed this dainty sisterhood who had come to imperil their digestions in my society with chicken-salad and chocolate and French cakes, how each of them in sweet self-abandonment had tripped prettily up to the Pro-

crustean bed, resolved to bear like lovely heroines whatever excruciating piece of surgery its limited accommo-
dations might require of the occupant ; and how, victim by victim, each had borne with unmurmuring lips
the inexorable lopping-off which followed.

Here is a sample of the conversation at this morning's
luncheon : florid phraseology is in vogue nowadays,
and it is the proper thing to pile Pelion upon Ossa,
Diary, whenever one opens one's lips. Among the
maidenhood of our Best Society (my capital b and my
capital s are both intentional), not to make every sentence a farrago of superlatives is recklessly to court the
charge of being called slow and poky :

Belle Dillinger : "Girls, who *do* you think had the
astounding brass to dare join me in the street this morning ? You might guess till you were all black in the
faces, and then never form the remotest conception."

(Universal perplexity, everybody turning a puzzled
face to everybody's neighbor.)

Margie Cartwright (breaking the deep silence) :
"Come, Belle, we're mad to hear. Who was it ? "

Belle : "That loathsome wretch, Johnny Bigsbee."

Omnes : "Ugh !"

Susie Montgomery : "Thank Heaven, I've never
had the fearful fate of knowing him. They say he actually drivels at the mouth when he talks to you."

Omnes (with uplifted hands and a nauseated grimace) :
"Oh, Susie !"

Kate Effingham : "He was really engaged to a girl
out West ; Mrs. Fullerton knows it to be a fact. She
died very soon after the engagement, which, of course,
was only to be expected. I can't conceive how she
ever let him kiss her. I should *so* much rather be flayed
alive. Wouldn't you ? "

(Universal preference to being flayed alive promptly manifested.)

And so on, interminably. Mamma, who had been lunching away from home, returned at about four o'clock in the afternoon, and found me prone to say rather satirical things concerning my just-departed guests.

"Don't be morose, Helen," she at length sharply reproved. "I have recently observed with regret that you are showing a very crabbed distaste for society. You should overcome the foolish feeling at once; it is very unsuitable to the future wife of Fuller Dobell."

Mamma seems to think so; but I fervently hope that she is wrong.

*Oct.* 31.—The night before my wedding-day! Fuller has departed very early and I have been sent upstairs very early also, the coming fatigues of to-morrow requiring that I should take deep draughts of preparatory slumber. However, I am in this case like the proverbial horse, which can be driven to water, but must afterwards become a free agent as far as regards his drinking or his not drinking.

Sleep! I wonder if any brides ever do sleep much on their ante-nuptial night.

## CHAPTER XIII.

OV. 1.—No doubt Mrs. Fuller Dobell ought to feel entirely fagged out after the wearying events of her wedding-day; but somehow she doesn't feel anything of the sort. Just at present she is seated before a gratifying little fire, armed with her diary and her pencil, and clad in a commodious wrapper which is indeed a comfort to the flesh after her smart tight-fitting travelling-dress, worn all the way from New York to Philadelphia.

Fuller has engaged charming apartments for us here in the Continental Hotel. The chamber in which I am now seated wouldn't precisely shock a princess even if it did not thoroughly please her; and on the other side of yonder closed door is the attractive little parlor where we have recently had our dinner served to us. There I left Fuller, with destructive intentions toward a cigar, some moments ago. Whilst amputating its end he said something about my probable exhaustion and need of rest; so I took the selfish hint and left him alone. He supposes that I am not beginning anything half so wakeful, Diary, as a chat with you. Doubtless it would rather worry him to know of my occupation; but then that cigar was long, and experience has taught me that he isn't a fast smoker. So there is no danger of his discovering me just at present, and I shall have ample leisure to follow his suggestion before the clutch of Vice (smoking *is* a vice) has had the kindness to release him.

There have been various accounts given, during the past few hundred years or so, of how it feels to get married. Speaking strictly on my own responsibility, I affirm that it is a very disagreeable feeling indeed. I am morally certain that if, whilst I was being conducted altarward through that thronged church this morning, anybody had shown any portion of my person the fullest stabbing-qualities of which the largest-sized pin is capable, I should have been thoroughly ignorant of such a demonstration. I was in a kind of torpor from my scalp to the soles of my feet, though a torpor which permitted me to move tolerably well and to give my responses with creditable clearness. People said afterwards that I made a very successful bride. Their complimentary comments would perhaps have been much the same, however, if Mr. Dobell's betrothed had had a mild touch of hysterics at the altar or had gurgled incoherently when it became proper to say " I will."

Walking down the aisle again, arm in arm with Fuller, and feeling myself possessed for the first time of that strong strange and sweet right so to walk with him— well, this was rather an improvement upon previous sensations, it must be admitted. It was indeed very .much as though, after writhing in the dentist-chair, with hair all tumbled and face flushed hotly, I had been allowed to take up my bonnet and walk, cheered by the professional information that my mouth was now in excellent order, and not at all cast down by the professional advice regarding a call once a month or so in the future. I was still being stared at, it is true, by the hundreds of sharp searching eyes; but every moment brought me farther away from that keen scrutiny and nearer the merciful carriage which waited outside, ready to roll me comfortably home between drawn window-shades.

The reception promptly followed our return. I shook hands, and Fuller shook hands, with every member of a prodigious throng who approached us for that amiable purpose. I also smiled, and Fuller also smiled, with the conventional prodigality. A good many people held long conversations with me, of the devotional ultra-affable order ; I have forgotten nearly everything which everybody said, except the kind speeches of a few whom I believe to have spoken with unaffected sincerity. John Driscoll was among this honored minority. He held my hand and looked me straight in the eyes, whilst he was telling me how strong were his wishes for my future happiness.

" But you appear as solemn as an owl whilst you are saying these pleasant things," I objected.

" Do I ? " he returned, with a fractional smile. " It is because I am so much in earnest, Mrs. Dobell." And then somebody displaced him. I believe, by the bye, that he was forced to abdicate in favour of one of Melville's sisters ; the youngest, a tall pale girl, not without a certain sluggish tallow-colored beauty. She congratulated me copiously ; I felt sure, some time before the end of her pretty speech, that Melville had not made whatever feelings my note might have produced in him, a matter of family confidence. He was not present, I am glad to relate, at the reception.

My ultimate release from the drawing-room was very refreshing. Blanche and Marie combined their powers of handmaidship in the matter of my second toilette, and disenthralled me from all bridal braveries with mar-

vellous speed, either babbling in my ears, as she did so,
melodious French accounts of what Mrs. That, Mrs.
This, and Miss The Other had been overheard to say
about my costume, my superb array of presents, and
everything which concerned the nuptials.    Such a pearl
necklace as that which Mr. Dobell had given his bride,
was never seen before ; as for Mrs. Jeffrey's gift of
silver, and Mrs. Walters' emerald set, and the countless
costly tributes of affection, not to say policy, which the
Messrs. Tiffany and others had assisted an amiable circle of friends in offering me, these were all pronounced
nothing less than magnificent.

I wonder if Blanche and Marie didn't understand
perfectly what buncombe they were guilty of when they
chattered so volubly about Madame Dobell's many
dear friends.    They are themselves a pair of shrewd-
brained worldlings, it is fair to suppose, and for this
reason able to scent hypocrisy in others.    Possibly they
were well aware that nine-tenths of the expenditure
involved in my very beautiful assortment of gifts had
been money told out with coldest and cunningest
motives.    Possibly they could translate, with a skill
quite equal to my own, the luxurious language of a
certain table groaning under its rich burden : how Mrs.
A. had here sweetly testified, in this shining salver,
that she wanted our acquaintance to take the profitable
shape of an intimacy ; how Mrs. B. had there shown an
entire claret-jugful of disinterested regard for mamma's
social triumphs ; and how in yonder brooch sparkled the
earnest hope of Mrs. C. for much future entertainment at
the house into which her precious trinket had found its
way.    Friends !   Ah me, what a sirocco of satire the little
word carries with it, when used in the hard heartless
sense of our drawing-room deceptions, withering and

shrivelling before its breath the fresh green lusty life of real friendship, and leaving in its dreary wake only the harsh dry ashes of selfishness, guile, vanity!

Blanche and Marie were just reaching the terminus of my toilette when mamma entered the room. Discovering that I was dressed, she turned and spoke to Henry, as yet invisible. "You may bring it in, Henry."

"It" proved to be a bronze of considerable size and of considerable seeming weight. Henry placed it on a table and retired.

"From Mr. Delano," mamma enlightened me, handing me that gentleman's card.

The subject of the bronze was a young girl, not clad in anything of a strikingly cumbersome nature, with her dishevelled hair making flexuous erratic lines along shapely shoulder and firm bounteous bosom: one exquisite arm supported her drooping head upon a jagged picturesque mass of vine-wreathen rock. At the statue's base was carved the name *Oenone.* As I watched the figure these lines from Tennyson's poem— that chaste pastoral which tells with such masterful melody how the poor Trojan shepherdess lamented her lover's falsity—murmured itself through my memory:

> "She, leaning on a fragment twined with vine,
> Sang to the stillness till the mountain-shade
> Sloped downward to her seat in the upper cliff."

"It's altogether too pretty a gift for you to frown over," presently commented mamma.

I *had* been frowning, but smoothed my forehead very promptly on being told so. "How queer that he sent it at such a late hour," I murmured. "It's very pretty. By the bye, mamma, you remember who Oenone was, don't you?" Just here I laughed, a trifle harshly. "He might have chosen a more suitable subject. Perhaps he meant to hazard a little downright disagreeable prophecy, you know."

"Pshaw, Helen," was the soft reproval. "I came up here, my dear, to bid you good-by, and so avoid anything like a public leave-taking." After which mamma folded me to her bosom. The folding lasted six good seconds. She then kissed me, with gentle deliberation, upon each cheek. The kissing possibly occupied six seconds more. She then remarked "God bless you." Very soon afterward I went out into the hall and found Fuller waiting for us.

I can't remember half the people, women, and men, who made me most impressive adieus in the hall. It was a delicious relief finally to discover myself alone in the carriage with Fuller, being driven fleetly dépôtward. I felt very much as some cat would feel for which a dozen or so of affectionately-disposed children had been exhibiting their several artless modes of regard, in holding it now by the tail, now by the ear, now by both together ; but which has sprung away from all such innocent fondling, and somewhere safely ambushed, licks itself in grave displeasure.

Well, the cars rattled us to Philadelphia, and here we are. I wonder if Fuller's cigar has approached annihilation by this time. Perhaps he has an instinct, an intuition, that I am disobeying orders, and doesn't like it. I shouldn't, if I were he and had any such suspicion. Undoubtedly it behooves me to recollect that a certain promise about loving, honoring, and *obeying* is not yet twenty-four hours old.

## CHAPTER XIV.

OV. 12.--After considerable wandering we are home at last. We staid in Philadelphia four days, and from Philadelphia journeyed to Baltimore, where we made another pause of four days. Thence to Washington, and from Washington home.

Mamma has had a whole floor charmingly fitted up for us in our absence. She has given me a lovely sleeping-room with boudoir attached, and adjoining this a sleeping-room for Fuller, and still further on a cosey study or library or smoking-room, or whatever is the proper name for it. I can't help preferring smoking-room, as my husband's personal habits are not, after nine days of honey-moon, wholly unknown to me ; and I usually like to call a spade a spade.

"I am so glad you telegraphed yesterday about getting home to-day," mamma informed me, not a long while after our return. "I've been arranging a pleasant little dinner for this evening."

I moaned, but she did not hear me. The spirit has its voice of silence. "I'm glad it is little, mamma. Travelling, you know, rather unfits one for ponderous entertainments."

"Certainly, my dear. You shall take a rest this afternoon" (the quiet command of her tone seemed as natural now to my married ears as it had once seemed to my ears maidenly), "and by six o'clock you will feel in every manner refreshed again. After dinner we are going to the theatre. I suppose you have heard about those horrifying ballet-dancers at Niblo's : we are going to be horrified."

"But mamma—"

"The thing is done constantly by nice people, my dear," was her august interruption. "We shall have a box, you know."

"Has Fuller heard of the arrangement?" I questioned.

"Oh, yes; I spoke of it this morning, just before he went out. The idea seemed to please him. By the bye," mamma added, producing a little packet of letters from her pocket, "your husband's name reminds me, Helen, that these should have been given him immediately upon his arrival. My forgetfulness is to be blamed for the delay. Please say this, if you see him before I do."

She placed the letters upon a table near at hand. "How odd it seems for Fuller's letters to be sent here," I laughed, approaching the table and taking them up. "This envelope is directed with some rather important flourishes. I'll open it and see who writes so pompously."

My own hand was on the point of breaking open the envelope, when mamma's caught it firmly by the wrist. "Do nothing of the sort, Helen," rang her shrill trenchant tones. "It is idle to suppose that Fuller would be anything but annoyed by such a proceeding on your part."

The old cowardice which has made me succumb so often before that imperative voice and face, was waving its white flag now from the ramparts of my will; but suddenly a prompt bold resolve sprang forth and struck down the craven signal.

"Pray let go my wrist, mamma. And pray remember that as Fuller's wife I choose to follow the promptings of my own judgment in all such matters as this." The words were steadily given, but I felt my throat quiver as I spoke them. "If I see fit to open this letter, or any letter addressed to my husband, only he has the right either of reprimand or veto."

Her clasp on my wrist tightened. "But in your husband's absence I shall assume the right of preventing so stupid an action!" The next instant she had snatched the letters from my hold by means of her disengaged hand, the movement being made with such crafty suddenness that until its object was fully gained I did not even begin to realize what had been done. Then, however, I am sure that my face grew very white indeed.

"Return me those letters, mamma," I just murmured and no more.

She swept toward the door, with knit brows and back-thrown head. "They shall be returned to you only with Fuller's consent. I scarcely think that the gaining of his consent will be a very easy matter, by the bye. If I understand him, he is not the man to permit any such absurd terms of matrimonial confidence as these which you propose inaugurating."

"But surely," I made effort to answer with calmness, "my right to possess these letters and to use them as I may please, surpasses your right to prevent me from doing either."

Mamma gave a lazily sarcastic laugh, whilst pausing just at the threshold of the room. "Of course, Helen, if I were to see you in the act of depositing your head among those blazing coals yonder, it would be brazen presumption for me to interfere." After that she lifted a warning finger and let it slowly oscillate, for a moment, midway between mouth and eyes. "Be careful, my dear, or at some future time you will commit some worse folly than this, from whose consequences it will not be in my power to save you."

I sat down in front of the fire, after she was gone, and stared into it. Its blaze and its crackle seemed girding at me. More than once a fierce impulse swept burningly through my blood, to rise up and find mamma and tear, if possible, those letters from her keeping. But when I did rise up it was only to pace the floor with swift nervous steps. It needs vast power, sometimes, for one "to burst the bonds of habit." Here were my rights of wifehood being insolently scoffed at, and beyond the mere natural disclaimer which will leave the lips of one wronged and trampled upon, I had made no effort to assert myself, to hold my own, to throw down the gauntlet before injustice and tyranny.

"And yet," presently counselled that prudence which so often treads upon the vanishing skirts of passion, "you have acted wisely in avoiding all violence of defence. When next you see Fuller, let him hear your story and judge your cause. Even if he disapproves the action you meditated, he must likewise disapprove your mother's unauthorized counteraction. He cannot—believe with entire faith that he cannot—take part against you in a matter of such decisive import."

It was about at this stage of my reflections, and whilst I was still pacing the floor from end to end, though now with slackened progress, that my foot struck against something almost too light to be called an impediment The something proved a letter, evidently one of those for the possession of which mamma had esteemed her little touch of brute force clearly justifiable. The envelope was white and of rather dainty texture, I noticed. As I read Fuller's name upon it, a conviction at once possessed me to the effect that I had seen the same handwriting somewhere before now. I have always prided myself on my memory for nearly any handwriting once seen. Years ago in school I had made parade of this accomplishment and won for it much applausive notice..

I had seen before the handwriting upon the envelope which I then held. But where had I seen it? Perhaps the postmark of the letter might tell me. I looked, and discovered the post-mark to be "New York." No; there was not any clue here. At length I fell to pacing the room again, with a hand pressed against either temple, trying hard—somehow trying very hard indeed—to remember.

"It's a woman's writing, of course," left my lips, presently, in tones of low deliberation. And then it all flashed across me. I saw the croquêt-ground at Pineside, lit cheerily with the bright autumn weather; I saw a servant handing me a letter; I saw Fuller and Melville Delano and Selina Matthers standing not far off.

The next instant I had paused in the centre of the room, and was holding the letter tightly compressed between both palms, and was staring straight into an opposite mirror with very very startled eyes.

"Oh, no," I heard and saw myself whisper, in a frightened husky way; "oh, no, no, no! It can't be; it isn't." Then I held the letter at arm's length from me, and glared upon it.

Not a chance of my being in error. I should have known the shape of those gliding willowy characters

7

anywhere, momentary as had been my last meeting with them.

I laid the letter upon the table, and sat down again in front of the fire. It had seemed right enough to break the seal of that other envelope ; but not for all the world would I have broken the seal of this. Here was perhaps something which Fuller *wished* to hide from me. Even the possibility of such a wish transformed those two thin walls of paper into a very fortress of defence.

Immediately after seating myself this second time, I made a spasmodic and abortive attempt to pooh-pooh the whole matter, the whole matter having, of course, a sufficient understanding of its importance obstinately to resist being pooh-poohed. After a while I took the much wiser course of asking myself what good and legitimate reasons I had for feeling (as I did feel) anxious, nervous, dispirited. The result of this self-questioning was more satisfactory. There was only a dim doubt possible that the letter which had reached Fuller from the hotel during his stay at Pineside, had not been written by the woman in whose company I saw him a few hours later. Admitting to my own mind that she had written this letter, I must also admit Fuller's account to mamma of her having done so with no other right than such as may be assumed by persons of her lawless character toward one with whom, if acquainted at all, she is only on terms of slight acquaintance. And now, if this creature had written once from some such daring motive, might she not have written again from a motive precisely similar ? There lay the bright side of the matter : on the bright side I must determine to look. Never mind what dark views could be taken : let my eyes refuse to accept them.

Fuller had said something, before he went out, on the subject of returning to dine at home. Just before he left the house, mamma must have mentioned her plans for the evening. As he had agreed to these plans, there was every chance of my seeing him privately at some time during the next few hours. I longed, heart and soul, for that private meeting. I felt that all occupation was impossible until it took place. I wished that I might bridge with sleep the interval between then and now.

Presently Blanche came to tell me that lunch was ready, and I sent her away with the intelligence that I cared for no lunch whatever. Not long afterward I threw myself on the bed, and tried to make the recollection of last night's clamorous jolting experiences in a sleeping-car operate persuasively toward the enjoyment of a little real slumber. The attempt was at length successful. I fell asleep. And during my sleep I dreamed an ugly ugly dream.

No matter what the dream was, Diary. Dreams take such hideous liberties with the probable, sometimes. They are a kind of blurred and cracked mirror, very often, in which we see those whom we love the best distorted and misshapen almost beyond recognition.

I awoke in a state of miserable shivering, and knew by the room's dimness that it was quite late. Through the half-closed door which led into Fuller's room there was streaming a volume of gas-light. From the same direction came Fuller's voice, carelessly humming a melody.

I sat for a little while on the edge of the bed, trying to shake off the dismal effects of that ugly ugly dream. This was not at all an easy operation, I soon learned. At length I rose and went up to the table on which I

had laid a certain letter. The letter was there still.
I placed it in my pocket, and entered my husband's
room.

He stood before his dressing-table in full evening
costume, evidently having just completed his toilette
for dinner. "Awake at last, Helen?" he called out,
on seeing me. "I was bound I wouldn't spoil your
siesta, for I knew you must be tired. Blanche came
upstairs to dress you for dinner, but I sent her away.
By the bye, it's ridiculously late, if you've anything
special to do. We're to dine a half an hour earlier than
usual, on account of that theatre-party. Your mother
said she'd told you all about it."

"Yes," I assented. "Mamma told me." I had begun to feel certain, by this time, that mamma had mentioned nothing to Fuller of what had transpired in the
morning between herself and me. Since she had left
me to break the ice, I quickly determined to break it
with one decisive stroke.

"There are some letters for you, Fuller," I commenced, the carelessness in my manner being a trifle
overdone, possibly. "Did mamma give them to
you?"

"Yes."

"Indeed?" Silence. The ice needed a second blow.
"Perhaps she didn't speak of—of a little matter which
occurred between us with reference to those letters," I
presently went on, my voice having grown rather unsteady by this time.

Fuller looked at me curiously. "A little matter,
Helen? Do you mean anything unpleasant? I should
judge so from your very grave face."

"Then you would be judging correctly. Mamma
came into my room this morning with some letters,

Fuller, which she said were for you. I wanted to open one of them; but before I could do so she snatched them—snatched them as we would snatch anything valuable from a mischievous child—and quitted me in full possession of her spoil. Of course I was very angry. I think that I had every reason for being very angry, Fuller."

This last sentence left my lips between two quick catches of the breath. His face had been hardening through the past moment or so, and I knew for a clear certainty the fact of his displeasure, now. But was it displeasure because of mamma's interference, or because of something widely different from that? If *only* it should prove the former! My anxiety, whilst I waited for his answer, was a keen pain to me.

The answer was not long in coming. "You wished to open one of my letters, Helen? Did you suppose that I would approve such a course on your part?"

My heart sank within me, at that. "No, Fuller," I murmured. "One may act without thinking, as I acted then."

He shrugged his shoulders sullenly and gave his head an impatient toss. "Thoughtlessness is so near culpability, sometimes."

I felt the tears rush to my eyes. "You can't accuse me of any wilful desire to displease you!" I burst forth, passionately and bitterly. "I have no feeling for or against *your* opening *my* letters; it just seems quite a matter of course that you should act precisely according to your pleasure as regards them, Fuller. For this reason I have been thoughtless; and for this reason only."

"I have not the least desire ever to open your letters," he coldly stated, though the hard look had now nearly left his face. "Pray let it be understood for the future that what the postman brings you is yours unexceptionably; that what he brings me, is mine in the same manner."

I felt chilled through and through. "Certainly, if you wish it, Fuller. I have one question to ask you, however, before we drop this subject. Do you consider mamma justified in snatching those letters from my hand?"

He walked toward his dressing-table and appeared to absorb himself for a moment in what the mirror had to tell him about his white necktie. Then he folded his arms, faced me, and said firmly:

"She was not justified. You had a better right to open the letter than she to interfere."

If my face wasn't brilliant, after that, it ought to have been. Before answering him I had reduced the distance between us to an inappreciable quantity. "Almost my own words, Fuller!" I cried. "I was sure you couldn't take part against me. I—" And then tears quite destroyed my voice, as I laid a hand tenderly upon his shoulder.

"My dear," he tranquilly began, taking out his watch in a businesslike way that somehow made me withdraw my hand at once and not let it steal about his neck as, a second before, it had wanted to do—"My dear, there are just fifteen minutes left you to dress in. I really think you had better ring for Blanche, unless you mean to dine with the Walters and John Driscoll just as you are. And I don't honestly think that such a costume would be at all suitable."

"Nor I." A little laugh followed my words. He might slight me like this if he chose, but he should not have the satisfaction of seeing my wound. "By the bye, Fuller, you were wrong in letting me sleep so late. I hope dinner will not have to be postponed on my account." Then I moved toward the door, pausing after I had gotten a few steps away from him.

"In mamma's forcible seizure of those letters," I added, quietly, "this one chanced to fall upon the floor. She didn't observe it; nor did I, until after she had left the room. Here it is."

I held out the letter. He came promptly forward and took it from my hand. I tried to command every muscle of my own face whilst I watched his. I cannot say that I succeeded perfectly in this. Anyhow, a little betrayal of feeling mattered nothing, for the moment. His eyes were otherwise engaged than in watching me whilst he read the superscription upon that envelope.

When he lifted them again and looked at me fixedly, searchingly, I had every feature under control. Let me tell the plain hard truth: his color had heightened beyond the possibility of a doubt; his mouth showed one or two queer nervous twitches; added to this, his head moved ever so slightly from side to side when he began to speak, as human heads will sometimes move when the grip of a strong embarrassment has them well in its keeping.

"All right, Helen. Much obliged." He walked quickly away from me whilst uttering the words, (whilst uttering them in a voice that tried hard to be careless, unaffected, natural; but failed completely) breaking the envelope as he did so.

I waited to hear nothing more. I had heard and seen enough.

I went into my own room, and before being fully aware of my occupation I had rung any number of ab-

surdly loud bell-peals for Blanche.     She appeared,
presently, looking alarmed beyond language.

Was madame sick ?    Had anything happened.

" Yes, Blanche," I broke forth, loud-voiced and with
a certain brisk dash of manner, happily not characteristic of me.    " Yes, something has happened.    I've overslept myself and want you to dress me before it's dinner-
time."

Blanche didn't precisely execute this latter command.
I suppose that I kept dinner waiting about five minutes.
They were all in the drawing-room as I entered :
Mamma, Fuller, John Driscoll, and the two Walters.

" We've been sorely tempted to commence dinner
without you, Helen," rippled mamma, all smiles and
suavity.

" But I refused to countenance the arrangement,"
added John Driscoll, whilst I was having my hand
shaken by himself and Louis Walters, and being kissed
by Cornelia.    " It would never have done on the
evening of your return."    Somehow I felt that John
Driscoll's eyes were dealing very observantly with my
face, although they gave no pointed indication of any
fixed scrutiny.    " If so, he is familiar enough with my
various shades of expression," I remember. thinking,
" to form a tolerably accurate judgment of how I feel
just at present."

" Isn't she looking delightful ?" cried Louis Walters.
" Dear, why don't *you* do your hair like that ? " this
latter question being amorously addressed to his wife.
Louis Walters always makes love to his wife—in public.
Even privately, by the way, he professes to adore her.
People tell me that he usually sings her praises in the
ear of whatever foolish female happens just then to be
the recipient of his compromising devotions.    And

Cornelia plays her part in the odd conjugal travesty with a gusto that never flags. Tradition recordeth not whether she, for her part, ever entertains with impressive eulogies of her husband the dynasty of devotees who regularly succeed each other in her esteem; but it is certain that she will mention "darling Louis" in the hearing of friends, to a degree of audacity that sometimes makes the repression of an amused smile nothing except painful on the part of her auditors. What a glaring farce it all is, when you understand the goings-on of this curious couple! Assuredly one of the unenlightened, meeting them for the first time, might be prone to cavil at their excess of matrimonial fondness each for each. On all occasions when together, they combine to form about as abominable a whited sepulchre as I know of.

My place at dinner was between Louis Walters and John Driscoll. I fancy that neither gentleman found me specially entertaining. I sighed a great mute sigh of relief when we ladies at last rose from the table, leaving Fuller and his two guests to their coffee and cigarettes. "It shan't be anything but cigarettes, we promise," declared Louis Walters, with emphasis. "As soon as the ladies have gotten their bonnets on they shall find us prepared to join them. By Jove! it's time we were at the theatre now!"

"You don't say so, dear," moaned Cornelia. "Then we shall hurry our very best. I didn't want to miss a bit of the performance. I haven't had the pleasure of being really shocked at the theatre since I was in Paris, you know. Come, Mrs. Jeffreys! Come, Helen!"

I made hasty work of getting my bonnet on, prompted, possibly, by a delicate sympathy with Cornelia's refined impulses; and (let it be hoped for similar reasons)

7*

mamma did the same. Some very brisk driving brought our carriages to Niblo's in time for us to secure the last half of the first act. Our box was of the proscenium sort, close upon the stage, and containing possibilities of extreme privacy for any one with a desire to see and not be seen.

I confess that some such modest inclination possessed me when, not yet having taken my seat, I looked down at the stage and discerned three or four female figures exchanging pirouettes, prances and caracoles with each other. A first glance at these figures necessarily resulted in the observer's discovery what their costumes were *not :* it was only after a little while that one could determine with any accuracy at all how far they had managed to escape entire nudity. Then by slow degrees one became aware that their lack of normal clothing was replaced by an amplitude of flesh-colored tights and an apologetic yard or two of silk or satin daintily occupying the physical region between hip and arm-pit and generously spangled. All these ladies were smiling as though each was anxious to impress her audience with two facts : first, "I am not cold;" second, "I am not ashamed."

"Of course you must take a front seat, Helen," insisted Cornelia, seeing me remain in the background. "Come, now; no nonsense. Recollect that you're as much married as either your mother or myself. This won't do at all; will it, Louis, dear? will it, John Driscoll?"

Cornelia meant that the rapid selection I had just made of a chair well withdrawn from anything like conspicuousness, would not do at all. Louis echoed his wife's opinion on this subject with a husbandly promptitude sweet to hear and see. As for John Driscoll, he

seated himself at my side and drawled out a very indifferent response about everybody being allowed to sit
where preference dictated.

Cornelia tossed her head and took a chair beside
mamma, who appeared serenely unobservant of the
whole matter. " No, Louis, love," she presently burst
forth, in a most decisive half-whisper. " You can't sit
next to me, dear. That seat is reserved for Mr. Summerby. I saw him buying a ticket as we came in, and
of course he will presently pay us a visit."

" Very well, love," acquiesced Louis Walters, resign-
ing all claim to the seat with instant amiability.

I gave John Driscoll a glance more full of disgust than
amusement. " This farce has for me its melancholy side
no less than its merry," I murmured.

" Do you mean what is going on there," (pointing toward the stage) " or here ? "

Just then my eye caught sight of two shameless pan-
taletted coryphées dashing at each other with voluptu-
ously-posed arms. " Both," I made answer, smiling a
derisive little smile.

" You are out of humour to-night, Mrs. Dobell."
His grave eyes were full upon my face. " I trust from
no serious cause."

That last sentence made me start ; it was so unexpected, yet hit me so surely in a tender place. " Certainly from no serious cause, Mr. Driscoll." I managed
to look a trifle shocked, a trifle mystified, by his question. " But is there any valid reason for your inquiry ?
Suppose I venture to contradict you about my humor ? "

" Ah," he laughed, gently, " you know that I know
you too well for any such contradiction to mislead me.
I used my eyes at dinner, pray remember: and **my**

tongue, too, now that I think of it. You made me talk so copiously; me who am not gifted with any social trait, except it be the power of graceful listen ing."

His words were ordinary enough, but his low voice had the rich ring of something that Cornelia might have thought concealed sentiment; that I chose to call re- vealed sympathy. I suppose the iron school of flirta- tion has taught him so perfectly to manage the mellow music of that voice as to make for him the task of say- ing nothing and meaning much comparative baby-play. Well, it is an ill wind, et cetera. I knew, just from those few trivial words, that he guessed how miserable I was. And I longed to tell him that I knew, whisper- ing in his ear whilst the music deafened those about us and the "hired animalisms" behind the footlights were earning their bread and cheese with such gymnastic en- ergy: "You are Fuller's friend. You are my friend. If he has judged me injuriously, right me in his esteem. If I have suspected him rashly, prove to me that I am a fool for doing so."

This is what I longed to say. And there seemed a protective helpful influence about John Driscoll's mere presence, this evening, which sorely tempted me to say it.

Perhaps Summerby the Insufferable, entering our box with his ultra-urbane manners, and his hard coarse beauty and his general suggestion of one struggling beneath vigorous disadvantages to be a gentleman, was a reason for my keeping silence. When, after the in- terruption necessarily caused by his entrance, John Dris- coll and I resumed our conversation, the rich ring had somehow lessened in his voice and the protective help- ful signs had faded from his manner.

By this time dancing had given place to a more strictly intellectual species of entertainment, viz. : drama.   It was a relief to observe that there were a few ladies in the company who did not scorn the hum-drum propriety of wearing dresses below their knees.   But the dramatic section of the piece, meagre as it was, appeared to contain very few energetic performers.   The leading lady both by speech and by movement seemed desirous of telling the audience that she felt keenly how impossible was her hope of pleasing them in long clothes ; the leading gentleman rounded his rythmic periods with devil-may-care elocution, as though bitterly conscious that he was putting his fine genius to the base use of affording the dancers time to change their dress.   " I should be so much funnier," seemed to remark the funny man, " if you good people wouldn't consider that I was postponing a platoon of Legs every time my lips are opened."   As for the villain, " how can my villany freeze your blood," he seemed to grumble, " when these rampant Bacchantes are doing their best to make it boil ? "

Presently we had a touch of lyric art from a jaunty little female of the soubrette type.   " Don't you think her lovely ? " Cornelia wanted to know, turning round to address John Driscoll and me.   " And do you happen to have that wonderful lorgnette of yours with you, John Driscoll ?   I'm so miserably near-sighted.   It is always delightful to my poor eyes."

" I fancy Mrs. Walters wants to rake the house a little," my companion remarked to me, whilst he produced from a side-pocket the lorgnette Cornelia desired, and handed it to her.

" Is it so very wonderful ? " I asked.

" It has great power.   At least everybody agrees with

me in thinking so. I picked it up in Paris some years ago."

Cornelia verified his prediction, occasionally levelling her lorgnette at the little cantatrice, but principally employing it in ocular voyages through the neighboring orchestra seats, whilst Summerby, with his glossy black moustache (suggestive of bountiful pomading) not many inches from her ear, kept up an inaudible current of whispers to which her indulgent smiles inaudibly and eloquently responded.

Somehow my own eyes followed Cornelia's during her raking process. Here and there among the orchestra-seats I discovered a familiar face. Then my gaze wandered toward the opposite boxes, two in number. The lower box contained a family group : an evident mamma, a no less evident papa, and a bevy of glad-faced children. The upper box contained three ladies, whose escort (if it is presumable that they had one) must have occupied a position more retired than my own, since he (or they) could not be discerned from where I sat.

My eyes are good far-sighted eyes. I required the assistance of no lorgnette in ascertaining whether I had ever seen any of those three faces previously. My recognition was made almost on the instant. I mean my recognition of a certain face seen twice before now : once on the piazza of the hotel near Pineside, once at the glove-counter in Stewart's.

"Talk of the devil," says the old proverb. "Think of him," I might have altered it, then. Very shortly afterward the first act ended. Three or four men took prompt advantage of the curtain's descent to enter and pay their respects to mamma, Cornelia and myself. Aleck Sheffield and Charlie Minard made conversation an imperative matter with me for fully ten minutes. The orchestra had begun its sonorous prelude by the time they left the box. Released from their society, I glanced about me to discover that Fuller was absent.

What was it that sent a sudden stablike pain through my heart as I made this discovery? Assuredly his absence had nothing in itself to cause a jot of surprise or alarm or annoyance. Ah me! did the coming event cast its shadow?

The prelude ended; the curtain rose. There was a thin layer of drama and mediocrity; there was a thick layer of dancing and indecency; there was again a thin layer of drama; and so on, till another act had elocutionized itself badly and pirouetted itself nakedly, to completion.

During all this time I sat with a miserable dread gaining force moment by moment. Fuller was still absent. The place occupied by that woman in the front of the box had been vacant for some time past. I don't know that I allowed myself to admit any definite sequence between these two facts. But they remained to haunt me, nevertheless. A loathsome probability *would* press itself into my thoughts. "The play is beginning to interest you, I should fancy," John Driscoll remarked, as the curtain fell for a second time. This is what he read (he who knows me so well!) from the two scarlet spots which I felt burning on my cheeks and the brightened light which I knew was filling my eyes.

"I am going to borrow your extraordinary lorgnette," I stated, for answer. "I want to discover where Fuller is hiding himself all this time."

He leaned toward Mrs. Walters, who appeared, just then, to be having something especially sweet whispered in her car by Summerby the Inexhaustible.   I can't say whether or no John Driscoll broke one of the creature's compliments cruelly in half by his remark to Cornelia; anyhow Cornelia so far forgave this act of violation as to hand him the lorgnette languidly over her shoulder, a few seconds later.

Just as I raised the lorgnette to my eyes after receiving it from John Driscoll, mamma addressed a remark to my companion which made him turn momentarily away from me.   I seized the opportunity thus given, and levelled the instrument full upon that upper box. Heavens, what power it had !   I could almost read the programme which one of the occupants held in her hand. As for the rear of the box, that could have no secrets from me, though the gas was burning rather dimly; perhaps made dim with intention.   Every object which could be seen at all, I saw unmistakably.   The two females who had been the companions of that other were still rather conspicuously seated in the front of the box.   Behind them was utter vacancy, unless carpet and chairs deserve a more dignified name.

But on a sudden I received a forcible reminder that there was a certain corner of the box which did not come within my field of vision.   One of the two females —a vulgarly-dressed beauty, though a beauty undeniable—turned her head away from her companion and smilingly moved her lips.   The lorgnette gave strong evidence that she was talking, but it had no power to reach that section of the box occupied by whomever she addressed.   I continued my scrutiny.   Presently a laughing face (a face I have gotten to know rather well by this time) was thrust forth from obscurity.   Its owner was evidently saying something funny, from the mirth with which her words were received, and had leaned for-

ward to say it.   Perhaps a minute afterward, somebody
else leaned forward also.

A man, this time.

Fuller.

The face was visible only for a second ; then withdrawn.

It seems odd to state it, but the next thing that I
recollect after having made this discovery was seeing
John Driscoll close at my side whilst he held up the lorgnette I had been using and spoke in brisk pleasant
tones.   "A very little more, Mrs. Dobell, and my
wonderful lorgnette might have taken an injurious trip
from your lap to the floor.   Hereafter you will oblige
me by handling it less carelessly."

I turned my face toward his, trying to smile.   It
must have been ashen pale, and the smileless smile
must have rendered it paler.   "Good Heavens !" he
broke out, in anxious whisper; "you are ill.   Let
me—"

" No, no," I objected, faintly, putting my hand upon
his arm.   Somehow that was all I could manage, just
then.   And after that my eyes went straight toward
the box again.   I knew that his own followed them.
She had reappeared, and was occupying her former
conspicuous place near the two others.   I heard John
Driscoll make a short sound, something between a sigh
and a groan.

" Did you discover Fuller, Mrs. Dobell ? "

I turned and faced him, at this.   "Yes.   He was in
that opposite box—the upper one.   Do you know any
of those "—" ladies " stuck in my throat—" people, Mr.
Driscoll ? "

He avoided my look instantly.   "I think I have seen
them before."   Then in a sort of eager impatient way

he searched my face, asking sharply: " Do *you* know them ? "

I smiled bitterly. My self-possession was coming back to me. " I am not so fortunate as you are. I have only seen one of them before."

His brows gathered themselves in puzzled style. " May I ask where and when ? "

I might have answered him with entire candor, such a cold careless apathetic feeling had begun to possess me : but just at this moment the door of our box opened. We both turned quickly round. Fuller was entering.

" Where have you been for this age past, Fuller ? " called out his sister.

" I've been to London to see the Queen," he laughed, taking a seat directly behind Cornelia.

" Pshaw, Fuller," she persisted, " I hope it isn't *a secret* where you've been. Helen, I certainly should not tolerate such reticence, if I were you, at this early conjugal period."

" Very well, Cornelia," he responded lightly, " if you will have facts, I met an old friend who detained me for an entire act. A man. You don't know him."

" Let us all be thankful that it was a man," murmured Mrs. Walters fervently, again placing herself under the light of Summerby's smile.

How glibly the lie had left his lips ! I tried to hold steadily the programme that I was staring at ; no one but John Driscoll saw my hand tremble.

The curtain rose three more times before the performance ended and we all prepared to go. This is the thorough extent of my knowledge regarding what passed on the stage after Fuller's return. John Driscoll did not once speak to me (or if he did I failed to hear him) during those three acts.

"Helen, you don't look a bit well," commented Cornelia, as we were leaving the box.

"I am tired," I stated, placidly.

Tired! ah, how true that was! I recollect glancing at Cornelia and wishing that we might change natures, she and I. Yes, if I could only shuffle off my conscience, my sense of decorum, my power of loving, just as though they were worn-out garments, and take in their stead all which helped to make Mrs. Walters happy after her kind of happiness—even including Summerby the Adhesive! It did not pay, I told myself, to have what is called soul. With refinement of feeling, comes a proportionate power of suffering. Sensitiveness so often means agony that the downright jelly-fish bluntness—perhaps "the straitened forehead of the fool" himself, was better in this world of shocks and wounds and wickedness.

Well, that is what I told myself then. I don't tell myself so any longer. Certain moods give birth to certain ideas. No; I prefer my own miserable identity to anything a whit more callous. Cornelias and people of her sort have their "lower pains," perhaps, but they have their "lower pleasures" likewise. They cannot love as I have loved.

As I do love still! Thank God for that! Fuller could do nothing so vile that it would alter my love for him. Last year I would have laughed at the possibility of my writing down this sentence about any living man. Now I see that with myself, at least, once to love is always to love. Not if he lied a thousandfold more shamelessly than I heard him lie to-night; not if he stole, drank, cheated—

Pshaw! what am I writing? It is very late. I ought to have been in bed long ago. Let me think:

there isn't much more to tell. Mamma and John Driscoll and I took one carriage; Cornelia and Summerby occupied the other. "Fuller and I are going to walk up town, if you'll let us," Louis Walters announced to mamma and myself. "Mr. Summerby very kindly offers to go home with that dear Cornelia of mine, and John Driscoll agrees to take Fuller's place here."

"You are a pair of wretched deserters," gracefully succumbed mamma. "I suppose you are going to smoke. Well, it isn't the first time that Helen and I have been ignored for a cigar. Good-night."

So they left us. During the ride home mamma talked, John Driscoll talked, I talked. I have forgotten what everybody said.

John Driscoll left us at our door. He pressed my hand as he bade me good-night. I suppose it meant sympathy. He pities me; but his pity does not gall me as some men's would.

After we had gotten indoors mamma gave vent to a few suave commonplaces. I suppose that they were suitably answered; and then I came upstairs. The greater trouble absorbs the less. I feel rather forgivingly toward her when I recall this morning's occurrence.

Fuller came in some time ago. I can hear his heavy breathing in the next room, when I stop my writing. It sounds like the sleep of the just.

*Is* there yet a chance that all may not be so very dark for me? I wish I had made an effort to get the truth from John Driscoll: he must know. Anyhow, I do not yet deal in certainties. Relations of the sort I dread may have once existed between Fuller and that woman previous to his marriage; and what now looks so culpable in him may be but a final snapping of the chain.

I wish I could believe this. Faith should be born. of love, and my love passeth understanding. Indeed, till to-night I have never dreamed of its depth.

It is very strange. I ought to feel angry and bitter: I can only feel miserable beyond words. But reflection, introspection, will advantage me nothing.

## CHAPTER XV.

OV. 13.—I had some coffee brought to my room, this morning, at a very late hour. But when the beginning of one's sleep dates from about dawn, one is apt to breakfast unseasonably. Fuller was in the reception-room, reading the paper, when I went downstairs; so much I discovered through the crevice of the opened door, before entering.

He bade me good-morning with all his old cheerfulness. Yesterday I would have gone forward to get his kiss; nor not one, but half a dozen. To-day, after having gently returned his good-morning, I pretended to be looking for a book in one of the little low bookcases at the back of the room. With the corners of my eyes I saw him stare steadily in my direction for several seconds. Then he resumed his paper, giving it a rather vigorous rattle.

I stood there beside the book-case with an open volume in my hand and a falsehood on my face—the falsehood of appearing engrossed by the volume. In reality it was all the dumbest of dumb shows. I creased my forehead meditatively and pursed my mouth interestedly, seeming to be detained at one page by an attractive sentence, then hastening over a few more pages at full speed, then being detained again. The

book may have been Dickens or it may have been Rus-
kin : I believe we have both authors in the library.

I had come there with the fixed resolve that I would
make an effort to find out from Fuller on what terms he
stood with that woman. If he had deceived mamma
and through her deceived me, and was now casting
pitch at my wifely name, I at least deserved to know it.
Indeed, I was quite able by this time to look firmly in
the face all the probable facts which might be deduced
from his present culpability—if culpability in truth it
was. He had wanted money. Mamma's flattering
courtesies had tempted him into the Newport intimacy
with me ; an intimacy whose motive was the ultimate
getting of money. Hypocrisy in his courtship ; hypocrisy more vile in his marriage ; hypocrisy and cruelty
and insult in the masquerade marked out for himself
after marriage ! His arms were to hold a wanton one
hour and me the next ; his lips were to pass from hers
to mine ; his voice was to phrase tender thoughts for
me to-day, for her to-morrow, in horrible alternation.
Or else he would neglect me utterly, out-Cornelia his
sister in conjugal carelessness, and make the world lift
its eye-glass compassionately at me, with some touching
comment like " Poor thing ! She might have known
how none of that family ever *do* really marry."

So much for the facts whose certainty must follow my
conviction of Fuller's guilt. If, on the other hand, I
should hear that suspicion had wandered all too perilously near the edge of calumny ; that whatever any
woman on earth had been to him before meeting and
knowing and loving me, now no longer was such woman
of the lightest worth in his thoughts ; that although he
had once or twice given rise to just suspicion, in reality
he had been far from deserving blame ; that what I saw

had been merely the sundering of ancient ties, too
strengthened by years for a single wrench to break
them—if only I should hear all this, how should I dare
disbelieve, dare even to doubt it? How could I blame
him, either, for having stooped to a lie that he might
spare me pain? Ah, to what a golden ending of these
last few dismal hours my devout hopes pointed!

But were they not deceiving me? Fuller's paper
seemed wholly to absorb him. Whither had flown that
firm resolve of mine about making an effort to get from
him the truth? I continued the dumb show a little
longer, asking myself, with quickened pulses, why my
courage had ebbed into· such shallowness at this, the
vital moment. Did I dread hearing the worst that I
could hear? Did I dread meeting some caustic rebuff
that would wound keenly whilst it still left me in the
same dreary state of doubt?

Well, I must speak, anyhow. Let it be about the
weather, about the moon, about Kamtchatka—I *must*
speak.

"Did you like the play last night, Fuller?" I was
still ostensibly engaged with my book.

"It was very gorgeous in the way of pageantry and
all that," he answered, "but I can't say that it deserved
any great praise."

My heart gave one or two furious beats as I framed
the next sentence. "You staid away for quite a while.
Indeed I began to wonder if you were ever coming back.
Didn't you say to Cornelia that you had met a friend
who detained you?"

"Yes." The monosyllable came curt and cold. A
little silence followed. Then he commenced speaking
again in wholly altered tones, quick and light and careless. "I told your mother this morning, Helen, that I

regretted the line of conduct which she pursued yesterday. Of course I can't answer for your future freedom
from her interference. I believe, though, that she was
impressed by what I said to her."

I had lain down the book and drawn nearer to him
by the time that my reply was given. " Thanks, Fuller, for having spoken to mamma. As for my desire to
open your letters, I trust that the explanation which I
gave has satisfied you."

" Explanation ? " he questioned, with raised brows.
" I did not hear any, Helen—that is, nothing at all
adequate. However, we will let the matter pass, if you
please."

" But I don't please ! " I stormed, crimsoning. " The
coolness which you adopted toward me last night was
simply contemptible, after what I said in self-defence.
I did not believe you capable of holding ill-feeling
against your wife because of so trivial a matter."

He met me, anger for anger ; only, his anger was of
the curbed smouldering sort ; the antipodes of my own.
" What you choose to term a trivial matter, I choose to
term one of great importance."

A laugh left my lips, bitter and discordant. " Perhaps it isn't difficult to guess why."

He fixed hard eyes upon my face. " I don't understand you at all."

" No ? I mean, then, just this : probably you have
excellent reason not to let me into the secrets of your
correspondence. I dare you to tell me with frankness
from whom was the letter which I handed you last,
night."

After that I glared at him defiantly, in too much of a
downright temper to shrink before the effect of my own
words. He wore no guilty flush, now ; he had only

8

grown a shade or two paler and had started up from his chair.

"Helen, you know me well enough to know that I will not bear this sort of thing. I suppose that when you become more reasonable you will regret having attempted it."

Something in his clear firm voice made me see the disadvantage at which I had placed myself. Women generally cry when any such revulsion of feeling begins. I did not cry—at least not before Fuller's face. I dashed from the room, rather, so that he might not witness my tears.

Whilst I was hurrying upstairs mamma met me in the second hall. I knew that her eyes swept my face, and could not doubt that she saw there its fiery agitation. When I had reached the door of my own room, I stopped before entering. Mamma was going downstairs at the time I had met her: she would probably find Fuller where I had left him, in the little reception-room.

The impulse to run down and listen for a moment or two was not a particularly high-toned one, I am ready to admit. But I wanted right eagerly to learn (now that my passion, having shot up rocketwise was falling stickwise) whether Fuller's frigid impervious manner had not been a kind of stubbornly-worn mask, and would not drop from him the instant I had gone. Anyhow, I expended very few reflections upon the right or wrong of the matter, but darted downstairs just in time to lean over the banisters of the lower hall stair-case and see ,mamma entering the reception-room.

"What is the trouble with Helen now?" I heard her ask, in a voice touched by surprise. And then, instead of the answer for which I waited, keenly expectant, came the sudden disappointing sound of a closed door.

I made no attempt aurally to overleap this obstacle, but went upstairs again with a new feeling of discomfort added to my former ones. Could it be possible that mamma received confidences from Fuller which were withheld from me?

An hour or so spent in my own room brought, as a matter of course, calmness; and with calmness reason generally walks arm-in-arm. Reason rebuked me for having shot forth that sharp little shaft about the letter. Such a shaft should only have sprung from the bow of a certainty in Fuller's wrong-doing. And I wasn't yet certain. "Not certain, not certain," I mentally repeated many many times, catching at my frail straw of hope.

Of course, I found myself arguing, he could not have told me from whom the letter had come after I had dared him to tell in such furious fashion, even if his tailor or his boot-maker had been the real correspondent. No; I would not add wrong to wrong, in this stupid style. "The little rift within the lute"—provided it were no more—should not go on widening and widening with every hour, when a few brave self-forgetful words on my part might prevent such rapid ruin.

By the time that I went downstairs to lunch I had made an adamantine resolve. The next opportunity which offered itself of an interview between Fuller and me should prove beyond all chance of error how falsely or how fairly I had suspected. I wasn't a woman in a novel, I told myself, with a merciless author to make her miserable for a certain number of pages because his art imperatively demanded that there shouldn't be a reconciliation till the last chapter. I was going to kick down the barrier of mutual misunderstanding, if any such blessed impediment waited for the opportune kick. I was going to tell Fuller simply and plainly—

Well, never mind what. The dining-room was vacant when I entered it, and continued so whilst I ate my lunch. An inquiry of Henry resulted in the intelligence that Mr. Dobell had left the house at about twelve o'clock, and that Mrs. Jeffreys had gone out in the carriage a little while afterward.

And so my lunch was eaten in solitude, and with an atomic appetite. When would my opportunity come? I asked myself. In the afternoon or evening?

Neither afternoon nor evening brought it. Fuller returned just in time to dress for dinner. During dinner I found it hard work to be occasionally audible in the way of what are called general remarks. Without specially addressing me, Fuller showed a willingness to do so. If it had not been for mamma's presence at table we would probably have answered each other's commonplaces with more personal directness: as it was, we both talked mammaward.

"Now my opportunity has arrived," I thought, as Fuller, lighting a cigarette, rose from the table. After he had left the dining-room, I waited for perhaps three minutes, then rose and followed him. I had confidently expected to find him smoking in the reception-room. Instead of this I found him overcoated in the hall, appearing there just as the boom of his up-springing opera-hat informed me, by means of its laconic basso-profundo, that he was going out.

"Wait a few moments, Fuller, please," was on the tip of my tongue. Something kept the words from getting any further, however; perhaps the fear that he would refuse what I asked of him. It was better not to run the risk of a refusal. I had no reason to suppose that he would remain out all the evening.

And so I walked quietly past him and went upstairs;

and presently the hall-door clanged behind his departure.

Well, it is after eleven o'clock now, and he has not
yet returned.   At about nine, mamma sent for me to
come down and see some people.   I replied in a message to the effect that I was not very well.   My message was no falsehood.

I shall not wait up any longer; I am going to bed.

And yet, just a word more before I go.   Fuller's
treatment of me at dinner, negative as it was in character, amazed me for one reason.   There was no sign of
anger about it; no evidence that he wished not to resume terms of friendliness.   If I had merely flown into
a passion this morning, his after-demeanor would not
puzzle me; but I had cast an open slur upon his faith—
I had said that to him which, if innocent of the charge
implied in my words, he should feel bound to resent as
an unmerited insult.   How, then, can I account for his
serene   angerless   conduct   during   dinner?   Henry's
presence in the dining-room might have prevented him
from keeping frownful silence, but he would not have
made that a reason for cheerful spirits.   Is it some effect
of mamma's counselling, or is it the brazen indifference
of guilt?   If that suddenly-closed door, this morning,
kept from me anything which might throw one comforting ray into the darkness of what my thoughts are
now, I bitterly regret not having been allowed to play
the eavesdropper as long as I wanted.

For Heaven knows I am in miserable enough need of
comfort !

## CHAPTER XVI.

OV. 14.—"It is a fortunate matter for Helen and myself," mamma was informing Fuller, with her grandest manner, as I appeared at breakfast, this morning, "that they have given me the box I wished; otherwise I should have staid away from the opera throughout the entire season, as I told them last week. I seriously suspected from the first," she went on, buttering a morsel of toast as though conferring upon it a papal blessing, "that this special box had found no absolute lessee, but that there was a strong chance of some operatic potentate's friend deigning to engage it. I left the Academy the other morning, with severe signs of displeasure. 'Red-tape' expresses the whole matter, I am quite confident, little as I generally countenance slang. However, the manager writes me this apologetic note," (glancing down at an envelope propped slantwise against the coffee-urn) "and I shall so far waive dignity, since it is for my own advantage, as to send him a cheque. Helen, will you have tea or coffee?"

"Tea, thanks." Just then, Fuller, who had finished his breakfast, rose from the table. Whilst leaving the room and rolling a cigarette in languid concert, "I must say you are sensible in not missing the season," he observed. "Everybody says that the opera was uncommonly nice on Monday night." Then he disappeared.

"I forgot to mention, Helen, that opera had begun," mamma presently stated. "But no doubt you saw the advertisements, or somebody told you."

"No one told me, and I'm not an inveterate newspaper-reader, mamma, as you may have noticed."

Mamma smiled whilst making my tea. "You say that very indifferently, Helen. You used to delight in the opera. But many of your tastes seem to have changed—I won't say since your marriage; that, of course, would cover too short a space; but since your engagement. The change is hardly pleasant to witness, I must own. Indeed, it displeases me. And before long it will probably displease Fuller."

I hesitated for a moment; then my answer came fluent enough: "You are quite right. I am not fond •of parade and pretension any longer; and that is about all that New York society seems to consist in, as far as I can make out the meaning of it. Not that I want to turn preacher and launch philippics against the morals of the day; don't suspect me of anything so grandiose, please. You expressed the case very clearly, mamma, when you inferred a change of tastes."

"And it is a most lamentable one," was her austere enunciation. "However, I refuse to recognize it," went forth the solemn fiat. "If you have these feelings, I must insist upon their concealment. No woman of your youth and health and surroundings should shirk the responsibilities (to call them by a most severe name) of her Social Position. If you do not enjoy Society, you can, at least, assume a liking for it. I suppose you will go with me to the opera this evening?"

My tea was made. Mamma, her breakfast concluded

and some pointed token of her noteworthy displeasure
being doubtless considered necessary, rose from her
chair, which Henry, with courtly obsequiousness, drew
back.

"You know that I am very fond of the opera," I acquiesced.   "Is Fuller going?"

· "I really haven't asked him.   He may go with us ;
he may drop in afterward ; he may not go at all:  Fuller
is liable to all sorts of engagements.  I have no wish to
pry into his affairs."

"*Nor should you have,*" that last sentence plainly told
me, though any such words were unspoken.

"Of course not, mamma," I made answer, with much
calmness.   "You are not his wife."

She was leaving the room, but stopped to reply.
"If I were his wife it would be the same.   Any other
course, depend upon it, is eminently absurd."   Then
she, too, disappeared.

I didn't eat much breakfast.   Although far from expecting the minutest sympathy in this quarter, I was
not well prepared for such an early disavowal of it.
Whilst drinking my tea (gulping it down in hot swallows, might better be written) I tried to banish from my
thoughts the little that she had said, the much that she
had meant, and occupy them wholly with the coming
interview between Fuller and myself.

Presently I quitted the room, passed into the hall,
drew near a certain open doorway, and knew by the
clouds of smoke issuing thence that Fuller's presence
would make such an interview promptly possible.   Provided, that was, mamma had not joined him since leaving me.

She had not joined him.   He had no society except
that with which tobacco and the morning paper com-

bined to furnish him, this duo of entertainers proving so fully the strength in union that he was not aware of my being at his side until I had stood there for a good half-minute.

As soon as he turned and saw me, I spoke. "Fuller," I broke forth, without proem or prelude, " I have come to end, if possible, the bitter feeling that is between us. A few plain words on either side ought to accomplish this. Let me ask you a question—agree candidly to answer it."

He flung the little smoking fragment of his cigarette rather adroitly into a distant cuspedor. "There is no bitter feeling, Helen, on my side, at least. I advise you not to nourish any : it certainly won't be the cleverest policy."

"This cold and measured way of speaking, Fuller, must be assumed with you," I returned, my eyes fixedly observant of his face. " I cannot believe that you feel the indifference you are showing. Perhaps you want some evidence of contrition on my part for what I said yesterday morning. Understand, then, that I am sorry, and genuinely sorry, for having spoken as I did. I have no sense of humiliation in telling you this. Why should you have any in explaining—?"

"All my private personal affairs because your curiosity requires that I should do so," he interrupted, his voice ringingly hard. "There is but one sort of settlement, Helen, that can ever be arrived at between you and me. I am to mind my own business and you are to mind yours. That is, perhaps, a very discourteous way of putting it; but plain words are necessary, once and for all. I wish you to ask no question of the sort you have hinted at ; I refuse to answer any such question if you put it."

8*

He had been looking steadily out of the window all this time ; if his manner had not a grain of softness, neither had it a grain of anger. He appeared to be simply stating his opinion in bald passionless deliberate terms. I could not find an answer, though a hundred were rushing to my lips. Of what use was indignation against this marble of immobility? Through every vein seemed running the slow icy realization at what fearful odds I waged my contest. If he had ever loved me that love was gone now—gone already—gone after a few poor little days of wedlock. Ever loved me ! My thoughts had hardly shaped those words before their desolate mockery became apparent. I don't exaggerate one jot or one tittle when I say that it was with me, during those few moments, as though some mocking devil had his horrid lips close against my ear and was sneering that I had been fooled, duped, used for a passing purpose and thrown aside when that purpose was gained. "They were all lies," sneered the devil; "his smiles, his suave speeches, his kisses—all lies, lies, lies ! At Newport he was a hypocrite, at Pineside he was an arch-traitor. And you, you have been merely a fool."

Presently I became conscious, in a sort of numb lethargic way, that Fuller was speaking again. "And now, Helen, if you wish to remain here and talk with me on some other subject I shall be quite pleased to have you do so. But any more useless parleying to no purpose whatever, I must decline to engage in."

He was still looking streetward through the near window, and so he did not see my face whilst I stood there at his side for a second or two before quietly leaving the room and quietly going up to my own. I seemed moving in a dream, then. I remember seating myself near the little centre-table in my dressing-room and leaning my head on my hand; but I don't believe that any thoughts came to me afterward, though I sat there for quite a while. No; I was too stunned to think. Against the opposite wall ticked my clock with sharp monotony; outside rumbled the wheels of omnibus and coach; "Oranges, oranges! fresh *Hava*na oranges!" appealed a Celtic voice from below my windows: all these trivial sounds branded themselves upon my mind, and are inseparable from my remembrance of that void sensationless interval.

At length I must have reached out a hand mechanically and drawn toward me one of the books of poems that fill my table, and parted its pages. It chanced to be Christina Rossetti's poems—a book that I have read and re-read, and learned passages from, and loved dearly. Possibly the mere sight of these familiar well-prized pages went far toward waking me from my stupor. But it so chanced that the first lines my listless eyes fell upon were :—

> "It is over.  What is over?
> Nay, how much is over truly !"

That was enough. I read no more. I could not read any more. The rock had been smitten; the living waters gushed forth. "Like summer tempest came my tears." Down against the table fell my head : with lips close upon those very lines, with arms outflung in an utter self-abandoned recklessness of wretchedness, I sobbed great heavy sobs.

. . . . . . . . . . .

Fuller dined at home to-night, but did not go to the opera with mamma and myself. "I shall probably happen in upon you," he told us, carelessly. We left him lounging in the reception-room, with a novel.

It was a splendid house, as far as attendance went
There was boxful after boxful of people whom we knew.
Mamma bowed here, there, everywhere; I followed example, scattering my smiles broadcast.   Nor were they
smiles that fell in barren places; for during the first
entr'acte we were besieged with devotees, all in ostensible
seventh heavens of delight at our appearance.    I talked,
I laughed; I was more than once nearly noisy.   The
devotees no doubt thought me in glorious spirits; some
of them said so, I believe.    If they could have seen the
embittered sickened heart of their entertainer, how they
would have shuddered to their pearl-kid finger-tips,
these throngs of elegant opera-going gallants !

Not long after the second act had begun, and whilst
Ludlow Inmann was being murmurously conversational
at not more than an inch from one of my ears, I chanced
to discover Melville Delano in a distant box.   Kellogg
was singing a delicious air deliciously, and I had been
managing to appreciate her, notwithstanding Mr. Inmann's close adherence.   He is like a great big pot on
a slow fire : you can let him hum with impunity whilst
you attend to something else.   An occasional stir is
merely optional.

I gave him such a stir now.   " I see that Mr. Delano
is in the Effinghams' box."

" Yes.   He isn't precisely an enemy of Miss Kate's,
you know. · Don't feel authorized, myself, to say how
the affair will turn out.   Do you ? "

" No, indeed ; " (with a shoulder-shrug.)   " If you
see him this evening, by the bye, just give him a message from me.   On the score of old friendship I claim a
morsel of notice, provided Miss Kate isn't too selfish a
monopolist."

Ludlow Inmann made a very prompt Mercury.   At

the end of the act I saw him in the Effinghams' box : by not many minutes later Melville was shaking hands with me.

I know that mamma was amazed ; but there was not in her manner a gleam of anything except cordial courtesy.

" You got my message ? " I opened conversation.

" Yes. Inmann told me what you said. I was doubly astonished. I hadn't yet seen you. You are looking very well."

" Should that astonish you ? " I laughed.

" No. My other reason for surprise was that you sent for me."

" It was rather bold, Mr. Delano. I should have waited for you to come of your own accord. Which you would perhaps never have done."

" Quite right." His black eyes left off looking at me whilst he went on : " I was not thoroughly sure that your invitation had any serious meaning to-night. Sometimes people send each other invitations, you know, that are mere matters of form."

His innuendo was plain enough to me ; he meant the note which I had sent him with the wedding-cards. A keen pang followed my remembrance of hours so recent yet so unutterably happier, when that note had been written. But he saw nothing on my face of what I felt.

" You are very kind to bear me no grudge on account of that little matter," I murmured, not caring how near to each other we had gotten our respective countenances, how absorbed was my manner, or how reciprocally absorbed appeared his. Was I not to-night one of the same frivolous world that fanned itself and babbled and played with its salts-bottle and devoured the unwholesome flatteries that were poked at it, all about

me ?   Had I not made an effort to lift myself from these
surroundings, and had not the hand which might have
helped me suddenly denied all help ?   Let me satisfy
Fuller and mamma, and being still a dweller in this little
Rome of flippancy, recklessness, laxity, where fate seems
bent upon my staying, do as my fellow Romans do.
Let me flirt in simpering contiguity with other women's
husbands, just as other women will probably behave
with mine.   Let New York say of us : " He married
her for money ; she married him for position ; and they
really seem to have made a very friendly exchange."
Who knows but that Fuller and I shall one day possess
the precious metropolitan fame of giving the selectest
dinners, the most carefully-sifted balls in Society, and
thrill with the happy consciousness that hundreds of
strugglers are elbowing their difficult way to our throne-
foot ?   Noble ambition !   Blissful prospect !

Just then the nearness of Melville Delano had a
special importance for me.   If Fuller was coming it
was time that he came.   In that event I should not be
wholly weaponless as far as concerned the striking of at
least one sure blow.   Coming, he would find Melville
at my side.

He did appear, presently.   I saw him at quite a distance off, advancing loiteringly toward our box, stopping a second here, a second there, all smiles and bows
and affability.   I saw him, and then a fierce sort of
boldness seized me, and before I knew it Melville was
asking for a rosebud out of my bouquet and I was smilingly telling him that Kate Effingham would never forgive me if I granted such a favor.

" Is her pardon of so much importance to you ? " he
whispered.   " I am sure it isn't to me."

" Then what people say is all wrong ? " I made mur-

murous answer, disengaging from its pale-pink sisterhood one of my freshest rosebuds.

By this time Fuller had reached our box. He had
nearly entered it before he recognized Melville. There
was no sign of greeting between the two men. Fuller
drew back in abrupt style, his brows momentarily knit,
thrown off his guard by the suddenness of the encounter. Melville shot one sidelong look at the new-comer,
discovered in that look who he was, and went on talking, a trifle confusedly, to me. As for myself,

"Have you just arrived?" I questioned, with beaming composure.

"Yes," he returned, shortly, ignoring me for the
little group of men that were surrounding mamma.

"Had I not better leave you?" Melville confidentially wanted to know, whilst fastening in his button-
hole the rosebud I had just given him.

"And pray why?"

His eyes made quick eager search of my face. I am
sure that they found there only placid pleasant encouragement. "Because," he hesitated, "because—but
pshaw, you know perfectly well."

"Know?" with raised brows I responded. "You're
wrong; I don't at all know."

"Somebody is looking terribly cross. I should say
that a coming curtain-lecture was casting its shadow
before.

"Then you're a very stupid prophet," I laughed.
After that I cleared the subject with a flying leap, as it
were, and landed upon something widely different.
Another act began. Melville remained at my side.
The group of men about mamma lessened by several
members. Fuller was among the departures. Presently
I saw him in close converse with that little yellow-

haired Gerald woman, who smiles so much and whilst she does it shows you such very white teeth and such very red gums.

It was about now that I began to observe in mamma pronounced signs of annoyance; I should say uneasiness, but the word hasn't enough dignity. Evidently she considered that Melville was outstaying the conventional time—that is, for Melville. Evidently, too, she disapproved of my exclusive and concentrated civility. More than once a kind of extra sense told me that her eyes were scanning us. I affected entire unconsciousness. In reality I only grew more determined that Melville should not leave me.

Nor did he, until the opera was over. Fuller at length quitted his yellow-haired charmer, and went among fresh boxes and entertainers new. When the green curtain fell on the melodious misery of tenor and soprano he had not returned.

" Mr. Delarro is going to get us our carriage," I coolly told mamma, as we rose.

· Which Melville did. I bade him good-night with just enough warmth not to make my cordiality seem over-done. Mamma gave him no hand, but smiled courteous farewell. And as the carriage rolled us away from the Academy, I caught a glimpse of Fuller coming down the steps with a white-cloaked companion on his arm.

Would mamma attack me, I wondered, on the subject of my civilities to Melville? But though I steadied myself to meet such an attack, none came. We had not been home ten minutes before Fuller arrived there. I had thrown myself into a great chair in the reception-room, and had just told myself languidly for the fourth or fifth time that I had better ring for Blanche. Fuller

entered the house with his latch-key, and came immediately into the reception-room. I supposed mamma
had gone upstairs ; anyhow, she was no longer visible.

The instant that my eyes met his face I knew what
was coming. He planted himself directly in front of
me, staring hard ; not scowling, not showing any sign
of concealed passion.

"I don't know why you acted as you did to-night,"
he presently began, "unless it was solely for the purpose of causing me annoyance. Don't affect that look
of surprise, please. You know very well what I mean."

"Do I?" (O bitter masquerade! my forehead was
creased in one or two puzzled lines ; my lips were just
bent, and no more, in the least downward contemptuous curve.) "Please excuse the stupidity, but I really
don't know."

This was the way to meet him on his own ground,
marble for marble, ice for ice ; this way and this only.
It had been widely different when I had believed that
some love-warmth slept beneath his coldness ; now,
when I knew that he cared nothing for me, that he was
all coated in the dense mail of indifference, that I could
merely wound him through his arrogant self-love or
vanity—now the fight must be fought with merely a desire to deal such wounds and nothing more.

Evidently my unlooked-for coolness ruffled him,
threw him off his guard. "If you don't know," he
stated, with a touch of roughness, "then suppose you
learn. I mean that you are not justified in receiving
the attentions of a man whose acquaintance I do not
recognize—Melville Delano. In future I insist that you
shall give him reason to understand—even if you fail to
cut him outright—that his society is not desired."

I rose, at this, gathered from the chair my fallen opera-

cloak, and threw it over my arm as though I was a little
afraid of wrinkling it by the operation.   Then I spoke,
with much easy quietude of manner.   "You seem to
make rules, I must venture to observe, only for the
purpose of breaking them.   Not many hours ago I was
to mind my own business (though I believe you did me
the favor to add that this was a rather discourteous way
of putting it) and you were to mind yours."

He measured me quickly from head to foot ; he
gnawed his lip nervously once or twice ; he looked
down at his oval magnitude of flawless shirt bosom ; he
reinstated a spray of lilies-of-the-valley that was about
precipitating itself from his button-hole ; he was plainly
taken aback, amazed, shot at from a battery that, a moment or two ago, had seemed quite incapable of opening
fire.

"I said that, Helen, and meant it.   I mean it still.
But this is wholly an outside matter.   You may know
whom you please, provided you know respectable people ; but—"

I stopped him there.   Not with any hastily passionate sentence, not with irate eyes, not with any indignant demeanor.   I only laughed a trenchant caustic
mocking laugh.

"Respectable people, Fuller ?   Do I hear you *quite*
correctly ?   And is that condition to be mutually im-
posed ? "

He grew paler by a shade or two and looked angry
enough to strike me.   For a little while at least I was
mamma's daughter.   My head was high-held ; my pose
was august ; my stare met his with austerest dignity.

"Come," I at length went on, after placidly watching
his answerless discomfiture, "suppose I undertake to
canvass your conduct this evening, since you have seen

fit to adopt a like course as regards mine. I noticed that
you spent quite a while in Mrs. Gerald's box; that fast
little lady with the yellow hair whom neither mamma
nor I are willing to know. Not that we have quarreled
with her, understand; not that we have taken any un-
reasonable prejudice against her; not that she has ever
caught either of us in a breach of propriety; not that— "

"Stop, Helen! You are going too far." He
growled out the words with savage force, and came a
step closer to where I was standing.

But I held my ground with calm hardihood. 'After
all,' shot through my mind, 'it would not matter much
even if he should strike me.' So many of the idols in
my temple have been tumbled over: what matter if the
iconoclast shall assault another?

"You see my meaning, Fuller? I am glad of it."
I gave a gentle laugh. "Quick perception and a guilty
conscience go together very often." And now I glided
past him, moving composedly doorward. "Regarding
this question of my letting Melville Delano talk to me
as long as he likes and as long as I like, you must really
permit me to exercise my own choice. He is an old
friend and a sincere. Sincerity is such a supremely
rare virtue, remember, in this world where such gross
deceptions are practised every day."

By this time I had reached the hall; and whilst my
foot was touching the first step of the staircase, I turned
to see him standing on the opposite threshold of the
reception-room, angrily handsome, a slight flush replacing his past pallor, his blond head back-thrown.

"Explain your meaning," he demanded, "about
gross deceptions."

"I would rather not," with keen-pealing voice, with
unwavering eyes, I made answer. "It would merely

be what you yourself have already named useless parleying to no purpose."

I ascended three or four steps. He thrust both hands
pocketward, half turned his back upon me, as though
re-entering the room, then abruptly changed his mind
and faced me again.

"You are right. I believe as little as you do in the
wasting of words. I shall not waste them now. I insist upon your discountenancing all marked attentions
from Melville Delano."

I bit my lip a second, to subordinate the devil that
wanted to possess himself of my voice and hurl forth
fiery language therewith. Then I spoke, measuredly,
deliberately.

"Make yourself worthy of issuing such commands
and they may perhaps be obeyed." After that I went
upstairs.

And so it has become war to the teeth—war flinch-
less and uncompromising on both sides. I am glad of
it.

Glad! Ah, miserably misused word! I shall be
glad of nothing any more. How much better if I had
died of some swift sickness at Pineside, this autumn,
believing that he loved me! And yet, no; for in that
case my soul might have had eyes to look down into
his soul where I had left him, seeing all its black
shameful fraud. And then Heaven would have turned
horrible to me, since there would not be any waiting for
him, any hope that he would one day join me there
in divinest re-union. No; better if I had passed away
then into utter nothingness; stiffened, crumbled, rotted
and not known it. I should have had my day; should
have cheated fate of its power to torture me like this;
should slumber blankly, voidly, pulselessly, and dream

never a dream of how he had not shed a tear over my dumb inert body.

These are wild words. I am in a wild terrible mood. If there was only hope that I have judged him with too great haste—that he has not, after all, flung in my face this enormous insult, this cruel awful jeer! But there is no such hope.

# CHAPTER XVII.

OV. 15.—We have met each other again; we have spoken; we have even been polite to each other. Evidently he has decided (with laudable magnanimity) to overlook my bad behavior. Perhaps he thinks I am going to yield ultimately, after a little rebellious sputter, in this affair about Melville Delano. Perhaps mamma has been counselling him as to what is the most " advisable " policy. She may indeed have promised him her full co-operation whenever it shall be needed. I grow sick at heart, ragefully and frenziedly sick, when I think of this. . . .

*Nov.* 16.—" Any admittance ? " appealed a feminine voice at my door, this morning, a little while after lunch.

I rose and let in Cornelia.

" My dear," (giving me a sort of pouncing salute on each cheek) " why are you moping here so ridiculously this divine day ? "

" Is it divine ? " I wanted to know.

" The heavenliest kind of Indian summer. One feels as if one ought to go about in beads and feathers and things—like a squaw, you know—just to be in accord with the season. How do you like my new suit? Fresh from Worth's yesterday."

I admired, conventionally.

" And my bonnet ? " she progressed, planting herself where the light was strongest and revolving slowly, like the automatic wax-work that sometimes lures passers-by in hair-dressers' windows. " *Was* there ever such an odd shape ? I met Mrs. Georgie Buckland and she giggled in my face. What will Virot make us wear next ? " Then Mrs. Walters took a seat, showing the most gingerly solicitude about tumbling her vestments. " I heard of you at the opera last night."

" Yes ? From whom, Cornelia ? "

" Summerby told me you were there—that is I believe it was Summerby. He didn't say whether he talked to you or not." (Looking unconcernedly away from me, and looking also as though Summerby would have received the most gracious reverse of frigid treatment if he had really come.) " Anyhow, I heard that Melville Delano monopolized you most of the evening."

How the words jarred upon me ! How, a few days ago, I would have haughtily resented them ! What could I do now ? What but smile and murmur " Ah ? Yes ?" in bland acknowledgment ?

" An early beginning, Helen—a scandalously early beginning," denounced Cornelia, trying to make her red laughterful mouth mock-solemn. " However," (breaking into most audible mirth, right here) " one knows one's own affairs far better than anybody can counsel one. For my part, I'm rather pleasantly disappointed in you. I was ready, somehow, to see you commence all manners of strait-laced pruderies. And it would have been such sheer stupidity, if you don't mind my telling you so, with a man like Fuller."

Whatever may be my faults, Diary, I don't think that I deserve to be called a termagant ; and yet it is the truth that just now my right hand was itching to make a scarlet print of its breadth and length on that nice delicate cheek of Cornelia's. The desire, let it be recorded out of common compliment to my self-respect, would not have reached consummation even if no knock had sounded at the door and I was not obliged to call out the conventional "come in." Whereupon I was amazed by the appearance of Fuller.

He kissed Cornelia and then turned toward me. "It's such a fine day, Helen, that I thought you might care to take a drive. Do you?"

I felt myself turn tomato-color under his calm eyes. I don't know what I should have done if Cornelia had not been in the room. Perhaps I should have started up from my chair and burst forth "Oh, Fuller, do you really want me to go?" emotionally, passionately. As it was, I managed something like a decent acquiescence, too dashed to do more than just save myself from a pitfall of stammering confusion.

"Upon my word," pouted Cornelia, "your incivility, Fuller, is quite brazen. I suppose you mean to go out in that two-seated arrangement that Louis says you've lately bought. But I deserve some slight vestige of an invitation, nevertheless, considering that I'm present and not stone-deaf. I've a good mind to express perfect willingness in the matter of perching myself on the coachman's seat behind you and Helen. You ought to be obliged to cart me along with you in some such style, as a punishment for bad manners."

"Pray come," laughed Fuller. "If Helen has no objection I have none."

By this time I had made at least reputable patchwork of my tattered self-possession. "When shall we start, Fuller?" I asked.

" Shall we say at three o'clock ? " he suggested, taking out his watch. " It is nearly two now. John is waiting for the order."

" Very well," I agreed—" three o'clock."

Fuller left the room, presently, and I did not see him again untill just before we started on our drive. Wild thoughts had been at work in my brain whilst I was dressing, watched with languid interest by Cornelia. I turn back now, Diary, to some words which I wrote in you at the end of yesterday's record : *If there was only one hope that I had judged him with too great haste.* Could it be that I had really so judged him ? " O my God," I thought, " is this man's feeling for me not wholly the loveless void I believed it ? Does he regret what has passed ? does he wish to re-establish those sweet terms of happy harmony ? does he truly care, after all—? "

" What a perfect-fitting corset you have on, Helen," criticised Cornelia, ignorant of the dreadful irrelevancy. "It looks as if some Frenchwoman had muttered a spell and there it was."

Blanche, who was assisting at my toilette, gave this compliment more of a smiling reception, I am afraid, than her mistress did. " Perhaps," my thoughts went on, taking a gloomier turn, " Fuller has merely meant his invitation to ride as a counter-blow against my stony indifference. If so he has indeed meant it, I must use wary eyes in keeping clear of the snare thus set for me. If he wants to show me that he can forget to-morrow the wound dealt yesterday, that he cares to have the world see us on apparently amicable terms, that he shall maintain the outward form of marital civility and ignore any displeasure on my part as he would ignore the displeasure of a petulant child ; then—."

9

"Your collar-bones don't show a bit, Helen," decided Cornelia. "I wish mine didn't, but somehow
they have ever since Archibald was born.   I suppose I
shall have to wear the most ponderous neck-gear with all
my low dresses, this winter.   It is so trying!"

Ah, me! one's collar-bones haven't much reason to
show, as I mentally answered Cornelia, when one has
fed upon the nutritious diet of intense happiness.   No
doubt my own emaciating period (something a trifle
wofuller than the birth of an Archibald) is among the
very near probabilities.

At three o'clock I was ready; at three o'clock we
started.   There was no necessity for any remark on my
side until we had gotten quite a little distance up the
avenue; for each of the polished bays Fuller was driving seemed bent on doing its restive best to occupy
his full attention. · Presently they went along more
tractably; whereupon I eulogised the day with a little
moderate enthusiasm.   Fuller agreed that the day was
a delicious day.   Then silence again.

After that I cast a sheep's-eye toward John, making
myself momentarily conscious of more or less shirt-collar,
the rather roseate nape of a neck and a segment of hat-rim.
The collar, the neck and the hat-rim were a trifle further
away than I had thought them.   John might not be
sharp-eared; there was a steady clatter of passing
wheels; I was going to run the risk of having John hear
what I should next say.

"Your asking me to ride surprised me a good deal,
Fuller."

"Yes?" whilst he bowed to somebody in the Gor-
dons' window.   "Did you expect I was going to ask
Cornelia?"

"Not that.   Your earnest request might be taken,

you know, in two or three ways." I spoke with entire placidity. "It might have meant that I hadn't it in my power to offend you for any length of time, because what I thought or said was quite unimportant to you; or it might have meant the precise reverse of this, as regarded my opinions and words." Here my voice quivered a little under the stress of pure unmanageable feeling. "Recollect that mine isn't a hard grudge-bearing nature. If you care to win back whatever is—is lost, Fuller, you must see that the means of doing so are not difficult."

I waited for his answer, looking straight before me at a little glittering swinging ring over one of the bay's sheeny backs. Presently Fuller spoke.

"John."

"Yes, sir."

"Charlie goes better, I think, on the off side; and next time remember to give him a little looser breeching, by the way."

"Yes, sir."

Silence. I had gotten my answer. I knew now why he had taken me to drive. It was better that the discovery should have been rapidly made. I had hoped against hope; my folly had found swift cure.

After a little while I talked commonplaces. Fuller gave glib and prompt enough replies; he even volunteered subjects more than once. At length the Park was reached and the bays were made to quicken pace.

"The horse on my side," I presently commented, "seems to be on the look out for something to get frightened at."

Fuller laughed, rather acquiescingly. Just at this time there was a close carriage right in front of us—a bulkily respectable-looking affair that might have borne

some such occupant as a fleshy dowager with more than
one chin and a pedigree which had ramified itself straight
from the central root of Knickerbockerism. We were on
the verge of passing this carriage when I was suddenly
conscious of a violent sidelong lurch. Something (I
have no idea what) had supplied the horse of which I
had just spoken with his desired excuse for rank rebellion.

But the sidelong lurch did not end matters. A grat-
ing crushing sound instantly followed, and there was
one of our wheels locked in ruinous junction with a
wheel of the contiguous carriage. One of our horses
reared horribly ; the other made a short furious bolt
forward. I suppose Fuller's fine driving saved at least
a single life—Fuller's fine driving and John's quick
presence of mind added to this. For whilst I was on
the point of perpetrating a most plaintive sort of shriek,
our condition looked suddenly much less perilous, because of John having sprung out and darted to the
horses' heads.

Somebody did shriek, however, and with decided
shrillness. The voice came from the carriage at our
side. A woman's face, white with alarm, was thrust
forth from its open window. I recognized the face as
one familiar to me, but that was all, just then. Not
until I had contrived to scramble down to firm earth
with what mingled speed and dexterity terror gave me,
did any realization of whose the face had been enter into
my consciousness.

It was her face ; that woman's—Fuller's—no, I won't
write the word. " Oh, help ! help ! " she was shouting.
" Let me get out ! I shall be killed ! Help ! help ! "

She had reason for terror ; the horses of her carriage
were plunging frantically. I had stationed myself at

one side of the road, out of the way of all passing ve-
hicles. In a moment more the wheels were unlocked
and both pairs of horses were considerably quieted ;
but still that voice kept on calling for help. What
people name common humanity, I suppose, prompted
me to advance, now, toward the door of her carriage
and open it.

"There is no danger," I stated, looking anywhere
except at her face. "You are perfectly safe." Then
I drew back, leaving the carriage-door still open.

Out she rushed, immediately afterward. Just then I
glanced toward Fuller. He had quitted his seat and
was coming in our direction, leaving John at the horses'
heads.

It is my belief that she had not recognized me when
I spoke to her through the carriage-door. She was
then in a wildly frightened state ; my veil was down ;
my voice she had never heard. I believe also that the
first real sense of her real situation dated from her recognition of Fuller.

He was only a few yards distant when she sprang
toward him with thrust-out arms, her alarmed eyes blazing from her dead-white exquisite face.

"Oh, is it truly you ? Where have you come from ?
How did you get here ? I expected every instant to
be killed ; " hurrying forth her sentences in maddest
pell-mell, with a hand on each of his shoulders.

He bent his head so that his lips nearly met her forehead. What he answered was very low ; but I heard it.

"Edith, for God's sake don't make such an infernal
noise. Don't you see how I am placed ? "

With that the blood leapt up scaldingly to my cheeks.
I stood like a statue, scrutinizing the pair. Fuller went
**on** speaking. He whispered, now ; I could not catch

a word more.   Presently he left off addressing her and
took a step in my direction, laying a hand on each of
her hands as if to displace them from their hold.   But
she clung harder, as a scared child might cling, at the
same time giving her nobly-poised head a quick turn
and sending me across her shoulder one fixed angry
shameless, contumelious stare.

I felt every fibre of my body quiver, then.   I can't
remember much else until I had gotten to John's side.
" John," I was questioning, " is our wagon badly hurt ? "

" It ain't hurt at all, ma'am.   You see, ma'am, the
wheel was so heavy and strong.   But the other carriage—"

" Never mind the other carriage."   Before my next
sentence was framed I had begun to ascend into our
own.   " I want you to get immediately in here with
me, John, and drive me home."

" Mr. Dobell, ma'am— ? "

" Leave Mr. Dobell where he is."   I was seated, now.
" You hear me.   Do at once as I tell you."

John obeyed.   Two carriages had stopped near us,
the occupants of each keenly observant of the accident.
One was a dog-cart ; Ludlow Inmann was driving it,
Belle Dillinger sat by his side.   I saw them both bow
whilst John was turning the horses homeward.   ' This
will be town-talk to-morrow,' sped through my mind,
as I bent my head in answer.

" Make them go fast," I commanded, sharply, the
instant the turn was effected.   Poor John ! he looked
frightened out of every wit, and was on the point of executing the order, when

" Where are you going ? " called out a voice directly
in our rear.

Fuller's voice.   The next instant he was at my side.

I caught the whip from its place before I spoke. Then I levelled most savage eyes upon him, leaned down as far as the high seat would let me and flung at him these words, fiercely whispering them in a voice clogged with passion :

"I am going home without you. I am going to leave you with your mistress."

And almost whilst that last hateful word was leaving my lips I laid one cutting blow across the back of the horse nearest me. The effect was like flame touching powder. We had left the place of the accident a good distance behind us when John had the startled team well in hand again. For my own part, I relished the rushing speed that had followed my blow. I should not have cared if those horses had dashed me to destruction. We were being trotted peaceably out of the Park when I turned to John :

"Drive home by the Sixth Avenue way."

"Yes, ma'am."

It was dusk when we finally turned into Fifth Avenue again. I question whether anybody for whose observation I cared saw me then. I had just entered the house when mamma met me in the hall. "Aren't you home rather earlier than you expected to be?" she wanted to know. "By the bye, where is Fuller?"

I was pulling off my gloves as though they were poisoning my hands. "Mamma, I must speak with you about something. Will you come upstairs into my room, please?"

I hurried up, after that, never pausing to see if she would follow me. Once inside the room, I flung myself into a chair, discovered that it was a rocking-chair and rocked it exaggeratedly, waiting for her. Presently I heard her dress rustle in the outer hall.

Her face had a peering puzzled look, as she came and stood beside me in the softened light.

I broke silence at once, rattling off precisely what had happened, and never stopping an instant until I had finished the story. "Perhaps my behavior was stupid, all things considered," I made end. "A woman of the world would have behaved differently, I suppose. But I am not a woman of the world; I'm an insulted, outraged wife. Please remember this, before you tell me what you think of the occurrence."

I was scanning her face in search for some sign of sympathy, or sympathy's opposite. One might as well have studied a sheet of white paper with similar motives. All that I met there was grand inexplicable gravity.

"It is a very unfortunate occurrence, Helen."

"Rather," I assented, with a kind of dogged satire. Then I made every word firm and hard and clear. "He and I cannot live together any longer, mamma. I won't be pointed at by the world as a fool and a dupe. Let me go away from this house, or make him go. I demand it in the name of decency."

These sentences seemed to pierce her mail of composure shaftwise.

"Nonsense, Helen." Her words came fluent enough, now. "Excitement makes you view this affair in wrong colors. You tell me that she was the same woman whom you saw in his company on the hotel-piazza, this autumn. Remember how he met her then. You agreed long ago not to consider that meeting unpardonably culpable. But in the present encounter what was there except the sheerest force of circumstances?"

I laughed with loud bitterness. "Doubtless I should be just the same fool I was at Pineside, mamma, but for what has passed since that time. If Fuller Dobell really told you what you then told me, his statements were lies."

" Helen !"

"Helen me as augustly as you choose. I'm not rhapsodizing; I deal with sober facts. Among the letters which you snatched from me here in this room, the other day, there was one which escaped you—which fell upon the floor. I picked it up afterward. It was from this same woman."

" You read it, then?"

" No. But the address was in the same handwriting as was the address of a certain other letter which I handed to him on the croquêt-ground at Pineside. Besides, his embarrassment on receiving that second letter only strengthened my certainty. This is not all, however. You recollect his absence from our box the other night at Niblo's ? *She* was in a box opposite ; he went there. John Driscoll's excellent lorgnette helped me to discover him, though he was well withdrawn into the background." After this I rose up, with eyes riveted on mamma's face and with cheeks that were burning like two fire-coals. " I tell you, mamma, that it must all end. I am human and I won't bear it. See him when he returns home to-night. Tell him what I tell you. Say that I desire to live apart from him—that he has not married a dolt and an idiot, but a woman with a womanly spirit, capable of resenting insult and intolerant of having herself soiled by his vulgar disrespect. I mean what I am saying. As sure as my name is Helen Dobell I will leave the house in a week's time if before then he has not left it."

The room had grown so dark, now, that I could scarcely see her face. This is what she answered, however :

9*

"You talk like a fool. I shall carry no such message. If, as you say, he is acting stupidly, he can be
brought to his senses. Do you fancy that I shall
permit any such disgusting social scandal as your separation? Remember, please, that I have a position to
support" (O the enormous majesty of that pronoun
as she uttered it!) "and I do not intend that either you
or Fuller Dobell shall cheapen me before the world's
eyes. This affair can be settled in a very different way;
to-morrow, to-night, an hour or so later, you will think
as I think."

"It shall NOT be settled in any way but as I propose to
settle it," my voice cried forth, quivering, shrill, defiant.
"If *you* won't speak to him, *I* will. And if he refuses
to go then, I shall go myself. You can't keep me
here, either of you! I would a million times rather
earn my own living than—"

"Hush, Helen. The servants must have heard you,
as it is. I command you not to raise your voice so
loudly again."

One of her hands was on my shoulder, the other
gripped my wrist. She pushed me with quick force
back into my chair, standing over me, after doing this,
with her face so close to mine that I felt her breath
come and go against my cheek. "Whatever you mean
to do, pray have the goodness not to scream out your
intentions in any such absurd key. Shall I help you off
with your bonnet?" (releasing me and drawing away
from me, whilst speaking with softer tones.) "Where
are the matches? I will light your gas."

"No; do not light the gas. I prefer the room as it
is. And I should like to be left alone, please."

"Very well." She moved doorward. "It will be
dinner-time, shortly."

"I am not going down to dinner. I don't wish any."

"I will have something sent up to you." There was no touch of sympathy in her manner, though its concession verged upon humility. It seemed so odd to hear her changed voice, now ; to see her royally willing to step down from the throne and play amiable. Tame vassal of her wishes as she has found me all these years, she has heard in that passionate threat of mine the voice of a spirit which her majestic vetoes cannot awe into silence ; she knows this and trembles for results.

"If you have my dinner sent to me I shan't eat it," brusquely enough I returned. She made no reply ; she merely quitted the room, closing the door behind her.

Of course she had not been gone more than ten minutes before I had become much calmer of mood ; and of course, too, she had known this would happen and had therefore left me alone. People in tempers occasionally yell out wild resolutions which they regret afterwards but to which obstinacy bids them cleave. I had yelled out one resolution with all the eloquence of hysteria. I might attempt something more in the same line ; anyhow, the less of such rabid rhetoric the better. And so (with what I don't doubt were very nearly thoughts of this description) she had made her politic departure.

Hours have passed since then. Fuller is not home yet. Can it be possible that he will dare to resent my conduct of this afternoon ?—dare to leap up on any pedestal of insulted dignity regarding what has occurred ? Well, he shall find me no coward when the attack comes. Hotly as I flung down the gauntlet before mamma, no cooler mood will make me stoop to pick it up again. There let it lie.

To all that I said I adhere, only leavening the hardness of my determination in one slight way. This :

If he promises that always hereafter he will be to that
woman as one stranger is to another, never holding
communication with her by word or by letter, then, half
because our living apart from each other will injure
mamma before the world she worships, and half because I myself shrink from the scandal and publicity of
such a separation, I will consent to remain in this house
and show society at large how harmoniously he and I
can manage to meet among the babblers and gossips,
during ball and opera and dinner-party. If he refuses
to countenance this condition, I go.

My eyes are thoroughly open, now, to the folly of my
recent behavior. The whole proceeding was stupid in
the extreme ; it was even, in a certain sense, grossly
unjust to Fuller. But I do not admit, for this reason,
his right to assume the defensive. That meeting in the
Park, with its attendant circumstances, was the natural
result of the scandalous wrong and outrage to which he
has been subjecting me since the earliest days of our engagement. There would have been provocation for ten
times my reckless fury.

I dread to-morrow intensely, and yet I long for it
with a sort of savage anticipation. I am carrying you
through turbulent times, Diary, am I not ? Ah, if
there were only a dim glimmer of hope that in the end
a little comfort might reach me ; that, although I could
have no sweet sunburst after this opaque darkness, there
would be at least a faint flickering light, less vivid than
some clouded moonrise ! But no ; where is the vaguest
possibility of such change ?

Why cannot my love turn into the contemptuous hate
he deserves ? Some women, placed as I am placed,

would loathe him by this.   My cheeks burn with shame
when I think of how I must love him always.   Such a
little while ago I would have laughed to hear any one
say that my love did not find its deepest root in respect
for his moral worth !   What a fool I should have been !
Here his character is laid bare to me in all its ugly
naked selfishness; I know him what he is, cruel, un-
principled, no man of men, but almost fit to rank
among those churlish charlatans who soil "the grand
old name of gentleman."   And yet if to-morrow I heard
that any terrible danger threatened him I should have
wild fears for his safety, should long to reach him helping hands, should be willing to give my very life for his.
What fustian the wiseacres talk who say that real love
can only spring from devout faith in the worthiness of
its object !   I see now that in many a case, though the
idol be changed from gold to clay, the worshiper must
yet kneel; that love will sometimes bear the most
brutal blows without falling ; for love—

Goodness ! one might prose like this for pages, and
then get no further than the simple truism that love is
—love.

# CHAPTER XVIII.

OV. 17.—Fuller must have gotten home very late last night; or rather very early this morning. He did not appear whilst mamma and I silently breakfasted together. I was on my way upstairs a little while afterward when I met him descending, face to face. He just glanced at me, and so quickly that I had not time to judge of his expression; then, with averted head, he passed downward.

I had no sooner entered my room than I rang the bell for Blanche. The breakfast-room had been no place to hold a discussion with mamma, and I had not chosen to break silence before Henry with anything so domestically ominous as a request that she would allow me some private words upstairs. A message to this effect, however, I sent down by Blanche immediately she appeared.

Whilst waiting for the answer I walked the floor sentinelwise. I was calm, but with no self-forced composure, no exciting effort not to be excited. At best, at worst, I had little to gain or lose. My chief triumph was to be in making Fuller understand that he could not trample upon me without feeling some slight resistance. For the rest, whether I lived with him or left him, what did it matter, after all? There would still be the same deep gulf between us, not narrowing with years—broadening, perhaps.

Blanche did not come back at all. Mamma came in her place. I neither hemmed nor hawed. There was the ugly unmanageable bull right before me ; I had only to seize it by the horns and show my grappling-strength.

"Mamma," I made beginning, not seating myself, though she sat, " you remember, possibly, everything which I said yesterday. Everything then said I adhere to. I am willing to place one condition, however, on my separation from Fuller. Let him promise faithfully never to hold the slightest communication with that woman, and before the eyes of the world, at least, I shall remain as much his wife as I have been since our marriage. I strongly prefer that you should make him this proposition. If you consent to do so, please strip the matter of all sentiment. Offer it to him as a mere business arrangement, and say that I desire as early an answer as may conveniently be given."

She heard me through with a graciously condescending heed. Once or twice whilst I was speaking I saw her vivid eyes look their keenest into my face ; but for quite a while after I had finished she sat with eyes floorward and with hands resting serenely on her lap. Presently she raised her head and became audible in steady tranquil tones.

"I shall not make any proposition to Fuller which would take it so impertinently for granted that he is as culpable as you declare him. But I will acquaint him with your resolve, speak of you as one whose suspicions may or may not approach correctness, and tread upon the subject with the gingerly feet that common courtesy makes requisite. And I will admit that your reckless hot-headedness bullies me into acting as mediator.

Any child may seize some article no less frangible than costly, stand at a safe distance from its elders, and threaten complete destruction unless it is given what it demands. You hold in your hand our family respectability. I don't choose to remain perfectly inattentive whilst that is being dashed into fragments."

"How you can doubt that Fuller is guilty of what I accuse him, seems wholly dark to me," I returned. "But since you have such doubts it will be best for me to take upon myself the duty of seeing and talking with Fuller. Perhaps I have been weak and cowardly in wanting to shirk such a task. He will have finished breakfast in a few moments, I suppose?"

I was moving doorward when she sprang up with an activity which her slow majesty of carriage permits, I should judge, about once every five years.

She caught my arm firmly. "Helen, stay a moment. You must not see Fuller Dobell this morning. I shall see him for you."

"Very well," left my close-shut lips; "as you please. Only, will you consent to bear him the exact message I have already given you? If not, I am my own war-ambassador."

We were staring at each other, now. I had a queer thought about those bold men who brave lions and tigers in their cages before thrilled multitudes, always fixing upon them an unvaried eye-power. "Show me one gleam of timidity," her eyes seemed to inform mine, "and I will have you back in the old abject place which you have held under my rule through all the past years of your life."

Were her next words meant to try my courage? "Helen, you will please remember that all patience has its limits," between drawn lips she gave warning.

Either of her thin nostrils quivered a little, and her face came much nearer to my own. I suppose it was sheer force of habit that pushed me several steps away from her, then. In other days I had dropt my eyes so often before those dark intense ones of hers, that now I dropt them again. Only momentarily, however ; and yet she took these slight changes for signs of intimidation, nerv-ousness, fear. I was her chattel again—the thing she could move about at her own proud pleasure ; the poor obsequious creature that not long ago, if she had said " Helen, I forbid you to think," would have esteemed the command more or less sacred and made cerebral efforts to obey it.

One of her hands caught each of my shoulders. She shook me with violence. " You are a little fool," she began, in a voice that seemingly came from deep down her throat ; " a little headstrong fool and idiot. I have never let you dictate to me yet and I shan't now. I tolerated your hare-brained nonsense for a time, just to see how far you would carry it ; from this morning it shall end."

I sprang backward, then, with a face that I know was lividly white, with a laugh that rang bold bitter defi-ance.

" End it if you can ! Your cowed cringing child is a woman, who dares assert herself and doesn't care a fig for your superb tyrannies any longer. I am going down-stairs now to tell Fuller what I told you. This, I trust, will be proof enough that I am the sort of headstrong fool who means to carry out her obstinate designs."

As I turned to leave the room she darted in front of me, closed the door noisily and planted herself before it. The fine majesty of her attitude made a grand pict-ure. Just a little change of costume—say a ruff about

her throat, a coronet or a few pearls on her white hair—
and she might have been some dead-and-gone celeb-
rity being historically ill-mannered to some pitiable victim.

But I didn't behave much like a pitiable victim, by
the bye. I turned away with a sneer.

" There is another door, you know, leading from the
dressing-room, if I chose to take it. But I don't choose.
Your remaining there a few hours will not prevent my
ultimately seeing Fuller." After that I supplied myself
with a book and sat down near the window.

Complete silence whilst I pretended to read; a silence
that possibly lasted three good minutes. She had tried,
I was telling myself, to reinstate between us the old
slave-and-master terms. She had failed. What would
be her next course? Concession? I could hardly believe that; it was sheer flying in the face of the probable.

At length curiosity drew my look doorward. As it
did so she spoke, still standing in the place where I had
last seen her.

" Helen."

" Well, mamma."

" I suppose you will not hear reason. One must
meet you on your own ridiculous ground."

She came slowly towards me whilst these words were
being pronounced. It was a full unconditional surrender. I had no sensation of triumph, however; indeed,
I felt a slight blush warm my face as she approached
me. She has been so high-handed a tyrant for so long
a time, in her dealings with me, that I had a kind of odd
sympathy with her humiliation; sharing it, even, in a
vague reflected way.

Her next sentences showed that they were not uttered without a touch of difficult effort. " I will bear

Fuller the message which you desire me to bear. Are you satisfied ? "

" Perfectly," I responded, rising. " You promise me that you will forget no word, mamma ? "

She bit her lip, gathered her brows, looked for a second as though on the brink of some stern answer, and finally bowed, coldly acquiescent. " I promise. Have you any further cross-questioning as a sign of your distrust ? "

" None," I returned, carelessly curt. " But please add that I should like to get his reply as early as possible. This afternoon, if convenient."

That was all that passed between us. Very soon afterward mamma swept serenely from my room, not looking in the least as though she left me victor of the field.

I wanted immensely to steal downstairs and listen, if possible, to her interview with Fuller. But wanting was all I could do : decency kept handing me back my intention like a bad coin, every time I tried to put it in use.

My next meeting with mamma was at lunch : Fuller had gone out. Whilst Henry served us we talked elegant nothings, mostly about the marked change in the weather, if my memory be trustworthy just here. When Henry had departed on some momentary mission, however,

" I have spoken to Fuller," mamma plunged.

I left off being surgical to my cold bird. " And he has given what sort of an answer ? "

" He is very sore about your conduct of yesterday," she stated, with hardening face. " He believes himself merely to have been the victim of circumstances. He blames you for vicious and vulgar behavior."

I leaned back in my chair with a chilly smile. "He is a little unjust. If my behavior *was* vicious I am quite sure that its vulgarity didn't very far surpass that of the person whom I heard him address as Edith, telling her not to make such an infernal noise for God's sake, and asking her if she did not see how he was placed ; since this person screamed and carried on to a really painful extent." I laughed my satiric best, right here. "Possibly there was so much ambiguity about the form of address adopted by Fuller that I drew most unjustifiable conclusions ; nor had I the least reason to draw them, you will perhaps insist, when past experiences tended to exculpate him so honorably."

Mamma went on precisely as though she had been seized with a transitory deafness during the delivery of my sarcasms. "I had hard work, I can assuré you, in even making Fuller listen, at first ; he was so bitter about the whole occurrence. But after a while he got to look at the matter in a proper light—to see what sad results your dare-devil temerity might occasion. Let me cut it all short. He accepts the arrangement which you propose for him. When you and he next meet you are to meet civilly—pray understand that."

"Yes. And now let me understand one thing more, please. Does he deny the charge implied, if not made, in the message I sent him ?"

Enter Henry. Consequent silence on mamma's part.

I saw Fuller at dinner. There was between us no directly personal exchange of remarks ; we talked mammaward again ; that was all.

I am victorious, but ah, how sad, how worthless a victory it is ! How much more I should value a little grain of love added to an infinitude of humiliation ! What a meagre satisfaction is it when only your sense

of justice has been appeased, and your empty heart
yearns as wildly as mine yearns for the one sweet unattainable comfort!

He will keep his word, I suppose. Fear, if nothing
else, will make him keep it. I have frightened him,
just as I have frightened mamma.

If people had called to-night I would have gone down
and seen them, merely to escape my gnawing thoughts.
But it is a wildly stormy November night, full of chill
rain and sad windy sounds, and no one has come.
Somehow whilst sitting alone I have let my memory go
back among past years, and have recollected one girl, a
school-friend, Mary Gray, whom I used to love dearly
and have long cosey talks with about both our futures.
She was poor and a nobody, was Mary. She may be
dead now. Mamma made me stop visiting her, and we
have not met since I was fourteen. But I can see her
rather homely bright-eyed face as though I had looked
upon it yesterday. I hope she is not dead, but married
and happy; married and making some man happy too,
whether her lord be carpenter, grocer or drudging clerk.
For she was all heart and sympathy and warm impulses
—worth a hundred Margie Cartwrights and Kate Effinghams, with their trunkfuls of Parisian wardrobe and their
hollow souls. O, Mary, if I had you here to-night, to
wind my arms about, and lean my head upon, and tell
all my bitter troubles! I think you could make me cry.
As it is I can't cry a tear.

Yes, I have conquered, but after all what was there
to fight for? A battle-field that was choked with my
dead already—my dearest dreams and hopes, all slaugh-
tered in one sad calamitous massacre!

## CHAPTER XIX.

NOV. 27.—I haven't had the heart to touch you, Diary, for—let me count: ten whole days. Ten days of opera-going and dinner-going and dinner-giving, and here and there a party; for parties have begun already and mamma makes her magnificent toilettes in which to startle dowagerdom, and I let myself drift along with the social current.

Melville Delano entered our box at the opera on the Monday evening which followed Fuller's acceptance of my little domestic plan. My husband was not there at the time of Melville's entrance. He came in with an air of placid confidence, taking the little stool at my side which somebody had just vacated.

I leaned forward so that my face was quite close to his. Then I fixed serious eyes upon him, and murmured in the bosom of my upheld bouquet:

"You mustn't do this any more, please."

His sombrely black eyes caught a sudden glitter under a sudden frown. "Do what any more?"

"Come here."

He looked as though on the verge of springing up from his chair. I put forth a hand, resting it lightly, momentarily, upon his arm. That seemed to say "peace" to the troubled waters, somehow.

"Don't go now, Mr. Delano—not just yet, I mean. You *must* understand;" (giving my shoulders a little impatient shrug.)

"Understand what?" he wanted to know, in a sort of gruff mutter, strengthening my belief that the majority of men are able to whisper about as well as a lion is able to mew: and low voices were requisite, by the bye, as it was during a musicless entr'acte, and just at my elbow in the next box sat a bony girl in yellow, with large ears and no male society.

"Why, simply that I don't send you away from any dislike. I am compelled to do so."

"What compels you?"

"People—the world—propriety."

His face was like a thunder-cloud, with eyes that were lightnings. Luckily his seat was low enough for this change to escape public notice, and his back was turned from mamma and the box's other occupants. "Did people or the world or propriety," he growled, "dictate such a course to you the last time we met here? I was quite in favor then; I was sent for and made much of through an entire evening. What does this change mean? Some reconciliation with your dear husband? some—"

"Don't be insolent, Mr. Delano. You know me well enough to know that I will not stand it."

"I know nothing about you, except that you are a very weather-vane for whimsical changeability. You blow hot and cold; you play fast and loose; and you expect that I am tamely to stand your countless shades of treatment."

"I forgive you because you are absurdly excited," I whispered, still addressing my bouquet, "and evidently don't understand the full force of your statements."

"Pardon me. I understand it thoroughly. I was the slave of your caprices before you married, and I still am to remain so, it seems, now that you have changed Jeffreys into Dobell, I was a fool to let you use me as you did use me the other night. Do you fancy that I did not *know* you were using me then?" His passionate eyes, try as I would to avoid them, drew the color into my cheeks, just here. "But I came to-night because a smile from you has its value to a poor fool like myself, even at the price of self-respect. The old story, you know, of the moth and the candle. I had little reason to fancy that I would not continue your cat's-paw for one evening longer, especially since recent events made such a condition of affairs seem highly probable."

My cheeks were crimson, now. I forgot his bold impertinence in the sudden curiosity he had pricked to life. "Do you mean to tell me," I faltered, "that everybody has heard about—about—?"

"That dramatic collision in the Park on Saturday?" he sneered. "My dear Mrs. Dobell, it is town gossip."

This sneer brought me to my senses at last. I made myself all haughtiness and icy disdain. "Mr. Delano, we must end this discussion at once. There is only one way to deal with ungentlemanly rudeness."

A single water-spurt merely aggravates some fires. "Yes, yes," he hastened, "I am ungentlemanly now, but it was a trifle otherwise when I saved you from insult last autumn, on that hotel-piazza. You were so stupid in learning the lesson I tried to teach that you deserve all sorts of punishment hereafter. When you told me, whilst we were saying good-by to each other in the hall at Pineside, that you meant to marry Fuller Dobell, it was on the verge of my tongue to warn you, in the

most disinterested compassionate spirit. I should have
done so, but for your mother's appearance—should have
verified the words which I had just spoken. Do you
recollect them? They were : " treat me like a friend
and you shall find me worthy of all trust." Not that
you *had* treated me so, by the bye, but I would have
served 'you, nevertheless, in the fearless statement of a
few plain facts. More than once during your engagement I thought of still proving myself your benefactor
before it was too late. But you were so hedged in, by
then, with bigoted beliefs, that no doubt my efforts
would have been mere futility. Perhaps I did best to
hold my tongue."

" As you will oblige me by doing now," I murmured,
freezingly.

He sat quite silent for some little time, after this,
staring at his opera-hat. Suddenly he lifted his face to
mine again. I saw at once that he had grown calmer.

" You think me ungenerous as well as ungentlemanly," he recommenced, in tones far less emphatic,
" to have spoken like this. Perhaps you are right; I
saw the misery on your face to-night, knowing the face
so well, though doubtless it is hidden from others.
Perhaps you are wrong ; there are such things as playing with edged tools ; you should have left matters as
they existed between us when you returned from your
wedding-tour ; you were not justified in trying to make
a worse fool of me than I am already. However,"
(and his voice deepened with such tenderness, at this
point, that I shuddered lest the bony girl in yellow
should hear him) " I am your friend always, in spite of
yourself; and who knows but you shall have occasion,
one day, for using me to some real advantage ? Good-
night."

10

He rose abruptly, offered me no hand, bowed with rather strained courtesy to mamma, and left the box. A few moments later Fuller re-entered. Had he seen Melville? His manner evidenced no displeasure, if he had.

# CHAPTER XX.

ALL this happened on Monday evening. I somehow went home with kindly feelings toward
Melville. "*Plus on aime quelqu'un, moins il
faut qu'on le flatte*" ran through my brain when I
thought of him. He had roughly rebuked me, yet had
I not deserved all I had gotten? And his very bitterness of accusation and reproach, had this not sprung
from a devout loyal love? The man is as much in
love with me now as he was at Pineside. I think that
until that first night at the opera, his love had grown
like a torpid serpent under such a winter of indifference
as he had received, poor fellow, and when the burst of
sunshine came, the serpent found itself suddenly tingling into activity again. It was sheer folly and gross
cruelty for me to make him the servant of my own
selfish ends. Melville has a large noble heart, and—

Stuff and verbiage! I made much the same moral
inventory of some one else, once. I think I shall never
write or speak praisefully of any character again. I am
going to turn a Vivien of backbiters and leave "not even
Launcelot brave nor Galahad clean." How do I know
that Melville Delano is not a deception, an apple of
Sodom, a whited sepulchre? Surely not because truth
and honesty seem to have made his eyes their especial
stronghold; not because he seems to speak what he

means ; not because I have never caught him in fraud or falsehood. These are no proofs. There is a kind of Gorham plate virtue, I find, that stands immense wear but at length shows, of necessity, its base alloy. For all I know, his may be of this durable but imitative kind.

Two days went on almost eventlessly. By that time the relations between Fuller and myself had grown what they are at present, and what they shall probably remain (I have no reason to think otherwise) till one of us is out of the world and death has set his dark signature to the divorce which only lacks our own. We both occupy, when alone together, a kind of middle camping-ground between coolness and civility : when with people (mamma excepted) we are gently cordial, each to each. I tell him nothing that occurs from day to day ; with me he is similarly reticent. Unconfidential half-ceremonious courtesy—that just about defines it. A marriage that is a tragic sardonic jest ! I envied passionately an organ-grinder's wife whom I saw yesterday, her lord's conjugal accompanist on the tambourine. Perhaps he wasn't her legal lord, by the bye. Well, they made their discords companionably, and in any case her right to call him husband was a diviner one, doubtless, than all my pompous wedding-pageant ever gave to me !

On Wednesday night I dined with Fuller at the Chamberlanes'. It was a colossus of dinners, given for two English lords to whose sacred names I don't dare offer the insult of incorrect spelling. One of their mightinesses took me into dinner and bored me very keenly through a sort of repast that nobody could have eaten, course for course, without bursting, or drank, wine for wine, without besotting himself. My blue-blooded neighbor stared mutely at the épergne in a

manner which I at first took for haughtiness but afterwards discovered to be stupidity.  I can't help confessing, too, that the hands and feet possessed by this engaging peer seriously shook one of my theories regarding the physical results of aristocratic parentage.  But
for all that is known to the contrary by our vulgar
transatlantic minds, my potentate may have been exchanged in his cradle, to the detriment of the rightful
heir ; a species of misfortune only too common among
select English circles, if their native novelists are credi-
ble authority : and alas ! these are the one means we
can command of gaining an occasional precious glimpse
into the abodes of Birth.  For when we go to England
ourselves their lordships would almost sit at meat with
their head butlers, I believe, rather than invite us
among their holy gatherings.  It is of course an immense pity that they shouldn't have us ; but it is truly
an enormous pity that we should take the refusal so to
heart, and when they visit our own shores conduct ourselves before them so much as though we were bent
upon working out our salvation in social British eyes,
and upon reaching, some fortunate day, after long wandering through the desert of their disfavor, the happy
Canaan of their esteem.

Cornelia Walters was among the guests.  Whilst the
men were wine-bibbing after dinner, I managed to get
Cornelia into a corner of the drawing-room.

" Well," she opened conversation merrily, " what do
you think of his lordship ? "

I shut both eyes very tight indeed, and yawned
cavernously.  " What gross irreverence," she commented, with a bubbling laugh.  " Had you any idea
that he owns nearly a whole county and has three or
four other titles besides being an earl ?  Louis knows

him quite well; met him in Switzerland. It was Louis who wrote him down at the club, the other day."

"Louis is in luck. I suppose Lord What-you-may-call has given a little practical aid in the cultivation of his broad acres ; his hands and feet are the only evidence of such toil that I had to judge from, but they formed evidence of a rather solid sort."

"If the Chamberlanes could hear you they'd gnash the family-teeth in furious concert at having let you go in with one of their dear aristocrats. You're a perfect · communist, I declare ! If I get you a little red cap will you promise to wear it, Madame Robespierre ? "

"Don't make me more notorious than I am, Cornelia," I murmured, meaningly. Cornelia looked at the carpet, with sobered face. "No doubt I am enough in people's mouths as it is."

Cornelia did something that was half coo and half titter, whilst smelling with immense olfactory diligence her share of the bouquets which we ladies had all gotten at dinner.

"Especially as I had Belle Dillinger and Mr. Inmann for an audience," I persisted, confident that if I bored Mrs. Walters deeply enough I should penetrate this amazing crust of prudence and reach language at last. "But I suppose the original story has been twisted into a perfect corkscrew of distortion, by this time. Doubtless if I should hear your edition I shouldn't recognize myself as its heroine."

Cornelia found a tongue then, and ceased to associate exclusively with Boston rosebuds. She smiled again, but it was a smile tart and unmirthful, making me remember that she was Fuller's sister. "My dear Helen, it would have been much better after all, as I think you'll admit, if I had availed myself of Fuller's permission to displace the coachman on that rear seat. I could have kept you in order so nicely, you know, when the necessary time came. What a pity one can't have glimpses of the future, every once in a while ! "

" Don't think me rude, Cornelia," I made prompt reply, " if I express myself keenly grateful that you did *not* go. I make no allusion, of course, to the creditable appearance you and I would have presented, trundling up Fifth Avenue panier to panier, back to back, chignon to chignon. I speak solely with appreciative recollections of John's good services in jumping out and seizing the horses' heads at just the important moment."

Cornelia gave a mass of marble nudity at her elbow much critical inspection. " It wouldn't have been the worst thing that might have happened, Helen, if somebody had seized *your* head a little while afterward. However, I don't wish to make malicious comments."

" An excellent resolution," I hastened. " Keep your sarcastic powers well in reserve, Cornelia. Scandal attacks the most innocent, you know, and even you may be called upon, at some future time, for a little self-defence. But suppose I take your witticism to have been seriously meant. Are you a representative of popular opinion ? Does the world consider that I acted stupidly, the other day ? Does it uphold Fuller and condemn me ? Don't spare me with your answers, please. They can't wound me. I'm quite panoplied with my own convictions."

Cornelia laughed rather unamiably. " If you're not afraid of the truth, nobody whom I have heard neglect to mind their own business about the matter has done anything except condemn you."

" And is it generally known who the woman was ? " I questioned, calmly.

" Oh, yes. An improper character. You are supposed, of course, to have had some knowledge that she
belonged among the indiscretions of Fuller's bachelorhood; but it hasn't been considered precisely good
style for you to have availed yourself of such enlightenment."

"Bachelorhood!" I jerked the word out between
sneering lips. "In other words, they assert that I merely
made a kind of hysterical fool of myself, having just the
ghost of a reason."

"That is about right, I fancy. Didn't you say that
my answers were not to spare you? Let me persevere
in taking you at your word. You are considered to
have given Fuller excellent excuse for being permanently furious, and the opposite course which he seems
to have taken astonishes everybody." Cornelia repeated her unamiable smile. "I wonder what they
would have thought of you abroad, in any of the European places. New York, you know, is a perfect Happy
Valley of propriety, when compared with foreign cities.
Here a man cannot go one hair's-breadth out of the
beaten track without hearing shouts of social indignation; whilst in London or Paris he may leave an actress
to join a princess, if he so desires. There Society is a
sort of pleasant restaurant, where one strolls in, calls for
what one pleases, and behaves completely as one wants,
the only stringent rule being that one must dress, talk,
and act generally like a person of culture. Here society
is a sort of ultra-strict church-meeting, where the
vaguest deviation from recognized statutes of decorum
sends a wrathful Bible journeying toward the offender's
head. It is very lucky for Fuller that people can produce no more powerful charge than the fact of his
having had his carriage jounced against a certain other

and finding this in possession of a rather objectionable occupant whom he had known before marriage. If scandalous report had seen fit to place him *inside* the carriage of the unconventional lady, lots of his female friends whom I know about would have been bullied by their husbands into cutting him; and I doubt whether even the men themselves would dare bow to him if Mrs. Grundy made the round statement that he had been seen publicly walking our streets in the same perilous company."

I suppose that I might have worked myself into quite a fury over the superb injustice of these remarks; but I chose to rein in any impulse toward self-exoneration. Cornelia was evidently in thorough ignorance concerning Fuller's conduct since his marriage, however much she may have known regarding it before then; and as this ignorance lay at the root of the censure with which she chose to treat my own behavior, natural enough was it that I should feel anxious to set myself right (yes, even in Cornelia's opinion) by the unfolding of a tale whose lightest word ought to weigh importantly to my advantage. But since matters had assumed their present condition between Fuller and myself, I felt deprived of the privilege to tell all that I knew. Before entering into that peace-treaty of which mamma has had the negotiating, I might have presented my sister-in-law with a few prominent if not silencing facts; but now my duty is to deal with Fuller's misconduct as with something which he has agreed to expiate by years of altered living. No matter how much of a farce was our reconciliation. We were reconciled; and I am bound to show the compact some sort of respect.

And yet it was hard work for me to leave Cornelia in such woful darkness about the real truth. I daresay

10*

that if Mrs. Chauncey Crawford had not joined us very soon afterward, my struggle would have cost me absolute pain. As it was, Mrs. Crawford's impassioned questioning about all that his lordship paid me the pointed honor of saying, brought with it an amused forgetfulness of more serious matters.

## CHAPTER XXI.

DEC. 15.—The last gap in you was a mere crevice, Diary, when compared with this great chasm of neglect. And yet what has there been which was worth the chronicling? To-night a dinner; to-morrow night a ball; to-morrow a theatre-party; and to-morrow the opera. Sometimes I look at mamma wonderingly, and ask myself if there is any chance that she will grow dead tired of it all, some day. Heaven pity her, if she does! For myself, I put on my purple and my fine linen with bored feelings and take it off with grateful. Lent is a sort of Avallon to me; a haven of rest that I shall find quite as refreshingly nice, doubtless, as though it were

> " Deep-meadowed, happy, fair with orchard-lawns
> And bowery hollows crowned with summer sea."

But the voyage thither is certainly very slow and stupid work. I often discover myself struggling intensely to take interest in my surroundings of " babble and revel and wine "—to compliment Mr. Tennyson by quoting from him twice in one page. Now and then, during a day or two, I flatter myself that the stone has yielded to the constant dropping at last, and that I am beginning to be a bird of the same feather with the flock among which I fly.   But it all turns out, very soon, to be a delusion ; a flash in the pan.   Most of the people whom I meet seem characterless—people of wood and putty.   They talk to me and their language, like some wretched shawl, " mere heaps of holes to one another stitched," appears wrapped about their thought's gaunt poverty in the vain hope of concealing it.   Some of them are dead levels of correctness; some are great plateaus of tedious badness ; but not one wears a single hillock of originality, personality, self-assertion : I of course except silly prejudices, which one finds in plenty.

But very possibly I am wrong ; perhaps I only see the world reflected in the cracked mirror of my own soul.   If a dyspeptic liver can make the brightest sky look dreary to us, why should not a broken heart bring about equally despondent changes ?

No doubt I should have gotten a kind of resignation by this time, if I had plunged myself recklessly into'that sea of flirtation, fastness, unmarried wedlock, with which a woman in my sphere of life, provided she doesn't possess a hump, a hair-lip, or any other such physical eccentricity, can easily familiarize herself.   Yes, I should have gotten the sort of resignation that

" Goes upon its business and its pleasure
And knows not all the depths of its regret."

I make no childish boasts ; but many a woman in my same situation would have gone tripping off arm-in-arm with the tempter weeks before now.   It bothers Cornelia Walters, I am more than half sure, to see how I resist every temptation to be fast.   The other day whilst we were lunching at home in the absence of both mamma and Fuller, Henry had no sooner made a permanent

departure from the room than my sister-in-law produced
a package of cigarettes.

"Don't look horrified, Helen, but please give me a
light; that is, if you refuse to join me."

"I shall not give you a light," declined I, a little
tartly.

"Then I can help myself," laughed Cornelia, rising
and looking about her till she had discovered some
matches.

"It is very mortifying, Cornelia," I began, to think
of Henry coming in and smelling smoke."

"Do you suppose that he'll believe I am responsible
for it?" she wanted to know, with much sarcastic anxiety. "I should be miserable if he did. Dear Louis
lets me smoke at home before the butler; but then our
servants always have to know more or less about our
little private vices, don't they?"

"A lady should be without vices," I moralized, severely.

"Oh, of course; in theory," was the glib retort.
"Ever so many of the women whom I know smoke.
The other day I was *so* much amused. You recollect
what a saintly meek-looking blond-haired madonna of
a creature Mrs. Chauncey Crawford is. Well, she gave
a divine little dinner to some bosom-intimates last Wednesday—just our set, you know, without a single one of
those tiresome foreign swells whom she is so fond of
entertaining. And it was such fun to see her jump up
at the end of dessert and inform the men that we ladies,
having been too long trampled upon by the iron heel of
male tyranny, had sworn for one evening at least to
break our bonds and remain for cigars and coffee.
Whereupon the men were served with their immense
after-dinner smokables—Henry Clays, I believe they

are called—and we ladies had the mildest and loveliest
little affairs, that a baby-in-arms might puff at with complete impunity ; Henri*etta* Clays ought to be their name.
It *was* so jolly ! "

"It must have been," I commented.

I meant it, too, in a certain way. Jolly to wear one's
womanhood like a cap tipped jauntily sideways with a
feather stuck therein. Jolly to make oneself forget that
life is life and sorrow is sorrow. Jolly to dance through
one's days, following the reckless philosophy that tells
us we are fools if we don't dash tears from the eyes
which waste time in shedding them, and use our mouths
to drown with loudest mirth the keen clear murmur of
intense regret—a regret like mine !—till it is only heard
now and then in the pauses of the merry-makings.
Jolly to clutch at pebbles when there are no pearls to
be gotten. Jolly to choke "the sob's middle music"
in our throats with a fate-challenging laugh that flings
defiance in the very teeth of misery. Jolly to flirt, to
smoke, to ape the worst phases of fast demi-monde
Parisian life, to get oneself talked about wherever one
may go, to do the things that set wise heads shaking
and send a shiver through all the tranquil soul of chaste
Conventionality—"whom," as Cornelia might insolently
remark, " our set only meets out at the big balls and
goes to see once a year, praying that it won't get in
when it does go."

Yes, jolly enough. I almost wish I could hurry
along in this mad sort of bacchanteism. I have only to
reach them a hand if I would join them. They are
most willing to admit me, though they have shut their
doors on so many, not rich enough, not powerful
enough, not well enough positioned.

But no ; something holds me back. Something

within me will not yield. Not very long ago (the first evening, it was, on which I met Melville Delano at the opera) I had almost resolved to do as these other women are doing—women whose husbands care for them about as much as mine cares for me and whose family influences have been similar to my own. But the resolve fell through, somehow. Who can change one's nature at will? I begin to think that your real skillful outragers of propriety are born, not made. It would be quite an easy matter for the Ethiopian or the leopard to perform those little difficulties we have all read about, compared with the feat on my part of making myself remotely like Cornelia Walters, in taste, in character, in morality—or in lack of all three.

## CHAPTER XXII.

EC. 18.—I was glad when John Driscoll, meeting me at a dinner the other day, asked me to dance the cotillon with him at the first Delmonico dancing-class. Glad because I have been thinking deeply of late as to whether, being still Fuller's wife, I should not make a sort of last effort to place ourselves on different terms, each toward each. I don't mean anything about trying to win his love ; I don't know that I would dare tell myself I meant this, even were such the case. I merely mean that our present relations together lack a little too glaringly everything which resembles congenial intercourse. And possibly I might gain some sort of direct or indirect aid from John Driscoll in the working out of such results. At least he could give me his honest opinion as to whether I would meet with any fresh disheartening rebuff. He has been such an intimate of Fuller's for so long a time that I felt nearly sure he must have been made more or less of a confidant regarding recent dissensions. And yet I could not believe that even if he had heard the most one-sided statements conceivable, his old-time intimacy with me, his clear knowledge of just what I am and what I am not, would do anything except prevent him from taking silent part against me.

The dancing-class, first of its series, was a really su-

perb entertainment. All the magnificent suite of Delmonico's rooms was thrown open to us. Many of the
toilettes were such things of beauty that one felt sad
whilst watching them to think how meagre a chance
they stood of being joys forever. The glorious main
ball-room, seen for the first time this season, spoke to
me like a voice out of my careless girlish past. That
spacious glimmering floor ; those brilliant-lit walls ;
those delicious wailing waltzes which Lander and his
colleagues in melody give with such matchless perfection—how much lighter this heart had beaten when I
had seen, had heard them last !

There was nothing of a positively conversational
character between John Driscoll and myself until we
took our seats for the cotillon ; nor did we get much
opportunity for talking before the first interregnum of
non-dancing. I find that I am apt to be on the floor
in nearly every figure, nowadays ; perhaps because
mamma is recognized as such a permanent entertaining
power.

"Are you sure that you will not take some ?" he
questioned, a little solicitously, as I refused the bouillon
that was being passed round.

"Quite sure. Do you think that I look as if I needed
a stimulant ? "

"No ; not precisely that. And yet, to be candid, I
will own that I have seen you looking better."

"No doubt you are right. You mean the dark rings
round my eyes, and the paleness. Don't deny that you
mean these. Remember there are such things as looking-glasses. And it would be very odd, surely, if my
face didn't show how miserable I am, for that matter."

"Miserable ?" he was evidently compelled to repeat.
"In spirits or in health ? "

" It is hard to be one for any length of time without being the other. But I specially meant in spirits. You must know why this is so."

He seemed troubled, but forced a smile. " Do you take me for omniscient ? "

" Pshaw. You are very intimate with Fuller. He must have told you how "—my voice trembled a trifle— " how we are getting on, or rather *not* getting on, together."

His face turned right grave on the instant : what a vast amount of quiet sympathy he can throw into those hazel eyes of his when he wishes ! " I am quite sincere in telling you that Fuller has not once spoken of these matters to me. But I have inferred many things. I could hardly fail to draw my own conclusions from what I have noticed."

Then I returned, in a slow whisper : " Fuller and I are not man and wife. We are just two people who live in the same house and treat each other with a kind of tolerating civility. I am sure that he has never borne me the least love ; that he married me for cold politic reasons. This discovery I made some time since ; you will probably understand *in what manner*," I emphasized. " The shock which it first cost me is in a measure abated. I have no hope, as a matter of course, that his feelings towards me will ever change at this late day— ever radically change, I mean. These are not the times of charms and love-philtres, you know, " (whilst I laughed a little laugh.) " But I have thought very deeply and very often upon the present state of affairs, and I have grown to believe it possible that some slight alteration for the better may be brought about in our relations. Do you think that I judge rightly ? or do you consider my plan worthless ? I want your advice."

There was a touch of vague inoffensive humor about the gravity his face wore, now. "You see Fuller on an average about twice a day, I suppose?"

"That isn't what I mean at all. It is our *way* of be having to each other when we *do* meet."

He crossed his legs, bringing one of his big-bowed low shoes and a glimpse of crimson-silk stocking into marked prominence. Then he began devoting himself with studious scrutiny to one of his gold waistcoat-buttons.

I sat and smelt flowers. How little the people, passing and re-passing, babbling, laughing, flirting, pleasure-hunting, dreamed of what a solemn topic John Driscoll and I had entered upon the discussion!

He was not, for his part, at all a zealous participant in the discussion, I soon had reason to remark. More than once, during the silent interval that followed between us, I stared impatiently at his handsome drooped meditative head. At length I made up my mind to continue talking until he himself gave some dim indication that he would care about being listened to. And so I re-commenced, whilst he sat the picture of attention, lounging in his chair as only very handsome men ought to dream of lounging, his shirt-bosom making a huge white bulge forward, both eyes fixed upon one of his sheeny shoes and his hand still having digital relations with the waistcoat-button.

"Don't suppose, please, that I've any wish to try and make Fuller stay from the club evenings, or come away on my account earlier than he comes now. Not a bit of it. Those and similar actions grow to be painful sacrifices when a man isn't in love with his wife. What I want is something warmer than this dull mutual politeness, whose monotony wearies one desperately, even if

it has no other unpleasing feature.  Do I want an im
possibility ?  Remember, I don't mean anything like
love-making ; let us call it love-making's eighth cousin.
Only, it is not sheer dead indifference."

A burst of music just then reminded me with some
little force that the ball-room at Delmonico's was not
solely designed,. that evening, for my own and John
Driscoll's convenience.  Everywhere about us the cotillon had re-formed itself.  We were among the first four
or five couples and therefore must dance as soon as the
leader called upon us.  Which the leader almost immediately did, by the bye, with that indestructible suavity that makes Willie Gregory a complete prince of co-
tillon-managers.

Leaving my question still unanswered, John Driscoll
rose with me and began his easy delightful Boston that
I suppose I couldn't help finding enjoyable if I were due
at my own execution five minutes afterward.  Our little
turn finished, he left me in silence.  I had begun to feel
considerably piqued, by this time, and rather lost my
head in selecting a partner for the forming figure : it was
only after irrevocably taking out that little Bartholomew
man that I remembered what dire discomfort as a partner he had caused me before now.  Through the figure
went little Bartholomew and I ; then came the ordeal of
dancing with him ; then at last came the blessed privilege of seating oneself.

John Driscoll was already in his chair when I sat down
beside him.  I let him look amiable and remain speechless for a little while, and then I spoke, with sharp petulance.

"I asked you a question some time ago.  I trust
you're going to have the manners to answer it."

Just then up floated Aleck Sheffield and held out a

hand to me.   I did not rise on the instant but gave him
my own hand whilst turning eagerly toward John Driscoll ; for he had begun, in a low slow way, to favor me
with his answer :

"I must tell you that I do not think you can change
matters at all to your satisfaction.   I advise you to let
well alone."

"Your Boston is the most delicious thing I know of,"
Aleck Sheffield was murmuring in my ear, presently.

"Thanks," I laughed.   And the laugh seemed to
come right from the central pang of a heartache.

## CHAPTER XXIII.

DEC. 20.—I have been thinking over the advice John Driscoll gave me. It springs as much from the man of the world as from the friend of Fuller Dobell. He is right. There should be love or there should be nothing; I was a fool to think otherwise.

How strange that Fuller's invariable coldness does not alienate me from him ! There are times when my spirit seems to start up with clenched hands and cry: " I *will* hate him ! " A sort of resolve follows, usually forgotten two hours afterward. Surely there is nothing beautiful, nothing honor-worthy in a love such as mine. It is like a slave smiling in the face of a brutal master ; like a dog licking the hand that has beaten it—like anything which is the simile of undignified and contemptible humility.

Well, I have one satisfaction, if it can be called that. He does not dream that I am *not* wholly alienated. He must believe that I do not care a fig, now, for his affection or his lack of it.

—Fool that I am ! Only a few weeks have elapsed since I wore my heart on my sleeve before him as we drove to the Park, just previous to that miserable meeting. Had he not the opportunity then of snubbing me shamelessly, and did he not use it with unpitying promptitude ? " If you care to win back' whatever is lost, Fuller, you must see that the means of doing so are not difficult." Those were my words ; and how did he answer them ? By that horrible horsey order to John.

'Whom the gods hate they first make mad.' What celestial prejudices I must be the object of ! A March hare or any other recognized symbol of insanity is a light of reason compared with me. To care for him now is sheerest craziness, beyond any doubt. But fortunately all mental maladies are not incurable. Some day the tie may weaken and snap, leaving me blessedly emancipated. And yet I have already written in these pages that nothing can ever change my love. Perhaps I was right ; and I frame the sentence with bitterest dread ; for to love him has verily grown my curse.

*Dec.* 22.—" If you've no other engagement, Helen, be good enough to give yourself bodily up to me for the morning."

Miss Margie Cartwright was responsible for this remark, having dropped in at about eleven o'clock to-day.

" What are you going to do with me, Margie ? " I asked.

" I am going to take you shopping. Mamma at last has given her consent for me to get an India shawl— one of those pretty little square ones, you know, and I want you to come and select something that is decent as well as cheap." It is a pet foible of Margie's to talk like a pauper. She makes the same parade of her poverty that some people do of their wealth. She is proud of it, indeed, with a kind of queer left-handed ostentation that is funny from its pure originality ; just as though a peacock which had been despoiled of all but

a single caudal feather, should solemnly lift that and
strut about with it, in unabashed importance.

. " I shall be very glad to do what I can," I consented,
after a moment's reflection as to whether the getting on
my bonnet and the walking out would be an exertion at
all worth the making : a sort of sensation, by the bye,
which has only come upon me of late and which I cannot find it difficult to account for.

Margie's shopping lasted precisely three hours.   An
infinite amount of vacillation among five or six different
shawls finally reduced itself to a steady vibration between two—one pretty and very cheap, the other cheap
and very pretty.   Provided I once received the whispered intelligence that "mamma would be furious if,
etc.," there is no doubt that I received it at least fifteen
detached times.   Finally I got a little irritable over a
round statement which Margie made the clerk who
waited upon us, to the effect that she was ' one of those
people, you know, with whom every dollar, more or
less, told decidedly."

" For Heaven's sake, Margie," I rebuked, in a rather
excited aside, " pray make your purchases without
giving the clerk *too* perfect an idea of your income per
annum."

Looking quite a great deal hurt, Miss Cartwright followed my advice, taking the shawl that was cheap and
very pretty, and affording me the sort of relief which is
only expressible in a huge sigh of gratitude.   Margie
isn't of at all a sullen disposition, however, and her
annoyance was over almost before we had left the store.

" Do you know," I presently asked, " that it is after
two o'clock ? "

" And I'm so desperately hungry," Margie returned.
" Aren't you ? "

"I feel as if I wanted my lunch. Suppose we go in here and get some."

I said it more than half jestingly, whilst we were passing the Fourteenth Street Delmonico's, and anticipated a prudish little scream from Margie, or some similar mark of dainty horror. Instead of this, however, there was merely :

"Oh, Helen, it is so fast for ladies to go in *any* restaurant; don't you think so ? "

"I've heard people say so, Margie, and I suppose it is. But if one were very hungry one couldn't help feeling that the impropriety was materially lessened. Think of it: sometimes people eat each other, when they are famishing, and it isn't considered murder, you know."

"But we're not in any such cannibalistic state," laughed Margie; "and we're so near each of our homes."

By this time I had gotten to feel a certain amount of evil pride in the result of my temptations. "Pshaw," I generalized, "nobody can denounce it as precisely criminal in a married woman and a young girl. The most they can say is that it isn't especially swell."

"It would be such a lovely spree," half-yielded Margie. "But now I recollect, mamma once told me—"

I didn't wait for the valuable intelligence which mamma had no doubt imparted, but walked toward the Fourteenth Street entrance, (I suppose it would be simply amazonian to go in by the Fifth Avenue one) confidently expecting that Margie would follow me. And she was presently at my side, making not a few low-voiced fluttering protestations which I feigned that I didn't hear.

We entered the salon and selected a seat well re-

11

moved from any window. A very courteous waiter came promptly forward, handed me a carte and disappeared. "What are you going to take?" I wanted to know, glancing Margieward across the table; but as my eyes made this little journey they fell upon the face of some one who was directly behind Margie. There she sat, in all her serene superb loveliness—the woman because of whom I have suffered so bitterly!

"I haven't any preference for anything," stated Margie. "Pray order what you think best, and I shall fervently try to do it justice."

"Omelette aux tomates," I began to read, murmurously, having just the minutest idea what words my lips were pronouncing, "chicken croquettes à la maître d'hôtel, côtelettes à l'italienne—"

"Don't, for Heaven's sake," interposed Margie. "Do you know, Helen, I think we ought to get rice or hominy or something very plain—as if we were miles away from home and nearly starving. It is so sort of—of demi-mondish, don't you know, to come here and take these French dishes."

I glanced up from the carte for a second, fascinated by a desire to see whether that woman was still looking at me. Yes; those marvellous light-lashed eyes, colored so that Swinburne might have admitted them to be "the greenest of things blue, the bluest of things gray," like the eyes of his own Félise, were fixed with unwavering steadfastness upon my face. About her ripe-lipped rosebud sort of mouth played a smile delicately insolent. She was not eating; she had apparently but just entered the salon and had not yet been served. My rapid glance told me these things. Her sneering smile drew the color to my cheeks almost instantly. I suppose Margie would have noticed this at once if I had

not begun giving a reckless kind of order to the waiter,
who just then appeared with ice for our goblets.

" Helen, aren't you ordering a great deal too much ? "
inquired Margie, with anxious astonishment, after listening to several items.

I gave an excited little laugh.  It was *so* hard to be
natural, knowing how those two cold critics of eyes
were levelling their fullest scrutiny at me.  " Am I,
Margie ?  Well," (to the waiter) "that will do, then."

The man bowed with meditative courtesy, evidently
committing my order to his practised memory whilst he
did so.  Just then a voice came from the opposite table, commandingly loud, and yet refined, musical,
through and through the voice of a lady.

" Waiter."

" Yes, madame."

" I have been here some time before these two ladies,
and am entitled to be served before they are, on that
account.  Do you not agree with me ? "

" Yes, madame.  It was somme meestek."  The
waiter looked apologetic to his finger-tips.  " I will
send somebody at once."

Two o'clock is not an hour, I suppose, when there
are many people to be found in the salon at Delmonico's.  A glance about the room satisfied me that there
were very few people there now.  I could not but feel
certain that she had spoken merely from motives of rude
bravado, as one who had nothing to lose by making
herself stared at, and could render me uncomfortable
for this very reason.  Yes, such must have been her
aim, I rapidly concluded : the insolent smile had served
as mere prelude to her present behavior.  My best
course was quietly to ignore her demonstrations.  They
sprang from a kind of baffled hate, I could not doubt.

To this woman I was the wife for whom Fuller had in-
alienably deserted her; she did not know, possibly,
that our wedded bliss was not of the most perfect, by
this time.    Illicitly, shamefully, in whatever way the
world chooses to consider it, she had once held him; I
had stolen him away from her and bolted him up tight
with the double fastening of matrimony and propriety.
I was therefore fair game in her eyes for whatever mis-
sile she could hurl at me.

It was all very well for me to look here, there, anywhere, and seem to treat the matter as one which concerned the waiters, not myself.    Had I been alone, this
course might have had a somewhat arrow-blunting
effect.    But Margie, whose back was opposite the
speaker, made rather rude work of nearly revolving in
her chair for the evident purpose of getting a good
glimpse.    Her stare resulted in an impulsive turn toward the waiter.  "We are really quite sorry," she
hurried, "to have been the means of annoying that
lady."    Then to me: "My dear Helen, it *was* disagree-  •
able, I've no doubt.    You see, she must have been
waiting some time before we came in."    Margie's eyes
were sparkling with discovery.    She was telling herself, I could clearly perceive, that she had just seen a
charming creature, charmingly dressed; no self-assert-
ing vulgarian, but an offended lady who had had the
spirit and dignity to resent culpable neglect on the
waiter's part.

My featureless sort of gravity she took, doubtless, for
lack of sympathetic feeling.    If Margie had merely
fancied herself the indirect means of annoying a fellow-
creature, she would scarcely have been disturbed, I
fancy, by the ghost of a conscience-twinge.    But here
was a person who could absolutely afford to set the im-

mense moral disadvantage of never having been seen
anywhere against the irreproachable good-style of her
whole appearance. Margie was flattering herself that
she knew a lady when she saw one; I had felt in a
mood of similar benevolence toward my own detective
powers, on that hotel-piazza, last autumn, and could
now understand her sensations perfectly. With me
there had been, however, the damning influence of Melville Delano's behavior; with her there was nothing of
this powerful kind.

I daresay that my sober manner piqued Margie, who
took it for indifference, if not the desire to inflict a
slight snubbing. She is a self-willed little body at
times, with at times a touch of real temper. Doubtless
because she believed that I had already judged her conduct to be too loud and demonstrative, she determined
now to show me how positively we disagreed upon this
point. And so, half rising from her chair and turning
herself wholly round, she began to address that creature.

" We are very sorry indeed to have been the means
of—"

" Margie !" my hand fell graspingly on her arm as I
leaned across the table ; her name left my lips with a
kind of vetoing emphasis, very imperative and sharp.

A word can say volumes, sometimes, dreary a truism
as it seems to state this. Margie turned toward me
again, read it all in my face (quick-witted vixen that she
is) and reseated herself suddenly, bumpingly and ridiculously.

Alone, as it were, I was left to face the foe. Of
course I had made an unexampled fool of myself, acting
from hot impulse, never pausing a second to consider
the pure folly of my course. But now it was too late
for repentance to advantage anything. There the foe

was, having risen from her seat, glaring at me with haughtiest fury. I myself sat down, then, pale and frightened. The waiter stood and stared. This creature had me thoroughly at her mercy; all that I could do was to trust that her wrath would not take the form of speech.

But I leaned upon a broken reed. She spoke almost instantly, and in tones high from rage yet filled with a rich quivering harmony. Every word was flung straight at me.

"You are quite right. Keep your friend from the deep injury of exchanging a sentence with myself. *I* have the misfortune to be immoral under less pleasant circumstances than you. Mrs. Fuller Dobell can commit indiscretions without greatly shocking society, but everybody isn't as luckily placed, perhaps. What is a crime in me, becomes in you only—"

I did not hear another word; for by this time I had started up and was calling out to Margie, "Come, come, for Heaven's sake!" whilst I made fleetest exit from the place.

I did not know until I had gone nearly a block that Margie had joined me and was asking excited questions. "Helen, Helen, why will you not answer?".

"What, Margie?" I waked up.

"Why, who is that person? Tell me all that you know about her."

I reflected for a moment, then lied. "I know nothing, Margie, except that she's improper."

My voice had betrayed me. Margie had heard the story of the Park adventure, and is capable of using that shrewdness popularly known as an ability to put two and two together. Whilst we walked on in silence I concluded that this numerical feat was being performed.

"But it's so strange," was Margie's single comment on the occurrence, after I had spoken and shown her my secret. "I should never have addressed her if I'd dreamed about it, you know. As far as appearance goes she doesn't look as if butter possibly *could* melt in her mouth."

## CHAPTER XXIV.

EC. 23.—I have not mentioned to mamma, of course, and of course I have not mentioned to Fuller, what occurred yesterday. Margie Cartwright, too, has made me a solemn promise that she will consider it a secret between us; and Margie will keep her word.

That woman's headlong audacity has agitated me more lastingly than I had believed it would do. I kept seeing her beautiful scornful face all last night, and hearing her sweet rich angered voice casting every sort of impertinence at me. I have a morbid curiosity to learn whether she truly considers that I am immoral. Was that statement of hers regarding Mrs. Fuller Dobell's indiscretions even vaguely connected with any remnant of report that may have reached her ears? I cannot believe that it was. I must believe it a matter of furious fiction, having sprung purely from her own malicious desire to insult.

I daresay that her rage would not have run away with her prudence so absolutely, if it were not for the separation now existing between herself and Fuller. I have torn him from her possession and she hates me with a reason. I am possibly a perpetual thorn in her side. What keen delight she would have felt, had we both lived a few centuries ago, in negotiating with a skilled toxicologist relative to my taking-off. Sex and surroundings both stand materially in the way of my sympathizing with her, or even finding the dimmest probable excuse for her present life : I fear that I am an unalterable martinet about this sort of things. However, there is just a chance that some frightful tornado of temptation, not realizable to me who am of another social clime altogether, may have swept her away with it. And then that faultless dressing—that lovely voice —that cultured English—if she picked them all up with the collective tact of an adventuress one cannot but admit the deep-lying refinement underneath such tact ; but if she were born to them all—then God help her, one ought to pity her ! In spite of my martinetism I clearly recall certain big tears during clandestine feasts upon *La Dame aux camellias.*

Perhaps my grasp of Margie's arm and the " propriety, prunes and prism " in my face, stabbed her with intense sharpness, not merely wounding because of her jealous hatred, but for other reasons as well. She could not have gained any powerful hold upon a man of Fuller's cultured tastes, I should suppose, if she were greatly touched with coarseness ; and it may be that she has lost nothing of the sensitive pride that often goes with innocence. There was something in the recklessness of her rage (provided it *was* this, and not mere cold-blooded insolence) that rouses a sort of admiration in me whenever I think of it.

Can it be that she loves Fuller ? If so, there would be no use in trying not to pity her : she amply deserves pity. I had always believed this sort of woman, outside of unwholesome French novels and plays, to be a mere money-spending automaton,

11*

" A love-machine,
With clock-work joints of supple gold,"

such as we are told that the magnificently sinful Faus-
tina has become, of late centuries.    But there is a
chance that I am wrong; surely she has the face for a
fallen angel, throwing a fallen woman completely out of
the question.

Let me put a supposititious case, in this wise :

Say that she loves Fuller passionately.    Say that she
knows him passionately to love her in return.    Say that
because he needs money and she has none to give him,
she has consented, after great struggle, to his marriage
with me.    Say that my requirement from Fuller builds
a sudden inseparable barrier between them.    Then, saying all this to be true, is she not worthy of something
like pity ?    Indeed, yes !

Not he, however.    He deserves no vestige of pity.
If my case were really a true case, I should no doubt
find myself bitterly exultant over the thought that his
promise binds him from being near her ever again.

Well, if he suffers in keeping the promise, that is my
revenge.    He is keeping it, will keep it, I am certain.
If I dreamed otherwise—But pshaw ! my imagination
has worn wings quite long enough, for the present.
And matters are bad enough as they are, Heaven
knows.    It is of course silly policy that I should gravely
set myself to the task of imagining them far worse.

# CHAPTER XXV.

EC. 28.—Something occurred, to-day, which has strangely startled me.

It began at dinner. Fuller came in a little late, and was rather talkative after taking his seat; vinously so, I could not help suspecting. As is usually the case, a good three-fourths of his conversation was pointed at mamma. No doubt I was wretchedly out of sorts, to begin with. Anyhow, I felt myself getting more and more irritable, by silent degrees, as Fuller and mamma laughed and chatted the moré, became the more interested in each other's society. Their subjects of discussion were purely composed of gossipy trifles—how A, B and C had done or said this, that and the other. Mamma gave closest heed to her son-in-law's fluent personalities; perhaps because they mostly dealt with notable people, in whose sins, peccadillos and mistakes she felt a sort of sisterly concern. Without specially caring to sound my own trumpet, I can't help feeling that I have heretofore behaved with some slight patience and self-government when, on occasions like the present, my existence has been so coolly overlooked, in a social sense, by the rest of the dinner-table. But to-day I was cross and ugly, and ached, moreover, to give them both a pronounced hint of my condition. Fuller happened at last to touch upon Charley Bertram, who is getting

to be quite an intimate of his, I fancy. With the cor
ners of my eyes, I saw them lounging most fraternally,
yesterday, in the club-window. Now Charley Bertram
is one of my abominations. Accordingly I saw fit to
make this fact the base of a little harangue.

"Charley Bertram bestowed some of his precious politeness upon myself, last evening, at the Merediths',"
I set forth, whilst mamma and Fuller both turned surprised eyes upon me. "How long since he has gotten
back from England, by the bye? And, poor fellow,
why has he ever gotten back at all? If it's a question
of his not having money enough to remain, I do think
that he is a most deserving object for some rich friend's
charity. After years of patient study how to talk, walk,
dress, laugh and breathe like an Englishman, it truly
seems hard that he should be forced to live among such
savages as Americans."

"Charley is a very nice fellow," stated Fuller, a little
sharply. "Has his faults, perhaps, but is a thorough
gentleman."

"We don't harmonize on that point," I returned.
"But perhaps the majority of Americans are not cultured up to his fine foreign standard of breeding, and
are therefore not the best of judges."

"Very possibly you're right," muttered Fuller, with
a fair amount of ill-humor.

"Pray recollect, Helen," mamma saw fit to rebuke,
"that it is far easier to satirize people than justly to
praise them."

Fuller spied his little niche of opportunity and jumped
into it. "Helen seems to be of a very different opinion
from that. Anybody can flourish a bludgeon; but to
use the scalpel requires a trifle more skill. She infers
that Charley Bertram is ungentlemanly; and yet I

challenge her to recollect a single occasion within her own experience when she has been called upon to observe a trace of bad breeding in him."

I took two or three quick sips of coffee. "One need only to repeat one's former statement. We benighted Americans are possibly no judges of what is proper breeding and what is not. For example, when I saw him at about two o'clock, the other Sunday morning, being driven, with a cigar in his mouth, up Fifth Avenue in Carroll Montgomery's dog-cart, I was doubtless laying myself open to keen ridicule by venturing to consider the action at all unbecoming."

"Are you aware that I was in that party of which you speak?"

"Perfectly aware. I saw you from the window of the reception-room. I could not help but feel relieved when I discovered that you were not smoking."

He made a shoulder-shrug and a sneer very intimately associate with each other. "I had just thrown away my cigar. I lighted another almost immediately."

"Under Mr. Bertram's advice, I suppose. His countenance of the impropriety no doubt gave it a certain caste."

I saw Fuller's eyes sparkle faintly; a sure sign, with him, that his temper is going, slow as he usually is to lose it. "A person who is so particular about propriety of behavior," he rapidly returned, "should herself be more guarded, now and then. It is thought fast, for instance, if a lady lunches at Delmonico's in the morning, unattended by any gentleman."

Luckily dessert had been placed upon the table and Henry had recently left the dining-room. I should not have liked him to see me, after Fuller had spoken. First I flushed hotly; then all the blood died away from my face, leaving coldness in its track, like a breath of air blowing against my cheeks and forehead. I fixed my eyes on Fuller's face and let them stay there.

"Who told you that I was at Delmonico's?" I questioned, with hard-voiced calmness.

The unsheathing of a banana seemed so deeply to absorb him that I could not get his attention, somehow ; at least he would not look at me, would not answer my question.

"It could hardly have been Margie Cartwright," I went on, with a ringing stress on every word ; "for Margie is a very truthful girl, no matter what other faults she may have, and she faithfully promised me that she would not mention the occurrence."

"Dear me, Helen," put in mamma, with stately amiability, "it wasn't quite like robbing the treasury, you know. For my own part, I rather disagree with Fuller in even considering it more than merely—let us coin a word—fastish. Had you and Margie both been unmarried I should have liked the proceeding much less, as a matter of course."

Then my eyes left Fuller's face, but only for a second, sweeping mamma's. "It was not on account of propriety or impropriety that I made Margie promise. It was for another reason." My eyes were back upon Fuller, now. "I wonder if Fuller knows that reason."

He met my look coldly, at this. "Margie Cartwright did not tell me," he stated.

"Then who *did* tell you?" I wanted to know, huskily, with gathering brows.

"I do not like your manner," he bristled, roughly dignified. "When people require questions answered they are apt to be more politic in their style of framing them."

"Answer or not, just as you please," I retorted,

loudly careless. "If you do *not* answer I can draw my own conclusions."

I was watching him narrowly, in spite of assumed unconcern. Nothing that I saw upon his face had precisely satisfied me when he responded:

"I daresay you can draw your own conclusions. I hope they will be sensible ones, showing proper consideration for the fact that Fifth Avenue and Fourteenth Street are thoroughfares in which passers are occasionally seen and that Delmonico's is a place now and then patronized by some few occupants."

"I will admit that someone may have observed me enter; but there was nobody in the salon whom you are at all likely to have known, except—" Hesitating here, I cannot tell what I should have added; probably I should have called a spade a spade with boldest freedom. As it was, Fuller took occasion to speak and so leave my sentence incomplete.

"You do not deserve, after your incivility, to hear that John Driscoll saw you enter the restaurant. However, there is the fact, and you may make what you choose of it."

Whilst finishing that last sentence he rose from the table. I can't explain the impulse of doubt that instantly seized upon me as he was passing from the room. His manner had been plausible enough, and yet there was a touch of conciliation about it, a suddenness of change from haughty annoyance to grim concession, tormenting me with the belief that a certain purpose was at the root of his recent statement. The purpose, I mean, of deceiving me—lying to me—making me believe that John Driscoll had told him when John Driscoll had not told him. When "Edith" had told him.

There was no use in trying to banish suspicion from my mind, now—in telling myself I doubted unjustly and for little cause. I had told myself that before, and what sorry comfort had resulted from such gingerly slowness to admit that guilt was guilt !

I felt nearly consumed with a desire to see John Driscoll before Fuller should see him. At half-past ten we were going to a ball at the Gregorys'—mamma, myself and very probably Fuller, though his departures and returns have grown to be matters concerning which is observed a most questionless household quiet. If he went with mamma and myself to the Gregorys' my chances of seeing John Driscoll before Fuller could talk at any length with him were quite satisfactory. But if Fuller followed an occasional custom of his and left the house between nine and ten, afterward appearing at the party, then there was little hope that he and John Driscoll would not see each other, at the club or somewhere.

As it turned out, Fuller did not leave the house until he left it with mamma and me.

" How your hand trembles, Helen," commented Susie Montgomery whilst I was pinning an insecure portion of her toilette in the dressing-room at the Gregorys', before we had gone downstairs. Somebody once said of Susie that she would be a charming girl at a party if she would only take time to dress before she came, and not follow the plan of constantly mislaying herself all over the room.

" Yes ; I'm a little nervous to-night, Susie." Which was not half true, for I felt on literal pins and needles of nervousness regarding this matter of seeing John Driscoll before Fuller could see him.

We went downstairs, presently, Fuller and I entering

together, mamma following behind, in magnificent oneness. Up glided Charley Minard. "Pleasure of a turn, Mrs. Dobell?"

"I shan't dance till the cotillon, thanks. By the bye, we're engaged for it, are we not? And I am to thank you for this exquisite bouquet. Where did you manage to pick up these divine Marshall Neils? They are nothing if not heavenly."

Just then Fuller slipped from my side. I had put forth no effort to detain him, feeling sure that it would be purely useless provided he had made up his mind to go away for any such purpose as to communicate with John Driscoll. If I should show at all a marked desire to detain him, this course might simply agitate suspicions that were now, perhaps, unborn. For, provided there had been any deceit used, Fuller might very possibly believe that I would believe without asking corroboration of my belief from John Driscoll; and so he might not have intended exchanging a word with his friend on the subject of what he had told me.

As soon as Fuller was gone, however, I made prompt work of beginning my search about the rooms for John Driscoll. "You must let me walk round with you till I'm tired," I told good-natured Charley Minard, who immediately presented his arm. "I'm in one of my nervous fits, to-night, and can only cure myself by walking it off."

And so we walked, and walked. But at first John Driscoll seemed to be nowhere. Presently my eyes fell upon a certain corner where sat a lady whom I had never seen before; dark-eyed, handsome, foreign-looking. By her side was the object of my search.

"To whom is Mr. Driscoll talking?" I immediately asked of Charley Minard.

" That is Madame De Something—I forget the other two-thirds of her name. A Frenchwoman, whose husband is here, I fancy, in some diplomatic way. Enormously swell, and very nice into the bargain."

" You know her, then ? "

" Oh, yes. So odd that I can't recollect her name. It's—it's——" with the commencement of some emphatic forehead-tapping.

" Never mind, please. I'd just as lief not know, Mr. Minard. I want to secure this seat right opposite, here, before any one gets it ; and then I shall ask you to do me a favor."

After I had gotten the seat, one commanding a fine view of John Driscoll and his Frenchwoman,

" You will go and say a few words for me," I began, "to Mr. Driscoll, please. Tell him—" Here I stopped, abruptly. Fuller was the cause of my having stopped. He stood not three yards from where John Driscoll was sitting. He was not talking to anybody but appeared to be dividing attention between his friend and a certain monstrous basket of flowers at his elbow. Was he lying in wait to secure John Driscoll at the earliest chance ? It certainly looked so.

" Well, tell him what ?" questioned Mr. Minard.

I went on, then, in a kind of roughened voice. " That I particularly wish to speak to him for a moment, without a second's delay. In other words, take his place with Madame De Somebody and send him instantly to me. Then I'll be immensely nice to you, if you value such a reward, all through the cotillon ; and when we meet again I shall make you throw away that ugly boutonnière and take one of the loveliest roses out of your own bouquet."

" An irresistible bargain," he commented, begin-

ning to go; "I must strike it with you." And he
went.

Fuller had not yet seen me; of that I felt nearly certain. As Charley Minard put out his hand to the
French lady, Fuller drew a step nearer the group: he
was almost near enough, now, to hear what they were
talking about. I saw my error, then. The shadow of
coming failure already darkened my spirit.

Charley Minard said something to the French lady,
and then addressed several sentences to John Driscoll. I
watched a surprised look cross his face. A moment
later he turned, glanced in my direction, saw me, bowed
and rose. Meanwhile Fuller's eyes followed each movement.

I was like a general who observes under the most
favorable visual circumstances the complete defeat of
his army.

John Driscoll had bowingly left the lady and was
advancing toward me, when Fuller slipped up to his side
and caught his arm. He turned, met Fuller's face, and
the two friends began talking. I yearned to jump from
my chair and join them. 'Women cannot dash through
ball-rooms without male companions,' I seemed to hear
Conventionality reprovingly murmur. I looked again
at John Driscoll and Fuller: my husband had gotten
an arm in that of his friend and was slowly leading him
away from me, whilst talking with vehemence. I felt·
that I could bear it no longer—or wouldn't, whether I
could or not.

Up from my chair I sprang, and was just preparing
myself to sail in unattended grace through the room,
when lo, a fresh obstacle!

Mrs. Gregory, glorious in her bediamonded Roman-
nosed hostesship.

" My dear Mrs. Dobell, the Marquis de Lanzolle has just asked to be presented. A marked honor, I assure you," she progressed; and by the bye, she is about the most unconscionable snob in New York. " They are great people, you know, and only here for a very short time. His wife is talking with Mr. Minard, just opposite us. Is she not lovely-looking ? "

Whereupon the marquis (a really charming elderly man, with exquisite manners,) was made to know me, and even my final forlorn hope regarding Fuller and John Driscoll suffered absolute extinction.

But later in the evening, during a pause of the cotillon, John Driscoll came and sat down beside me. " I received your message," he promptly opened conversation, " but somebody seized hold of me just as I was fulfilling it."

I did not even look searchingly at him. I understood that it would be a thorough waste of time and words for me to make the remotest semblance of an attempt toward knowing how much he knew. John Driscoll is a man whose immense natural gifts of ready wit, clear-headedness, facial control and every similar trait which belongs under the general labelling of Tact, have all been cultivated so tellingly during past worldly years that they form a fortress against which I should not think of hurling my frail arrows. However, the chance remained of his not having made Fuller any promise, of Fuller's entire silence on the subject we had discussed at dinner. If this were the case, I was sure of hearing the plain truth—yes or no. If Fuller had really forestalled me, then his friendship for my husband would have exerted its force, good friend of mine though I well knew him to be.

" I worded the message rather urgently," I commenced. Then I asked him the roundest, the most un-varnished of questions. " Fuller says that you saw me go into Delmonico's, the other day, with Margie Cart wright. Did you really tell Fuller this ? "

He laughed with pleasant quietude. " It is not very nice of you to doubt Fuller's word."

Then, with a sudden passionate impulse, I tried to put my soul in my eyes, asking: "Will you give me *your* word that you said this to Fuller ? "

He shook his head with some low laughter. " By Jove, I couldn't think of giving my word about anything of that sort. You know what a traitor my memory has always been. I merely am willing to state that I did see you, and that I did tell Fuller I had seen you, when you entered—"

" That will do," I broke in, giving my fan reason to collapse so suddenly that I just missed breaking it. "If you're deceiving me, I don't suppose I ought to blame you, under the circumstances. Mind, I don't say whether you are or not. Only, pray let us drop the subject."

Which we were almost immediately compelled to do, by the bye, as the cotillon recommenced, and Charley Minard came up to take his lawful seat by my side and depose Mr. Driscoll.

I went through the first figure that followed, with a tear of rage in each eye. It is to be hoped that nobody saw two such inopportune strangers amid so much festivity.

What are my feelings now, when I think it all over? Do I give Fuller the benefit of the doubt? I must, in common justice ; but that is all.

## CHAPTER XXVI.

AN. 4.—Suspicions gnaw me. I am sick for their ceaseless tormentings. Sometimes the thought that I am being made a fool of sweeps over me surgewise. At such times I feel like rushing to mamma, or even Fuller himself. But of course I control such impulses. It would be merely a simple method of forewarning and forearming. If he has lied to me, it is assuredly his wish to keep on lying; and were I to show him my present state of mind, whole handfuls of dust would immediately be thrown at my eyes.

I have thought of a certain means to a certain end. Melville Delano will tell me anything on the subject, provided he knows anything. And I might bring myself, too, to ask him, though I have given him a cold enough sort of bow since that night at the opera. I suppose he will be at the Romeyns' on Monday night; he has been going to all the gayeties lately.

*Jan.* 8.—Something has at last occurred worth chronicling; but very possibly I am wrong in attempting to write it out. My head becomes fire at the thought of such attempt, and my heart begins to beat with a long strong throb.

Fuller did not go to the Romeyns', this evening. At

dinner he told us carelessly that there was a chance of
his being there very late and a chance of his not being
there at all. For my own part, I would have given
much for the energy to put down my foot before
mamma, and myself refuse to go ; but although somehow feeling wretchedly unfit for any sort of festivity,
(and I have been having miserable weak feelings every
day for some time past, mixed with dreary touches of
headache) I lacked, just then, the fortitude to brave
her displeasure, and so temporized, stating that I wanted
to be home early, since I was not engaged for the
cotillon and did not intend letting anybody have me
for a partner.

"Very well, Helen," mamma acquiesced. "You
know I haven't any special passion for sitting among
cotillon-spectators unless the figures are strikingly odd
or the whole entertainment strikingly splendid. And
by the bye," she murmured, touching one of her gray
puffs in queenly meditation, "I don't feel absolutely
certain, my dear, that these Romeyns will do much
more than just succeed in having the right sort of people at their house. However, Mrs. Montgomery and
Mrs. Cartwright and Mrs. Chamberlane all promise to
be there, and with myself added that will give the affair
a certain sort of—of—" (ever so little on one side went
mamma's majestic head ; ever so little upward were
lifted her grand shoulders)—"tone, I suppose, is the
word. We had better order the carriage, then, for
twelve ? "

I had not been in the Romeyns' rooms more than five
minutes before I discovered Melville Delano among the
guests. Then, whilst allowing Ludlow Inmann to pull
his string and subject me to his mild shower-bath of
trifles, I made believe that my mind was engrossed with

what I was letting this young gentleman do for me and not giving final consideration to the subject of whether I had best speak or not speak to Melville Delano.

I at last concluded to speak. Ludlow Inmann looked a little blank when I asked him to go and tell Melville Delano that I wanted a few moments' conversation. He had been my messenger on a similar errand at the opera, not long ago. But he has amazing good-nature : or is it that most of these dancing-men, modeled after his not very intricate or subtle type, like me with the sort of prejudiced liking that permits me to impose upon them, every once in a while, and not receive the curt reverses of gallantry that some women are unlucky enough to encounter? I think yes. I seem to have drifted, since I first came among these people, into a current of quiet popularity that has been bearing me along ever since. Perhaps this valuable popularity explains why what Cornelia Walters no doubt considers my unnatural treatment of Fuller in the Park, that day, has *not* made Society regard me with such very shocked eyes, after all.

Ludlow Inmann disappeared in the throng and presently I saw Melville elbowing his way to me. He made no attempt to shake hands, but just speechlessly seated himself in the chair I had been saving for him.

" I sent for you," was my unnecessary opening statement, made purely to make words.

He nodded faintly. " Otherwise I should not have come. And I suppose you had a very important reason for sending."

" Yes," I plunged ; " very. I wanted to get some friendly information from you—that is, if you're willing and able to furnish it."

"Well?" His dark face, that I have seen so passionful, was set in lines of hard serenity. He leaned forward a trifle, fixing his black steady eyes upon me in cold inquiry.

"It is about that woman—the hotel-piazza woman."

"Yes."

"I want to know whether you know if Fuller—" Then I stopped, and felt that shame had hurried up to me with her rouge-pot and rapidly begun operations on either cheek. It was such humiliation to ask him!

"I can guess how you wish to finish your sentence," he presently stated, in a voice very much as though there were a counter between us and our relations were of a character strictly mercantile. "But I prefer running no risks until I learn precisely what you mean, Mrs. Do-ḩell."

"This then," I hurried, with a sort of 'now-or-never' air. "Do you know whether Fuller is at all intimate with that woman at present—ever sees her, in fact?"

"I have no doubt," came the glib response, "that they are very intimate and that he sees her constantly."

It is trusted that no one noticed me grasp Melville Delano's arm, right here, and hold it for two or three seconds afterward with tightening fingers. The rooms were just then packed with people and we occupied seats close against the wall, shut in by the babbling smiling human crush.

"You will be careful, please, how you deal in reckless statements," I blazed, though my tones were of the conventional key. "Remember, I speak of the present, not the past. Of the present within a month or so. They *used* to be very intimate, perhaps: are they intimate *now?*"

My excitement only seemed to make him more col-

12

lected. He had, evidently punished himself with yards of sackcloth, bushels of ashes, for that furious evening at the opera.

"I have heard of no change," he murmured, his voice gentle and even-toned. "If there has been such a change I can perhaps find out the exact truth for you within a very little while."

All this calmness and precision from a man with whom neither is characteristic, nettled me rather keenly; nettled me, too, because I saw behind it a fixed intensity of hatred for Fuller and a savage willingness to act as informer against him.

"No doubt," I broke forth, "you will go to any lengths in what you consider such a fine cause. I wish you had snubbed me when I first made known my desires, this evening. I half thought you would, to be sincere. You ought to have done so."

This had been a telling shaft, as I soon saw. Much of his calmness vanished on the instant; but his tones had a sharp touch of anger, notwithstanding.

"I have shown a willingness to aid you in discovering what you have a thorough right to know. You first endeavor to use me and when I evidence a disposition to be used, begin an attack upon me. Whose conduct is the more consistent?—the more generous?" He rose abruptly and stood at my side: I could see that his lips wanted to sneer and that there was within his ardent Spanish sort of eyes a kind of dulled fire that would have matched a sneer very nicely. "Helen Dobell, when will you learn to treat me as if I had a remnant of human feeling?" he slowly asked. "I don't think your nature is a cruel one, but God knows I seem to have the benefit of every cruel impulse that ever visits it!"

"You're very good at melodrama," I retorted;

"only please recollect that I've received some proof of your powers before now."

He stood for a moment quite quietly, after that, looking away from me. I fanned myself. At length he bent down (just as I saw Aleck Sheffield, beaming with discovery in the distance, on his way toward me through the throng) and quickly murmured :

" I shall let you know to-morrow whether the answer I gave your question to-night was correct or no." Then, whilst Aleck Sheffield shook hands with me, he slipped away.

"How unfortunate that you shouldn't stay for the German," Mr. Sheffield lamented. " I'm going to lead, you know, and I never saw such glorious material as they have for the flower figure, not to speak of the immense originality about certain favors and things of that sort. Each man has to jump through a paper hoop and scream *houpla !* before he can dance with his chosen partner."

But our carriage was ordered for twelve, and I would not be tempted, and should probably have behaved with forcible bad-humour if mamma had wanted the order changed : which mamma, for reasons that were manifest during the first portion of our homeward drive, clearly did not want.

"A mixture," she commented, as our hack rolled through the chilly streets in the chilly January midnight ; " a melancholy mixture, Helen, was it not ? The Romeyns could entertain so brilliantly if they only chose to be—"

" Snobs," I put in, dragging my opera-cloak closer about me, and staring through the uncurtained window at my side.

" Precisely. Which, be it said to their discredit, they

are not.    Helen, why don't you pull down the curtain ?
Do you consider it nice style to be seen glaring out into
the street ? "

"Who could recognize me, mamma ? " I laughed.
"Did you ever know such intensely bright moonlight ?
How lovely Stewart's house looks !   One might almost
fancy oneself in Venice, if this carriage were more
like a gondola."

" Pray pull down the curtain, Helen."   She spoke so
sharply that I lifted my hand to obey her.

Just then a carriage came rumbling past us, going in
the same direction.   For a moment it was so near that
I could look into it through its uncurtained window.
And I did look.   And I saw a face that set my heart
beating wildly : Fuller's face.   I also caught a glimpse
of another figure seated beside him : a woman's figure,
I more than half fancied.   This latter was so obscure,
so momently seen, that it left the vaguest sort of im-
pression.     .

After that the carriage rolled rapidly beyond us.

Decision more instantaneous than mine was then, has
not often been made, I think.   Mamma was on the
back seat ; I on the front.   Right behind me was the
little glass window by means of which one may hold
communication with the coachman, if so desirous.

I sprang up, turned toward this window and quickly
slid it down, using both hands.   Through the aperture
I thrust head and shoulders.

" Coachman," I called, " coachman."

He heard me at once, slackening the horses' speed
and leaning down to hear what more might be said.

" Coachman, do you see the carriage that has just
passed us ? "

" Yes, m'm."

"Very well. Follow it. Follow it at a little distance, wherever it goes. When it stops, stop too, but
not near enough to let them notice you. Do you understand what I mean?"

A pause. Was he never going to answer me?

"*Don't* you understand?" I presently repeated,
querulous-voiced.

Something pulled sharply at my dress from behind.
"Helen," came mamma's awful murmur.

With it came the coachman's reply. "Yes, m'm, I
understand." At this I drew in my head, closed the
window and threw myself back into my seat.

Mamma's dark eyes were shooting fire at me through
the dimness. "Helen, what *does* this mean?"

"It means that Fuller was in that carriage," I cried,
"with somebody. I am going to find out who that
somebody is. Don't try and stop me. I *shall* find out."

"Change that-order instantly!" she pealed forth,
placing herself at my side and reaching out an arm toward the window I had just closed.

But I caught her hand by the wrist and pulled it back.
Our faces were quite plain to each other. I think I
could have killed her easily, in a very little time, just
then; I felt so fierce and strong. I am sure that I would
have fought and struggled with her if she had made
another effort to address the coachman.

She made no such effort. Our faces, I repeat, were
quite plain to each other. She must have seen the
tiger of opposition in mine. Once or twice she seemed
on the point of speaking and then checked herself with
a look of mixed contempt and consternation; as though
I was much too crazy for the hearing of any rational
statement. And in such opinion I believe her to have
been wholly right.

Meanwhile the carriage rumbled on. We had left the Avenue and were in a side-street. Presently we stopped.

I caught the door-knob, got the door open and stepped out into the street. Behind me I heard a voice that I hardly recognized, plead in deep despairing tones : "Helen, Helen! Please come back!" (Was ever such monarchical overthrow !)

I saw the other carriage the instant I looked for it, standing on the opposite side of the way, not a hundred yards off, and distinct enough in the long empty moon-lit street.

If I had really cared for Fuller's recognition of me I don't suppose that I would have done anything except break down miserably, now, feeling my courage collapse into the limpest kind of cowardice. But I did not at all care. My firm purpose was to find out who occupied the carriage with him. One's own eyesight was better proof than all the most precious testimony of a Melville Delano.

My white dress and white cloak made me very con-spicuous whilst I stole across the street ; but as I did not court detection, at first, I found it easy to avoid being seen. Their coachman had not seemed even to notice the presence of our carriage on the opposite side of the way ; and as I sped across the street the bulk of Fuller's carriage hid me from those who were alighting. And then, for a little space, I stood in complete ambush, feeling that the instant she appeared on the sidewalk I should discover who she was—or was not.

But I was wrong, here. For when Fuller helped her from the carriage (I confess, by the way, to an odd kind of satisfaction on finding that there really had *been* a woman inside) all that I managed to see, somehow, was a mass of dark silk draperies and the back of a bonnet.

And the owner of these hurried up the stoop of the nearest house, still giving only a rear view to my strained eyes.

As she did so Fuller bangingly closed the carriage-door and at once turned to ascend the stoop, without holding any words with the coachman.

Whereupon away rolled the carriage, just as I stepped audaciously upon the curb, following Fuller with I don't know what mad idea of entering the house itself, provided only my purpose were carried out and I saw his companion's face.

Over the lower part of my own face I drew the netted worsted-work which I wore about my head. It seemed to me now, whilst I stood directly at the foot of the stoop, staring up at them, as though one or the other must look down and discover me before their summons at the bell was answered. A glance at the woman's face would have made me certain who she was, (or was not) in that brilliant winter moonlight. Already my convictions were strong. The large easeful pliancy of her figure and the floating sort of grace that marked her movements could not well belong to other than one certain woman.

They waited for the bell to be answered. The coldness of the night made them both draw close against the dark door, ready to enter the house the instant it should be opened. Fuller's face was not entirely averted ; hers was turned fixedly doorward.

I felt as if a true devil of recklessness had gotten into my blood, now. Having gone thus far, I should not be driven back from the very verge of discovery. Then, also, what had I to lose ? Nothing. What to gain ? Much : if it be much to learn whether anyone has shamelessly hoodwinked you or no.

And so I sprang up the stoop three or four steps, with the network drawn closer across my face.    Then I coughed loudly.    After that I saw her face with much plainness.    And her voice called out to me just before I turned to descend the stoop :

" Why, Flora, is that you ? "

I think I had reached the curb of the sidewalk when one rough hand caught my arm, another my shoulder. Without looking, I knew the assailant was Fuller. Whether he saw me or not I did not really care ; and yet I tried to free myself ; simply, perhaps, with the aim of baffling his curiosity.

But he held me hard, ruffianwise, tearing my cloak with his savage clutch upon it and bringing his face round so as to gain view of mine.    And then, with a little bitter laugh, I used my free hand to tear away from my face all covering.    " Look as long as you please," I cried.    " I was determined to see who that woman was, and I've succeeded !    You have proved yourself a liar—nearly the last bad thing it was left you to be ! "

He had drawn back and ceased to hold me, almost from the instant that he saw my face.    Doubtless they had neither of them recognized me when I had coughed them into the noticing of my presence, a little while ago.

" Helen, I shall make you pay for this."

He looked ghastly in the moonlight whilst he glared at me, muttering those words.    For my own part, I was all tremulous with passion and felt my blood burn with an insane fierceness.    But I had sense enough to see the queer tragi-comedy of our position, if one may name it so.    Just as I thought, I spoke, receding further from him at every word.

" I have gained my point, and that is all I cared to

do. I have found out that you have not one spark of honor. That you are a liar."

The carriage waited just where I had left it such a very little while ago ; for I suppose, by the bye, that this whole wild proceeding did not really occupy three minutes.

Mamma's face looked stonily severe as I entered, after telling the coachman to drive home. But not a syllable left her lips all through our homeward ride. Her fall was worthy of a great tyrant. She accepted it in superb silence.

After we got home I passed upstairs to my room and have been here thinking and writing, writing and thinking, ever since.

I wonder if mamma leaned out of the carriage-window and saw, and heard. Something of this sort must have occurred : otherwise her lack of curiosity would have been purely marvellous. She probably knows the very worst : knows, I mean, that I am going.

For I am going ; that is certain, unless Fuller goes. They cannot keep me here, now. Let mamma refuse to help me, if she chooses ; I shall help myself ; I have a little money saved and Madame Langlois may get me or else give me some situation as teacher. Anyhow, I am going if Fuller does not go ; whether to sink or swim, starve or prosper—I am going.

If Fuller had come in whilst I have been writing in you, Diary, I should have appeared before him at once, and have stated my intention, even at the risk of having night made hideous to the next-door neighbors. But he has not come. I daresay he will not appear until to-morrow, sometime ; or rather to-day, for it is long long past midnight. And I am sorry not to have seen him whilst able to deal, as I feel myself able now, with any-

12*

thing he might dare to bring up, offensive, defensive, palliative.

It is true, there are sharp queer pains darting through my head at intervals, and now and then light shivers seem to pass and re-pass from my head to my feet. But I am quite sleepless, and could use my brain to good purpose, if called upon. Perhaps I am going to be ill; I hope not. All my best energies are needed now.

I do not suppose mamma will ever consent to my leaving the house. She will force Fuller to go, in all likelihood. Still, I am ready. There must be a separation. Ah, that pain. . . . I shall try and sleep, but I do not believe that I could compose myself in one position for ten minutes' time, if it were a matter of life and death.

## CHAPTER XXVII.

AN. 8.—It is nearly ten o'clock at night, and Fuller is not yet home. All day I have been asking for him—that is, whenever my blinding headache would permit me to think of anything but its own agony. I ought not to touch you now, Diary. Every moment I expect a recurrence of my sufferings to pay for such imprudence. I was so ill this morning that mamma made me see the doctor. Perfect quiet was prescribed among other medicines of a somewhat stronger character.

Can Fuller really have returned and mamma not have told me? I think it quite probable. Well, well, I must use despatch in getting better, so that I can be thoroughly my own mistress. The worst of it is, I am so weak : to-day I grew tired and dizzy after merely walking from one room into the next. I wish I could sleep ; but my brain seems to burn when it does not ache, so keeping me always wakeful. I found myself in such a strange stupor this morning. I know my eyes were open and that I was not asleep ; and yet Fuller seemed to be walking with me through fresh keen-aired October country, and Pineside was somewhere near, and we had only been engaged a very little while. I had just slipped my arm within his, and had

gotten a strange thrilled feeling whilst we walked on to
gether through the early autumn evening.　And he had
just called me darling, and a little spot on one of my
cheeks was tingling yet from the soft assault of his warm
lips.　And westward, above the " quiet-colored end of
evening," there was a tender slender crescent-moon ;
and many katydids were talking very dreamily together.

　" Headache seems to be her principal trouble, Doctor," informs mamma, promptly silencing the timid
katydids.　After that I wake up and have my pulse
felt, and exhibit my tongue, and ask Doctor Prentice
whether he thinks I will get over it soon.　Of course he
thinks yes.　When did a doctor, under like circumstances, ever deviate from thinking yes ?

　But I am omitting to chronicle the only real event of
to-day : Melville Delano's note.　It came this evening,
at perhaps eight o'clock, and was written on his club
paper.　I suppose it may be said to make assurance
doubly sure ; although I was in need of no such forceful
testimony.　This is the way it runs :

" My Dear Mrs. Dobell :—I have had the means of finding out what
you desired to learn and I have availed myself of these means.　The intimacy of your husband with the woman Edith Everdell still continues
wholly unchanged.　I am glad to have been of service in this little matter,
and beg you to believe me

" Sincerely your friend,

" Melville Delano."

　Was ever such arrogant boldness ?　This man has the
fearless intense hate that murderers are often made of.
I do not believe it would do anything else but put an
insolent glitter in his black eyes if Fuller were to show
him that note, some day.　Perhaps he half thought
that it might get to be seen by Fuller at some future

time, and cared slightly enough whether it did or no.
But it shall not.  I have just thrown it from my chair
into the fire and watched it whilst devoured by the red
greed of the flames.  As ashes, it can do no mischief.

Mamma seems to bear me no ill will for last night's
mad prank.  She has been very attentive all day.
Once or twice I have caught her looking at me with a
steady puzzled look.  Perhaps she thinks me very ill ;
or wonders if I shall not soon be so ; or reflects upon
her own future in case I should die.  Her excuse, then,
for getting to those balls she is so dearly fond of would
even have grown slimmer then than it grew when I was
married.

I can't help asking myself what she would do about
the crying, if I should never get over this.  There would
be times when common propriety would insist that she
melted, if ever so little.  But she could not melt  The
nearest she would ever come to shedding a tear would
be when somebody pushed her down a little from the
social place she has almost sweated blood to get.  Well,
I suppose she would manage, if I were lying anywhere
stark and sheeted, to perform, whilst she showed me to
people, something so successfully woebegone with her
handkerchief that public opinion would feel itself amply
satisfied.

Ah, what wildness and ghastliness am I writing,
Diary ?  I don't really know ; my pencil dances over
your pages as if it were leaded with quicksilver.  Think
of it : you, that are insensate white paper and morocco,
are my confidant out of all the world—my one real
friend whom I meet in maskless intimacy.  And what
bitter bitter things I have had to tell you of late !  You
were like a stream, not long ago, that lapsed through
laughing lands ; I never dreamed but that your bank

would grow lovelier, lovelier, almost with each new day; but suddenly they faded, saddened, blackened into boglike waste and dreariness. Yet never mind: some day I shall read over all your pleasant pages and take a kind of joy in the reading; for I am not one of those who believe that

"A sorrow's crown of sorrow is remembering happier things."

No; it is the one comfort that the poor sorrow clutches at and wears on her chilled bosom amuletwise. I believe it is Memory who gives us the merciful medicine that often saves our brains from ruin. Well for the mourners that they can feel those impalpable kisses of their dead—kisses that were and that therefore yet are, divinely! Mothers, wives, fathers, husbands, be thankful for that "dewy dawn of memory" which can visit your benighted lives, now and then. The soul that has had its better days should be proud of having seen them. Helen Dobell is glad that she was once Helen Jeffreys: glad that there is a library at Pineside where the wood-fires can burn right blithesomely; glad that it is a pleasant thing, when a woman loves a man with sweet surrendering passion, to walk beside him through the yellow-lit autumn evenings. Golden recollections are only dross when one is rich in golden realities.

Why do I not stop, Diary? If some one doesn't come in and stop me I shall probably ramble on all night in this haphazard way and . . . . .

## CHAPTER XXVIII.

EB. 19.—There is the broken sentence, and more than a month has passed since my hand failed in finishing it. They came in, a little while afterward, and found that I had fainted. I recollect breaking off in you, Diary, because of a sudden horrible weakness, and staggering with you miserably toward my desk and locking you up, and then knowing that I was going to faint but not being able to call Blanche or anybody. And after that I cease to remember everything.

For three weeks I was only conscious in a vague misty way, at intervals. Then came a time of intense weakness, with a full knowledge of what went on about me, though an entire inability to think of these occurrences. And now I am bolstered exorbitantly in a huge chair, looking like the shadow of a ghost, as I feel very sure, without needing any toilette-glass to support me in the statement.

I have been knocking at Death's door, they seem to think. At one time it was even as though they actually heard Death's responsive drawing of the bolt and the awful hospitality of his " come in." But the dark hinges that move so willingly for some stood immobile for me. And down among the damp dismal purlieus of Death's abode it was even as though the white Life-Angel wandered to find me and to bring me back, like a child that has strayed into noisome and unwholesome places.

I wonder what was the use of saving me. There are so many others who might have gone back to life gladder themselves, more gladdening to those about them. *Tu sais choisir*, I recall how Alfred de Musset tells death, in a bitter lamentation that those for whom life wears her chief charms are the first to be taken. "Not this man, but Barabbas," they cried out long ago in Jerusalem. "Now Barabbas was a robber."

Mamma seems to be majestically overjoyed at my recovery. She honors me with a great deal of magnificent pulse-feeling. I wish she wouldn't. It was no surprise for me to find myself under the guardianship of a hired nurse, who, by the bye, will leave to-morrow. Mamma was not made for the undignified drudgery of pouring medicine into feverish mouths. I daresay she swept through my sick-chamber, now and then, with stately sympathy, or charmed the doctors by any amount of superb solicitude. But hard matter-of-fact nursing is quite another affair.

I have received some lovely flowers from Margie Cartwright, Cornelia and several other kind friends, wherewith to beautify the hours of convalescence ; and John Driscoll has just sent me the most adorable lot of loose violets. One has only to bury one's nose in them and shut one's eyes and feel sure that the nineteenth of February is a fantasy, the middle of May a fact.

I know nothing about Fuller. There ! the tears have started ; I thought they would.

Perhaps he is gone. Perhaps mamma has made him vacate the room next this and take some other, for fear of disturbing me. I am nearly certain that he has not occupied his old room during three nights past ; for whilst Mrs. Blackman thought I was sound asleep, these three past mornings, I have been listening, listening, with closed eyes, for some evidence that he was there. I ought boldly to ask her ; but I dare not trust myself to frame the question, in my present state of nervous weakness. I do not know what surprising physical result may take place. Already the writing of this has given me a burning spot in each cheek and set my heart fluttering queerly.

Mrs. Blackman has just come in and stared at me with dumb disapproval. And so, Diary, we must part, for the present.

*Feb.* 25.—I am so much better and stronger ! They will not let me leave my room yet, but I have seen quite a number of people. Everybody seems to have put on her (I have only had experience, thus far, in lips feminine) best smile. Margie, Cornelia, Susie Montgomery, Kate Effingham, poor Selina Matthers—they all showed such pleasant warmth of congratulation.

The last time that I wrote in you, Diary, I had a most wretched sort of hysterical attack ; but that was five days ago. I am doubtless better able, now, to touch on a certain subject.

And yet what is there to tell ? Nothing. Mamma has not spoken ; I have not spoken. Of one thing I feel confident, now : he does not occupy the next room. I have made up my mind to ask Blanche about him twenty distinct times ; but each time the ugly question sticks in my throat. Why show my wound to Blanche ? Mamma is the one to deal with. I must speak to her ; but it shall be after I have grown a jot or two stronger.

One reflection haunts me so often : after lying so long

" Within the hollow of the hand of death,"

how much better if the cold fingers had tightened about me crushingly at last! "How much better!" my thought keeps repeating to my thought. I had nothing to wake up and be well for. Nothing unless to suffer! For has it not become with me, in spirit at least, even as though some hidden hand had cast upon me "the bitter water that causeth the curse?"

*Feb.* 21.—To-day I went downstairs to dinner, at mamma's suggestion. I have been well enough to leave my room, if I had chosen, for fully three days past. But I dreaded to go, just as I dreaded mentioning that one subject to mamma.

I was glad when mamma gave me the gentle push downstairs, as it were. She advised me to dine with her this evening; that was all. With her; the word "us" was not used. When I went down I was prepared not to see Fuller. And Fuller was not there.

A little while after soup mamma put forth a palpable feeler. "Mr. Dobell will not dine at home this evening," she told Henry, and then shot a swift glance at me, of which I was supposed not to have the least consciousness. "Ah," she went on, "I see that you have set no place for him. I must have told you before. I had forgotten."

After dinner mamma and I went into the reception-room. It looked very cosily pretty and was a delicious novelty after the sameness of my sick-chamber. There was not much light except what the fire made, leaping and curling about two or three huge black blocks of coal in the low hearth-place.

I was determined, now that the ice had been broken, to speak. I had not been seated more than three minutes when I began with these words:

"Fuller does not occupy his own room at present."

I was staring into the fire. I did not see her face when she answered :

" No. We both thought it best that he should change during your illness. I gave him my sitting-room on the second-floor."

That was all, for a little while. I waited for her to continue, knowing that she would. And she presently did.

" He has spoken often, Helen, of seeing you. But I have prevented him from going into your room until I had talked with you a little."

I did not answer for some time, still staring into the fire, watching the yellow turmoil of flames and hearing their sharp crackle. At length, I turned toward her, looking hard at her in the uncertain light.

" You did well to delay his coming, mamma. I don't want him to come. I think it would be better if we never met again. I half believed that he had left the house ; and permanently. I am disappointed to hear that this is not so."

The words were just finished when a sound came to us from the adjoining hall. The sound of some one entering by the front door with a latch-key. I knew that it must be Fuller. I sat quite still. There was utter silence between us.

The door was presently shut with a sharp noise. Steps sounded in the hall. Some one stood there for a moment, and then entered the dim room where we sat.

Mamma rose. " Fuller," she murmured, " here is Helen."

I sat perfectly still, staring at the fire. I heard him come forward, and knew that he was standing near me a little while before he spoke.

"I am glad to see that you are better," his voice addressed me.

I did not look up at him. "Thanks," I just returned, and no more.

"You have had a hard time of it."

"Yes." My eyes were still fixed fireward.

"Will you not take my hand? I am offering it to you," he whispered.

And then I behaved like a fool. Ah, me! how weeks of sickness can alter one! I buried my head in my hands and began to sob terribly.

It was a sort of mild hysteria. When I had gotten over it mamma and I were alone together.

"Give me your arm, Helen," she instructed, "and we will go upstairs."

We went.

## CHAPTER XXIX.

ARCH 9.—We meet constantly, now. We speak; we are, in a certain horribly mocking way, friends. He has returned to his customary room. And I—ah, why did I ever live through the peril of that sickness?

I am not really recovered from it yet. I have not half my old firm self-reliant feeling. Every day I tell myself that I ought to assert myself; but each resolution ends in tears, and sometimes a wretched headache will follow. Still, I am better. The doctor has ceased to come for a week and more.

Fuller is so courteous and gentlemanly. Now and then I find myself wondering whether he does not regret all that iniquitous past and really long for something widely different; whether he has not abandoned *her;* whether he does not wish for my pardon and for all the sweet joys that might result from it. Ever so many times I have been on the point of asking mamma if this is true; but the thought of how she would assuredly put the best face upon matters, delude me as I feel sure that she has deluded me before—as she has deluded me, most certainly, at Pineside, when she spoke of his real relations with that woman—deters, chills, and discourages me from holding any such interview.

Sober reason always tells me that his kindness and

his courteousness mean nothing; that he is only trying
to make me trust him as I trusted him once before; that
he persists in treating me like a blind incredulous fool.

Well, I must rouse myself, sooner or later, in some
sharp telling way. I am not really duped; I can never
be duped again. Action must come before very long.
My nervous forces, shattered as they have been, are
gathering for it.

What a bitterly galling fetter my love has grown to
me! If only I hated him! Maimed as I am now, how
well I could deal with him! It would be no sacrifice,
then, to go away at once. Apart from him I should
gain the very strength and energy that I require.

*March* 24.—The days slip on. I am still irresolute.
Still a coward.

*April* 1.—To-day has brought with it a most unlooked-for development. I feel like one who has crept
to the edge of some gloomy pit and looked tremblingly
within and seen serpents crawling there. And yet in a
certain way, I am glad because of my bitter experience.
It has roused me from my torpor: I am at last determined on doing *something*. Then, too, it has shown me
that my illness has not effected so deep a physical change,
after all. Perhaps I shall not be my old self for many
many months; but I still have a fair share of force and
endurance. I can act. And I mean to act.

This is how it occurred: Every evening, of late, I
have followed the plan of leaving the table after dinner
and going upstairs into the yet-darkened parlor on the
floor above, and there coiling myself in the hollow of a
deep tufted sofa and ceasing to be of the world worldly
for at least an hour. Henry generally wakes me up by
entering for the purpose of letting there be light, illum-
ining one gas-jet, discovering by means of it my inno-

cent repose and being on the point of a respectful retreat. As yet neither mamma nor Fuller have any
knowledge of such after-dinner proceeding.

This evening I left the table as usual; as usual I went
upstairs, stole through the little roomlike hall that sepa-
rates our two drawing-rooms, and found my soft coil-
ing-place in a shadowy corner of the front one.

I fell asleep; for since my sickness sleep at this time
renders up her drowsiest poppy-wreath after a moment
of solicitation; but I am sure that when I was awakened
my nap had only lasted a little while.

What roused me was the distinct sound of mamma's
voice in the hall between the two rooms. Some slight
light was there, but its effect upon the darkness surrounding myself was vague exceedingly.

"I am opposed to nothing, Fuller, within the bounds
of reason." Mamma was evidently at her majestic best.
"But now you are passing those bounds, and you cannot deny it."

Fuller's voice, low and slow and rather expression-
less: "I do not pretend to deny it. I am abusing your
kindness. Our contract has been violated most abom-
inably—and I am the violator."

"That is to me a purely hateful subject," loudened
mamma, though her voice was still not forcible enough
to be heard at any marked distance. "You have mentioned it in this way more than once, Fuller, and more
than once annoyed me by doing so."

Then he spoke, with a kind of bitter bravado:

"What is there to be ashamed of in the whole proceeding? The thing is done every day in European
countries. God knows what you saw about me to make
you want me for a son-in-law;" (jarring these last
words with a faint ironic laugh.) "But the bargain was

struck squarely and fairly.    Needing money, I found
myself saleable.    And I sold myself."

(Greedily listening, whilst my heart-beats were making me fearful that I should not gain every least word
of such loathsome disclosure, I sat with thrust-out head
and locked hands, motionless amid the darkness.)

"You will oblige me by keeping silent, Fuller.    I,
for one, have no pronounced anxiety that either Helen
or the servants should hear you."

"Helen is two floors above us, and one might just as
well go through the farce of believing that servants don't
possess ears.    I daresay they all listen at the cracks and
crevices whenever they choose ; but it certainly makes
us more comfortable to try and think the opposite of
this.    I repeat that there is nothing in our contract to
cause the remotest shame.    Abroad, they almost cry
such things from the house-tops."

"And abroad they do so much one cannot do here
with the least social safety."    Mamma's voice had
roughened huskily, somehow.    "Since you wish to
mention the terms of a certain agreement, why not
recall them in full ?    You know very well what I mean.
Apart from having given Helen every reason for indignant outcry, you have recklessly exceeded the large
allowance I made you in the beginning."

"I know it.    I offer no denial of your statement.
And after a whole winter of your generosity, I come
again with brand-new demands upon it.    I am incorri-
gible" (repeating that bad harsh laugh).    "It is just as
though one were to put a beggar on horseback, and after
his beggarship had ridden the animal to death he were to
shout out, with all the grandeur of Booth in *Richard
Third,* 'Give me another horse.'"

A short silence.    Then mamma's voice, full of trenchant emphasis : "You spend money extravagantly ; everyone knows that. But not more than a quarter of the large sum total I have given you, Fuller Dobell, has been spent upon yourself. You need not attempt any denial of this. There is that woman."

No answer. After a little time mamma proceeded :

"Helen was right in the resolve she made just before her sickness. On this side of the water, whatever foreign customs may be, it is nothing except a shameful outrage to any woman for her husband to do as you are doing. And mark my words, Fuller : even if I should so far forget dignity as to supply you with these fresh funds for which you ask, and even if I should afterward continue to uphold you in the sad falsehood of your present conduct (a falsehood, because the chief clause in our little compact was your total future abandonment of a certain connection)—even if all this should happen, I say, the real end of such unjust proceedings would arrive much sooner than you now suspect. Helen's mind was resolutely made up when the sickness seized hold of her : every day is now giving her new bodily strength ; and notwithstanding those half amiable terms which exist at present between yourself and her, she has not forgotten the past, and she means, before many weeks, to assert her recollection of it. I call such assertion on Helen's part the real end of your gross misconduct, and I do so for the simple reason that if it came to a question of whether you or she left my house—"

He interrupted the august tones right irreverently, at this point. "I should have to go, of course : I know that well enough. And the money would stop with my departure."

"Precisely."

More silence. The sound of advancing steps. Was

13

he coming toward my retreat? No; his steps had
turned away from the parlor threshold, were taking an
opposite direction.  I soon knew how' it was; he had
begun pacing that small circular hall in which they had
met together.

And now mamma again spoke, her voice all frigid
severity, yet having a vague touch in its tone of something like entreaty :

"I have no doubt, Fuller—I cannot have a vestige
of doubt—that all this has occurred to you, has been
food for certain reflections long before now.  You must
have thought, also, that the end of your difficulties
could easily be brought about.  It was not hard to do
before Helen's illness; it is still not hard.  If you were
willing to make the attempt, your success would be
rapid and thorough.  There need be no self-humilia-
tion; no absurd asking for pardon.  You could go to
Helen and state facts plainly.  You could tell her that
although you had once broken your word to her in the
matter of continuing to know that woman—"

"I never broke my word."  He was still pacing the
floor with quick firm steps.  "I never once promised
that I would cease to see her.  The only lie (to call
things by their exact names) which I have ever told with
regard to this affair, was told when I promised you that
from the time I became engaged to Helen I should
date my cessation of a certain intimacy.  But when you
came to me after that adventure in the Park, with news
of how furiously Helen had put her foot down, I would
not, nor could you make me, repeat the promise which
I had not formerly had the strength to keep.  Whatever you then told Helen you told on your own responsibility."

"Strength to keep!" mamma iterated, in harshest

murmur. "Your strength is tenfold greater than that part of it which you merely choose to exert, Fuller."

His answer seemed to me wrenched out of a tormented spirit. "You understand nothing of the case. I might be strong enough, myself, never to go near her again, if only she would aid me. But she doesn't and will not aid me. She—"

"Pray curtail any such explanations," broke in mamma's shocked voice. "Of course you know that they are not for My ears. Moreover, we had better at once end our discussion. If the one powerful result of your present behavior does not affect you on hearing it prophesied, I know of nothing that will."

"Do you think it an easy matter for me to break loose?" He spoke the words in a kind of devil-may-care undertone, so low that I could just catch them and no more.

"You can break loose, as you term it, to-morrow, if you desire. I am simply sure that you can. And it is boyish, it is doltish for you to rush headlong into such complete social disaster. You are not a man who can afford to pooh-pooh the world : you love its good opinion too well for that ; you would be miserable if deprived of its countenance. Already your misdemeanors are stealing into public knowledge, though I will admit, gradually. There is a nucleus, perhaps, of some fifteen men (most of them your professed friends) who are aware of that intimacy. This nucleus may enlarge before long, into something like notoriety. Some people affirm, now ; but some deny. Whilst this difference exists, whilst you have the vast advantage of being publicly seen in Helen's and my society, and whilst you are possessed of liberal funds, you hold at your command a perpetual refutation of scandal. But you know

New York. Let all this end to-morrow : let it be said to-morrow that Fuller Dobell no longer lives with his wife and that his pockets narrowly escape emptiness. What would follow ? The name you bear might get you noticed at your club, perhaps, but though fathers and sons bowed to you, mothers and daughters would soon look another way when you met them. You know New York, I repeat, with its curious conflicting laws and by-laws :—how it frowns here and winks there ; how it will swallow this criminality, and make mouths at that peccadillo ; how it is a sort of Paris in hobble-dehoyhood, with some pruderies that are its vestiges of virtue and with many laxities that are its inroads of corruption. You are safe to-day ; you may be in dire danger to-morrow. Put forward one stout effort—break loose as you yourself have called it—and the result is certain."

It was some time before he answered her. Whilst she spoke I could hear that he had stopped walking. Presently he murmured :

" I do not think there is any use of our talking any longer."

" I agree with you. There is not." Mamma's tones were icelike. " I do not doubt that you saw your future just as clearly before I tried to show it you."

" I did."

" Very well. Our conversation began, I believe, by that request of yours for money. You have largely overdrawn what was stipulated in our agreement. Still, I will give you a cheque to-morrow morning. I cannot say that I will do so again ; I cannot justify myself in doing so now ; I merely give, and that is all."

" I shall not call upon you again. You have my promise to that effect ; and you have never known me to break my promise but once. I think that is the only

time I have ever done it in my life, miserably though I
may have behaved as regards other matters." After
this a little silence, during which I heard the silken rustle of mamma's dress as she went upstairs. Then, in
growled savageness, these words left his lips :

"And if it hadn't been for that curséd golden bait
you fished for me with, I shouldn't be the damned
scamp I am now."

Of course she did not hear him : she must have gotten well out of hearing distance by then.

I have written too much, far too much. My hand
trembles, my head begins to ache ; I scarcely dare write
a page more.

What I have heard has worked strange change in me.
I find myself pitying Fuller passionately, now, and
yearning intensely to aid him. Perhaps I owe him disdain for his weakness ; but I feel the debt of a bitterer
disdain toward the one who so vilely tempted him ;
and by comparison he stands forth almost guiltless.

There is a knowledge for which my inmost soul
thanks God. Coldly and lovelessly as he holds me now
and has held me all along, I am glad with great gladness that his faults are faults forgivable. Not that I
forgive him ; but that *I could* forgive him if, having
once made me his wife with the miserable motives I
know about, he had afterwards learned to love me and
regretted past misdeeds. And among those misdeeds
I no longer place the shrewd sordid cunning of a contemptible aim to marry me. No ; I am sure now that
he went to Pineside with no such aim at all ; that
mamma, in the full armor of her calculating heartless-
ness, fought the battle with his best manly prejudices ;
that she fished for him with the golden bait of which
he spoke, selling me to him. . . . No, no ; I must not

think of it. I must set myself, body and soul, against thinking of it. Such thoughts help to fill mad-houses.

She pointed out Fuller's possible future to him to-night in words of telling force. The idea of saving him from it is going to possess me night and day, I feel certain. If he leaves that woman I will live on with him as his wife. I shall have no further reason to go, then —none, at least, in the eyes of the people we know and mingle with. And even if hurt pride would take a certain cold comfort in our separation, I will deny myself such comfort and accept the sacrifice of sharing his home with a man who holds me, perhaps,

"Something better than his dog, a little dearer than his horse."

But if he still cleaves to her, we must separate. And with our separation comes to him all the calamity mamma prophesied.

How, then, to spare him that calamity? How to devise a means of parting these two? He is not strong enough to break loose of his own accord; I have heard his own lips say so. He is like the drunkard who needs some one to drag him from the fiery lure. If only I could do it all myself, without aid! Yet ah, if only I can do it at all, with aid or without!

The thought flashes across me, right here—' Did ever woman attempt so strange a part as this I long to play? Am I not a sort of monstrosity among wives?— making pity bloom up where only "the red venomous flower" of jealousy or revenge or something of that fierce sort should flourish?'

But how should it concern me what other people would do or think or desire? Let others be others; let me be I.

## CHAPTER XXX.

PRIL 2.—I am really writing this on the morning of the third. It is nearly twelve o'clock
and I have just breakfasted, having taken all
my sleep (dead-tired sort of sleep, too) since some time
in the early morning. What hours for one who was last
week calling herself an invalid! But how much worse,
in a sanitary point of view, are the racking excitements
through which I have just passed!

It makes such a strange story; perhaps the strangest
of any I have yet told in these pages, where I fancy that
since my marriage fact has been trying to get itself
mistaken for fiction. Let me begin at the beginning,
Diary, like a good conscientious tale-teller.

After hearing that conversation from my corner amid
the darkness, I slipped upstairs to my own room.
When mamma followed a regular custom she has adopted during my convalescence of paying me a visit just
before bed-time, she found my door locked and was
curtly told that I had gone to bed. It was true; but
in any case I would not have seen her that night. My
nerves needed a little bracing before we met again. It
was like taking some dreadful dose; one cannot toss
that off bumperwise at a moment's notice.

"I am sorry," she was good enough to lament,

whilst I sneered in silence and was answerless.    That
night I got much more sleep than I had looked for ; the
weakness of recent illness, I think, gave it me.    In the
morning I felt fit for the bracing-process, more or less
accomplished it, and went downstairs.    Mamma was
there alone ; Fuller usually appears at about eleven
o'clock, nowadays, and then (as I heard him state not
long since) goes and breakfasts at the club.

Mamma was pointedly gracious and affable, it occurred to me.    She made my coffee with something
very like a full-blown smile, and though she had finished
her own breakfast deigned to watch mine, leaning back
in her chair with much reposeful magnificence.    I tried
not to be anything but my ordinary self ; I daresay that
I succeeded, for she seemed to detect no atom of difference in my behavior.

" I suppose you don't feel like going for a little while
to-night ? " she presently murmured, in suavest interro-
gation.

" To-night ? "

" You have certainly heard that Lent was over yesterday and that there is the opera-ball to-night at the
Academy ? "

" Oh, yes." I shook my head right decisively.
" But I should not think of going, mamma."

" Just as you please, of course," she acceded.    " It
is for you to judge whether the excitement will be injurious or no.    One of the tickets will remain unused, so
that if at the last moment your mind is changed you can
avail yourself of it.    The ball will be quite a superb
affair and they tell me, too, strikingly select."

" You will not be downstairs among the masquers, I
suppose.    You will have a box."

" Yes.    Cornelia Walters and I are going together.

I daresay Cornelia will desert me for a domino during the evening; it is so like her."

"If there is a shred of respectability attached to the wearing of a domino," I returned, "be sure that Cornelia will never let the occasion slip. It is much too tempting a one."

"Have you seen the tickets?" mamma wanted to know. "If not, stop in the parlor on your way upstairs and take a look at them. They are so pretty."

"Whereabouts in the parlor?" I asked. I had no special interest in seeing the tickets; it would be hard to say why my question was put. But I had reason to remember it before many hours had passed.

"In the cabinet between the front windows; I forget exactly which drawer."

I did not see Fuller all through the day until dinner-time. And during the day, just as I had felt sure on the previous night that they were going to do, thoughts persistently possessed me regarding a means of saving Fuller. "I might be strong enough, myself, never to go near her again, if only she would aid me. But she doesn't and will not aid me"—how those words went and came, came and went through my mind's perplexity, with stubborn persistence of iteration !

Was there not aid somewhere, which needed merely a shrewd enough searcher to find it? I believed so; I could not help believing so. Again and again I paced my floor with hands pressed against either temple and with carpetward eyes. A hundred fragments of expedients were formed and thrown aside—maimed worthless applicants for the work I desired done, not one of them puissant enough to serve as the real knight-errant in my cause. Some little while before dinner-time I had at least reached this understanding with myself: As a

13*

powerful means toward effecting my wishes it was requisite to gain some trustworthy knowledge regarding
the character of the woman, Edith Everdell. Possessing such knowledge, I might have found a stepping-
stone wherewith to mount up toward success. Failing to secure it, my design might miss a most valuable
aid.

Could not Melville Delano supply me with precisely
the knowledge I wanted ? Remembering how prompt
had been his information on this same subject, not long
ago, could I fail to think yes ? As for John Driscoll, his
friendship with Fuller forbade my making an attempt in
his direction. I do not mean that he would ever absolutely serve Fuller in any work against my happiness or
my interest ; I am convinced, in truth, that our present
life together is a keen discomfort to him. But the intimacy exists ; and although Heaven knows he would be
filling an almost sacred office in helping me to serve his
friend, still there is no denying that his part might be
an awkward one. And then that falsehood he told me
about the Delmonico restaurant : or was it a falsehood ?
Well, I cannot blame him badly, and yet pique will be
pique. Anyhow, I was resolved not, if possible, to try
and make him my coadjutor.

It was strongly improbable that I should have a
chance of seeing Melville for some time to come. Parties are infrequent, just now, I told myself, and I should
doubtless not find my way to any more at this fag-end
of the season. How then to bring about a meeting ?

At dinner there was quite a great deal said regarding
the ball. Fuller stated that he would not be able to go
with mamma. He had an engagement at about nine
o'clock ; should probably stop at the club afterwards
and go with some of the men.

"At what time do *you* go, mamma?" I wanted to know. For I had gotten an idea.

"Cornelia is to stop at eleven precisely, though I told her it was too early for a great public ball like this."

"Cornelia doesn't want to miss an atom of the fun," laughed Fuller, whilst annihilating an olive. (I wonder, by the bye, if Cornelia could commit any misdeed, short of homicide, which in the eyes of her brother would not be food for lusty laughter.)

At nine o'clock, or near it, Fuller left the house. A little while before he went I had given a note to Blanche, with instructions that she should attend to its being taken immediately to the club. If the gentleman was not there, I further instructed, they must be told to forward the note at once to his residence. And this is what I had written :

"MY DEAR MR. DELANO:—Can you arrange to come and see me for a few moments after about eleven o'clock this evening? I specially wish to meet you. Come if the Bal d'Opéra, or any other possible engagement, equally pressing, will permit. *There will be no one at home except my-self.*

"Yours very truly,

"HELEN DOBELL."

April 2nd,——Fifth Avenue.

I felt sure that he would come, provided only the note reached him in time. Mamma doubtless expected that I would appear in her dressing-room whilst her toilette was being made ; but I did not go. My mind was in a mood to employ itself upon other matters beside the nice disposition of diamonds and the proper allotment of laces. Somewhat after eleven, Cornelia's carriage arrived, Cornelia herself not alighting. Presently I heard mamma descending into the lower hall. Seated in my own room, just then, I looked at my watch.

It was a trifle more than a quarter past eleven. 'Rather what the thrilling novels, in their fine language, would call an unexpected rencontre,' I thought, 'provided mamma and Melville should meet at the hall-threshold.'

But no such meeting took place. I had waited fully ten minutes after mamma's departure, and was on the brink of ceasing to expect him, when there sounded a ring at the street-door. Presently Melville Delano's card was brought up to me.

I at once went downstairs on receiving it. I found him in the front drawing-room. As he rose and gave me his hand, it flashed across me how handsome a man he was, after his own dark Southern-seeming type. Most men look well in full evening-dress; but those who look very well never appear better than when apart from their own sex.

I seated myself at his side, on the same sofa he was occupying. He first broke silence.

" I have come to you again at your request," he smiled, very quietly.

" Yes. I am glad you came." My words were shortly given. The old feeling was upon me, I suppose; the feeling that has nearly always made me shrink from Melville Delano ever since I knew Fuller at all likingly. His hatred seems to express itself in the mere sound of his voice, and within my own nature a kind of responsive antagonism always rushes to arms.

" In what way can I be of use just now ?" The sneer was perceptible, though very vaguely so, amid this murmured question.

I stared floorward. It had to be spoken ; it might as well be spoken straightforwardly and so gotten over. " I wanted to ask you to tell me about that woman—that Edith Everdell."

" Tell you about her ? "

My cheeks were fiery, by then. I kept my eyes still floorward. "Yes. I supposed that you were familiar with her real character and surroundings. Is there any-thing at all "—the words would hardly come, but I jerked them forth—" good about her ? "

He laughed sharply and briefly. "There ought to be, certainly. I am an optimist, myself, more or less. Anyhow, I don't believe what the cynic says somewhere in Tennyson :

> " Every heart, when sifted well,
> Is a clot of warmer dust,
> Mixed with cunning sparks of hell."

If every heart were that, I wonder how many sparks hers would hold ; " (whilst he laughed between the words.)

" Is she so very dreadful ? "

" She ruined your husband, and other men before she knew him ; though he will not believe as much—indeed, would refuse to believe anything really bad of her if all the world stood as witness for her depravity. It is what people call an infatuation, I suppose."

I somewhat ceased to glare upon the floor, about at this stage of the interview. One can get used to nearly everything, I should judge : I was beginning to lose my first intense diffidence. Possibly, too, because an intenser curiosity was being roused within me every moment.

" Has she no redeeming points ? " Here my voice quivered a little for very eagerness. " I mean, do you not think that one might have it in his power to work on her better nature by force of argument or entreaty or both ? "

He began a faint tattoo on the crown of his opera-hat. "From what I personally know of the woman I answer : it would be impossible. There are different opinions, however. I have heard it stated by some that she has a heart somewhere, deep down in her nature : very deep down, I should fancy. One might say of her as of ' Madame la Marquise ' :

> " Could we find out her heart thro' that velvet and lace !
> Can it beat without ruffling her sumptuous dress ?
> She will show us her shoulder, her bosom, her face,
> But what the heart's like, we must guess."

"Briefly, if you want my own opinion, a person might as well try to discover cardiac symptoms in that bronze young lady on the mantel yonder."

"Do you know her personally ? "

"I used to know her."

"Ever at all well ?"

"Not very."

"Then your statement is open to contradiction."

"I have told you what some opinions are."

"Would you advise me to make any attempt toward persuading her in the matter of giving Fuller up ? "

He answered rapidly, with most emphatic stress on each word : "Indeed I should not! Such an appeal would be nothing except a great triumph to her."

"Are you *sure* of that ? " I asked, with keenly-questioning eyes.

He spoke rather tartly in reply. "Do you doubt the sincerity of my advice, Mrs. Dobell ? "

Disheartenment had irritated me a little, perhaps ; then, too, his words struck a sensitive place—my conviction of his loathing for Fuller.

"Doubt you ? " was my slow response. "I try not

to do so. But then I remember that you hate Fuller; that you must clearly see how he is slipping step by step into a miserable future, now that as a young married man he still dares to pursue, here in New York, the same courses which he pursued as a young unmarried man; and that the thought of any help to him from any quarter must not at all please you."

I spoke whilst staring straight past Melville, only letting my eyes dwell upon his face when I had finished. And then I saw that his face, but for its naturally olive tinge, would have been as white as the cravat he wore.

I half expected one of his passionate eruptions, from the fiery indications his eyes gave me. But none came. I thought then, as I think now, that he found himself in the position, just at this moment, of a man who sees suddenly laid bare some motive which he has believed hidden with complete secrecy; and that Melville had really meant, in discouraging the plan I proposed, to gratify the demands of a hard personal hate.

No; instead of a noisy explosion there was only a moderate shoulder-shrug and a dimly satiric smile; though the paleness went rather contradictingly with these signs. "Do you remember what I said to you at the Romeyns' party this last winter?" he wanted to know, with a voice deep down in his throat. "Surely, if I am worth using I am worth treating civilly; and since you stoop so low as to make me your confederate, you should understand that your own condition suffers a kind of corresponding declension." After that he paused for a little time, his face hardening in every feature. "You are right in telling me that the thought of helping your husband does not at all please me." And then suddenly the very fierceness that I had believed he would not show, leapt into the man's voice and manner. "I do hate Fuller Dobell, just as you are convinced that I hate him. But my hatred has not prevented me from pitying you ; and if, in making you one jot happier I could aid him, you wrong me thoroughly by thinking that I would not sacrifice every personal feeling in your husband's direction."

I laughed coldly, seeing all the while how cruel I was. (Query : is it only the fact of his hatred for Fuller that makes me so often so cruel to this man ? Or is it the knowledge of his persistent unsmothered smouldering love for myself, that sometimes frightens me, sometimes chills me, always keeps me on my guard against an outbreak ?)

" I am afraid that your hatred is the one feeling uppermost," I affirmed, after that cold laugh.

" Try me ! " he burst forth, bringing his lips close to my face. Then all on a sudden I knew that he had seized my hand and was deluging it with kisses many and hot. By main force I dragged it angrily away.

The action seemed only to lend him fresh passion. " No, Helen Dobell," the heavy bass murmur of his voice was now tremulously telling me, " love is uppermost, not hatred. How could I fail to be glad that you knew of your husband's treachery, his rascality, his complete unworthiness ? Like a wretched fool I kept silent when they were marrying you to him ; like a wretched fool I did not speak the words that you must have believed and that would have saved you all this misery. For after a little time, in that case, when the wound of your discovery was well healed, who knows but that this deep love of mine might have found— "

I sprang away from him just as his hand was touching my arm. I must have been colorless to my lips whilst I stood facing him, with furious eyes.

"Mr. Delano," I cried, "pray remember who I am."
He was not a whit daunted, but rose also and made an
eager though futile grasp at my hand. I was frightened, then. Something almost like madness seemed to
look at me from his black lurid eyes. I stood quite
still whilst he spoke again, staring away from him, trying to make my face rigid and frigid as stone.

"Oh, Helen, the idea that you do really care for me
—that you see the bitter mistake of your marriage—
that you regret your hard treatment and are willing, in
so far as you can, to amend it—that you hide under all
your coldness and cruelty and the seeming wish to make
me your servant, feelings of a far different sort—the
idea of these things, I say, has stolen upon me by slow
degrees since the first time we met after your marriage.
I told you, on our second meeting at the opera, that I
was your mere tool during the night previous, and that
every smile you gave me was given for some politic
purpose of your own. But I did not wholly believe
this then ; I do not wholly believe it now. Perhaps my
uncertainty is better than complete despair, but I long
for the real truth. Think a moment before you answer.
Now that Fuller has shown himself so meanly unworthy
of you, does your memory never revert to the days
when my intense and lifelong love waited for your least
sign of encouragement, not daring to put itself in
words ? Have you no regret—?"

I stopped him, then, not expecting that I could really
succeed in doing so. The result, as it proved, amazed
me.

"Do you remember the note which you received
from me to-day?" I broke in, making my voice ring
cold and clear as smitten metal will sometimes do. "In
it I wrote these words : *There will be no one at home*

*except myself.* I think it was that which brought you here. Otherwise I believe you would not be the coward you show yourself now."

Yes, the result of those few words was a matter to amaze. All the fire and force seemed to die out of the man on the instant. He shot me one reproachful look from those superb eyes of his—a look that I was far too angry, no doubt, to value at its pathetic worth. Then he threw himself on the sofa and buried his face in both hands.

I began slowly to walk the floor. He gave no evidence of any tearful weakness; he merely sat quite still, with buried face. I suppose that fully five minutes passed in this way.

At length he abruptly uncovered his face, rose and drew near me. I saw that he was quite pale and that his eyes had a dulled saddened look, in sharp contrast with their previous fervor.

"Good night, Mrs. Dobell. I daresay I have been very rude. If any apology will be taken I am ready to make it. You probably do not want me to stay any longer?"

I did want him to stay longer. "If you will behave yourself," I conditioned, severely, "you will please me by answering a few more questions."

There was a faint irony in the smile that just rimmed his lips. "I promise to behave myself."

Somehow his changed manner had at once restored my confidence, frightened as I had been a little while ago. Doubtless it was because I saw that the change had been genuine and radical; that my slur-tipped arrow had told; that the odd reckless headlong creature I have always found him was for a time restored to his senses. He would be tractable now, I felt certain, through the rest of the interview.

And he was. We seated ourselves again, presently. "I wanted to ask you more about this woman," I plunged. "How long has she known Fuller?"

"Seven or eight years, I believe."

"Can you tell me anything about her life before she met him?"

"No. I know nothing of her origin. It would be hard to find anyone who does, I think. She burst upon New York suddenly one winter."

"And her life since then; has it been worse than Fuller believes? Does she deceive him at all, or is he aware of the exact truth regarding all her actions? Pray think a moment before you answer these questions."

"It is not in the least necessary;" (with a light laugh.) "She is well known to make Fuller Dobell believe that black is white, as regards her own personal behavior. Grosser deception was never seen. He thinks her a kind of Eloise; inprudent, if you will, but pardonable because of her love, although surrounded by associates of her own sex whose character he well knows. Whilst in reality she is much more like a sort of modern Messalina. It is a joke among not a few of Fuller Dobell's friends."

"Why does no one open his eyes?"

"I cannot tell. No one does. Men are so punctilious before each other's faces, you know, about minding their own business."

"But there is John Driscoll, at least—Fuller's most intimate friend."

"John Driscoll is a man of the world; the most complete one I ever met. He knows the folly of making trouble by unsolicited interference. Do you suppose that if John Driscoll attempted to undeceive his friend, that friend would at first believe him? Indeed, he might not ever succeed in winning credence at all. Anyhow, there would be a long fight between Edith Everdell and John Driscoll. If I were betting on such a contest I should give odds on the woman's side."

A silence. Melville took out his watch. "It is nearly twelve o'clock," he told me. "I am afraid that I shall have to leave you. I promised, as it is, to be at the ball this evening by eleven."

"Fuller and mamma have both gone," I made words, whilst in a sort of reverie. Melville's late intelligence had set me thinking.

"Have they gone together?" he wanted to know, with rather strong emphasis.

"No." I glanced quickly into his face. "Why do you ask?"

"Oh, nothing." He rose, then. "I must say good-night once again."

"This ball is to be very select, is it not?" I asked, ignoring his good-night.

"They tell me so. But I have heard, by the way—"

"Well, what have you heard?"

"It was a mere rumor, and a whispered one at that."

"What was it?"

"That Edith Everdell was to be on the floor, among the masquers."

"And you do not believe it true?"

"It is quite possible. If she expressed the wish to go, there is one person who has just the daring requisite for getting her there."

"You mean Fuller?"

"I mean your husband—yes."

A silent interval. Melville moved away from me. Presently, with his face and voice the soul of composure,

"Whether I have lost the right to offer you advice or not," he murmured, " I cannot help feeling that you wrong yourself miserably by continuing to live with that man. No woman's dignity should stoop so low." Then, seeing me toss my head intolerantly, he turned, and without another word walked from the room.

I forgot him nearly as soon as he was out of sight. I do not even remember hearing him close the lower hall-door. My mind was full of more important things. Because this man had counselled me to cease living with Fuller I did not the less feel intense longings to save him. Had I not sent for Melville Delano as a means of helping myself toward this end?

And what chances were found open to me? Ah, what, indeed! He had painted her a hard cold-souled creature, on whom all persuasion would be wasted. He had shown up her moral life in the vilest colors, making her really unreachable in the matter of an interview. Before, there had seemed a spark of possibility that I might meet her face to face and plead Fuller's cause; but now there could be no such meeting.

Except at the ball to-night: that would be a meeting not face to face, but masque to masque.

I fell to pacing the floor presently, with my chin pressed into the palm of my hand. Dare I go? And yet why not dare? It was my one opportunity of exerting this ardent new-found strength, rooted in my ineradicable love for Fuller. Better that I should try, even against such ponderous pressure of failure. Better any kind of effort than effortless and tame surrender.

I could go to the ball if I wanted. There was no fairy godmother needed to get me ticket and masque and domino and carriage. A moment's search among the drawers of the cabinet mamma had indicated,

brought the hidden ticket to light.    Upstairs, among
my wardrobe, there was a great voluminous black-silk
domino and its concomitant masque, which I had worn
only about a year ago at Mrs. Chamberlane's masquerade.   (Ah me ! how time has slipped along, bringing merciless changes !   How I thrilled triumphantly
under my disguise when John Driscoll, puzzled to his
finger-nails, at last groaned in my ear : " If you only
satisfy this craving curiosity of mine and tell me who
you are, I absolutely promise to be your lifelong
slave ! ")    And as for the carriage, could not an immediate order be sent to John for the coupé ?

It was just for a moment after this that I stood, ticket
in hand, bracing my courage, as the runner stands
bracing his muscles before he starts.    Then I walked
toward the bell and rang it.

Enter Henry.    In a little while I had given the order
about getting the coupé.   " And send Blanche to me
immediately," I added.

I do not at all doubt that Henry believed me quite
out of my head as he left the drawing-room.    But he
was his usual obeisant self.    Being such a perfect servant, very possibly if I had gibbered and made a mouth ·
at the end of my order, he would merely have replied
with the most respectful of bows.

## CHAPTER XXXI.

"I SHALL want you to go with me in the carriage," I told Blanche; "but that is all. It is not very nice to think of coming home alone in a common hack, but one is obliged to take the first carriage that offers at these public balls. I should like to have you in the dressing-room whilst I take off my cloak, and have you go with me as far as the ball-room door, but that cannot be, I suppose."

Blanche looked virtuously appalled. And was it possible that madame would dare to go into the ball-room quite alone?

The thought did give me a faint chill; but my first step had been taken and I was far from feeling in at all a regressive mood.

"Remember that I shall be masked," I laughed; "and then mamma will be in the house, besides—" I was going to add "Mr. Dobell," but I felt the keen absurdity and stopped. "By the bye, Blanche, I have told you that I wish my going kept a strict secret from mamma, unless I myself choose to tell her. If she hears that I have gone I shall know from whom first came the information."

Blanche was very glib with her copious assurances of secrecy. My toilette lasted only a short time. I was ready some little while before the coupé arrived. After

Blanche and I had entered the coupé (myself already masked) I seemed suddenly to realize the daring of what I was going to do. It swept across me blightingly, as far as boldness went; I felt all my fine courage shrivelling leafwise under this abrupt frost of fear. What if my appearance attracted attention? What if I were grossly insulted? What if the door-keeper refused to let me pass, masked as I was and quite companionless?

But I fought against the growing cowardice. Nothing could be less noticeable than my dark commonplace domino. If I were grossly insulted my masque would be my safeguard. Should the door-keeper refuse to admit me I had only to murmur my name, or at best mamma's: years of opera-going ought to advantage me then.

By the time that we stopped at the entrance of the Academy I had nearly recovered my former nerve. I was unprepared for the staring crowd that besieged the door of the coupé: this set my heart beating a little. But then it would only be a brisk dash through the lane of persons up into the doorway beyond.

Just before we stopped I began rapidly to address Blanche. "I shall be home as near half-past one as possible. If mamma or Mr. Dobell reaches home before I do, say nothing about my absence unless it is discovered. And if it is discovered do not mention my having received any visitor in the earlier part of the evening. You may tell John that he is not to return for me. I could not find him, and they will not let people call for their own carriages at these great balls." ·

And then the coupé-door was thrown open by a stately policeman. For a half-second, perhaps, I sat motionless, feeling myself in the cold sudden grip of a severe dread. 'Shut the carriage-door,' something seemed to whisper, 'and be driven home again.'

Half a second is a mere droplet of time ; and yet I do
not think my hesitant state lasted as long as this. For
I rose with teeth clinched behind my masque, hurried
out on the pavement, shot through the throng that filled
it and reached the bright-lit regions beyond. The door-
keeper took my ticket questionlessly ; that supposed
peril was past. I soon reached the dressing-room,
where, owing to the lateness of the hour, I had prompt
attention.

And now, as I left the dressing-room and glided
downstairs among the lobbies to the ball-room, a feeling of strange courageous confidence began to glow
within me. It was almost as if I had just drunken a few
swallows of rich vein-warming wine. My first fears had
all taken wing. The people whom I met among the
lobbies passed me with scarcely a noticing eye-sweep,
all the men being unmasked, all the women masked.
Evidently I was free to move here, there, everywhere,
without my black unconspicuous domino doing more
than just form material for careless observance.

This confidence grew a reckless daring when I entered
the ball-room. The glitter and gayety would in any
case have excited me, after the utter quiet in which I
had been living. But added to excitement I felt a spirit
of bitter mischief possess and animate me. It was because of my dull heartache, doubtless. When one is
miserable as I was, the best amusement one can get is
a sort of cynic amusement, I suppose. Everywhere
about me were men whom I knew ; concerning many
of them I knew scandalous things.

Having had this whole quiverful of arrows handed me
by circumstance, so to speak, why not empty it whilst
I searched for her whom I had come to find ?

I did empty it. Just at my elbow stood Charley Ber-
14

tram, in a little throng of intimates. I fixed fearless eyes upon him.

"Well, Mr. Bertram," my disguised voice saluted him.

"Well, madam," he replied, with immènse civility.

"Can't you get *anybody* to help you back to England? It's really dreadful. You only need a few more years of training in the mother-country. As it is, you know, you're neither one thing nor the other."

I turned and slipped away just in time to see the smiles on his friends' faces and the half-controlled rage on my victim's.

After that I searched for a little while, scrutinizing every woman whom I met. There was not one who had her walk; not one whose height and figure and general movements made me do anything but doubt if it were she. Then I began to scatter my impertinences broadcast, still searching, searching. Here stood Aleck Sheffield, good pleasant nonentity, who has never done me an ill turn in all our ball-room acquaintance together: yet I was merciless, craven-hearted. "Is it true that you wear stays?" I wanted to know, tapping him on the shoulder. "I've never believed it, but nearly everybody else does." And I vanished from him just as the color was surging up furiously to his blond hair.

Search, search.

There stood that pompous old Jacob Holladay, who ranks himself about the supremest social potentate in all New York, having himself fawned upon by a little court of men and women. Respectability diffused itself from the feathery gray of his chin-divided beard to his golden festoon of watch-chain, and thence downward in a rather curved course (for he has marked stomachic attributes) to his lustrous shoes. "Nobody can understand what you see to admire in that ugly little actress at Niblo's," I dared to rattle off, as I darted past him ; and by the glance shot over my shoulder I saw his Olympian brows gather and his face take quite an apoplectic hue.

Search, search.

" They call you Mrs. Louis Walters' bouquet-holder," I snarled in the startled ear of Summerby. . . . " Give up fortune-hunting," I hissed to Johnny Wilcoxson, " and perhaps you won't be jilted nearly every season." . . . . " Why are you such a thorough-going snob ? " I wanted to know of Winny Westerveldt. " It's currently reported that you boasted of passing through college without speaking to but three men in your class."

Search, search.

" Is it a fact," I questioned of Harry Averill, " that you cut an intimate friend for presuming to import and wear a pair of trowsers precisely like one of your own ? " . . . . " If you wish to know why everybody asks you to lead cotillons everywhere," I sneered in the ear of Willie Gregory, " don't look an inch higher than your heels for the reason." . . . . " Have you found out the cause yet of your being so badly treated at parties ? " I confidentially murmured to Fred Martelle. " Don't ask ladies to dance with you after more than two glasses of wine ; depend upon it, that is about your limit."

Search, search.

It seemed as if I had no chance of finding her. Perhaps she was not there. Melville Delano had merely spoken of her coming as a probability, and not a very strong one, either. Presently I caught a glimpse of Frank Meredith's bluff queer little person. He would be sure to know if she were on the floor, provided any one knew. Dare I ask him ?

But I was in just a mood to dare do anything, then. Up to his side I glided.  "Mr. Meredith?"

All his handsome wine-reddened face, with its jaunty little brass-colored moustache, broke wrinklingly into one large smile.  " At your service, Mrs. Anybody."

"Mrs. Somebody, eef you please," I objected, in the Frenchest sort of broken English I could master.  " I want to ask you a dreadfule question.  Ah, it ees so dreadfule !  Will you promise to answer it for me and then to let me go in peace?"

He peered into my masque as though his funny black eyes could pierce it needlewise.  " I shall do all that I am able, pray believe, my charming little Frenchwoman. If I could only say with one of your own poets :

> *" Ah fine barbe de dentelle,*
> *Que fait voler un souffle pur,*
> *Cet arpège m'a dit :  " C'est elle !*
> *Malgré tes réseaux, j'en suis sûr."*

But I can't, unluckily."

"If I were to seeng anything for you," I laughed, " it wouldn't at all favor the recogneetion.  My voice could wreeng contempt from a peacock.  Are you ready for ze question, monsieur?"

" Entirely."

" Well, I want to ask if you know a certaine not nice woman by sight ;—not nice at all.  Edeeth Everdell, she is called.  You know her?"

" Perfectly."

" Is she here to-night?"

" She is here."

" Will you point her out?"

" She is just at your elbow, madame.  There is no mistaking that figure and carriage, especially as her domino shows both very plainly."

No mistaking them indeed ! I had not seen her until now. I am nearly certain that I should have known her, had we met previously, without Mr. Meredith's help. Two or three men were about her. I hurried away, keeping her in sight, not wishing, if possible, that Frank Meredith should see me addressing her after what had just passed.

A sudden disheartenment had seized me. After all, I asked myself, would it be possible for me to get her attention as long as I wished it ? And even then how wild, how vain the hope of even changing her by word of mine !

Well, well, I could but try. Presently I slipped up to where she was standing. Frank Meredith was some distance off, by this time. I drew nearer, nearer. A sweet rich rippling laugh was just leaving her lips, clear-heard above the music, when I at length stood beside her. "I want to speak with you for a little while, if you will let me," I murmured. I did not disguise my voice, feeling that there was no need.

"With me ?" was the low response ; too low for her surrounders to hear. "How odd. I didn't suppose that any of my own sex here this evening were anything but oppositely inclined." (Then a light little laugh.) "You see that I dare to hint who I am."

"I know who you are," I answered. "Will you come ?"

"Come where, Madam Mystery ?"

"Not out of the ball-room, but where we can talk together a little more privately—away from these gentlemen."

How her eyes fixed themselves upon mine ! I almost quailed under their cold bold brilliance. "Very well," she presently murmured, in slow puzzled style. "I will go with you."

I moved away, at this, looking across my shoulder to
see if she would follow. She left at once the small
group of men, waving one or two of them back with a
little gesture of disdainful grace.

I found an almost vacant line of seats near the wall,
under the ceiling of the upper tier, and beyond the real
limits of the ball-room. My heart made rapid throbs
as I watched her seat herself at my side. No one could
overhear us ; we were unnoticed of anyone, now ; we
were virtually closeted with each other, private amid all
this publicity.

How should I begin ? Let there be no wordy flourishes. Hopeless as my cause was, let me at least urge it
with hardy straightforwardness.

" You are Edith Everdell," I plunged.

" I am Edith Everdell."

" Did Fuller Dobell bring you here to-night ? "

She shrugged her shoulders. " I choose to answer
no such questions. I came here ; that ought to satisfy
you."

" You refuse to answer any questions concerning Fuller Dobell ? " I made my voice even-toned, tranquilly
emphatic. " Then you will not tell me why you are
doing your best to break his wife's heart."

I knew instantly that my words were an unforeseen.
lunge to her ; the sudden start she gave told me this.
Yet a little laugh, like nothing but the quintessence of
scorn, broke through the lace-fall of her masque almost
instantly.

" I feel honored at being considered of so much importance in Mrs. Dobell's eyes."

" You are of great importance," I stated, stifling the
anger that began at once to swell my heart. " She
recognizes and admits your beauty, your cleverness,

your power over her husband. She would never have married that husband if she had known you held such power."

"Pshaw!" A sneer mixed itself harshly with her mellow melodious tones. "She would have married him anyhow: pray don't try and deceive me with any such plausible stuff as that."

"I assure you she would have done nothing of the sort."

"But in any case her mother would have made her. It was a matter of plain give and take. Those Jeffreys wanted the prestige of the connection. I know Mrs. Jeffreys' type, if you please: I have seen it before now —occasionally, too, (in different times and in a different city) laughed at it as we laugh at amusing inferiors. I suppose you are some friend of Mrs. Dobell's. It hardly seems possible that you can be Mrs. Dobell herself."

"You have guessed rightly. I am a friend of Mrs. Dobell's; I am also a friend of her husband. I desire to aid them both, but chiefly him. He is on the verge of a most miserable condition. If his intimacy with you continues many weeks longer, his wife will have ceased to live with him, he will have lost money and caste, he will hold an almost pitiable place compared to that which he holds now. For this reason I have resolved to plead with you in his behalf. I have resolved to beg of you that you will cease knowing him. Mrs. Dobell does not require her husband's love: she merely requires that his infidelity shall not render her marriage the burlesque it has become, and that the world shall not make her a laughing-stock because of her husband's behavior. Fuller Dobell has only to take one step in freeing himself from danger. Will you counsel him to

take that step, or will you coldly lead him past his opportunity ?   God knows he deserves to be far less leniently dealt with ! "                          •

   " Less leniently dealt with ! " she iterated, in stinging mockery of voice.   " And by whom, pray ?   By
the wife who is most probably his match in all wrong-
doing, although she plasters her deeds over with a trifle
more discretion ? "

   I felt my cheeks burn tinglingly beneath my masque.
I was angry with much anger.   I think it marvellous
that I kept my passion within bounds, right here, considering how it tugged to break restraints.

   " Have you an atom of proof," I asked, finding strong
difficulty in getting the words spoken, " that Mrs. Dobell's character is not quite above suspicion ? "

   "Proof!" she laughed, with caustic force.   "Who
cares for proof?   Not I, indeed !   I am no such fool
that I cannot use the few senses I have had given me.
I know the kind of life she lives, and the men and
women who help her live it.   They are all alike, and
she is one of them.   They have immense resources of
concealment—that is about the only way in which they
differ from other sinners.   They are *so* respectable, you
know, and *so* finely educated !   Who *could* suspect them
of any real harm ?   Fast ? oh, yes ; undoubtedly fast.
But fast, after all, means so little !   Meanwhile their
wealth and that farce of their position covers multitudes
of abominations."

   I ought to have gone away then—before then.   An
excellent safeguard against making a fool of oneself is
to know precisely when one is going to do it.   I had
such prescience, beyond any doubt.   Whilst she was
speaking I had experienced the infallible signs of having cheeks that had grown fire-coals and a heart that

has gotten to beat gallopingly and to feel as if it only lacked about an inch of your throat. I should have understood these symptoms; I have had them before, in greater or less degrees.

Instead of going away, I staid and answered with all possible heat:

"You merely show an absurd ignorance when you talk like that. All women of your stamp talk so, I have often heard. I suppose it is a way they have of easing their consciences for the atrocities they commit. Then, too, things are apt to appear pretty black when we look at them through the burnt-glass of our own depravity."

Every vestige of music had left her voice, as her reply rang rapidly. "Whatever stamp I may wear now, I once wore the stamp of your so-styled respectability. I have known the classes to which you doubtless pride yourself upon belonging; and I found them liars and hypocrites through and through."

"I don't believe you," I flashed. "If you had ever belonged among really respectable people you would still bear some moral traces of your past life. You would at least not be the gross deceiver you are."

"What do you mean?"

"Do you suppose that you can continue much longer to throw dust in Fuller Dobell's eyes?" I rushed on, without noticing her quick hoarsely-spoken question. "You know very well that he believes you love him and that he believes this love the only stain upon your purity. And in reality you are the precise horrible reverse of what he thinks. No wonder that you dare slander Mrs. Dobell." (I rose here, for a dim gleam of prudence had begun to break skywise through my storm of passion.) "How should such a creature as you are do anything but deal in falsehood?"

14*

It was just as I finished speaking that she sprang up from her seat and came very close to me. "Perhaps you think you can say these things with safety," she hurried, her voice sounding all husky and rage-choked, "because I am here where I have no business to be—here among your own company of *more success-ful* evil-doers. But I warn you—"

And then I was out of hearing, having slipped away from her and hastened toward the multitude. For a little space I wandered about, (passing Fuller, just at this time, with some unknown masque on his arm) whilst bitterest qualms of self-reproach momently assailed me with greater force.

And so I had made a most wretched failure. Was not the failure more than half my own fault? Had I not thrown away recklessly even my one vague little chance of influencing this woman? Now that the "heat and flame of my distemper" were cooling, I began to call myself fool with despondent emphasis.

Suddenly a hand touched my shoulder, I looked quickly round. She had followed and found me again. Her voice seemed more husky, more rage-choked than ever, as she now addressed me.

"Whoever you are, whether Fuller Dobell's wife or some messenger of hers, I want you to know this: I shall hold fast of Fuller Dobell as long as I can, and I do not mean that anybody in all New York shall frighten me into giving him up. As for his wife, who doubtless married him with an idea that I was an en-cumbrance of no possible importance and that I was promptly to be suppressed and put out of the way after his marriage, let her and let that grand old snob, her mother, (now fanning herself so superbly upstairs in yonder box) understand that each has reckoned wrongly in her shrewd matrimonial scheme, and that I am not quite so easily waived aside and forgotten as some few other of Mr. Dobell's bachelor-peccadilloes. I naturally hated Mrs. Dobell, not for being his wife but because her influence drew him away from me a little while, and made me fight to regain him. But I never really feared her; and I tried to show her this three or four times: once in Stewart's store, once during that absurd break-down in the Park where she behaved like such a child-ish fool, and once again when we met in Delmonico's. No; I never feared her. Bear this message, if you are not Mrs. Dobell herself, as I believe you are not. Say that I am a rock, and she needn't bruise her nice white fingers trying to budge me."

"You need have no fear that she will try," came my response, in a kind of composed mutter. "There are other ways of working besides with one's fingers. Fuller Dobell may be grossly infatuated, but black is black and white is white, and he must believe his own senses. There is such a thing as convincing a man against his will, provided he be of sound intellect."

I was hurrying away when she caught the sleeve of my domino. "Who are you?" Her voice was that of a woman whom fury has well in its hot hold. "I must know. I *shall* know."

And whilst speaking she made a sudden dash toward my masque with her right hand, as though to tear it from my face.

Luckily I saw her hand lift itself just in time for the proper evasive swerve. I remember feeling miserably frightened as I sped through the crowd after that, eager to mix myself therewith and so permanently escape her. All my past daring and hardihood and confidence had vanished mistwise, now; for they were all a bravery that only had root in my incognita, and the assault upon this struck them a life-blow.

There had been something tigerlike in the woman's gesture. She was in a passion and had nothing to lose : under circumstances of this favoring character it would be difficult to say what limit of recklessness she would pause at.

I should have gone immediately out into the hall and made an attempt to obtain a carriage, had not a feeling of dread prevented this step. How could I tell that she might not follow me and commit a fresh assault, in her headlong fury?

No ; it was best to make sure that I had lost myself to her. Then home with all the expedition attainable. Home without even getting my cloak from upstairs. Home, indeed! And why had I ever at all been idiot enough to leave home ?

At length, after liberal gliding about here, there, everywhere, I came to a stand-still, looked around me and waited. Heavens! there she stood also, not ten yards off, evidently believing herself in efficient ambuscade behind a stout blue domino, and evidently watching me.

I did more hurrying about, with similar results. For a third time I made myself the most active sort of nomad, and a very will-o'-the-wisp, besides, in the matter of deceptive turns and transits. This final effort lasted quite a while, half because I had resolved that it *should* be final, and that after it I should in any case make an attempt to get home ; and half because I dreaded to stop and take my third outlook.

As it was I stopped, but no outlook followed. There was none necessary. For I had no sooner ceased moving than something caught my sleeve, and there she stood, unescapable as fate, close at my side again !

I dragged my sleeve away whilst she burst forth in the same low roughened rageful voice :

" I *shall* find out who you are. I know I'm a devil when I'm angry, and your fine threats have made me so now. Or if not angry, curious to—"

She would have finished her sentence by tearing off my masque. Heaven knows how I ever had the quickness to escape for the second time that sudden and swift dash of her hand. I think that the fact of my having survived the first attack unscathed was a reason for my having defeated the second. Anyhow, I know that before she had more than quarter accomplished her ugly fierce faceward plunge, I had gotten well beyond her reach.

After that I rushed blindly, dizzily, straight against a gentleman.

" Pray excuse me," I murmured, not looking up.

" I thought I knew your walk," whispered Melville Delano, quietly, " when you passed me a little while ago. But I am sure now that I know your voice, Mrs. Dobell."

I caught his arm with force. "Since you know me, help me."

He lifted puzzled brows ; doubtless because my voice was so fearful and tremulous. Then a slight smile played about his mouth. " I am doubly fortunate this evening, am I not ? In what way do you require help ? "

I motioned with my head toward where she was standing, her eyes leveled in hard stare upon Melville, and seeming wholly undismayed at my present course, to judge from her nearness and a certain defiant poise of her head. " That woman," I galloped, " has twice tried to tear off my masque. I came here because you told me that you thought she would be among the guests. We had some conversation together, and it has resulted in this."

"In what?" His brows had begun to knit themselves darkly, and those thin nostrils of his to quiver queerly.

"Why, in her following me about wherever I go and making these dreadful assaults upon me. She says she is determined to find out who I am. I feel afraid, because of her behavior, to leave the ball-room. And I want to get home with all speed. Can't you put me into a carriage and send me there?"

"Certainly." He offered his arm, which I took with glad eagerness. "I will ride home with you myself. It was a wild idea, your coming alone!" Whilst speaking his eyes were steadily riveted upon Edith Everdell, who stood immovable, staring at him in return.

Melville drew me directly toward her, as if to show how resolved he was in the matter of protecting me against any further insolence. She never budged as we passed her, only following us with her eyes, in an unlessened scrutiny. I was on the side farthest away from her and relieved to be there.

We had perhaps taken twenty steps, after that, when I turned and glanced across my shoulder. "Heavens!" I murmured, nervously, "she is close behind us."

Melville wheeled about on the instant, whilst I clung to his arm. He was in one of his passions, unless his fierce clouded face told a wholly wrong story.

The music had just stopped. Above the babble of many encompassing voices Melville's voice rang out harsh and hard.

"You have no business to follow this lady and insult her as you have done."

She drew suddenly backward, as though his abrupt attack was a most unforeseen one. Several people about us who had heard Melville's loud aggressive voice if they had failed precisely to catch his words, began to draw nearer and to stare very curiously.

But after that sudden withdrawal and after standing for a moment as though irresolute, she tossed her head with an impetuous force and came several steps forward again. Then she spoke in that same low furious voice : I have never known a voice express deeper rage, half smothered though it was :

"The person you are with insulted me first, if you please, under cover of her masque."

"Come," I whispered, excitedly, to Melville. "People are beginning to notice us. Pray come."

"She offered you no personal violence, whatever she may have said," flashed Melville's sharp retort. "And you will oblige us both by ceasing to follow us." *

Whereupon she drew nearer yet. "I shall go where I choose to go, and ask from you, sir, no permission in the matter of my going."

Both voices had been very loud. There was quite a little audience gathered about us, now. "For Heaven's sake come," I moaned at Melville's side, pulling at the arm which did not yield a jot.

"You dare to tell me," he cried, "that you will again attempt to unmask this lady ?"

"And suppose I do dare," she flung back.

"Only this : that if you make such an attempt once again I will have you removed from the floor. Most of the committee must be much mortified as it is to know of your presence here to-night. And whoever brought you here deserves the censure of all respectable attendants."

"I beg of you to come," I faltered, getting weak with alarm; for now we were the centre of a thick throng.

My voice seemed to touch him with a sudden sense of what needless fright he was causing me. Leaning abruptly toward me, he glanced down at my black-satin face and doubtless saw with pity the intense appeal that I tried to make my eyes give its ugly featurelessness. After that I am sure that he was on the point of turning with me and using all admissible speed in quitting the ball-room. As it was, we had even half-turned when somebody parted the circle of people about us and hurried up to Edith Everdell's side.

The somebody was Fuller Dobell.

It was the hotel-piazza scene intensified;—this thought swept through my mind, pointed with a kind of frightful humor. Here were we four actors in that other scene brought together again under such different yet such similar circumstances. Here were Fuller and Melville Delano glaring at each other, just as before; here were that woman and myself, with the strange change of being both masked: but in place of the spectatorless quiet which then surrounded us—oh, when I think of that neck-craning crowd I turn numb, in horrible memorial respect to the numbness that pervaded me last night!

Fuller was dead white and had blazing eyes. Whilst giving his arm to the creature he had come to defend, his look measured Melville with an arrogant composure. You saw at once that although both men may have been equally enraged, Fuller was the man who had his anger best in leash.

And his voice was all evenness and iciness. "This lady, sir, is here under my protection, and for whatever

impertinence you offer her you will be answerable to
myself."

Melville instantly sprang nearer the speaker, dragging
me after him. For the moment I was too weak to resist : I let myself be dragged.

"This lady, as you choose to call her, is a disreputable person and has no business to be here this evening."

"What you say is a lie, and you shall be made to
retract it," came the fleet retort.

"Suppose you make me retract this as well."

So much Melville Delano said. What he did simultaneously was to lift his right hand and to snap with
sharp sound across Fuller's cheek the loose glove he
carried.

I saw Fuller square himself like a pugilist, on the instant ; saw him shoot out a quick blow with his left
arm ; saw three or four hands seize hold of the arm before it had more than half reached its place of aim ; saw
Fuller pushed violently backward ; and lastly found
myself pushing wildly forward through a wall of people,
whilst gasping out "Let me pass ; let me pass !"

Presently I got through, somehow, anyhow. My
weakness had given place to a fierce unnatural strength.
I rushed across the less crowded part of the ball-room
at headlong speed. "O if I could only get myself into
some sort of a vehicle and feel myself being driven
home !" was my silent yearning.

It chanced that I did not leave the ball-room by its
main entrance. Instead of doing this I found myself,
nearly without knowing where I was, in one of the side-
lobbies. I had hurried along for quite a distance and
had almost reached the lobby's end, when a certain discovery brought me to an abrupt standstill.

Mamma and Cornelia Walters, surrounded by several

gentlemen, stood directly before me, unmasked, of course, evidently on their way to a carriage and evidently pausing to hold a little conversation before they proceeded further.

How long would they pause ? I dared not pass them. Commonplace as my domino is, mamma had seen it before, Cornelia had seen it before, and then, too, if Melville Delano had recognized me how probable that their keener women's eyes would not be less observing than his had been. Anyhow, I had best draw back a little and so remain unobserved until they moved onward. They could not be waiting for any special carriage ; they must be going presently. And so I drew back and prepared to wait. The idea of again entering the ball-room and finding some other means of egress was not at all a pleasant one. Indeed such an idea sent a shiver through me whilst I was dismissing it.

And so I waited. Where I stood I could hear them talking with entire distinctness. Clearly above Cornelia's rather purposeless chatter sounded mamma's voice.

" Yes," she was telling somebody, " Helen has really been dreadfully ill. No one knows how I have suffered during the miserable interval. Poor child ! she is very weak and nervous yet, though altogether past her convalescence. You will hardly believe me when I tell you something."

Somehow I wasn't an atom curious to hear what he would hardly believe, whoever he was. If he would only hardly believe it somewhere else rather than just there, and give me a chance to get away, provided the getting were possible ! since I had begun to think that fate was objecting insurmountably to any such procedure.

" Well," progressed mamma, " I have not said a word

to Helen regarding the entertainment I give to-morrow night. In the morning I shall of course tell the dear
child, and if she thinks herself quite able to dress and
come downstairs she shall do so. But in her present
state so little excites her that I have fancied silence a
far better plan. All her intimate friends have received
instructions from me, so that she is at present wholly
ignorant of the affair. By this means, you see, I spare
her much useless worrying as to whether she is strong
enough or not strong enough. Now don't you agree
with me that I have acted quite wisely ? "

Mamma's tones grew a trifle more distant, then.
"Thank Heaven ! " I mutely commented, "they are
beginning to move away ! " At this I stole a little
further forward and reconnoitered, so to speak. They
had stopped again, only a few steps further down the passage. Evidently mamma had just met old Mr. Chamberlane and had something of supreme importance to
tell him, whilst she tapped his shoulder with her fan,
in tenderest chastisement. O it was too torturing !
Would they never give me my chance ?

In my nervous fluttered perplexity, after having made
this second discovery, I turned directly round and let
my eyes sweep the opposite end of the passage. There
were so many people moving hither and thither that
I did not at first perceive what very soon became plain to
me, viz. : that Fuller was advancing in my direction with
a domino on his arm. And when the domino had gotten
a few steps nearer I knew that it was Edith Everdell.

I drew close against the wall, hoping that they would
not observe me. I wonder now that I did not dash
past mamma where she stood at the other end of the
lobby and so reach the street-door. Of course I should
have done this. But in my then excited state I must

have been powerless to reason at all beyond the fact of Melville Delano's having already recognized me. I felt, in my trembling insecurity, as though someone had indeed torn off at least half my masque and left me with the remaining half as a mere fractional means of disguise. A little cool reflection must have changed all this. But I was in no mood for cool reflection. If Melville had known me, why would not mamma and Cornelia know me? If they, why not Fuller? And so I stood, huddled up against the wall, making the show of having a torn domino which needed pinning, and feeling like a trapped rat.

Would Fuller and that woman pass me not know-ing—or, if knowing, in peace? I grew numb again when I thought of how her rage might break all bounds, this time, made even hotter by previous defeat and by the thought of how I had been the means of the recent disturbance.

But after all, the chances of that very same disturb-ance having scared her into a tractable and sober state, were decidedly strong. Yes, even if she recognized the drooped stooped bundle I was making of myself, she would probably vent her fury in nothing except an insolent stare.

But why did they not pass? It was certainly time for them to have reached my standing-place and gotten beyond it. Had they gone in some other direction?

This idea had no sooner occurred to me than I had lifted my head and looked searchingly toward the spot where I had last seen them.

They were there no longer. But they had gone in no other direction than that which I believed they would take. Here they stood;—here, not five yards from where I stood myself, both staring at me with curious fixity.

" I told you it was the same," muttered Fuller's companion, turning suddenly toward him as soon as I revealed myself.

After that I made no further attempt at concealment. Will it be unpardonably fine writing, Diary, to say that I have a vague understanding, now, of what a stag's feelings are just as it knows that it can fly no further and feels the breath of the murderous crimson-tongued mouths all around it ? Well, be this hyperbole or no, I simply stood and looked back at them, without any idea of escaping.

Fuller had disengaged her arm from his. In a voice too low for her to hear, he seemed making certain emphatic statements. He was very pale still, with a certain queer grayish drawn-down look about his mouth, which I had never seen till now. His vivid-lit eyes had lost nothing of their fire.

" And I am to wait here ? " she suddenly asked, the question seeming to be an ill-humored objection. And then her eyes were turned from Fuller's face to fix themselves on mine.

" Yes," he promptly retorted, and with some sternness. " You will please wait until I return. I shall possibly be gone but a short time."

After that he left her and came directly toward me.

I was quite calm. It was the calm of desperation, I suppose. I never doubted, in my dazed odd state of mind, that he would at once discover who I was. Perhaps he had discovered already. Well, after all, what did it matter ? I had come here to do him a service. It was only fair that he should recompense me by getting me home as quickly as he could, and saving me from that woman's further assaults.

When he was very close to me I saw that his face had

a strangely changed look—storm-swept, if it isn't an
extravagance to say so.   I do not mean the paleness,
precisely ; I do not precisely mean the brilliant eyes.
There was something else.   Melville Delano's glove-tap
had been too light to leave any mark.   And yet it had,
in its noticeable unnoticeable way, left the mark as of
an athlete's fist.

His voice, as he addressed me, was gravely courteous.
" Madam, I have not the pleasure of knowing if I know
you.   But as you seem without escort, and as you are
doubtless anxious to reach some friends, I beg that you
will let me offer my services."

How those few words changed everything !   He did
not know me.   He had come to do me a kindness.
Yet stinging under Melville's blow, he was generous
enough to go out of his way in extending aid to Melville's late companion.   To think of my being proud of
him then—here, in the presence of that creature !   I,
whose right to feel proud of any deed he might do has
grown so utter a mockery !

My silence lasted so long that he took it, doubtless,
for distrust, and presently went on, with a vague smile :

" Be assured, madam, that I shall make no attempt
to discover who you are.   But perhaps I am mistaken,
and you wish no assistance of this sort.   If so, I will
not trouble you any further."   .

Just then Cornelia Walters' laugh floated through the
lobby.   They were there yet.   They would probably
remain there five or ten minutes longer.   Fuller's arm
was being offered me.   Should I take it and so get past
them ?   They would never dream of recognizing me
*with him*.   Besides, now that I was sure of Fuller's not
having recognized me, the old feeling of confidence was
beginning to return.   It was with me as though I had

gotten back that other missing half of my masque. Then also, the thought had just flashed through my mind : ' There was a *reason* for Melville's recognition. He suspected from the first that you would come here, having told you what he told in the earlier part of the evening.'

But of all reasons for taking my husband's arm, this one was the most powerful : He stood a protector between myself and that woman's personal violence. He had ordered her not to follow him and she had obeyed. He was keeping her at a safe distance.

I slipped my arm very timidly within his, (ah, how I have leant there, during other hours, with all the bold glad dependence of one who trusts intensely !) and murmured in a gruff whisper that showed him not only what a palpable disguise my voice was using but what a laughable also :

" I only want a carriage. Thanks, if you will please get me one."

We reached the end of the lobby just as mamma, Cornelia and their little retinue of gentlemen had begun to move away. None of the party saw us, for the plain reason that they turned their backs upon us at precisely the opportune time. Then, however, Fuller undoubtedly saw, and took a wholly different course after we quitted the lobby, leaving the opera-house by a door as distant as possible from the one which they took.

He obtained a carriage for me with entire ease; there were so few people leaving at that comparatively early hour.

As he opened the carriage-door he again spoke. " I suppose you would prefer giving the coachman your own order."

" Yes," I returned.

"Just as you please." After that he spoke some words to the coachman which I did not exactly catch. Then he took some money from his pocket, whilst a few more words passed between them. Presently he turned toward me and seemed surprised that I was still standing by the carriage-door.

"Will you get in, please?" he proposed, very politely.

I did not stir. A new idea had entered my brain during the past moment or so. Still using my disguised voice, I abruptly burst forth with these words—for ah, how much bolder I had grown now that I was sure of being well freed from that creature's exposing clutches:

"Do you choose to give me your word of honor, Fuller Dobell, on the subject of whether you know or suspect who I am?"

"I neither know nor suspect," he replied, promptly, "and will give you my word of honor to that effect, if you so desire."

"But why are you behaving, then, with this kindness?"

At first he looked rather haughtily intolerant of my question. Then he fixed those oddly bright eyes upon mine and answered in cold steady tones:

"You were with Mr. Delano, I believe, at the time of that little trouble in the ball-room. I suppose you know that he has been arrested, or, if not that, forced to leave the house. I saw you without a protector, and chose to offer my services."

"It was strangely generous—almost chivalrous of you," I nearly forgot my disguised voice whilst I responded. "Not one gentleman in fifty would have acted so!"

After this I turned and entered the carriage. He closed the door, raised his hat, and I was driven off.

We had not more than passed out of Irving Place into Fourteenth Street when I managed to get the front-window of the carriage unclosed with all available speed and to tell the driver my address. "And I will give you a dollar more than that gentleman gave you," I added, "if you will make your horses go as fast as they can."

The result of this pecuniary goad to the driver's energy was my arrival home quite a little time in advance of mamma. I was relieved to have Blanche open the door for me and not Henry. Once upstairs in my room so intense a feeling of fatigue overcame me that I simply recollect being altogether indebted to Blanche in the matter of getting myself fit for bed, and then sleeping with a dead sort of soundness till I woke up and found the brightest daylight all about me.

I have not seen either mamma or Fuller yet. I suppose mamma will appear presently, to give the "dear child" tidings of to-night's ball.

Now that I have written it all out, Diary, I am going to read it all over and think about it. But I have written far too much. It is stupid to tax my strength in this needless way.

Fuller's face haunts me, as I left it last night. If anything dreadful *should* happen between him and Melville Delano I shall have been the cause. I do so hate to think of this! But pshaw! the days are past when men fight duels together. And yet they are both so high-spirited, have both hated each other so long. Who knows what *may* happen?

15

## CHAPTER XXXII.

APRIL 3.—I had just locked you up yesterday, Diary, when mamma made her appearance. This had been her second attempt to see me that morning, I was informed. My late rising had astonished her not a little. She trusted I was feeling quite well? Did my paleness mean no? for I hadn't a vestige of color and those rings had gotten about my eyes again.

"There's no denying that I don't feel exactly robust," I smiled.

"That is too bad," deplored mamma, "because of what I have come to tell you, Helen." And then she talked about her party that evening with much the same royally considerate manner (though more than a trifle toned down in one or two affectionate particulars) which I had heard her use at the opera-ball, a few hours ago.

"I may feel well enough to appear below stairs," I presently stated; "but there is no telling, mamma." For it had occurred to me, just here, that I might have cause to visit the drawing-room for at least a little while during the evening, and that it was therefore best to announce no exact resolution either way. "By the bye, was it nice at the ball last night?"

" Charming," declared mamma, " though not at all
select. One leans upon a broken reed when one expects
that sort of thing at entertainments where people pay
and go. Much to my satisfaction Cornelia did not wander away from me among the masquers. We left comparatively early. There were not so very many familiar
faces among the unmasked ladies ; but among the
men it was not at all easy to pick out the strangers."

All the while she was speaking I watched her face
narrowly for some dim sign that she had learned about
the quarrel and was keeping her knowledge hidden.
But face was never more baffling in its deception, provided she really knew. No ; I must conclude that she
had as yet learned nothing.

She left the room not long afterward, and nearly as
soon as she was gone I felt so intense a drowsiness begin its oppressing work, that I at length decided to
spare my eyelids any further waste of time as regarded
their blinking endeavors to keep open. I slept the
better part of the afternoon. It wanted but a little of
dinner-time when I woke up, literally gorged with
sleep and feeling refreshed therefor, the last vestige of
that tired ache gone out of my bones and my head
quite normally clear again.

Passing out into the hall, I noticed that the door of
Fuller's bed-room was open. I looked in as I went by,
seeing that it had no occupant. Then I somehow entered, for what reason I could not precisely tell.

Beyond lay Fuller's little sitting-room, separated from
that which I now occupied by a heavy dark-blue curtain drawn across its door-way. There was a wide
division in this curtain, just at present, through which,
whilst standing in the centre of the bed-room, I could
clearly see the room beyond. After making a certain

discovery I was on the point of departing with all haste : but somehow I remained and watched, filled with a kind of fearful curiosity.

There sat Fuller (knowing, of course, nothing of my presence here) before the large writing-table in the room's centre. I only saw his face in profile, but this view showed me well how sternly troubled it looked. His left hand propped his drooped head ; his right hand held a pen ; before him lay some writing-paper. I stepped forth from the bed-room, presently, with a sensation of nervous gnawing worriment.

At dinner his manner struck me as wholly unnatural. Now there was an evident effort not to be gloomy ; now an equally evident one not to be gay. Twice or three times I caught him staring hard at nothing, like one whom some thought of engrossing moment possesses and will not relinquish. The conversation principally concerned the coming party.

" Are you decided about appearing or not appearing, Helen ? " mamma asked of me.

" Not yet," I hesitated, crumbling my bread with nervous fingers. " Anyhow, don't expect me, mamma, or tell any one that you expect me. Please look upon me as an accident that may or may not happen." After a little silence, I added : " It will be about the last thing of the season, I suppose."

" No," stated mamma. " There will be the Barthol-omews' to-morrow night—Bessy Bartholomew's long-delayed Delmonico ball. The invitations have been out over a fortnight. I thought you had seen yours. I accepted for you, the other day, though not imagining that you would go. But of course, Fuller, *you* don't intend missing it."

This remark, sent suddenly Fullerward, made him

start, somehow. And he changed color a trifle, besides. " Miss it ? " he repeated, more rapidly, more
off-hand in style than is at all usual with him. " I hope
I shan't—I don't know—perhaps something may occur
—gracious ! who can tell in a place like New York ? "

" One may die."

For a second or two I kept my eyes on the table-
cloth after uttering this lively sentiment. Then I lifted
them, and shot a fleet stolen glance at Fuller.

He looked certainly a shade or so paler. Or was I
a nervous simpleton, bothered with stupid fears, incor-
rigibly fanciful ? Well, it might be ; or it might not
be.

By ten o'clock that evening I had gotten through
several chapters of a rather entertaining novel, and had
let myself gently drift into the resolution of not going
downstairs. But somehow, just at that time, the novel
became dull and savorless to me ; I got thinking of last
night and living all its terrors over again. I saw the
pressing crowd once more ; felt once more that dreadful ground-giving-way-beneath-my-feet sensation when
Melville dragged me toward Fuller in his reckless rage ;
heard once more the two men's mutual insolence and at
last the sharp snap of that assaulting glove.

And now what *was* to be the result ? If this is an
age when duelling has been flung in that rubbish-heap
where cluster so many " cold old crimes " of the past, and
if wounded honor is taught by law to appease itself
through some less murderous method than that of bul-
let or blade ;—if Fuller Dobell would call ridicule upon
himself were he to challenge Melville Delano, and run
the imminent risk of arrest and imprisonment were any
such meeting to occur, then must I believe that last
night's affair would be wholly devoid of all ireful conse-

quence ? It was hard, I found, to believe this ; and
the more I tried to believe it the more I found myself
haunted with nervous imaginings.

No ; there would be some result, surely. If to-day
had not brought it forth (and I felt nearly convinced
that to-day had not) then to-morrow would most probably do so. There had been a blow given, and Fuller
was just the man to feel himself on thorns until there
had been a blow returned.

If I could only find out precisely how the case now
stood between the two men !

Presently there began a rolling of carriage after carriage in front of our door, and sounds of feet hurrying
upstairs, and occasional sharp bell-peals, and at last the
long dreamy murmurous music of one of Lander's
waltzes.

By the time that the music commenced I had made
up my mind to dress and go downstairs. Blanche did
not appear until I had rung several times for her, and
then darted into the room, all volubility and smart ap-
parel. Madame *must* excuse ; there was such confusion
downstairs.

She helped me with my toilette as though beatified
that I should have made so noble a resolution, and
mingled with her satisfaction such nimbleness of speed
that I was ready much sooner than I had thought to be.

Well, whether the welcomes were sincere or no ;
whether or no three-quarters of them were fustian and
buncombe ; whether or no the kisses of the women were
Judas kisses and the warm hand-shakings of the men
were politic hypocrisies, and the congratulations in everybody's eyes and smiles and voices were three-quarters
of them hollow delusion ;—whether or no all this were
thus, I can't say and I don't much care. But notwith-

standing, it was pleasant to be treated as though one really were of some importance in the community, and as though the fact of how death had been recently threatening one with a permanent removal from it ranked slightly above the every-day commonplaces of incident.

I had not been in the room an hour before I began to observe one thing : nobody was willing to speak at any length with me on the subject of last night's ball. It would be "yes ;" it would be " no ; " and then, before I could well realize the change, it would be some quite earnest remark about something wholly different. Of course I made my own deductions, presently. Stories of Fuller's and Melville's encounter had flown on the wings of scandal here, there, everywhere. But had I no means of finding out from anybody how matters stood at present ? No ; I could not bring myself to question Ludlow Inmann or Aleck Sheffield or Willie Gregory or any of that Terpsichorean band. The weight of such a secret as that I had applied to him for such information would be simply a merciless imposition on my part, were I to thrill the gossip-loving soul of any one of these young gentlemen by a confidence so enormous. And then the humiliation ! No, no ; better remain in ignorance than purchase tidings at this price!

I did not dance the cotillon. Whilst it was going on and whilst I was seated in the back drawing-room, compassed with some half-dozen partnerless men, John Driscoll, also a non-dancer for the nonce, came struggling toward me through a barrier of occupied cotillon-chairs. I had seen him before, during the evening, but merely for a moment or two. When I saw him now, the determination to forget past pique and ask him a few questions grew suddenly strong within me.

John Driscoll had been standing before me for quite a little while in chairless devotion, when some penetrating female admirer of Winny Westerveldt's beckoned to him from the distant cotillon, and that gentleman's chair, just at my side, was temporarily vacated.

I motioned for John Driscoll to come and seat himself there ; which he did.  Knowing that Winny Westerveldt would presently return, and that the occasion must therefore be seized with marked promptness, I at once began.

" Do you know I am aware of what occurred at the ball, last night, between Fuller and Melville Delano ? "

He looked amazed, then quickly looked all composure again.  " Yes ?  I am sorry to hear it—very sorry."

" But I don't know if anything has occurred since then—or if anything is going to occur.  I wish that you would tell me whatever you know."  I made my whisper supplicatory as possible, without letting it be babyish.  " Will you not, please ? "  I made my " please " equal a whole sentence of pathos.  And whilst speaking I watched the man's face with a lynxlike narrowness that I am certain, however, he did not perceive.

Although for that matter, I pretend to no certainty in anything that concerns John Driscoll.  There is no doubt that some species of very difficult diplomacy lost a brilliant star when it failed to secure his membership.  Whilst he answered me I was simply sure of one thing : that his face and voice and manner were not going to tell me an iota more than he chose to have them tell, provided he were really on his guard and had good reasons for being so.

" My dear Mrs. Dobell," (with a vague shoulder-shrug and a little waving gesture from each hand) " in point of ignorance you and I are about quits here, I fancy.  But I confess you more than half puzzle me when you speak of what is going to occur. Have we any reason not to think the matter ended there ? "

" I hope it did," I murmured. " Do you really think it could? A man's opinion about these affairs is so much better than a woman's."

He gave a light slight laugh. " My opinion is not worth much in the present affair, I assure you. I had the misfortune to be upstairs, last night, when it occurred ; and there is always such a babel of conflicting accounts, don't you know ? "

" But understanding Fuller as well as you do," I pressed, in excited whisper, " how is it your belief that he will act, provided he received that insult and really hadn't time to retaliate before the two were parted ? "

Again the brief fraction of a laugh. " How will he act ? You want me to put myself in his place ? "

I was getting impatient. Distantly I saw Winny Westerveldt reinstate his admirer in her chair and glide forward to claim his own.

" Yes, yes," I returned, impatiently.

Did he see Winny Westerveldt also ? Was he trying to gain time ? He was John Driscoll ; I can't say.

" But I couldn't put myself in his place," he loitered, with rather a profound look.

" And why not, pray ? "

" Because—because," he continued to loiter, " Fuller is Fuller, you know, and I am—myself."

And then, whilst I gave an ill-humored little cry and clouded my brows, John Driscoll rose up because Winny Westerveldt was close upon us. And shortly afterward he left me.

I sat there among my partnerless adherents until the cotillon was ended and the departures were beginning. It was wrong for me to keep such late hours, but then

15*

I had fed myself upon sleep to such repletion during
the afternoon that the injury could not have been important.    I think I should have gone upstairs some
time before I did if it had not been that I felt a sort
of fascination in watching Fuller from a distance whilst
he danced with Belle Dillinger.    It seemed to me that
his face had never wholly lost its strange look of last
night.    He appeared in a perpetual mental state (to
judge from his eyes) of industrious wool-gathering.    I
could have sworn, after watching him for quite a little
space, that he was thinking of something else all the
time he danced, talked and smiled.

"Mrs. Tommy Meredith has been searching for
you, my dear," mamma murmured to me as we met
just after the cotillon.   "She is so anxious to congratulate you on getting well.   Don't you see her?   She has
just finished a turn with Fuller."

As mamma had left a great bevy of dowagers for the
purpose of communicating to me this vital intelligence,
I felt compelled to leave my seat and betake myself
Mrs. Tommy Meredithward.

The cotillon was just disbanded, and those who had
composed it were, "all that was left of them," prancing
and stumbling and dragging each other, as though trying to become convinced that they had not already tired
themselves nearly to death, and didn't want to stop,
and were not pushed about by that singular inertia
which makes some of us continue dancing long after our
wearied bodies have cried out, "Hold, enough."

I had talked to Mrs. Tommy Meredith until Charley
Bertram had seized and borne her away, disregarding
her simple statement that she should "drop dead if she
danced another step;" and I had found myself standing
alone in a retired corner, after that, watching the fagged-

out locomotion of the dancers, when suddenly I became aware that the two gentlemen, stationed almost in front of me, and evidently knowing nothing of my presence so near them, were Fuller and John Driscoll.

John Driscoll was speaking, and rather emphatically. "You have the support of my opinion, if you esteem it of any worth. Under the circumstances, I consider you justified in taking the course you have taken. But then, you know, my own ideas on these matters have always been what people would call peculiar."

"I remember," replied Fuller. "And that was my principal reason for calling upon you as I did. You will stop for me at what time?"

"I think we had better make it five o'clock; that will just about harmonize with the other arrangements."

Willie Gregory discovered me, just here, and hurried up to beg me for a dance: "Only one, please, Mrs. Dobell. It could never hurt you."

Fuller and John Driscoll moved away from me almost immediately afterward. My eyes followed them whilst I was framing a sentence of refusal for Willie Gregory. I am afraid he observed something strangely odd in my behavior; for to save my life I *could* not give him my attention during the next few moments.

In a very little while the rooms had thinned out immensely. "I am going upstairs," I presently told mamma. "If anybody asks for me, say that I was not very well and had to go."

Once in my own room, I burst into a weak flood of tears. But these lasted only a brief while. Then I sat down composedly and tried the plan of reasoning with myself to the effect that I had no real evidence of anything dreadful having been planned.

Nor indeed had. I. It might have been that Fuller

and John Driscoll were merely discussing some matter
as much the antipodes of what I had suspected as the
buying of a horse or the going out for a drive together.
Even the hour mentioned—five o'clock—might much
more probably mean five in the afternoon than five in
the morning.

And then I laughed—actually laughed aloud to myself, calling myself a silly terrorist. Five in the morning! Would I have ever dreamed about such an absurd hour being meant but for the novels I had read
with duels in them—the overdoses I had taken of Dumas
and Bulwer and Heaven knows who else, at various
periods of my girlhood?

Not quite pacified, but trying to make myself believe
that I was, I rose and rang for Blanche, and was soon
in bed. In bed, but not asleep, as the moments lapsed
along. For I could not sleep.

I had been in bed perhaps two hours, and the house
was now very still, when I became convinced that
Fuller, whom I had heard entering his room a long
while ago, was yet awake and had crossed its floor once
or twice during the past half-hour or so.

The desire to satisfy myself on this point became
simply intense ; and as for sleep, that seemed something
quite unattainable : I could only toss about feverishly,
and hear vague voices as of people talking together
on all strange subjects, and feel my pillow to be now a
mountain of height, now a valley of hollowness.

At length I rose up from bed, turned the gas from a
dim star to comparative brightness, unlocked my
door and stole forth into the outside hall. Drawing
near Fuller's door, I was surprised to find it wide open
and his bed-room lighted only with a faint reflected
light from the adjoining room.

Just as I had done during the afternoon I did now, stealing into the bed-room and looking beyond between the still-parted folds of the heavy blue curtain. A brilliant light filled the little sitting-room. Fuller was seated at the writing-table, dressed just as he had been when I last saw him.

He was writing rapidly, like one who has much to write and only a certain time to do it in. His head was so bent tableward that his face was nearly hidden from me whilst he wrote, wrote.

I felt at first like uttering a sharp and bitter cry : for it was a certainty to me, then, that my most horrible fears had, after all, been well grounded.

I don't know how long I stood, watching him, whilst he wrote, wrote. At length I stole back to my own room and looked at my watch. It wanted ten minutes of four o'clock. Was John Driscoll coming at five ? I did not at all doubt it, now !

Just then I heard Fuller's bed-room door closed with considerable sound. He had probably finished his writing and was going to get a little sleep before—

O God! I don't think I have ever really known till then how much I have loved him all along !

What should I do ? Should I go downstairs and wake up mamma and tell her ? How worse than useless as a preventive would be such a step ! How worse than useless as preventives would be all steps of which I might think !

I turned my gas up higher and made a sort of wild toilette. Bed was a thing abominable just then. I must always remember that wretched suspenseful hour until five o'clock. Sometimes I would walk the floor, with arms tight-folded and head bent groundward and gathered brows. And sometimes I would sit dead still, suddenly springing up and wanting to shriek out my terror. And once I flung myself down beside the bed and prayed, prayed, prayed. And once I caught myself reviling myself bitterly for loving him, for even caring what might become of him; and this mood ended in miserable tears.

At last it wanted only a few moments of five o'clock. I had heard nothing stir, as yet, in Fuller's room. What if, even yet, it should turn out that I had been mistaken? The thought set my heart beating delightedly. I drew near the door leading from my own room into Fuller's. This was shut, and there was a little passage between this and a second door. I dared not enter the passage for fear of the noise being heard by him at such an hour, and the suspicion of my wakefulness and watchfulness being roused in him. Listening, I heard no sound—not the ghost of one. And yet it was nearly five o'clock. O joy! perhaps after all I had been wrong! Or even if something *were* to happen, five in the afternoon was the time appointed; and there were yet hours, hours between now and then.

But whilst listening, suddenly I heard an unmistakable sound as of some one moving about the room. Ah, how awfully my heart fell, at this! Fuller had risen to keep his appointment. It must be true!

I got trembling with such violence that I was forced to sit down. My last doubt had been swept away, I told myself. And yet in saying so I deceived myself. There was still another proof wanted;—the proof of John Driscoll's coming.

The watch said five o'clock. I went toward the window and looked out into the dark dawnless avenue beneath. No sign of a carriage. Every moment told, now. Every moment took away the probability of my having rightly judged from what words they two had exchanged together. John Driscoll is usually the soul of punctuality about keeping appointments; I know him well enough to know that.

Presently I stood with the watch in my hand, staring at it, every sense on the alert, my hope and courage rising with each second that lapsed away and did not bring John Driscoll.

A minute past five: a minute and a half: two minutes: three minutes: three minutes and a half: (Oh, was it really true, after all, that I had been only a foolish alarmist!) four minutes: four minutes and a—

I lifted my head with a sudden jerk, then. I had heard something. And the something was a faraway sound of wheels rumbling along the still pavement.

Nearer, nearer. They were carriage-wheels. Nearer, nearer. I caught a glimpse of my face in the opposite cheval-glass and afterward remembered its pallor and its wildness, though neither impressed me then. Nearer, nearer. O my God! was it stopping? I reeled to the window. It had stopped by the time I got there. A man was getting out.

I absolutely remember nothing more till I found myself in the outside hall near Fuller's bed-room door. That was still closed. He had not come forth yet, evidently. Nor as yet had there been any ring at the bell —at least none that I had heard. But John Driscoll would not dare to ring the bell, coming on an errand like this. How, then, would he make known his presence to Fuller, whose room was in the rear portion of the house and who therefore could not be watching for him?

I had just asked myself this question when downstairs amid the intense stillness a slight sound like an opening door came vaguely to my ears. I leaned over the banisters, listening with most eager attention.

It was the front door, being softly opened and softly closed. Then came the sound of someone softly ascending. I understood it all, after that. Fuller had given John Driscoll a latch-key and had probably left a light burning for him in the lower hall ; and John Driscoll was coming upstairs.

The hall in which I stood was dimly lighted, just as it is usually kept throughout the night. I glided back into my own room and made my door very faintly ajar, so that I could see through the crevice thus formed, whoever might appear. The steps loudened by slow degrees, as they came higher, higher, though one could tell that the person making them tried his best to deal with a slight insubordinate boot-creak. Presently John Driscoll was making a vague summons at Fuller's door.

Almost instantly the door was opened. " My dear fellow," I heard Fuller whisper, " how odd that I didn't hear you come upstairs. I have been quite ready for some few moments." Then they both entered the room.

Very soon afterwards they emerged again into the hall. I suppose I did wrongly, recklessly, stupidly, in acting as I acted. But a kind of madness was upon me. I could *not* stand there and tamely see them go. I must make some effort to stop them, even if I knew before it was made that the effort would be worse than futile.

And so I had rushed out just as Fuller was on the point of descending, whilst John Driscoll followed close behind. Both of them started terribly on seeing me.

I cannot recall the exact words I used. They were

somewhat after this sort, my voice having a plaintive passionate break in it whilst I uttered them :

" Oh, Fuller, I know that this means something horrible. I am sure that I understand it. Think of what you are doing ! Oh, John Driscoll, *make* him hear reason ! Tell him to remember—"

And then John Driscoll had gotten hold of both my hands in both of his and was drawing me toward the room from whence I had rushed, with a force and firmness that I was just nervous, unstrung, terrified enough not entirely to resist.

We were much nearer the door of my room, and his body altogether shut out Fuller's from my view, when John Driscoll's deep murmur broke upon me. In the dimness I could see his hazel eyes take an unwonted fire and every line of his face drawn sternly.

" Mrs. Dobell, you will be trying to do your husband a great injury if you try to detain him now. Whatever you suspect, it is too late to tell your suspicions. He must go, and I must go with him, and you had far better let us go in peace."

Somehow the sound of his voice put rage into me at once. Perhaps I did not speak as loudly as I seem to have spoken ; but even if this be true, I marvel how nobody in that dead-still house heard me, admitting the somnolent effects upon everybody of recent fatigues.

" You are a wretch, and I hate you, John Driscoll. It was you who counselled him to go. I heard you last night. You have encouraged him, I daresay, in that other wickedness. I wish neither he nor I had ever known you."

He had left off holding my hand after my first irate sentence or two. And straightway he hurried toward Fuller, then, gently pushing him downstairs, whilst I

went angrily on.   When I had finished he made instant
answer, in a clear severe whisper, standing on the fourth
or fifth step of the stairs ; Fuller being now nearly invisible to me.

"One thing I must beg of you, and I am sure your
husband joins with me in asking it : Mention to no one
what you have seen or what you believe.   If you do so,
you may have cause to regret the consequences all your
life.   As regards what you say of me, Mrs. Dobell, I
know you don't, you can't mean a word of it."

It did not seem very long afterward that I heard them
open the lower hall-door and then close it again.   I
went back into my room, and as I went there was the
sound outside of the departing carriage.

It is now about eleven in the morning.   I have heard
the servants pass downstairs, but I doubt if mamma is
up yet.

Whatever was to be done is done, I suppose, by
this time.   One thought stabs me daggerwise whenever
I think it : if I had not gone to that ball, this horror
would never have occurred.   Shall I not feel like his
murderess if the very worst happens ?   But good
Heavens !   I went there in the wild hope of serving
him.

John Driscoll has sealed my lips with silence.   I shall
tell nobody—not even mamma.   If the man is not made
of stone he will bear me early tidings.   And yet perhaps he does not believe I would care much for anything
that might take place, having been chilled into unconcern by my doleful loveless experience.   But he must
have seen the truth, must he not, from my behavior
when they went this morning ?—from what I showed him
at the Delmonico dancing-class, a little while before my
illness ?

The truth ?  Yes, yes—the bitter dreary truth that I love as a beaten dog loves—that I would give years off my life now to see him well and safe—that I cannot starve my love to death, for it would rather feed on its own fervor than die outright, and wears a strength as of talismanic cause, blow-baffling as some surge-assaulted rock.

## CHAPTER XXXIII.

PRIL 4.—I am sitting in my room, waiting for John Driscoll to come ; he cannot well refuse to come after what I have written him and after what passed between us last night at the Bartholomews'. Whilst I wait, Diary, I may as well write it all out and so ease this agony of restlessness. Some women would walk the floor and cry, during a like suspense ; some would sit still and moan or groan. I write it in my diary.

Hard work it was to behave composedly, yesterday, when mamma and I met. If John Driscoll had not pronounced those warning words just as they two left on their mysterious unmysterious errand, I should doubtless at once have made her conversant with the thorough particulars about Fuller's going. As it was, I simply held my tongue on the subject and felt very like screaming with nervousness once or twice, whilst she discussed in terms of serene satisfaction the success of last night's party.

The day "crept along on a broken wing." I spent it principally in looking out of my three windows, one after another. Every time that a carriage stopped any-where near the house I grew cold and began to tremble. O day of misery ! I would rather die than live through another like you ! I would rather know, as perhaps I am going to know, that he is lying somewhere, killed.

Somewhere ! If somewhere, why not here in his own home ? Does John Driscoll think to hide such a crime as that would be from the world's scrutiny ? If so he is an arrant fool—and yet I know him too well to write him down a fool. But whether fool or knave, he is grossly cruel.

I had breakfasted so late in my own room that I easily escaped appearing at luncheon. But dinner was a different matter. If I wanted to conceal my anxiety from mamma it would be well for me to go downstairs, I told myself, when dinner-time came, and attempt the double hypocrisy of eating as if I wanted to eat and talking as if I wanted to talk.

Which I did. And whilst at dinner I made an easy discovery. Mamma was herself on evident thorns in the matter of Fuller's absence. Someone had brought her prompt tidings, doubtless, of the difficulty at the opera-ball, even though it had occurred just during the time of her departure ; and now she was drawing gloomiest deductions from his continued absence, and having vague fears as to what had become of him. But of course her anxiety was not a tithe of mine, unless someone had also borne her tidings to correspond with my own wretched experience of the night before ; and this, considering John Driscoll's marked desire for secrecy, was not at all probable.

It was right odd, our mutual masquerading, our mutual attempt to throw dust in each other's eyes. There was indeed an element of grim humor in it which made me feel, every now and then, like breaking out into a bitter laugh. She evidently thought that I knew nothing, and did not dream how far my knowledge surpassed her own.

Once, toward the end of dinner, I felt a kind of languid curiosity to see *how* she would act if given a good opportunity of confiding to me her fears. Henry had left the room. And so I asked:

"Don't you think it queer that Fuller should have been away all day and now not be at home to dinner?"

Instantly she was up in hypocritical arms. "Not at all, Helen; not at all. I daresay he has gone driving with somebody and then will dine at the club."

"I did not think of that," I succumbed, whilst she eyed me keenly with an assumed appearance of not eyeing me at all. Yes, she was ready to fight tooth-and-nail against my even having a suspicion of what she suspected. Perhaps if I had known nothing I should never at all have guessed her knowledge. As it was, I seemed to have anointed eyes, somehow, in the matter of reading her anxiety. Twice when the hall-bell rang I saw her color change, beyond any shadow of a doubt; and when Henry asked whether Mr. Dobell's dinner was to be kept for him, I watched her across the brim of my claret-glass and knew by her mouth (that most treacherous of all human features) how Henry's question was suggesting a train of thought at least not purely pleasant for his mistress.

"Are you going to the Bartholomews' to-night?" I abruptly asked, when we had gotten as far as dessert.

"Oh, of course," came her prompt response. Then it was plain to me that a certain recollection had suddenly assailed her. For the first time since I have known mamma, she stammered. "That is, I had intended—one can't tell if anything is going to happen, you know—or rather I don't mean this, precisely," (a soft laugh fluttering among her words, right here) "but —but—"

Then I broke in, my voice hard as iron. Henry had

permanently left the room. All during dinner I had been making up my mind that it was best, for politic reasons if for no other reasons, to empty before her my dismal budget of bad-tidings. And I emptied it after this fashion :

"The thought has just struck you, mamma, that if anything horrible has happened to Fuller, the Bartholomews' will be no place for you. Am I not about right?"

"Helen!" She looked all superb surprise.

"And so you have been believing me an entire ignoramus, all along, regarding certain matters?" After speaking so, I paused for a little space and laughed a hollow horrible laugh that startled me and made me hurry on : "I wish I had been! God knows I wish I had been!" And then I told her everything that has lately passed, from my wild ball-going to last night's wilder developments ; but I told only bare facts.

There came a long interregnum of silence when I had gotten to the end of my story. "Why did you not tell me this before?" she at last questioned, her stately calmness restored to her after having been lost more than once.

Long before finishing I had risen from the table and begun to wander here, there, everywhere about the dining-room. When I answered her now I was still this sort of mild nomad: "I suppose I ought to have done so, your interests being Fuller's in the matter of concealment. John Driscoll's parting statements deterred me, doubtless." (Ah, if she had only been some other kind of confidante than the mass of buckram-clad pride and coldness and self-love that I know she is! What delight, then, to wind arms about her and be comforted!)

Mamma sat speechless and unmoving for quite a while, with eyes fixed upon her finger-bowl. Then she abruptly rose up and came in my direction.

" Helen." Her voice rang with decision.

I replied with a questioning look.

" Helen, it will be best for both of us to go to-night. Indeed it is nearly imperative that we should both go. You understand, don't you ? "

" I think I do. You mean that we will seem to be aware of the whole matter if we stay at home. We must go and ask people if they know where Fuller is, I suppose. For my own part," (sighing an exorbitant sigh) " it seems as though I shall become mad if this suspense lasts much longer." Then I broke into my bitter laugh. "From what I have told you and from what you have seen, you must know by this time that I am still a fool in the matter of caring for him. I ought really to be callous and icelike, as far as affections go ; then your schemes at Newport last summer and at Pineside this fall, would have had a trifle more consistent results."

She turned pale, knitting her brows. " How dare you, Helen ! "

I tossed my head, with a reckless sneer on my lips. " Pshaw ! of course *you* do not dare deny that you grossly deceived me about that woman from the very first, telling me that Fuller scarcely knew her when you were right certain how well he knew her. There was never viler deception used ! " I dashed on, warming more ragefully with each new word. " You sold me to Fuller Dobell—sold me in return for the name you prized as so precious ! And more than this, he recognized the whole proceeding as a beastly barter ; for I have heard his own lips admit as much."

She gave a short choked cry, then, and came very
near me. "This is all a shameless falsehood ; and whoever told it you is a liar whom you disgrace yourself by
believing."

I broke into a broad ironic smile, right under the
shadow, so to speak, of her august face ; I took my ear
between thumb and forefinger and turned it toward her
with all the insolence of which I am mistress ; I cared
no more for her wrath, just then, than for the buzz of a
gnat.

"My own ear told me, and that I trust more than
certain people's words of honor. It was only two or
three days ago that you awakened me from a nap I was
taking in the front parlor, you and your respected son-
in-law, by a certain interview held a few yards off. No
information as to the real facts of my marriage could
have been much more explicit, I think ; all the repulsive details were gone through with ; I heard the whole
scandalous chronicle and felt myself tingling, of course,
with sweet filial reverence whilst it lasted."

My words by this time had wrought an immense
change in her who heard them. Ah, how marvellously
she has every passion under control, each obedient to
the common rein of policy ! I am reminded, when I
recall this, of a man I once saw at the circus, who dashed
in whilst riding more or less simultaneously five or six
galloping horses. Now two or three of them would
dart ahead at a seemingly tameless pace ; now these
would slacken speed and others rush to take their
places ; now appeared a dire confusion in their unmanageable midst, a turmoil of reared heads and jostling
fianks : but slowly out of chaos order would dawn, and
at length horse after horse moved along in tractable
canter, subservient to its rider's quiet compelling rule.

16

362       *PURPLE AND FINE LINEN.*

So with mamma : she lets her passions have their heads
for a certain distance, then comes the little decisive politic hand-jerk, and anger or spite or jealousy or revenge,
or whatever be the passion's name, falls into the ranks
again with all becoming docility.    Ah, she can be
queenly enough in her majesty of manner, I am learning, but can cringe and fawn and wheedle underneath it
all, with a most sycophantic suppleness.

(Ought I to write these things ?   She is my mother.
Well, well, she is also the woman who has set herself to
the task of maiming, spoiling, half-crushing my life, that
she, for her part, may hurry along at a more prosperous
speed, whilst I crawl through the rest of my days in
wounded weariness.)

The immense change I have mentioned was a grand
mild composure in place of all past fierceness.   When
she spoke I am sure that her altered voice made me
smile sneeringly.   "I am sorry you heard anything,
Helen ; but be sure that without knowing it you exaggerate the story of what you did hear.   And at least"
(with a superb straightening of her figure that looked
like the silent denial of some most undeserved charge)
"you must admit that my advice to Fuller was in every
respect admirable.   However, let us change the subject
and—"

"Yes," I assented, "let us change the subject by all
means.   What's done's done, I suppose, and you will
have to defend your conduct, no doubt, before a haugh-
tier judge than I could ever make myself."   These
words were spoken whilst I walked doorward.   Reaching the threshold, I turned abruptly round.   "I am going to-night," was my announcement, "unless something horrible in the way of news shall reach us before
then.   It will be easier to go than to remain at home."

('And perhaps,' my thoughts were adding, 'I shall see John Driscoll there. It may be that he dare not stay away, no matter what has happened.')

And so we went, mamma talkative though evidently depressed during the ride Delmonicoward, I simply dead quiet when not monosyllabic.

It was a huge ball. There had not only been sent an invitation to everybody who was worth inviting, but to the rural cousin of such everybody, I should suppose, and his maiden aunt. All the familiar faces were there, plumlike; and manifold unfamiliar faces, puddinglike. I raked the rooms for John Driscoll, not expecting to find him. I did not find him.

It was nearly one o'clock before the cotillon began. Three men asked me to dance it in the earlier part of the evening, and I gave to each of them the same answer:—It was uncertain whether we should stay or not. I meant that provided I could see John Driscoll and have a few words with him, all object in staying would be ended and all interest in these festal halls become veriest ashes of indifference. Then, too, something horrible might be told me by John Driscoll, which would make further stay impossible.

But when, just before the cotillon commenced, Clarence Sedgewick was the fourth to want me for a partner, (and Heaven only knows why! since surely I was dull enough and conversationless enough to be shunned rather than sought by my old dancing-friends) then I felt a yearning desire to stay still longer and not miss the chance, vague as it was, of John Driscoll yet making his appearance.

But for this yearning desire, five minutes of that babbling befurbelowed throng would have turned me deadly faint, doubtless. I should have gotten home, somehow, whether mamma vetoed my going or not. As it was, I would have insisted on remaining, even though mamma commanded me to depart. Which mamma, throned with numerous dowagers on a dais at the further end of the ball-room, plainly did not dream of doing.

Clarrie Sedgewick talks very well. His ideas leave the man on oiled wheels, and it isn't the glibness of flippancy, either. But oh, what efforts I had to make that he should be answered with the proper ' yes,' the appropriate ' no,' the suitable ' certainly ' !

The cotillon was more than half over. That vague chance of John Driscoll's coming—of his coming, even though anything dreadful had happened during the day, because of averting suspicion and keeping matters se-cret—had grown the merest speck of probability. I was tired of staring at the doorways. I had begun to feel the first mild torments of a fresh anxiety : perhaps horrible news had come to mamma or myself whilst we had been merrymaking here ; perhaps even John Dris-coll himself had gone to find me and had heard where I was and laughed to himself : " much she will care, any-how," or some such comment, and so delayed giving me the tidings.

Just then Ludlow Inmann flitted up to take me out. He offered his hand ; I took it whilst rising. Then, suddenly, I fell back into my chair, gasping forth : " You must excuse me, this time—I'm so tired—I've not been well, you know, and shouldn't overtax myself."

He smiled forgivingly and flitted off again. Truth to tell, my heart was beating with such wildness that I felt afraid to dance. For, standing in a doorway nearly opposite to where I sat, my eyes had lighted upon Mel-ville Delano.

He was talking carelessly, as it seemed, to three or

four men. I could see no change in his appearance, from where I watched him. I was sure that he had just entered ; otherwise he could never have escaped my detection.

It sounds silly, but I had to keep myself in my chair by sheer self-governing force, so that I might avoid rushing across the floor and assailing him with questions. As it was, I simply sat still, pale and quivering, with the " dancers dancing in tune " before me, and the *Beautiful Blue Danube* pealing plaintive and delicious in my ears.

Let me call my discovery of Melville shock number one. Shock number two followed perhaps a good minute later, and was the discovery of John Driscoll. He had emerged through another doorway, and was stooping down to say something in the ear of Mrs. Chauncey Crawford. I suppose that shock number two affected me homeopathically. Melville Delano was the bramble-bush by which I had scratched out both my eyes, so to phrase it ; and John Driscoll was now the means of my scratching them in again. I stopped trembling ; I daresay that a good deal of my color came back to me ; and presently, in rapid composed tones, I was telling Clarrie Sedgwick that it would be impossible, because of fatigue, for me to dance any more. " And you must take me over to Mr. Driscoll," I finished, lightly. " I've something to tell him."

" Why not bring Mr. Driscoll to you ? "

" No," I laughed. " The mountain will go to Mahomet, this time." I rose. " Give me your arm, please."

We crossed the ball-room, leaving it by a different door from the one near which John Driscoll was standing. I am quite sure that he did not recognize me, if even he saw me, whilst I was quitting. the ball-room. Presently I stood with Clarrie Sedgwick directly behind him, the doorway near which he was stationed being in front of me and the passage-way into which it led being behind. There was no escape for him ; it was a sort of stolen march. They had been forced to put double rows of chairs just in that part of the cotillon near which he stood, because of its immensity. If he wanted to avoid me he would find avoidance impossible—except by a brutal rudeness.

"Just go and touch Mr. Driscoll on the shoulder," I instructed Clarrie Sedgwick.

Which Mr. Sedgwick did, with obedient promptitude. Naturally John Driscoll turned on being so saluted. And turning, he instantly encountered me.

I did not need to raise my voice loudly ; we were too near each other for that. "I am going home in a few moments and want to speak with you before I go."

He stood utterly still, both hands resting on the back of Mrs. Crawford's chair, his face yet turned in my direction but his eyes not meeting mine.

"Mr. Driscoll." I spoke so sharply that he started, whilst Mrs. Crawford and three or four more of the cotillonites levelled inquiring stares at me across their shoulders.

For reply he came and stood very close to me. During a moment or so we searched each other's faces. Then he gave me his arm. "Let us go into the blue room," he proposed.

I felt as if I were walking blue-roomward along the crater-edge of a volcano. What horror might he be waiting to tell me of ? We had reached an extreme corner of the chamber before either of us spoke. He motioned for me to share a sofa with him, but I would not do it. I was going to drink my bitter draught standing, whatever it was. "For God's sake don't delay any longer," I made harsh appeal, glaring at him with hungriest eyes. "Melville Delano is here; I have seen him. So whatever has happened must have happened to Fuller."

Straightway, after that, he began speaking. "I should have seen you before now. It was my purpose to have gone at once to your house, but I have been detained—unavoidably detained—from doing so. I never dreamed of finding you here, but came because it was best, for appearance's sake, that I should come."

"End this maddening palaver," I cried, "and let me know whether Fuller is dead or alive!"

John Driscoll took both my hands in both his own, so drawing me toward the sofa. I am not sure whether there was anybody within fifty yards of us or not, whom the action might virtuously horrify. In this manner he forced me to sit beside him.

"I speak to you," he whispered, still keeping my hands, "as I would dare speak to hardly any one else. This morning there was a meeting between Fuller and Delano."

My heart stood still as he paused. "Well?" I managed.

"Fuller has been wounded."

"Badly?"

"Very badly. I ought not to give you any hope. There is just a chance and no more."

I remember wanting to articulate the question "where have you taken him?", failing, and then suddenly seeing the gaslights all dancing fandangoes with each other: and after this all was a nothingness until I found myself in the ladies' dressing-room, seated in a large

chair, with John Driscoll at one side of me and mamma
at another.  Beyond these there were a few more
faces.

" It was imprudent of Mrs. Dobell to dance, as she
herself told me this evening, just before she fainted,"
John Driscoll was lying to somebody.

" Yes," abetted mamma.   " To-night is the first time
that she has danced since her dreadful illness."

And thus it happened that I made a prudent return
to consciousness, if I may so term it ; asking no strange
wild questions concerning Fuller and Fuller's whereabouts.  Very soon afterward I was taken downstairs
to my carriage, leaning on John Driscoll's arm, mamma
following.  I never imagined that he was not going to
ride home with us.  As mamma, after entering, closed
the door, I made a sharp-voiced objection.

" No ; no ; " I cried.   " John Driscoll is coming.   I
*must* see him."

And then the carriage rolled off, just as mamma was
answering :

" He will see you as soon as possible to-morrow.  He
cannot come with us to-night."

After that I buried myself in one corner of the carriage, speechlessly wretched.  Mamma was very audible during the drive home.  John Driscoll had told her
everything that he told me ; but no more, as I soon
learned.

I will say nothing of the night I have passed.  I shall
always remember it shudderingly.  Of this I am sure :
no worse could possibly be in store for me.

Before nine o'clock this morning I had sent John
Driscoll two notes—one to his house, one to his club.
These notes were prayers for him to lose no moment of
time in coming to me.  And now it is past eleven and

he is not here yet. Perhaps after all he is not so cruel; perhaps he is only a coward and hates to come and tell me of Fuller's death.

Where can Fuller be now? As I write the question a loathsome thought enters my head. Oh, no, no, no; I will brush the thought away from me as we brush something black and beastly. John Driscoll could not have taken him *there*.

But if he has truly done so vile an action, and if God cares a whit for his creatures, whether they smile or suffer, whether they laugh or groan, then I am sure that John Driscoll must answer for that action to God. But ah, is there a God that cares? I am getting to ask that question, nowadays, again and again. At any time my faith would rise and fall like the sea; but now I am afraid it is nearly one perpetual ebb-tide with me, and—

A ring at the bell. This *must* be John Driscoll.

16*

## CHAPTER XXXIV.

PRIL 5.—It was John Driscoll. He was just entering the reception-room when I dashed up to his side.

"You must pardon my not coming sooner," he instantly began, on seeing me. "It was not possible. I have been with Fuller since I left you last night; except during a few moments."

"He is not yet dead, then?"

"No."

"But he is dying. I see it in your face, John Driscoll."

He shook his head decisively. "You may see worriment and sleeplessness in my face, but be sure that you see no such gloomy conviction there."

I gave a short glad cry, drawing nearer to him. "The danger is passing?"

"Not at all. He may not live, only there is no immediate danger." Then, marking my look of horror: ".Mind you, I say *may* not. I cannot precisely tell what the doctors think. I daresay they are afraid of giving an opinion. The ball has been extracted, but it is a bad wound, with danger of bad hemorrhages."

"But—where—have—you—taken—him? Why— did—you—not—bring—him—here?" I jerked out each word, pausing after it, dreading the answer that was to come.

He stared floorward; he would not look at me whilst that answer was given. " It was thought best to keep him hidden, you know. If he had been brought here the matter would have become public in a day or two."

" But you have not answered my first question," I persisted, a little gaspingly. " Where has he been taken?"

He spoke shortly, rather coldly. " You would not know if I should tell you."

" Are you sure of that, John Driscoll?" I cried, with raised voice and shrill. " Answer me at once. Answer me, for I *shall* know! Where have you taken my husband?" I caught his arm roughly, here. " Is he or is he not in Edith Everdell's house now?"

As the name left my lips he lifted his head suddenly. And suddenly, too, his eyes seemed brimful of sympathy, compassion, tenderness. " You must not blame me," he murmured. " Fuller *is* there. It was not my fault. By Heaven, I swear to you that it was not my fault. I believe she bribed one of the doctors to have his quarters changed last night, whilst I was absent: for at the risk of his life I found he had been moved when I got back." All this he spoke in his rapid earnest way, and with one of those abrupt little brisk-toned outbursts that in other days used. so to charm me—in other days, and upon oh, such different subjects! Afterwards he went on much slower: " But pray believe that he has every imaginable care. No means of saving him shall be left untried. If the worst happens it will happen because nothing could avert it."

There was quite a little silence before I spoke again ; certain thoughts had been darting through my head and so keeping me wordless. Presently I asked :

" Do you know Edith Everdell at all well ? "

His eyebrows went up. " I ? I know her ; that is about all."

" If you don't know her well," I hurried, sneeringly, " you are so rich that it is merely from lack of inclination, I suppose. Answer me : has she an atom of true womanly feeling ? Or is she just hard, luxurious, brazen, without one touch of human goodness ? "

His face was solemn and thoughtful ; all surprise had left it. " I think she is hard as granite," he stated, lingeringly. Then, after a brief pause, he added: " And yet her nature has one strange softness. Well, no ; I suppose, after all, it is not strange."

" What is it ? " I wanted to know, eager-voiced.

" Her love for her child ;—I believe she was once married somewhere and to somebody."

" This child is how old ? "

" About fourteen, I think."

" A boy or girl ? "

" A girl."

" And she is being brought up in the same surroundings as those of her mother ? "

" Indeed, no ! She is now a boarding-pupil at perhaps the most select school in New York. Scarcely more than four or five people have the dimmest suspicion of who she really is. Madame Langlois herself believes her to be a Baltimorean of irreproachable family ; —half of which is true, for nearly all her life has been passed in Baltimore. I have reason to know that Edith Everdell worships that child ; doubtless because she is a part of herself, one of her own possessions. Not to see her for years, as except by occasional stolen glimpses she has not seen her, must be a most bitter trial ; but she bears it with a stoic nerve for the sake of the child's after good. Then, too, she has given this adored daughter (who, by the bye, is already right beautiful, I have heard) the name of Adèle Tremaine, and she means to make the real story of her origin as utter a secret as such a thing possibly may be made. I should not be astonished to hear that she has hoarded, for years past, many an easily-earned dollar which was believed to have been squandered as soon as earned, and that Adèle Tremaine will some day be an heiress of no contemptible income."

"Oh, yes," I murmured, half to myself, "I remember. It is the beautiful pupil of whom Madame Langlois spoke to me when she called, just before my marriage. How little I dreamed, at the time, of whose child she was speaking!" Then I suddenly changed the subject, forgetting in a trice all about Adèle Tremaine and Madame Langlois. "John Driscoll," I cried, with imperative passionate force, "you *must* get me to Fuller, somehow."

"It is wholly impossible. Pray do not ask me."

"But I shall ask you, and I shall go," I stormed. "It is brutal for you to refuse. Help me there, or I will go myself. I can find the house where that creature lives."

He looked at me in my despairful rage, with a gentle pitying look that was wholly lost on me, then. "You cannot go. It is not even a matter to be discussed."

"But my husband is dying; you will admit that."

"I admit that he may be dying."

"Then what better excuse do I want for going to him, no matter where he is? Let me tell you something, John Driscoll." And now I clasped both hands together, and looked up at him with swimming eyes, and there were many breaks in my voice as I went on,

for the tears had begun to flow at last. " God help me,
I love Fuller Dobell as well now as I did the day he
married me ; and you know—you must know—how
little reason that love has ever had to live ! But it *has*
lived, John Driscoll, and it will not die, and the thought
of his lying wounded is as awful to me now as it would
have been on my wedding-morning. I know you are
going to help me get to him ! For old friendship's
sake, John Driscoll—" and then sobs choked me, whilst
he, having caught both my hands, was looking the picture of earnest sympathy, meeting my tear-blurred eyes
with his own warm-colored hazel ones.

" For old friendship's sake I would do a great deal,
Helen Dobell," his mellow murmur told me. " But
surely I shall need different sort of urging from that, if
I take you where you are too pure to go."

" But in such a cause," I pleaded, wildly, " what
matter if I soil myself a little ? I don't care a fig if
people sneer at me forever afterward. Those whom I
like at all (and Heaven knows they are few enough !)
must think as I think :—that it was right for me to be
near my husband at any imaginable hazard."

" The world could not discuss the matter, for the
world knows absolutely nothing of its occurrence. Fuller's absence from home must be explained by your
mother as owing its cause to certain business-troubles
with her Western property. It is well known that she
has property in Cincinnati and St. Louis; so the story
will be credited at once. Everybody who knows about
this affair, and could be bribed to hold his tongue, has
been so bribed, and liberally. And every unbribable
person has individual reasons, it happily occurs, for holding his tongue. The place and the time have both been
greatly in our favor, as far as concerns discovery ; but

what has been more in our favor than either of these, is
the glaring improbability that in this age and in this country any two men would presume to engage in a duel.
Duels are nearly as much out of fashion as white wigs
and tricorne hats—even in France, who used so to love
them. They are occasionally still talked about by men
of a certain stamp, but nowadays when a gentleman is
insulted by his servant or his equal, it is very much the
same thing ; he must cowhide both—if he can. If he
can't, why there are outrages beyond a particular limit
which a law-court may possibly remedy. No ; the
feeble likelihood of there having been a duel is going to
save us from discovery more than anything else, I feel
quite confident. If the suspicion once arose and investigation was made, I daresay that even our intense caution and secrecy would be of slight avail. But think of
it : New York—duel ; how the two ideas meet each
other like oil and water, refusing to unite ! The great
point, in a case of this sort, is always, not as much to
disarm suspicion as to prevent it from ever waking at
all.'' He seemed half addressing his own thoughts,
now, whilst he went on : '' It sounds right daring to say
so, but I firmly believe that the whole matter will remain (at least for many months to come) a profound
secret to the world. Unless, of course, poor Fuller
dies.''

'' When I spoke of the comments which might be
made,'' came my quick answer, '' I meant provided
Fuller should die. For I believe he is going to die ;
something tells me so. And in that case you could
keep nothing secret. Ah,'' (whilst I grew suddenly
fierce amid my tears) '' I hope they would hang Melville Delano for murder ! I should like to pull the rope
myself.''

John Driscoll gave a shoulder-shrug, his brow slightly clouding. "That is a wild way to talk, and quite unprofitable. However, though Melville Delano would doubtless be tried for murder, I question whether it would be possible to make any jury render such a verdict. True, he need not have accepted Fuller's challenge. Only a few men would have accused him of cowardice if he had not accepted it; and these would quickly have been silenced; there are always means of silencing anybody whose opinions run counter to the spirit of the age, modern progression, and all such high-sounding sentiment. Whoever presumed to consider the challenge worthy of notice would perhaps be told that he had recently fed himself overdoses of *Ouida;* that enlightenment and civilization shrank from duelling ; that it was a last remnant of· old-world barbarism. The forcing of men into armies and the slaughtering of them,· thousand after thousand, by ˙ mitrailleuse and needle-gun and chassepot, because two kingly gentlemen, each with his own private ambitious axe to grind, have chanced to meet at the same grindstone—this sort of thing has no barbarous flavor, it seems, to the fastidious. souls whom duelling horrifies. For my own part, I must confess that when Fuller came to me whilst yet quivering under the sense of grossest outrage, I could conscientiously give him no counsel except that which I did give. True, he might have gone about with a horsewhip, searching for Delano, and on finding that person have run the muscular chances of having the horsewhip seized from him and used on his own back; but I somehow didn't care to advise such a proceeding. I knew Melville Delano well enough to understand that, although he has the temper of a fiend, he has also a courage proportionate with it, and is just the

man of all others, in this age and this country, to accept
a challenge if he received one. Fuller was literally mad
after some satisfaction of precisely that sort, and nothing
different. And so I began arrangements at once, after
securing as help two or three of the cleverest heads I
know. As for results, I am sure there were no *deadly*
intentions on either side. What happened, happened
through accident. Melville Delano himself assured me
of this immediately after the meeting; and I believe
him. Indeed, the meeting took place with an understanding between all engaged that mortal wounds were,
in so far as was *possible*, to be avoided."

I was all tearful impatience when I answered him:
"Pray let us waste no more words on any subject but
one, and that is the getting me to Fuller's bedside."

"I cannot get you there." His decision of tone had
clear traces of harshness.

I moved doorward. "Just as you please," I told
him, between clinched teeth. "I shall go myself.
She dare not refuse me admittance. If she does, I am
not such a fool but I know how to snap her power like
a reed."

"Stop!" he cried, hurrying up to me. "If you
don't take good care you will expose this whole matter."

"And how should it concern me if all the world knew
it?" I questioned, laughing a little bitter laughter.
"Melville Delano and you and every other active participant *deserve* punishment and ought to get it."

"In God's name, don't speak so loudly!"

"For my own part, I do not care whether you get
punishment or not. I do not care for anything except
seeing Fuller. Whatever wild impolitic thing I do, you
mustn't blame me when it's done. You will have no

right to blame me then, for you refuse to help me now,
and—"

"Stay." He caught my arm whilst peering intently
into my face. "You speak of my helping you. These
are words rattled off at random. How can I help you,
as far as concerns the going privately to Edith Everdell's
house? Reflect a moment, and you will see the folly
of your demand."

"What do you mean by privately? Without the
knowledge of Edith Everdell herself? If so, understand that I am willing she shall see me at Fuller's bedside. Do you suppose that her presence there would
keep me away?"

Just as my querulous voice ended this question his
face got an absorbed look, he lifted his hand forehead-
ward, drooped his head a trifle and stared at the floor.
"Perhaps," he at length began to loiter, meditatively,
"perhaps—"

"Well," I broke out, with sharp haste, "perhaps
what?"

He fixed his eyes on me, then, and commenced rapidly to speak. "Rather than have you go as you
threaten going, I would resort to almost any deterring
expedient. One such expedient suggests itself, hardly
feasible, doubtless impossible."

"Let me hear it—that is, provided it be a means of
getting me near Fuller."

"It is a means of doing so; or rather might be, if
successfully used. But I warn you that it sounds un-
real, theatrical, novelish."

"Never mind that. Let me hear it."

"There will be a permanent nurse hired for Fuller
some time during to-day. I have the power of putting
any one whom I choose into that position—But pshaw!"

he suddenly broke off, smiling a broad smile. "The thing is not really worth a thought. You will guess the rest, of course."

"I guess only this much : that I might take the nurse's place. But how would such a plan prevent me from meeting Edith Everdell, who knows me by sight as well as I know her ?"

"You did not guess all." He walked away from me with folded arms, his smile nearly gone. "Nor, on the whole, were you stupid in not guessing."

"But tell me the rest," I persisted, following him for a few steps. Then I came to a sudden stand-still. "Ah, I see it, John Driscoll. You meant for me to go disguised, somehow."

He wheeled round at this and faced me. "Yes; that was the idea. The more I think of it the more absurd it seems."

After a little pause came my reply. "I don't agree with you. It might be done. Its being novelish and theatrical doesn't make it impossible. After the first ordeal of having her stare at me, there would probably be no chance of detection ; no chance if—"

"If the disguise were good enough."

"That is precisely the point. I think I could make it so, but I am not sure yet."

He shook his head in an intense negation. "I am sure. You could never accomplish such a thing. For a few moments and under a certain light it might be carried out ; but for days, possibly weeks—" and here he grew abruptly very grave indeed, as though the whole plan were appearing to him in new colors. "You in that house for days and weeks !" he muttered, harsh-voiced. "God forbid it !"

"Never mind *that* consideration, if you please," I

hurried, warmly. "It is trivial enough compared with the motive that takes me there. Let me think, let me think." And now I stood with bent head and a hand touching either temple. "I shall need a whole day for experimenting—the rest of to-day at least. You tell me that there is no immediate danger of Fuller's dying; and yet whilst I am testing my powers of disguise he may be cheating me of one last look at his living face. But I will risk it. I will begin preparations at once. If I am ever ready I shall be ready by to-morrow morning, as early as you please."

Trouble and incredulity were mixing themselves on his face. "No, no," he disapproved; "the scheme will not hold water three minutes. Remember, we do not deal with a fool."

I looked at him firmly, then. "Would you rather have me go disguised, with a vague chance of non-detection, or without the vestige of disguise and with the surety of recognition? Whichever you prefer I am willing to do. Only, let there be a prompt choice, please."

"I advise you to do neither. I beg of you to do neither. Twice, three times a day, I promise to send you bulletins—"

"Hush, hush!" I nearly shouted, putting a palm before each ear. "I will not listen to you. Go I shall, somehow. I am willing to make trial of the plan that you proposed, or that you only had half enough courage to propose. Shall I begin at once? Pray answer me immediately, yes or no."

He lifted both hands and let his head fall sideways, in a "do-as-you-please" sort of fashion.

"Very well," I hurried, "my preparations shall begin on the instant. If, when all is ready, it is all a failure,

you can but tell me so. Meanwhile, will you promise
to send me word if any change whatever takes place
in Fuller's condition ? "

" Yes."

" And will you promise to come here between nine
and ten this evening, so that I can show you what I
have done and get your approval or disapproval ? "

" Yes."

" Very well. Now you had better see mamma, since
she must be instructed what sorts of falsehoods to tell
about Fuller's absence."

" And your own also, if you carry out this mad
freak."

" Leave your instructions on that point until I am
well out of the house. If you do not, mamma will simply make a useless attempt to detain me. Indeed, she
might exasperate me to such an extent that loud talking
and possibly shrieks would go far toward the exposure
you seem to dread. So mind, not a word to her about
my purposed absence. When I am gone you and she
can arrange at pleasure some clever excuse." My hand
was on the knob of the door, now. " I will have
mamma told that you are here. Remember your promises." Then I left him.

After giving orders that mamma should be told of
John Driscoll's presence in the reception-room, I sped
upstairs to my own. A moment's pause, here ; thence
with good haste into my dressing-room and straight toward my dressing-table. After that came a long stare
at myself in the looking-glass.

Blond hair. Blond hair can be made any sort
of hair nowadays, so as to defy detection of the art
that alters it. This is the age of dyes and fluids and
wigs. There would be slight trouble about the hair's

thorough concealment. That might be already treated as a surmounted difficulty.

Blue eyes. What earthly art can change blue eyes to brown, black or gray? None. But there is a way of making them colorless, unnoticeable. That way is a pair of dark spectacles.

Next, complexion. I suppose there are modes of staining this; anyhow, whether yes or no, I shrank from the idea. Surely Edith Everdell had not seen enough of me, I told myself, to recognize me by any such slight means. But the tints were too fresh for an elderly female; and I wanted to be an elderly female, with spectacles and grey-touched hair. Well, here was a danger. A fresh-tinted elderly female, however, is by no means an impossibility. I would risk the complexion.

Next, costume. There must be a dark stuff-dress, not at all exaggerated in its primness of make-up. There must also be a cap; no suspiciously poky and capacious affair; but something shapely and pretty, with just a vague touch of nattiness.

So much for the physical disguise: assuredly it should be sufficient to a woman who has not seen me ten times in her life, if even that number, and who has not then once seen me much more than momentarily. As for the mental disguise, there the chief requirement is of course an assumption of far greater nursing knowledge and experience than I really possess. In this I may fail partially; it will be hard to fail absolutely. I know something of nursing; what I do not know I must try to assume.

Let us waive the details, Diary, concerning where I went and what I did to-day. It is late, and there is work for me to-morrow, beginning before daybreak.

This evening, between eight and nine, John Driscoll kept his promise about coming. Luckily, mamma was in the parlor with some guests. He asked for me and was shown into the reception-room, as I had given orders that he should be. I slipped downstairs (at the awkward risk of meeting somebody) in my full disguise of nurse, be-wigged and spectacled and aproned and capped. It seems absurd to write that he was so completely unprepared for my appearance in the reception-room as not only not to know me when I entered it, but not to suspect for several minutes after my appearance there who I really was. I might have deceived him a long while but for my keenness of anxiety to learn about Fuller's condition.

"The disguise is purely perfect," he commented, wide-eyed and in wondering tones. "I did not dream you could make it so good."

"Never mind the disguise till you have told me about Fuller."

"He sleeps nearly all the time. He is no worse and no better than when I saw you last. The doctors anticipate some decisive change to-morrow."

"And can I not go there with you to-night?" I wanted eagerly to know. "I have a portemanteau all packed and ready. There is a perfect opportunity for leaving the house whilst mamma is occupied with her visitors."

"No, no," he objected. "I have told them that the nurse will come at a very early hour to-morrow morning. My bringing you to-night might rouse just that first glimmer of suspicion which we wish to avoid rousing."

I sighed a great sigh. "Perhaps you are right."

"It is almost always customary," he went on, "for

men nurses to be engaged, in a case like the present."
Then, smiling with a queer humorous gravity : " But I
have represented you as a person of such extraordinary
skill that your sex is looked upon as a trivial objection.
Have you any skill, by the bye ? "

" Some. Not much. I shall be inspired, perhaps.
I wish you would let one of the doctors into the secret
of who I am, provided you can trust him."

" It is precisely what I have thought of doing. And
now to arrange about your leaving the house. You had
better leave very early. I will call for you as I called "—
He stopped short, averting his eyes.

" As you called for Fuller. You have the latch-key
yet which he gave you ? "

" Yes. And I will come at the same hour—five
o'clock. That will not be too early, I trust. No one
was wakened before, and it is fair to trust that the same
opportunity will occur again."

" There would be no use of my bothering you to call
for me," I made answer, " were it not for the portemanteau, which is large and heavy, and which I don't think
I could very well get out of the house alone. But for
this I could put on a veil and slip from the house at almost any time of day."

" Don't think of the bother, please," he responded,
kindly. " I will come at five, in a carriage. We can
drive about until six, and at six we can make our appearance where we are expected. You have but just
found yourself freed from a long engagement, and you
are entering upon your duties with the least possible
delay : that is about how the case stands."

" I shall be ready. You will not have to knock at
my door as you had to knock at Fuller's," I could not
help adding, in bitter afterthought.

"And do you feel any confidence in yourself? I trust so. Your disguise is just admirable."

I laughed a little. "My confidence is strong enough, for the reason that I am reckless and don't care much whether she finds me out or no."

He bit his underlip anxiously. "But pray don't let your recklessness make you wholly careless in the matter of exposure. Please be prudent and run no foolish risks of discovery. And trust that I speak the truth when I tell you one thing: this advice to you springs partly from a clear knowledge of Edith Everdell's nature, partly from a certainty that my judgment, just now, is cooler and better than yours. There is no use of thrusting one's head causelessly into the lion's mouth. Any act of temerity seems such a little thing to you now, but you may have reason to repent at leisure what you perform in haste. You are young yet: one's feelings and interests change marvellously as one ages. The world's malice and scandal seem a slight evil to you now, but some day all that may alter. And I should like to warn you with a certain formula of warning again and again: Edith Everdell is a woman whose malevolence is always worth the going a little out of one's way to shun."

Shortly after that he went. I have had no business, wakeful as I have felt, to spend all this time, Diary, in telling you what has passed. Five o'clock is so fearfully early. I must at least go to bed and *try* to sleep.

**17**

# CHAPTER XXXV.

PRIL 7.—I am in that creature's house. I have been here a day and a night.

John Driscoll found me ready and waiting for him. We quitted the house without rousing a soul, as far as I could discover. At a late hour last night, John Driscoll told me, he had left Fuller sleeping tranquilly. We drove about for a good hour, sometimes talking, sometimes keeping silent. At last, when it was full daylight, my companion gave his order to the coachman. As the carriage stopped, he turned toward me, murmuring :

"If your courage fails you it is not too late to change your resolution."

I laughed for reply. Then he got out and I followed him.

We had to ring three times before the bell was answered. An obese ugly woman finally came to the door, clad in a white sacque and petticoat and suggesting, with her disorderly hair and half-shut red eyes, recent arousal from slumber. John Driscoll pushed past her through the jealously-opened door, I following.

"Have you been sitting up with Mr. Dobell?" he questioned of this ill-favored portress, whilst we stood in the dim hall.

"Yes, sir," the woman answered, with an appearance of forced respect, just beginning to take into her sleepy brain, as it seemed, an idea of whom she had admitted. "That is, I've been dozin' on the lounge by fits and starts."

"How does he appear?"

"He's sleepin' all right, I guess. He hasn't woke up durin' the night, not as I'm aware of."

"You will please carry this portemanteau upstairs and show this lady the room she is to occupy. She is the newly-engaged nurse for Mr. Dobell." Then, turning toward me, whilst I was being searched by those sleepy eyes: "When Margaret has shown you your room, Mrs. Peters, she will take you to Mr. Dobell's. I will wait for you there."

Margaret at length left off her steady stare at me, and transferred it rather inimically to the portemanteau. Looking martyrlike, she presently stooped to her burden. John Driscoll hurried upstairs first, disappearing before Margaret and I had accomplished many steps.

I was taken into a little room on the third floor; a front room and neatly furnished. But mine was no mood, just then, for the examination of its details. After I had expedited in getting off my bonnet and shawl,

"I shall not need to remain here," I told her. "Show me, if you please, directly to Mr. Dobell's room."

"It's right next to this, ma'am," she gladdened my heart by answering. "You can open that door and go straight in whenever you please. That's why Mrs. Everdell give you this room."

"Oh, very well." I took a glance at myself in the toilette-glass. I was simply a commonplace refined-looking elderly person, with dark-green glasses ; nothing more. Who could remotely suspect me of being anything else ? By the bye, my glasses had already become a thorn in the flesh to me. It isn't at all nice, I find, to pass a bottle-green existence, the way some weak-sighted people must do, merely guessing at one's favorite colors when one meets them, and having little except the difference in size to assure one that a rose is not a cabbage-head.

" Shall we go in now ? " I asked of Margaret with my hand on the door-knob, which I need only turn to find myself in Fuller's presence. Then, without waiting for Margaret's acquiescence, I did turn the knob and enter.

A large room, lit with the early feeble daylight. The room was comfortable even to luxury, as one swift bottle-green glance assured me. When I looked at Fuller, lying in bed with shut eyes, I had to fight against letting a cry leave my lips. The green medium through which I saw his drawn livid face made him seem more awfully corpselike than he really was. The room had only one other occupant when we entered it—John Driscoll. Whilst he and I stood side by side near the bed, and whilst I found myself leaning closer, closer toward that wofully altered face below me, I heard John Driscoll murmur in rapidest French, as though alarmed and distrustful :

" Take care not to seem moved at all. Margaret is devoted to her mistress ; and it would be a bad thing to rouse her suspicions, you know."

I profited by the advice, which was needed, I must own. Doubtless I should have said or done something imprudent, without it. Very soon I became aware that Fuller was breathing with regularity. " Is he

conscious when awake ?" I presently asked, turning to
Margaret with a voice and manner all composure.

" Well, ma'am, he is after a fashion. He looks
round as if he knew where he was, sometimes, but he
don't never speak at all. The doctors say it's because
he's so weak."

" And has he slept like this all night ? "

" Oh, yes, ma'am. And most of yesterday he was
sleepin' ; only he'd wake up onct in a while and look
quite sensible. When he gets his medicine it don't
seem to rouse him much if he's sleepin' already."

Silence, during which I stood staring down at him,
praying that Margaret would go out of the room.
Which, to my intense relief, Margaret presently did.
The instant that she had closed the door I hurried off
my spectacles.

" That is imprudent," murmured John Driscoll.

" I can't help it. I hate them so. He is fearfully
sick. I am sure that he cannot live."

" You must not think that. Dr. Delmayne will
be here by seven o'clock. I have made them give him
a bed-room on this floor, and he has agreed to remain
here nearly all the time ; so that your office of nurse
will be almost a sinecure."

" And have you told him who I am ? "

" Yes. I saw him last night and told him everything. He has rude odd manners, but underneath them
there is the kindest heart conceivable. Luckily, he has
almost if not quite given up practice in consequence
of advanced age, and he is therefore willing, for friendly
reasons, to spend nearly all his time here."

" To think of that woman leaving Fuller in this
Margaret's charge ! " I murmured. " What do you suppose were her reasons for ever having him brought

here ?   One would suppose that she would have shrunk
from the risk of his dying on her hands.   Perhaps, after
all, love has been the ruling motive with her."

"Love," he repeated, in scornful whisper.   "Love,
indeed !   She chose to run the risk of his dying.   She
was clever enough to see what the alienating effects of
a long convalescence away from her house might be.
He is the goose that lays the golden egg, you know.
Other men might be (are, very often) her devotees for
a time.   But this man believes in her, and his faith has
a certain steady marketable value."

I shuddered, answering nothing.

At about seven o'clock Dr. Delmayne made his appearance.   He is a great bonily-gaunt man, more
than six feet tall, with a profusion of iron-grey hair
nearly muffling his entire face and leaving little of
any importance visible except a huge hawklike nose and
a small pair of dark piercing eyes.   Margaret being
present, I was introduced to him as the nurse, Mrs.
Peters, and greeted with an ugly grunt and the following mass of pell-mell mumbled sentences :

" Heard of you before, Mrs. Peters.   Splendid nurse,
I'm told.   Hope you'll help cure our patient here.
Going to try something in that line myself.   Trust we
shan't disagree.   Strength in unity, you know, or ought
to be, though 't isn't often there. is, because nearly
everybody's conceited enough to want his own way and
swear it's the best."   Then Dr. Delmayne shut both
eyes and chuckled resonantly, as though he had just
cracked a stupendous joke.   " I'm going to have *my*
way." (Opening his little eyes and glaring at me.)
" So that ends the story."

"No doubt you will find that we shall agree very
well, doctor," I replied rather cheerily.

This man had not been in the room five minutes before I began to repose in him a certain half-unconscious
confidence. For fully ten minutes he sat with his watch
in one hand and Fuller's wrist in the other, showing just
the suggestion of a sly smile under those bountiful facial
concealments. And it was a smile that cheered me,
whatever it meant to do ; a smile that seemed to spring
from some hidden hopeful conviction ; a smile that was
like a very low whisper, something to this effect: "I
know what I know, but I shan't tell you how nice it is ;
so that ends the story."

Between seven and eight breakfast was brought upstairs for Dr. Delmayne and myself. Just as we sat down
to it John Driscoll took his departure, promising to return in an hour or so. And then Margaret, who had
been bustling corpulently about the room ever since the
doctor's arrival, with no explainable motive except that
of curiosity, chose to make her exit. The doctor was
employed in shattering a boiled egg whilst I addressed
toward him a large relieved sigh. We were seated opposite one another at the little breakfast-table which had
been improvised for us.

"I am so glad that woman is gone,", I burst forth.
"She is such a nuisance. Can't she be kept out ? "

The little eyes went through me, to use a strong
figure. "Why is she a nuisance ? "

"Oh, doctor, I feel like asking you every five minutes how he is. And I can't do it—I don't dare trust
myself with my own voice whilst she is here."

The doctor threw back his head, ruthlessly executing
a roulade of chuckles. "Don't say ! Well, he's no
worse. That's magnificent news, my dear Mrs.
Peters " (lingering over the name, nearly chuckling
over it) " at least, you ought to think so, though I dare-

say you don't.   But *I* do; and  my opinion  isn't to be
sneezed at, in a  sick-room.   Now eat your breakfast,
Mrs. Peters."

   " I can't touch a morsel."

He jumped up from his seat as though I had pricked
him with a bodkin, or something.   He glared at me as
though I had just grossly insulted him.

   "What!"  he  evidently  wanted to scream, but did
not dare, because of his patient.   " You  presume  to
tell me, madam, that in my medical presence you
dream of refusing the succulent segment of beefsteak
with which I am about to provide you!   Or of declin-
ing the  nutritious egg!   Or of discountenancing the
pleasant potato!   Mrs. Peters, I am  not to be trifled
with.   Mrs. Peters, if it were not for the Human Stomach I should not have been able for years to practise
the  noble  profession  that has made me what I am.
Mrs. Peters, do you suppose that I will tamely sit opposite you and see the  Human Stomach insulted?   Mrs.
Peters, as the temporary guardian of your liver, I command you to eat.   And let that end the story."   Then
he sat down, still glaring at me with the little needle-
like eyes.

   "But you are evidently going to eat nothing except
that egg, doctor," I made  mild remonstrance.   " And
why should I—?"

   " You are a young woman," he galloped, in snappish
whisper.   " I am an old man.   Five years ago, Nature
said to me, 'Delmayne, your digestion is not what it
used to be.   Stop eating liberally three times a day.
Eat liberally once a day instead.'   Like the fool I was,
for the space of a year I told Nature to mind her own
business.   She did so, and racked me with dyspepsia
by the process.   She brought me round.   I am a wiser

man, now, with improved peptics, going breakfastless, luncheonless, in order that I may dine. Let me eat my egg, if you please, and don't throw my rickety old digestion in my rickety old teeth. For your own part, eat your own breakfast, Mrs. Peters. I shan't have you fasting ; so that ends the story."

It was hard work, but I managed to choke down some of the succulent beefsteak and a few spoonfuls of the nutritious egg. As for the pleasant potato, it rather stuck in my throat when I tried a swallow of it ; but I got down a good cupful of hot coffee. "Mr. Driscoll has told you all about me," I presently made bold to address the bearded eccentricity who sat opposite. "You know who I am. Consequently you must understand my intense anxiety to learn whether your patient is the least shade better or worse." After that I felt that two or three immense tears were trickling from under those horrible spectacles. "Oh, doctor, if you find he has improved only ever so little and there's somebody in the room, *will* you not make me a sign ? I have begun to trust you already, but I shall trust you so much more if I think you really feel for me in my wretchedness."

"Tut, tut, tut," he bristled, starting up from the table whilst in the act of flourishing his napkin against his leonine face. "Don't try sentiment with me, Mrs. Peters, *if* you please. I abhor it. The *argumentum ad hominem* is no argument at all. Excuse me ; you don't know a word of Latin, of course. No women ever do, nowadays, and hardly any men. Sentiment in a male mouth is usually maudlin weakness. In a female mouth it is usually deceit, pure and simple. Come, oblige me by wiping your eyes, madam. Mrs. What's-her-name may appear at any moment, so you had best

**17***

conceal those 'woman's weapons, water-drops,' as
Shakspeare neatly puts it. Mrs. What's-her-name's no
fool, I'm told."

Doubtless his gruff tones kept me from shedding
more tears. And it would have been ill luck indeed
had I done so, as not three minutes after he had spoken
the door was unclosed, and " Mrs. What's-her-name "
moved across its threshold like a splendid vision.

Heavens! what hearts this woman might have broken
if she had been positioned in the world Cleopatrawise,
or had had some bloated Roman emperor of a husband
to strangle in his bath, leaping up on his throne and
reigning there in his stead. What grace had the gods
not given this new Pandora? She had only knotted
her hair behind in a massive careless coil, letting it ripple back richly from either pure temple, with no elabo-
ration of ringlet, braid or puff. Her fawn-colored
cachemire morning-dress, touched here and there with
blue, showed all the lovely lines of her full-rounded
figure; which ought to have appeared creditably, by
the bye, in any earthly garment possessed of a waist
and arm-holes.

" How is he this morning, doctor ? " she murmured,
standing at Fuller's bedside and looking down at him
with those marvellous eyes. For myself, she had not
noticed me yet, or at least had not appeared to do so.

"Don't know," grunted Dr. Delmayne, very shortly,
not in the least appalled by her loveliness, as it seemed.
" Oblige me by never asking such questions. If he
were worse I should tell nobody, and if he were better
I should keep, at this uncertain state of the patient's
case, such a discovery to myself. Have you seen Mrs.
Peters, the new nurse ? If not, you might as well give
her the time of day, it strikes me : and so end the story."

Whereupon I was looked at, as I had been waiting to be looked at, whilst I stood at a short distance from the bed's foot. Her look had nothing specially curious, nothing unduly penetrative. And then, with the same voice whose suave music I had heard before we now met, (though certainly not during that wretched episode at the opera-ball) she spoke a few words to me.

"Dr. Delmayne's rebuke is scarcely deserved; don't you agree with me, Mrs. Peters? But then" (glancing Dr. Delmayneward, whilst a slow sweet smile seemed to light her lips at their extremest rosy edges) "he makes a point of snubbing everybody, I am told. And now pray tell me: is your room quite comfortable? for of course Margaret has shown it you by this time."

"Yes," I answered, with bold composure. "It is very comfortable, besides having the nice advantage of being so near" (I moved my head in Fuller's direction) "the gentleman who is sick."

"Mr. Dobell," she softly informed me. Then her brows gathered a little, whilst a slight smile held her lips; and she came many paces nearer to where I stood. "You have heard the name before now, Mrs. Peters, I suppose? Mr. Driscoll said that he would tell you everything and gain your entire confidence before engaging you. He has done so, has he not?"

"Oh, yes," I replied. "It is understood that I am to keep silence."

Her lovely eyes were scanning me with closer observance, now; I could perceive this right easily, though her wish that I should not perceive it was also evident. Had the sound of my voice roused in her some glimmer of distrust?

"Holding one's tongue with discretion is the rarest of human virtues," asserted Dr. Delmayne, between a pair of brusque grunts. "Glad to see, Mrs. Peters, that you're a woman and yet dare undertake such an awful work. You can't carry it out, of course. If you did you should dress in white ever afterward and wear a chronic crown of something. It is a fact that I was once called in on a case of paralysis of the tongue ; a female case. I grinned in the poor thing's face, at the consultation, and made her physician-in-ordinary so rabid that we've never spoken since."

During the next three or four hours no observable change took place in Fuller. Two other doctors appeared, one a "dilettante, delicate-handed" looking nabob of perhaps thirty, and the other an old man with a pure white moustache and magnificent manners. Dr. Delmayne snubbed the younger gentleman violently about every third minute. To the older gentleman he granted a hearing semi-occasionally. Almost everything spoken by this august medical conclave was lost to me, for I sat at a good distance off, beside the window, in the shadow of a full heavy pair of curtains. Edith Everdell was not in the room during the doctors' visit, nor did she return for a long while after they had gone.

I believe that Dr. Delmayne and I grow better friends every minute that we are left alone together. I have gotten somehow to feel, and to feel intensely, that he is already my stanch ally and wishes me well with much hidden warmth of kind-heartedness. I do not think that I am learning thus to like and trust him solely because of what John Driscoll told me about his real nature. No ; my trouble has given me a kind of instinctive perception. I see beyond the strange rough outer husk clairvoyantwise.

A little while after midday Fuller woke up from his* lethargic state and began moaning as if in bitterest pain, and turned glassy eyes here and there about the room. I was bending over him with quickened heart and misty sight, watching the doctor administer an opiate, when Margaret rolled herself loungingly into the room.

Dr. Delmayne's eyes took their sharpest glitter as he fixed them suddenly on the woman's waddling buxomness. "Did you come in here for anything particular?" he pounced, snappishly inquisitive.

Margaret looked all stupid surprise. "Not as I know of, sir."

"Then you'll oblige me by going out at once. If I want you for anything, my good woman, I'll ring for you. Understand? I'll ring for you."

The fat-face had hardened, by this, with an ugly brutish kind of obstinacy. "Mrs. Everdell told me to come in here every onct in a while and see how things was gettin' on, sir."

"Did she indeed?" queried the doctor, every word a kind of mild snarl. "Present my most respectful compliments to Mrs. Everdell, and repeat to her just what you have heard me say. Now go, if you please, at *onct*—to adopt your own corruption of a nice Saxon word. Go, my good woman; and let that end the story."

But Margaret ended the story with much scowling delay, casting one malicious glare meward from the piggish eyes, before removing her bulky sulky presence from the room.

"She suspects that I don't want her here," I murmured, a moment after she had closed the door.

"Let her suspect and be —— I regret, for only the third or fourth time in my life, that I've never learned to swear, Mrs. Peters. As it is, I must content myself with a *quos ego.*—Excuse me, by the bye; being a

woman, my elegant classic allusion is of course wholly
lost on you.    What a repulsive nuisance she is, that
Margaret, with her goings and comings !    But I think
I've exorcised her this time for you, and permanently."

"I hope so."

"See; he's quieter already.    The opiate is doing its
drowsy work very quickly."    Then, looking round at
me most abruptly, with the tumbler of medicine in one
hand and a spoon in the other :  "Do you want a scrap
of comfort, Mrs. Peters?"

"Oh, doctor," I quivered.    "Do I *want* it!    Can
you ask me?"

"Pshaw!    Don't be theatrical.    Yes and no for
ordinary bodies—emotional paraphrases for tragedy-
queens and such like.    This man here has got stamina
enough for a cart-horse.    Mind, I don't say anything
more.    'Hope springs eternal,' *et cetera*.    Draw your
own deductions, Mrs. P., and ask me no silly questions."

Which piece of counsel I followed by simply bursting
into tears.    It was a very quiet cry, and only lasted a
moment or two ; but the doctor contemplated me whilst
it did last as though I were of little more consequence
than a convicted murderess.    Then, just as I had gotten
myself well under control again, and just as he had begun to make me the victim of a merciless philippic, the
door was softly unclosed and in glided Mrs. Everdell.

I saw, the instant I looked at her, that she was annoyed.    She moved toward the bed in silence ; stood
watching Fuller for a few seconds ; walked toward one
of the windows, and finally spoke, addressing Dr. Delmayne.

"Margaret tells me, doctor, that you have just sent
her out of the room."

"Quite true for Margaret. Sublime virtue, truth; especially in women."

Her eyes began to glitter just a trifle. "Let me ask you for what reason you sent her away."

"Superb reason. Didn't want her here. Nuisance; awful nuisance. Pokes about; stares with those ugly eyelets—can't call 'em eyes—and makes herself generally a bore. Isn't it so, Mrs. Peters?" with sudden appeal to me.

"Perhaps you are putting it rather too strongly, doctor," I answered, with a half-smile.

And then I found myself subjected to a searching scrutiny from Margaret's mistress. "Do you share Dr. Delmayne's prejudice?" she presently asked. "Margaret thinks so, and feels convinced that the doctor has acted on your advice in sending her from the room."

Doubtless I was most imprudent to reply: "Nor is Margaret very far from wrong in so believing. I did not want her here. But I regret if her absence displeases you."

"How on earth can it," blurted forth the doctor, with far greater imprudence, "unless Mrs. Everdell wanted to make a spy of her?"

She turned upon him as if the words were a very dagger-thrust. "Spy, Dr. Delmayne! Be careful, please, what words you use."

"Thanks, ma'am, for the polite warning, but I generally am. Libel-suits are not pleasant things, as some people learn to their cost."

Instantly the color shot up into her face. He had touched upon some tender spot, doubtless, in her past life. But she answered him with bold promptitude. "It was my intention to have Margaret act as your assistant here, until I learned Mr. Driscoll's wish in the matter of engaging Mrs.—Peters. She is a servant in whom I have the greatest confidence, and would have made, I think, a capital nurse."

I felt, then, that I must play my part, or else bring upon myself, in all likelihood, stronger suspicion than that which now existed.

"I hope, ma'am," was my calm statement, "that you do not feel opposed to my remaining here."

Again the searching scrutiny of those exquisite eyes. "Opposed? Oh, no. But it struck me as peculiar that a *female* nurse should have been engaged. Are you often called upon to attend gentlemen? I should imagine that the office, for a lady, would be somewhat unpleasant."

"So it is," lied Dr. Delmayne, rushing to the rescue; "but Mrs. Peters has known me for a long time. Mrs. Peters and I have the honor of being very old friends. Mrs. Peters, I flatter myself, was induced to undertake the present case more through the mention of my name than through any other persuasions which Mr. Driscoll addressed to her."

I do not know what effect this ingenious tissue of falsehood produced upon her who heard it; for just then there came a moan from the bed where Fuller lay, and since that moment, all through the rest of the day and on through half the night, it has been with him as with one who walks very very deep into the Valley of the Shadow. His suffering has been intense; his gaspings for breath have been frightful to hear and see; a fever has taken possession of him whose hot force has turned his dead silence into occasional bursts of incoherent disconnected talk. Edith Everdell staid in the room through nearly all of it, and John Driscoll was

there also, and a woman whom I believe Edith Everdell
calls Flora—a handsome swart-skinned brunette, bad
style to her finger-tips—visited the room once or twice
and shuddered and went out again. The white-mous-
tached doctor came once in the afternoon and once in
the evening. As for Dr. Delmayne, if ever a man made
war-to-the-knife against Death, that man is he. I tried
to appear as little as possible like a neophyte and a
bungler ; perhaps I have succeeded ; perhaps not.
Edith Everdell was the last to leave the doctor and myself alone in the sick-room. Fuller was much quieter
by then—about twelve o'clock. The instant she had
left, Dr. Delmayne turned toward me.

" Go to bed," he commanded.

" No, doctor ; I could not sleep if I did."

" Nonsense. If you don't go I shall undress before
you."

" Undress ? "

" Certainly. Do you see those bed-clothes, there
beside the lounge ? I had them brought here this evening, whilst you were too scared to notice anything that
went on a yard from that poor fellow's side. I intend
to sleep there on the lounge. If he's worse, (but he
isn't going to be, before morning) I promise to call you.
Now don't look distrustful, and don't believe that I
shall go to sleep and not hear him if it's necessary. To-
night isn't the first time, Mrs. Peters, that I've only
slept with a single eye and a single ear. So please go
to bed, Mrs. Peters, without further pig-headedness ;
and let that end the story."

So I went into my own room, and somehow felt such
confidence in this man's efficient watchfulness that bodily exhaustion asserted itself and I slept tired sleep until quite late in the morning. On finding out the hour

I was spurred into a most guiltily expeditious toilette. The doctor was seated at Fuller's bedside when I entered the sick-room. "There is a little change for the better, *perhaps*," he admitted; "but only perhaps;" answering my eager question with evident reluctance. Then he went on to tell me that the patient had passed a tolerably quiet night; restless now and then, but on the whole, quiet. After that I was ordered to ring for breakfast. We have apparently conquered in the matter of Margaret's visitations. Breakfast was brought up by the same person who served us with luncheon and dinner yesterday; a tidy harmless-looking girl.

Fuller has been so quiet, and has seemed to need so little care for the past two hours, that I have stolen into my own room, and seated where I can see everything that passes in the next through the half-opened door, have written these lines in you, Diary, following my queer habit (now grown a very second-nature) of telling you every important thing that happens.

Whilst I have written there has been no worse change in Fuller's condition, and Dr. Delmayne has been dividing his attention between a newspaper, a novel and the patient's pulse. I suppose that John Driscoll, or one of the other two doctors, or Edith Everdell, may appear at any moment.

## CHAPTER XXXVI.

APRIL 11.—Nearly four days have passed since I touched these pages. And days of such poignant anxiety, such terrible torturing suspense! A very little while after I last ceased from writing, his sufferings came with what seemed sevenfold their former force. There was a slight hemorrhage, too, with awful danger of a worse one. All through that day I simply stood at the bedside, doing whatever the spirit moved me to do, and keeping my eyes now on Fuller's face, now on Dr. Delmayne's. I scarcely knew what people were in the room, for hours together. Once, when Edith Everdell drew very close to the bed and laid her hand (her warmly-white hand, tinged as I have seen the petal-tips of certain tea-roses) on Fuller's pillow, very close to his head, I felt a chill creep slowly through me whilst I watched her. But the instant her hand was withdrawn I forgot her presence, thinking only of that poor racked sufferer and hearing in my ears again and again, iterated knellwise : " He is dying ; he is dying. You can't save him. Nobody can save him but God ; and God will not."

It was toward evening of this same day that a most horrid thing happened. He had been uttering strange guttural incoherences for an hour or more. Dr. Delmayne and I stood, side by side, very near him, and as I watched his eyes it seemed to me that they took a glassier glitter with every new moment. John Driscoll had gone away for a little while. Edith Everdell, as I had a vague consciousness, was somewhere in the room. Near the door stood that Flora, staring at me with her bold black bad eyes, as she is fond of doing whenever we meet; I wonder, by the way, what makes her stare at me so.

It happened that I was nearer to Fuller than was Dr. Delmayne, at the time the horrid thing occurred. I daresay that if the doctor had been nearer than I, his hand might have been caught and the miserable mistake made regarding him; for Fuller was just delirious enough to make it.

Instead of that his hot hand suddenly seized mine and his dull-shining eyes swept my face for a moment, whilst he cried out, much loudlier and distinctlier than he had as yet spoken anything:

" Edith ! Ah, Edith, this is you at last. Where have you been keeping yourself? " Then he began fondling my hand excitedly, whilst I stood rigid, chilled, ignorant how to act, and feeling more keenly with every second the dreadful mockery of the situation.

Suddenly Edith Everdell pushed between the doctor and myself, and so, whilst standing close at my side, leaned down a little above Fuller. At the same time her hand made a rude effort to separate Fuller's from my own.

But tense muscles opposed her. I held his hand so tightly, then, that she tried and wholly failed even to wrench it away. And presently with high-held imperious head she stood glaring at me, a superb picture of ungoverned anger.

" How dare you prevent me from taking Mr. Dobell's hand," she cried, " when I hear him call me by name and when you yourself see clearly the mistake he is making ? "

I met her glare fearlessly through my green spectacles. I knew that my action had been a mere piece of insanity as far as prudence went ; but there had seemed something so maddening in the thought of this creature coolly separating those hands which God had once joined together, however shamelessly man had since broken them asunder, that were a greatly worse peril than discovery the price of my persistence, I should still have made my fingers cling with the same stubborn force as they were clinging now.

And as for discovery, I was filled with such a momentary recklessness that I cared not a jot about it, and should perhaps have even courted it, but for Dr. Delmayne's prompt interference.

" Mrs. Everdell," he stated, quietly putting himself between us, " if you place the least reliance on my judgment, please understand one thing : this room must be kept free from loud talking or " (lowering his voice in solemnest whisper) " there is no chance whatever for my patient's life."

Her tones were a trifle lessened, after that, but her anger was evidently unaltered. " I consider Mrs. Peters' behavior most impertinent. She refused to let me take Mr. Dobell's hand. I insist that you interfere to some purpose, doctor, if you must interfere at all."

" She has not refused," contradicted the doctor. " It is not so, Mrs. Peters, is it ? "

Prudence was pulling me by the sleeve, now. " Not at all," I lied, making the words come through my half-choked throat. Then I got my hand free from Fuller's and drew back a little from the bed. "I hesitated to let Mrs. Everdell take his hand because I thought it would be best to humor him in the mistake."

"Thoughtful creature!" murmured the doctor, with a whole heartful of admiration in his words. "I knew there was some such discreet reason for what you did."

At this there came a voice from the further end of the room. Flora, the woman who diverts herself by that chronic stare at me, spoke in hard clear semitone.

"Hesitate is a queer word to use, I think. It seemed to me much more as if she just gripped his hand with all her might and wouldn't let you touch it."

"Which is the exact truth," broke forth Edith Everdell, turning from her friend to re-level kindled eyes upon me.

What more she said I did not hear; for just then there came upon Fuller one of his sudden horrible attacks of gasping. The attack lasted a good half-hour. When I cared to notice whether those two women had left the room or no, I looked about me and found that only Edith Everdell remained. A little while afterward she too departed.

"You think that I behaved like a fool," I whispered to Dr. Delmayne. "I see it in your face."

"Never mind what you see in my face," he muttered, oracularly. "Perhaps it tells the truth and perhaps it doesn't. Anyhow, keep your wits under better control, next time. By the bye, let me feel your pulse;" (suddenly coming close beside me.) "Steadier than I expected to find it." The acute little eyes were ransacking my face. "Does it often strike you that you're doing about the queerest thing that was ever done by any female outside of two novel-covers?"

"Why don't you call it wild and crazy, Dr. Delmayne ?—as it is !" Then I made a little dreary gesture toward the bed. "If he only cared for me, you know, there would be some reason for this masquerade. But he even thinks of her whilst he is delirious."

Two flashes of fire left the wee eyes. "Don't blow your own trumpet," he growled, with right puzzling ambiguity.

"What do you mean, doctor?"

He wheeled away on one heel. "Stuff and nonsense! You know very well that if he were a bit soft about you the whole matter of your coming here would wear different colors. You know this, and what's more, you ought to know that I know you know it. Bad move, if you want sympathy, Mrs. Peters; very bad move indeed."

So ran his brutal words, and in tones rasping, compassionless. But I never thought, somehow, of feeling hurt or angry because of them. I am beginning to get so used to his grim acrid style that I verily believe a kindly-spoken sentence from him would not go far short of wounding me.

John Driscoll made his appearance, a little later. "I wanted to ask you about mamma," I took this chance of whispering ; for neither Edith Everdell nor her friend with the stare were present. "You have told her where I am?"

"Yes."

"Was the result very awful?"

"Rather," he smiled. "But her manner changed, ultimately, to a kind of magnificent despairing submission. Moreover, you must be sure that I put everything in the least ugly colors possible. For example, she merely thinks that you are in some place where an occasional meeting with Mrs. Everdell is a likelihood.

She does not know that you are here in the woman's own house."

"Well, for my part," I shoulder-shrugged, "it matters very little to me what you told her, so long as you let her understand that I am personally safe." Then, with the bitterest of bitter smiles I progressed : " I know it's bad taste to wash one's soiled linen even before so little of a stranger as you are ; but I can't help saying, John Driscoll, that it is she who has brought me to all this. It was she who first led me with blinded eyes into all my present misery. Do you understand what I mean ? If you don't, I mean that but for her my marriage—"

"Yes, yes," he broke in ; "I do understand. We had best not speak of this. Keep the old wounds closed if you can ; it is always good wisdom not to open them."

" Right," I nodded, after a little silence. " Only, they are not such very old wounds, after all. O my God ! to think, John Driscoll, that I have not been his wife six months, and am seeing what I see now, suffering what I now suffer ! "

" It is hard," he answered ; and answered no more ; and I knew from his words that he thought my own worse than futile, worse than waste of breath. So I kept silent and our brief talk ended thus.

That night was a dreadful night for Fuller. I would not leave him until nearly morning, though once Dr. Delmayne turned right savage in his kindly cruel desire to force me from the room. And all through the next day he was in deadliest peril of death, and a little while after dark so intense an exhaustion came upon him that I had not the dimmest hope he would ever wake from it ; but the frail dwindled life flickered and flickered flamewise, just burning on and no more, just not going completely out.

Before noon of the next day strength had somehow come to him, and a vague tinge of naturalness touched his fever-ravaged face, and I began to hope. He was struggling to be better. Perhaps he would not fail.

And that night I felt trustful that he would not fail. "You must go to bed now," Dr. Delmayne commanded, at about midnight. "You haven't the slimmest excuse, Mrs. Peters, for sitting up. Do you quite comprehend? Not the slimmest excuselet; so that ends the story."

I caught the doctor's hand, whilst he looked at me as though I were committing larceny upon him. "Tell me what you really mean, doctor. Is it that he is *going to live?*"

"Tut, tut, Mrs. Peters. We are none of us going to live. That is, we are all of us going to die, some day or other."

"Dr. Delmayne, if you know how to get me out of this room by telling me the truth, and don't do it, you're not very politic, certainly. I am sure you will not tell me a falsehood."

Whereat he chuckled an enormous chuckle, as at some enormous joke. "Upon my word, you're wise in your generation, my good Mrs. Peters—a perfect Solomoness, to put a famous proper noun in a grammatical petticoat. Well, I own you've made my professional reticence knock under. He's going to get well, to the best of my knowledge. You understand, ma'am?— My Knowledge! which isn't to be sneezed at, Mrs. Peters, except by the flippant nostrils of quacks and charlatans. Now *will* you go to bed and end the story?"

I awoke this morning to find every sign of his recovery still most hopeful.  He has had a good brief terrible fight with the Destroyer, and has come off wounded
sorely but still victor.  He will live.  How much and
how little those words mean to me !  Through all his
after-life he will never know whose hands helped him to
live ;—and by the bye, Dr. Delmayne whispered to me
yesterday that ' he didn't wish to flatter, but he *had* met
one or two clumsier nurses than I, and more grossly
ignorant.'  He meant that I was surprising him, every
little while, with my knowledge and skill.  I was right
in my prophecy to John Driscoll: I have been inspired.
Or is it only that the doctor was surprised to see me
capable of doing anything useful ?—me who am of a
class that usually bring up their women to be little except fair dancers and good flirts, with a languid taste
for fancy-work, and whole headfuls of unenlightenment
about darning a stocking or sweeping a room or cook-
ing a potato.

I think there is no doubt whatever that Edith Everdell has gotten heartily to dislike Mrs. Peters.  Whether
she suspects her to be any employee of Helen Dobell's
or not; whether or not she vaguely distrusts her appearance ; whether or not she is convinced that her disguise *is* a disguise—all this Mrs. Peters cannot and does
not care to determine.  Let her suspect or not suspect,
just as she chooses.  I shall of course take every pre-
caution against discovery.  And, by the bye, this
reminds me that I had forgotten, until a day or two
ago, about all my clothes bearing the initials H. D.  I
have consequently locked up everything that might lead
to detection, in the commodious closet my room possesses.  But possibly those pig-eyes of Margaret (who
arranges my room every morning, though she has been

permanently exiled from Fuller's) already have ferreted out the initials. And this may account for what quiet hostility I still see (when I have taken pains to notice it) remaining in Edith Everdell's manner toward me. It possibly underlies, too, the lynxlike vigilance of that Flora. Well, let them both rack their brains with misgivings about me. My one aim is to remain in the house with Fuller until he is well enough to need no further charge. Having this end in view, I must simply mail myself with self-control, and shun all such outbursts of personal feeling as that which happened the other day. It matters nothing to me what Edith Everdell or her friend thinks, so long as they both doubt and distrust at a respectful distance.

Now and then I have spasms of hatred seize hold of me when she is near. I suppose her presence in the chamber will be much harder to bear after Fuller's state begins more clearly to mend. Then she will have my attention, so to speak, and the nearness of her must perpetually irritate me. Already I begin to feel what truth Melville Delano and John Driscoll spoke: the thought of Fuller's death has never once touched her heart, as one could see plainly on her face. His death means to her the ceasing of a certain prosperous influx—the drawing of certain purse-strings; but no more than this. Seldom as I have noticed her, I have seen enough to make me discern how horrible an opposite from mine is the interest she feels in his living. Her face has mostly worn a bothered impatient look when I have watched it bending over his bed; the look of annoyance, dissatisfaction, disgust, but never of sorrow, solicitude, sympathy.

If she were an ignorant untrained creature, with little knowledge except the knowledge that she is beautiful

as a goddess and that men, for the most part, are sad
fools where it concerns the flinging away of money on
their own pleasures—then I should only despise her,
perhaps, and forgive whilst I did so. But it is her
training and her culture that madden me when I reflect
upon them, now. The thick rind of thoroughbred ease
which hides the rottenness within, makes her such a
loathsome deception. If she walks across the floor it is
a delusion; if she speaks, the sound of her voice is
treachery. She is a living lie. And to think that Fuller believes her! Should he get well, I feel that I shall
never rest until I have found some means of stripping
off the creature's audacious disguise and of showing him
the

"Serpent-heart, hid with a flow'ring face."

## CHAPTER XXXVII.

PRIL 15.—Through the past four days Fuller has been getting slowly better. The fever has now quite left him. He is so weak that he can hardly lift an arm, however, and yet he is disturbed by the slightest sound. Dr. Delmayne has forbidden anybody from crossing the threshold of his room. I don't think he would hesitate an instant to use forcible means if Edith Everdell should enter and refuse to depart. But his proclamation has gone forth through the household, and (excepting, of course, the servant who brings us our meals) they all seem to recognize the good policy of obeying it.

Last evening, however, between about nine and ten o'clock, a sound of laughter began below stairs, reaching us at intervals that momently grew shorter apart. It was a muffled sound because of the closed doors intervening ; but it had not been thrice repeated before Fuller showed signs of nervous wakefulness. Dr. Delmayne and I looked at one another. Presently there came a long loud peal ; then silence ; then a longer and a louder peal. I rose, just as Fuller commenced rolling his head from side to side with a faint plaintive childish whimper.

Dr. Delmayne wore so comfortable an appearance that I determined to spare him the trouble of going

downstairs and stopping the laughter. I would go myself. Of course the doctor would prevent me from going if he knew my real purpose. But I slipped into my
own chamber and so deceived him as to whither I was
bound : then, by the door communicating with the
outer hall, I hurried forth and made my way downstairs.

Several fresh peals of mirth guided me toward the
room whence these sounds were issuing. It was the
front parlor. The door was closed, but within there
was noise of high talking and the lower laughter of women mixed with men's heavier-toned laughter. Somebody seemed to have said something extravagantly
funny, just as I reached the door, to judge from the
applausive clamor that was prevailing. I shuddered to
consider the effect upon Fuller of this reckless uproar,
and felt glad that I had not waited to ring for a servant,
had not even waited to tell Dr. Delmayne where I was
going. And a little of the shudder, let me own, was
given to the thought of how heartless was this evident
merrymaking at such a time.

Boldly enough I knocked, and with some loudness,
too, because sure that I would not be heard unless I
knocked loudly. In an instant the clamor hushed itself
to dead silence. And in an instant later the door was
opened by that woman Flora.

She merely made a small aperture, thrusting her head
through this. " What is it ? " she asked, in sharp
tones. Then, discovering me, where I had drawn well
beyond the possibility of being seen by those within
the parlor if the door were opened widely, " Oh," she
murmured ; " Mrs. Peters ? "

" Yes," I murmured back, " Mrs. Peters."

By this time she had come out into the hall, shutting

the door behind her. She was gaudily dressed, with a certain theatrical magnificence in her costume's red satin complexities. Her cheeks were flushed to richest damask and her eyes burned brilliantly. Her bold bright-garmented beauty made a very gorgeous apparition. She silenced me for a moment with unwilling admiration ; long enough, indeed, for her to take the initiative in speaking, and to speak with a sort of surprised harshness.

"Well ; what is it ? "

" I have come downstairs to ask that you will cease your loud laughing at once. It greatly disturbs Mr. —— ''

" Hush," she broke in, with hurried whisper. "Don't you know that you shouldn't mention his name like that ? " Then a sudden ugly bravado seemed to possess her entire manner. " Are you *sure* that it disturbs him ? Or did you come downstairs of your own accord, just to pry ? "

This was irritating, of course, but it somehow didn't irritate me an iota. " Judge of that as you please," I made placid answer ; " only I beg of you and your friends not to let yourselves be heard again as you were heard just now."

I was moving away—had indeed taken several steps toward the staircase, when the door suddenly opened again. This time Edith Everdell appeared in the hall. Ah me ! how Flora's glories paled before this new arrival ! She was dressed in light soft blue, her marvellous charms all more dazzling than I have ever yet seen them. Even to me, who have gotten to loathe her as I would loathe a scorpion, her beauty was a perfect intoxication.

Flora gave her no time to speak. " Mrs. Peters has

come down to tell us that we must make less noise,"
she stated, an insolent drawl being evident even through
her whisper.

I had reached the first step of the staircase, having
neither the wish nor the willingness to stand parleying
with these creatures, when Edith Everdell's voice
stopped me.

" Do you mean to say, Mrs. Peters, that we have been
heard upstairs there, with all the doors closed ? "

" Distinctly," I replied.   Then I took another step
upward.   " I have not made my request in quite such
rude terms as it has been communicated to you by
that—" I was going to finish with " lady."   I had
every pacific intention of finishing with " lady."   I don't
know why I didn't, unless because the word abruptly
took me unawares, as it were, and refused to let itself
be spoken.   What I did finish with was " person."

Flora straightway gave her head an exaggerated toss,
" Oh, indeed," she satirized, leaving off her whisper
and curling her lips' full crimson with a beautiful vulgarity of arrogance.   " I'm ' that person,' am I ?   Why
didn't you say ' woman ' or ' creature ' or something
of that more contemptuous style ?   It would quite have
suited all your other confounded airs."   Then she
came forward five or six steps, with reddening cheeks
and brightening eyes, each fresh sentence seeming
to have inflamed her temper more violently, on the
principle, I suppose, that certain bonfires of passion
furnish their own fuel.   " It makes me mad just to look
at you ; it always has made me.   Do you want to
know why ?   Because you have no business here, and
Mrs. Everdell was a fool to have you come.   John
Driscoll bullied her into it and she let herself be
bullied ; that's just how it was.   You're a spy ; I know

you are. His wife got you here, or some of his friends
that are dead against Edith. You take notes of everything you see, and you mean to make mischief when
you go out of this house : I'll bet my life that's the
truth."

Her tones were far above a whisper, though in spite
of their malicious energy, I doubt if they had strength
to reach the occupants of the parlor. She had gone
only a brief distance in her tirade before I became
satisfied on one point : wine was making a fever in the
woman's blood and giving her boldness to speak out
her venomous ideas. It was not exact inebriety, but
rather an abandoned first cousin to it, of the brightened
eye and the heated head and the loosened tongue.

More than once after Flora had begun the attack,
Edith Everdell looked on the point of interrupting her.
But as the speaker progressed, a kind of reckless
sympathy seemed to draw her listener's mind away
from the fact that Flora was speaking at all, and only
to leave her aware that words were being uttered. And
in the end she broke in with so mild a reprimand that
the tones even surpassed the sentence itself in leniency.

"Hush, Flora ; be careful what you say."

I was fully mistress of my temper until that tormenting stroke of left-handed fellow-feeling ; then I forgot
prudence, and more than this, forgot fear. Quite
ignoring Flora, I turned upon Edith Everdell and burst
forth :

"These uncalled-for statements I don't choose to
trouble myself by denying. But I can't help saying
one thing, and that is : your forcing me to come down
here at all and stop your outrageous clamor, when you
well knew the condition of matters upstairs, has struck
me as thoroughly shameful. And whether you like to

18*

hear it or not, I frankly tell you that your want of common respect or decency is, beyond any doubt, shocking at a time like the present."

I spoke loudly enough, perhaps, for the inmates of
the parlor to have heard me if they had been listening ;
and whilst I spoke I saw Edith Everdell's face pale
noticeably either from anger or fear lest I should be
heard—from the latter, it is right probable. Almost as
the final word was leaving my lips, I turned with the
purpose of hastening upstairs at full speed. But even
whilst I did this, Flora sprang toward the banisters, and
reaching over them a quick savage hand, caught me by
the arm. When my horrified eyes met her face, I saw
something there that was closely like absolute fury.

"Don't have her in the house an hour longer,
Edith," she shouted, her voice raised to a right ireful
key and her grip tightened about my arm with a man's
own force. "Send her away at once ; she's a stuck-up
saucy thing, even if she isn't a spy. Make her go,
whether it pleases John Driscoll or not. How is it his
business, anyhow, who you choose to have in your
own house? Make her go straight off, or you'll feel
sorry, before long, that you did not take my advice."

By this time I had gotten enough over my amazement and terror to begin a vigorous struggle with the
horrid wine-excited creature. But her strength far exceeded mine, and my effort to break loose wrung a cry
from me, as its result only proved how much more
firmly her clutch could tighten about my arm. The cry
was sharp and keen-toned, though hardly enough of
either for Dr. Delmayne to hear it upstairs. An instant
after it was uttered I saw Edith Everdell seize the
woman's hand and drag it from my arm with a sudden
wrenching jerk, at the same time calling out :

" Flora ! Flora !  Behave yourself ! "

And at the same time, also, the parlor-door was thrown open, and whilst several men's faces dawned momentarily upon my bewilderment, I gathered my skirts together and rushed with all attainable fleetness upstairs. Straight on I sped, never pausing nor looking behind me till I had reached the door of my own room.  Entering, I locked this door and then sat down for a little while, resolved that I would quite recover my calmness before telling Dr. Delmayne the whole adventure.

But the calmer I grew the less inclined I felt toward telling him anything.  He had evidently not heard my rapid entrance into my own room.  How could I be sure that, on receiving any such confidence, his protectorship would not assume a most aggressive form of reprimand, making me more an object of spiteful suspicion than I seemed already to have become?  No ; I decided not to tell the doctor a syllable of what had just occurred.  Only John Driscoll should hear it all, when he came the next day.

And so I went into the sick-chamber, a little later, and found the doctor dozing over his novel, though he roused himself at the first rustle of my garments and favored me with the statement that those people downstairs had luckily stopped their abominable revelries ; and that they had stopped just in time, by the bye, to prevent a personal visit from himself.  "I was on the point, Mrs. Peters, of going down there and requesting, with some slight absence of ceremony, that they would immediately end the story."

' Oh, if I had only waited and let you go,' was my mental murmur, whilst I felt my aching arm where the effect of that bacchante's amazonian fingers were giving me no vague reminder of her brutal assault.

That night (which was last night, by the bye) Fuller passed so placidly that early on the following morning Dr. Delmayne told me his services as resident physician were no longer needed.

" You mean that you are going away ? " I faltered.

" I mean, Mrs. Peters, that I have a wife who considers herself an outraged woman and who has already taken five or six opportunities of telling me so ;—several times by letter, several times during my brief trips home." Then he caught my hand with a kind of gentle suddenness, the action being uncharacteristic enough almost to be laughable as well, whilst his voice softened from its usual gruff little whisper, and became, just for one fleet moment, all rich-cadenced as with ineffable sympathy. " Don't feel nervous about my going. I'll stop in three or four times a day, and make big visits at that. Remember, my dear Mrs. Peters, that the worst of your trouble is over."

" I am not so sure of it, doctor."

But I did not explain the ambiguity of those words, nor did he ask for an explanation ; perhaps he put his own construction upon them and believed that I was referring to all my future ; and perhaps I was, more than half.

When John Driscoll came, this morning, I told him everything that had happened last night. His face seemed to grow solemner and severer whilst I progressed in my tale. At length he broke forth, with strong grave appeal stamped on every feature :

" Let me get you away from here at once. Fuller is better, now, and—"

" Needs the most careful of nursing," I finished, with a dim firm smile. " I have grown erudite in nursing-matters, by this, and am a trifle vain of my powers, to tell entire truth. I don't think anyone could bring Fuller through *quite* so nicely as myself, just now, though this may all be hallucination. There is only one inducement for me to take your advice."

"And pray, what is that?" he wanted quite eagerly to know.

"My green spectacles. I hate them so. I am never free from a deep desire to tear them off. Riddance from them would be a right blessed emancipation, I assure you."

He made a great shoulder-shrug and walked away from the window, where we had been standing together for fully fifteen minutes past.

"And you really think there is a marked change for the better going on all the time?" presently I heard him murmur to Dr. Delmayne.

"No doubt of it," stated the doctor. "And he's going to have the best nursing in all Christendom ;— none of your hired kind, that does what it does like an automaton, and wouldn't much care whether the patient lived or died, provided the pay was poorer than usual or a little less sure. None of that stuff, sir ; but he's going to have instead (undeserving dog that he is !) a woman who would die two deaths, I solemnly believe, to gain for him this one life he has come so near losing. There's the kind of nurse that's a prize for us doctors when we can find her. Nothing makes a Florence Nightingale quite so quickly as a little of the genuine old-fashioned True Love—the sort that

" The more thou dam'st it up, the more it burns."

And by the bye, it's about the only good use which that disgusting little urchin with the arrows was ever put to ; ain't I more than half right? Well, out of that woman's weakness there has come strength, and she means to carry him through, D.V.—(free interpretation : 'Delmayne willing'.)  Yes, he's going to get over it, John ; and that ends the story."

# CHAPTER XXXVIII.

APRIL 22.—I have been so constantly employed in Fuller's room since Dr. Delmayne's residence here ceased, that I have had slight time, Diary, for accounts of how the days pass. Most eventlessly, at length let me chronicle. Fuller is well enough to be propped up in bed, now and then, but as yet the doctor positively forbids that he shall see anyone besides John Driscoll and—not *myself;* Mrs. Peters.

I think he has grown to place much reliance upon me, though he very rarely offers me a remark. Sometimes he seems for hours in profound thought, having wide-open eyes and staring ceilingward. Yesterday he suddenly left off this species of behavior and looked at me with more noticing scrutiny than he had yet approached toward showing.

"You're my nurse, are you not?" He asked the question with an abruptness that was not ungentle, somehow.

"Yes," I made answer.

"What is your name?"

"Mrs. Peters." Every new syllable that I pronounced gave me fresh fear lest he might recognize my voice, disguised though it was to the uttermost limit of its owner's skill.

Just the shadow of a smile touched his white lips. "Why are you not a man? You ought to be a man."

"They think me better than most man-nurses," I returned, growing bolder about my voice as its disguise seemed more trustworthy.

"You talk something like a man, with that deep voice of yours," he astonished me by murmuring, as though in a sort of soliloquy. "I suppose you are one of these manish females; but you don't look so. Am I very sick now?"

"Not very; but you will have to be in bed a long time yet. And the doctor has told me that if you began to talk I must try and prevent you from saying much."

"He told you that, did he? Well, the doctor is to be obeyed, I suppose." And a little later he fell asleep and slept more exhaustedly, I fancied, just because of having spoken and heard these few sentences.

I have had to send home by John Driscoll for some more underclothing; and to-day my trunk arrived, the H. D. on the outside having been carefully annihilated, as I had given orders that it should be. Speaking of John Driscoll, by the way, I am reminded of how charming his manner is with poor Fuller. He will not let Fuller give vent to more than ten words during their meetings, but all the words which he himself speaks are full of such cheerful unconscious sweetness that whilst listening I feel myself vacillate between envy and admiration. A few days ago Fuller woke up from a sort of stupor just as John Driscoll was entering the room.

"John, is that you?" he whispered, weakly.

"Yes, old fellow, here I am." By this he had gotten close beside Fuller's bed and had taken one of his friend's hands between both his own. "Getting along finely, I hear." (He hadn't heard anything of the kind.) "We'll have you well in no time, at this rate." And then followed a smooth stream of gentle cheering nothings that were more than his medicine to the invalid, I don't at all doubt.

Well, by the bye, John Driscoll ought to exert himself a little, now, in helping Fuller to bear his calamity. Heaven knows, he assisted him with enough gusto in going to meet it !

*April* 28.—Fuller's recovery is now very rapid. Three days ago he sat up, for the first time, in a great chair, and (ah, how I hate to write the words !) Edith Everdell paid him a visit.

Fuller's whole face lit with a look of unspeakable welcome the moment his eyes met hers. He stretched out both hands toward her before she had well entered the room. And then she, for her part, hurried toward him with a matchless deerlike gracefulness, and knelt beside his chair and wreathed his neck with both her arms. I saw them kiss again and again ; and heard them too. Both wanted me out of the room, very possibly, but I would not go. The thought of leaving him alone with her was torture—even worse torture than to sit (as I was then sitting) by a rather distant window and hear their low-murmured sentences, purposely made too low for my ears.

Only now and then I could catch a word or two. Once I heard her tell him this lie :

"Of course I knew that if you recollected me at all you would feel sure of how I was suffering and suffer yourself; and this thought has made me right miserable on your account."

It lasted a half-hour. Or rather, at the end of a half-hour I determined that it should not last any longer, for I had gotten a neuralgia that darted between my two temples, and had become so madly nervous, besides, that to sit still was grown a deed unperformable. So up I rose from my seat at the window, and came forward to where they were murmuring together with clasped hands.

Both stared at me with rather unangelic eyes. This was the first time I had met Edith Everdell since Flora's atrocious attack ; about which, I am inclined to fancy, John Driscoll said his say very soon after its occurrence. The man told me with much exactness of ocular expression : "You are a bore." The woman told me, with an increased exactness, if anything : "You are a bore, and I hate you."

" Mrs. Everdell, I must request of you not to remain any longer," I plunged. " The doctor left orders—"

" Oh, bother the doctor's orders," broke in Fuller.

" If I had not paid strictest heed to them, sir," I solemnly persisted, "you would not now be alive."

Edith Everdell gave the daintiest of shudders. " How sepulchrally she talks !" (uttering the words whilst her head, with all its glory of strange-colored hair, lifted the crimson charm of two parted lips until they nearly touched his.) " And in that queer harsh voice, too ! Have you a cold, Mrs. Peters ? "

" A little cold," I made answer, struck with a sudden fear lest this change which I am obliged to adopt in my voice when before Fuller would prove, now that she also heard it, provocative of fresh suspicions. Then I went on: " Mr. Dobell, please oblige me by doing as I wish."

After that I walked away from them, somehow feeling sure that my request would be heeded ; and in a very few moments it was heeded.

" I hope they'll allow me to see you every day, now,"
she whispered, with cooing wooing voice, whilst standing at his side and letting her hand linger between both
of his own. " If you only knew how I want to be near
you, and how long and lonely the days are ! "

" Do you go out often ? "

" Not often." Her eyes were all melancholy tenderness. " I have so little heart for anything, Fuller,
whilst you are sick."

" But you must not give way to such feelings, Edith,"
he made gentle remonstrance. " Recollect that I am
better now, and am mending very fast."

Then this sultana of hypocrites leaned down and gave
him a farewell kiss, looking goddesslike in her beauty
of stooped shoulders and long faultless thrust-out
throat.

I felt like shouting forth my thankfulness when the
door closed behind her, as at last it did close. But instead of this I let some words slip from between my
lips that I would have given worlds to unsay a moment
after their utterance.

" Are you quite sure that that woman cares for you
as she professes to care ? "

He stared at me with widest eyes of astonishment for
a second or more. Then his face, pale as it already
was, grew a shade paler. " What do you mean ? " he
muttered.

I was nearly frightened out of my senses, by this
time ; frightened for his physical sake ; frightened as I
would have been if I had made some bad blunder in the
giving of his medicines.

" Oh, nothing ; nothing at all," I hastened, a nervousness in my manner that just bordered upon out-
and-out agitation. " It merely occurred to me, as one

might say, to ask the question. *I* know nothing—of course not."

"Yes, you *do* know," he made stern response. Then, smiling a quick contemptuous smile, he went on : " Or rather, you think that you know. Come, tell me at once what you mean."

I was more collected, by this, and had begun to see a possible way out of the difficulty. If the first seeds of distrust for Edith Everdell were at all to be sown—the seeds from which valuable after-results might spring— why not sow them now, when the chance offered ?

I drew quite near to him. "If I tell you what I really do mean, you must first make me a solemn promise, Mr. Dobell ; the kind of promise that we intend to keep when we make it, you know."

" What promise ? " he questioned, staring hard at me, as though he would like to discover the color of my eyes through their opaque spectacles.

" This : You must never mention a word of what I tell you, to Mrs. Everdell or anyone who could repeat it to Mrs. Everdell. Will you make me such a promise ? "

He stared quite a while longer before answering. "Yes ; I make such a promise."

" Very well. I meant, then, that I have reason to believe that she does go out very often, and in the evenings, too, though she has just told you that she has little heart for anything whilst you are sick. That is all ; please believe that it is all. We had better not say anything more on the subject, just now. Perhaps—" but I paused there, wishing that I had not begun that new sentence.

" Well ? " he queried, sharply. " Perhaps what ? "

" Perhaps I shall try to give you some proof that I

have spoken truth, at some future time, when you are stronger and better able to hear it."

"I shall remind you of those words," he stated, sternly. And then, whilst he grew gloomily silent and remained so for fully a half-hour, until the arrival of Dr. Delmayne, I was visited by all sorts of dire fears that I had gone too far, said too much, behaved like an imprudent fool.

But during yesterday and to-day he has shown no signs of having retrograded. Perhaps he has been silently pooh-poohing all that I hinted to him. His faith in the truth and purity of that arch-traitress is strong enough to make him regard either as idlest malice or grossest error the statements of any such inferior order of being as Mrs. Peters, I have no doubt whatever. Well, such faith may have had good sanitary results. "It is an ill wind," and all that.

For two days past I have kept Edith Everdell from the room, and with Dr. Delmayne's authoritative veto at my service whenever I want it, shall be able to continue her exile at least a week longer. Dr. Delmayne assured me this morning that Fuller must have a month more of convalescence before he is able to leave the room.

A month! Undoubtedly for three weeks I shall not have power to keep her away: she can come and go when she pleases, after he has reached a certain state of bodily soundness. How I dread the thought of all this! And what a fierce animal feeling of ferocity possesses me when I recollect the work I am now well resolved to carry out—the work of disenchanting, disillusionizing Fuller. In good time I must have a talk with John Driscoll about this vaguely-formed plan of mine, and use all my eloquence in forcing a little help from him.

## CHAPTER XXXIX.

AY 8.—There is no keeping them apart any longer. I have done it for ten days, but this morning Fuller himself rose in open rebellion and told Dr. Delmayne that he was being made a fool of. "I am quite well enough now, doctor, to see whom I please," he stated. "And if you say not I shall simply believe you are trying to humbug me."

The doctor made snappish enough response, but that afternoon Fuller quietly insisted upon my sending for Mrs. Everdell, whilst he sat in his easy-chair, having a real touch of healthful color on either cheek and something quite noticeable in the way of a blond beard curling closely about his chin: doubtless the beard would have been a sharp surprise to me if I had seen it all at once, so to speak; but I have watched its gradual coming and am therefore grown slowly inured to the change it has wrought.

"Mrs. Peters," he informed me, "if you don't ring that bell for a servant I shall get up and do so myself: I am quite able, you know—able, for that matter, to march downstairs, if I want. And when the servant comes I wish a message sent to Mrs. Everdell that I should like to see her."

"Just as you please, sir," I succumbed, feeling that further opposition would be sheer purposeless kicking against the pricks, and that the loathed ordeal of those daily interviews must begin from now henceforward.

The message was sent, and Edith Everdell presently appeared, beautiful as one of the

> . . . . " Daughters of dreams and of stories
>     That life is not wearied of yet,
>   Faustine, Fragoletta, Dolores,
>     Fèlise and Yolande and Juliette,"

being all fresh rich coloring and willowlike grace and divine statuesque curves.

She was with him two good hours. I did not remain in the room much more than ten minutes after she had entered it, but forced myself to leave them alone together, feeling that there was less torture, after all, in putting a closed door between Mrs. Peters and that atrocious serpent of deceit.

After this, I suppose, she is to be with him for hours each day. Oh, it is almost beyond endurance! I am somehow free from all bitter thought when I think of Fuller's behavior; every spiteful, revengeful and malicious impulse seems to turn against *her*. Perhaps I even in a measure exculpate him, remembering his utter belief in her, and remembering also her marvellous unapproached beauty.

Before long he must surely remind me of the proof I promised him. It is odd that he has not already spoken. I hope his demand will soon be made; and that when it is made good luck will befriend me in adequately answering it.

*May* 14.—She is near him half the day, now. And every new hour that they are together seems to strengthen my resolve fourfold. If possible, I shall show her to Fuller in her beastly reality before I leave this house.

Meanwhile he does not even remotely aid my purpose by asking me for that proof.

Were it not for John Driscoll and Dr. Delmayne, I should doubtless be forced to leave here at once, by the bye. Two or three distinct times Fuller has thrown out hints, of late, pointedly suggesting that he is well enough not to need me any more. Edith Everdell has been at work, I feel confident, counselling him to assume this style. But it is quite useless. This morning I found an opportunity of button-holeing Dr. Delmayne, so to speak, just outside the door of the patient's chamber.

"Doctor," I stated, "they are trying to get me away from here; or rather that woman is trying it. I don't want to go yet; I shall not go yet. You must help me to remain." And then I told him precisely what I have gotten firmly to believe regarding Edith Everdell's persuasion of Fuller.

"Don't doubt it at all," he growled, in cross ellipsis. "Devil of a woman, I daresay, and up to anything bad, from a fib to a murder. Mrs. Peters, you shall remain here as long as there's a vestige of excuse for your remaining, and that ends the story."

Whereupon Dr. Delmayne, after standing for a second or two with meditative forefinger pressed fervently against one side of his nose, darted toward the door of Fuller's room and pounced upon his patient with the following language :

"Mrs. Peters tells me that she thinks of going. I have just answered Mrs. Peters to the effect that she will greatly displease me if she does go inside of at least —at the very *very* least—ten days longer."

"Why ten days, doctor ? " I heard Fuller's composed tones ask. "I am well enough now to do nearly everything for myself."

"You are nothing of the sort," contradicted the doctor, quite furiously. "It is Mrs. Peters and Human Ingratitude, combined, that lead you to the glaring blunder of such an opinion. Mrs. Peters has been to you for weeks past what the cord is to the bow, what the hand is to the arm, what the eyelid is to the eye. She has stood at your elbow in such perpetual readiness to be of service that you have grown to take her for granted, to accept her as an inanimate matter-of-course, like the chair you sit in or the spoon you drink your medicine out of. You are not aware, sir, how you would miss her if she went. I am. Why, what did one of my patients say, the morning after Mrs. Peters went from her bedside ? 'Doctor,' mourned the patient, 'I feel as if I'd lost three slats out of my bed.' That's the way you would feel. No, sir ; ten days longer ; ten days at the least—possibly fifteen, as I told Mrs. Peters a minute ago. I have also told Mrs. Peters that she positively must remain. And she is going to remain. So that ends the story."

I think my champion has gained my cause for me. Ten days are a long while. I may accomplish marvels in that time.

19

## CHAPTER XL.

AY 18.—And at last I have fairly begun the work of disenchantment. This morning, when John Driscoll came, I managed to have some words with him in the hall; words which I took care should be very low and cautiously-spoken on either side; for with Margaret and that disreputable Flora both in the house, there is no telling what deeds of eavesdropping might be attempted.

He heard my proposal with a blank bewildered stare. "Even if you were not treading upon such dangerous ground," he soon made earnest murmur, "even if you were not trying to dethrone Edith Everdell here in Edith Everdell's own house, how would it be possible for you to change Fuller's unchangeable faith?"

"Simply by making him an eye-witness of what would prove to him her vileness beyond any shadow of doubt. It seems to me that here, in the creature's own house, we should be able—"

"Oh, impossible," he broke in. "No plan could be more unfeasible than that."

I smiled sourly. "You said something of the same sort about my coming here. Wild and impracticable as *that* plan was, look how perfectly it has succeeded."

We separated not long afterward, by no means on the

best of terms. At least I was far from feeling very
amiably toward him, though doubtless he bore me no
special grudge for having made a somewhat successful
attempt to snub me.

All the rest of the day a little hand seemed perpetually tapping me on the shoulder and a little voice whispering in my ear. ' Begin now,' whispered the little
voice. ' Nearly every night she passes upstairs to her
room on the lower floor, sometimes bonneted, sometimes with wraps about head and shoulders, always
with unmistakable signs of having just returned home.
And yet she tells him that she rarely goes out by day,
never at night : she dares to tell him this, in her brazen
confidence that he will believe her. Begin now,' whispered the little voice. ' Your chance for beginning is
good. Why neglect it ? Don't neglect it. Begin
now.'

But I paid the little voice the tardy respect of not beginning until after dark this very evening. From early
in the afternoon of to-day until nearly six o'clock, Edith
Everdell had been with Fuller : I think it was this,
more than anything else, that spurred me into immediate action. I have gotten to hate the thought of leaving them together and to hate the thought of being
near them when they are together. To-day a sort of
compromise with these two aversions resulted in my
making incidental visits to Fuller's room, at distances
of about ten minutes apart. She had gotten for herself
a large tufted chair, much lower than that in which he
was seated, and had made her figure one superb languid
curvature over the side nearest to him ; and against the
dark back of his own chair her head rested, small, clear-
seen and of peerless waved contour, postured with such
luxurious grace of lazy ease that her pale sleek throat

bulged forward its chaste-colored roundness below soft-
molded chin and the rich moist bloom of lifted lips.
And his own face, a trifle above hers, was so near it
that he must have breathed her breath, she his.   There
was no chronic holding of hands; or possibly this was
the one scrap of notice which they paid my presence,
and some temporary manual divorce took place whenever I entered the room, to be annulled again an instant
after my exit.

At about dusk, just after I had come in and lighted
the gas, she uncurled herself, as it were, and raised from
its resting-place her head, with all its odd splendor of
prodigal hair, and presently stood at his side, having
taken one of his hands in each of her own and begun to
swing them gently that way and this.   " Good-night,"
she murmured.   " I must go now."

" And shan't I see you this evening, Edith?" he
tenderly wanted to know.   " The evenings are so stupid from seven till nine."

"They will not let me come," she answered, her
sweet voice seeming to tremble with plaintive regret.
" That bear of a Doctor Delmayne insisted, the other
day, that I should never visit you in the evenings."

" And why not, pray?"

A smile broke from her rich lips like a gold bee from
some crimson flower.   " You are not to be excited.
He ranks me among your excitements.   Flattering,
even though cruel; isn't it?"

" And so we must both pass stupid evenings because
of that despot."   I fancied that his face lost a little of
its easy amiability, just here, whilst lifted to hers.
" By the bye, you are not going out or anything, to-
night?"

She dropped his hands and gave her head a little in-

tolerant toss. "Fuller, I believe you don't believe me
when I tell you things, nowadays." There were almost
tears in her broken voice, and her smooth round chin,
with its one exquisite dimple, just vaguely quivered for
a second. "Why should I care to go out? and haven't
I told you that I scarcely ever have the heart to go,
even in the day-time? Oh, Fuller, you ought to believe me! When have you ever known me not to tell
you the perfect truth?"

For a moment, whilst the gaslight struck her divine
profile and showed me how the beautiful eloquence of
reproach in her face was mingled with an equal eloquence
of appeal, I found myself forgetting utterly that she was
a liar and a hypocrite, whilst I remembered solely that
she was a woman on whom heaven had showered the
most unstinted largesse of ravishing fleshly charms. It
was a kind of stagnant calm with me before the indignant storm burst over my soul. A moment later I had
set my teeth close together and the breath was making
quite an audible rush through my nostrils. Oh, with
what pure comfort I could have dashed up to her, then,
and shrieked forth: "You are nauseating with your
lies; and I dare you to prove that you have not gone
out four nights of this present week and never once returned till after eleven, at the earliest." Pure comfort
would it indeed have been, to shout out this fiery challenge! Instead of doing so I went from window to
window, pulling down the shades, one of which I gave
such a violent jerk that I jerked it from its roller, poor
blameless victim of my wrath!

And just as I accomplished this little piece of injustice,
Fuller was answering with an almost passionate force:
"I do believe you, Edith; I would believe you in spite
of all the world's counter-evidence, there isn't a single

doubt." Then, having caught her hand whilst she let it just linger in his hold and no more, turning away her head till he could only gain a side-glimpse of her milky throat, with the frail pink ear above it and the warm-colored fluctuant hair drawn back from the vague-veined temple, he progressed, in tones of intenser emphasis : "I admit, Edith, that I have been a trifle inquisitive about the matters of your goings and comings—almost enough so to make you fancy me distrustful. But I'm not distrustful. Don't be angry with me. Look round and say that you are not angry."

Whereat her face was slowly turned toward him, brilliant with a pardoning smile. "We will make an agreement, then, that you are not to taunt me again with these horrid unjust hints. Promise that you will not, Fuller."

"I promise, with all my heart ! "

The moment she had left the room I felt that my time for speaking out might far better have been postponed, perhaps, until to-night. Between eight and nine o'clock Edith Everdell would probably take her departure for somewhere. A little clever sentinelship in the outside hall would probably afford me a chance of making sure as to whether she really went or no. Then, armed with the certainty of her absence, I could at last use my tongue with far better effect after her recent daring false-hood to Fuller, and prove that

> "*Qui veut un jour bien parler*
> *Doit d'abord apprendre à se taire.*"

A little after eight o'clock, that evening, a carriage drove up to the door and stopped there. So far so good. I slipped into the outer hall and leaned over the banisters. My view well commanded a small space of hall directly in front of Edith Everdell's room. She would doubtless appear, presently, and presently she did appear, followed by Flora and going straight downstairs into the lower hall.

I made sure that it was she, after one good glimpse of her face in the bright gaslight. She was dressed darkly and bonneted, as was also Flora.

Then I slipped back into my own room, and waited near the window, not lifting the shade. Perhaps three minutes later there came the sharp sound of a shutting carriage-door. Then the sound of wheels, rolling away. She had gone to-night, as I have heard her go on many a previous night.

A little while afterward I entered Fuller's room. He sat in his great chair, reading, and only glanced up for a moment when I appeared. I came very near to him and stood at his side.

"Mr. Dobell," I murmured, in that odd roughened voice which it has gotten almost a second-nature with me to use.

"Well?" (rather sharply.)

"Some time ago," I began, in fearless prelude, "you stated that you were going to remind me of what I said regarding Mrs. Everdell's habit of leaving the house in the evenings. You have not done so, although I have been waiting for you to do so ever since."

His face was harshly darkened whilst he made harsh answer: "I let the subject drop, for reasons of my own. I didn't suppose you would resume it. And why do you resume it now?"

"Because I think you are deceived about the real truth, and quite contented in your deception. And because, if you choose, she has just gone off in a carriage, not five minutes ago."

He rose up from his chair whilst his eyes flashed

at me. "Be careful how you assert things, Mrs. Peters!"

I smiled. "You can prove it for yourself. Ring the bell and inquire."

Without another word he walked toward the bell and acted on my suggestion. Then he walked back to his chair and took up his book and tried to make me believe that he was reading, whilst his eyes were fixed on the print before him and his face was pale and sternly set.

Not long afterward there came a knock at the door. "Come in," Fuller invited, with short sharpness.

Enter Margaret, all fat dignity and ludicrous reluctance. "Jane's out," she mumbled immediate explanation, "and I had to come instead. What's wantin', please?"

"I wish that you would tell Mrs. Everdell," stated Fuller, "that I should like to see her as soon as possible."

I saw the obese creature conceal a surprised start. "Mrs. Everdell, sir?" (opening the somnolent little eyes about as widely as she could.)

"You heard me, didn't you?" was the rather brusque retort.

Margaret stood stone-still and speechless. Was she gathering together her fluttered wits? From her slow sulky answer, presently blurted forth, I should suppose yes.

"Mrs. Everdell's gone to bed, sir."

Fuller clouded his brows, then, and spoke with quick decisiveness. "It makes no difference. I wish to see her, all the same. Carry her my message. If she is asleep, give it, all the same."

"I don't like to, sir," came the glib lie from her

mistress's own servant. "She ain't well at all; that's the reason she's went to bed so early."

"Is it, indeed?" he cried, starting up, with irate face. "Are you sure, my good woman, that you're telling me the truth?"

A bad hard look came over the ugly fleshful face, at this. "Of course I'm tellin' the truth. I don't as usual tell lies."

"Oh, you don't? Then prove that you've told me the truth by going downstairs and giving my message, whether your mistress is sick or well. If she is too sick to see me I will go down and see *her.*"

Fright and ill-humor seemed to be waging war with each other, now, on the woman's face. What fresh unspoken lie rushed to her lips I can't tell. Evidently she saw that she had been cornered, checkmated, found out, and that the lie would be quite futile; for whilst scowling a great malicious scowl, she suddenly veered round with awkward bulky haste and bundled herself out of the room, slamming the door behind her.

Fuller sprang from his chair on the instant and hurried toward the door, opening it and going out into the hall beyond.

"You have a good place here," I heard him cry, "and I know you value it. But I promise you that you shall lose it to-morrow unless you tell me the precise truth: is Mrs. Everdell in at present, or out?"

Silence. Then Fuller's voice again. "Do you hear what I say? Is your mistress at home, or has she gone out?"

More silence. Presently a dull sullen unwilling sort of grunt, to this laconic effect:

"She's gone out."

19*

Very soon after receiving that information, Fuller reappeared. He seated himself and took up his book again, staring at it as before. Suddenly he laid the book down and glared at me.

"You have made the statement, I believe, that it is Mrs. Everdell's habit to leave the house every evening."

"Nearly every evening," I calmly corrected.

"You are prepared, I suppose, to abide by your statement when she returns to-night?"

"I should rather *not* do so," sped my prompt response.

"And may I ask why?" he burst forth, with the look of an inquisitor.

"Simply for this reason: Mrs. Everdell already dislikes me heartily. I wish to be mixed up in no quarrel with her. Perhaps I have acted unwisely in telling you the truth, even though I saw that you were being altogether deceived. Indeed, let me beg of you that my name shall not be mentioned during whatever discussions may follow. I think that when I ask this of you I am asking little else than a course of common generosity. I must ask, still further, that you will have the goodness to reflect on my request."

He kept silence for quite a little time after my words were ended, at first searching my spectacled inscrutable face so steadily that I almost had fears lest he would pierce beyond the exterior husk of Mrs. Peters and find the Helen Dobell hidden beyond it: and then he abruptly dropped his eyes, remaining thoughtful and absorbed until he at length lingeringly murmured:

"I think you are right. Provided your charges be just charges, you deserve my thanks. I shall shield you from Mrs. Everdell's ill-will, if thorough avoidance of your name can do that much. But—" and here his

eyes lifted themselves to my face whilst flashing faintly
—" if your charges be *un*just—"

" Then yours should not be more unjust," I broke in.

" What do you mean ? " he wanted to know, puz-
zledly.

" That you should not accuse me of telling what I
have told from mere contemptible motives of malice.
Moreover, if Edith Everdell denies that, this or the
other, *you* would be most unjust in accepting her denial as thorough truth. Because you believe in her absolute honesty you should not doubt mine. Hear whatever she says and take it, if you please, as evidence of a
certain weight ; but do not use it as a means of putting
my evidence to scorn ; for until you have clear proof
that I have spoken falsehood, it is my right to demand
from you something very like trust."

I knew that Margaret's brazen detected duplicity had
paved my way for me, and the boldness which I threw
into my words took origin from this consideration.
" Like mistress, like maid," was possibly ringing in his
ears, just then. How gloriously Margaret had abetted
my cause, against her own malevolent will !

" What do you call ' clear proof ' ? " Fuller presently
asked, with troubled face and troubled voice.

" Proof given you by your own senses of sight or
hearing. Proof that depends on no one's word of
mouth. As regards the matter of Mrs. Everdell's having gone out many times before to-night, such proof is
now of course impossible. But there will probably
come a time," I went on, feeling boldness enough to
utter the bold necessary words, " when I may prove to
you, in other ways, that her truthfulness is not what
you have evidently been believing it."

Again he started up from his chair, full of angry

fierceness ; (it is wonderful, by the bye, how little like his calm self, how excitable, how Melville-Delanoish his illness had made him. But I have slight doubt that although still weak, still nervous, he is convalescent enough to bear whatever shocks I have been causing him.)

" You are most audacious," he cried, " to stand there and infer slanderous things against a person in whom I have always put absolute trust. I will give you, however, one week to furnish the proofs you speak of—one week, during which I shall mention to nobody our conversation of to-night. At the end of that time, if you fail to furnish the evidence required, I shall lose what little faith your manner has somehow roused in me, and you must at once leave the house. Is this an agreement between us, or do you decline making it ? "

One week ! A short time, surely ! But in one week much might be accomplished—as much, after all, as in two or three. I had indeed best acquiesce ; and for that matter, what other course than acquiescence remained to me ? What other course except a forced departure from the house ?

" Very well," I gave lingering consent. Then I spoke much more rapidly. " In one week's time I hope to have satisfied you."

Fuller sat down again, pale and solemn-browed.

" I wish you would leave me alone now," he muttered, very gruffly. " I shall sit up until Mrs. Everdell returns. Do you feel able to prophesy when that will be ? "

" No," I answered. " Perhaps not until after eleven."

" Very well," he made dogged resolve ; " if it isn't till five in the morning I shall sit up for her just the same."

" Will not to-morrow do just as well, sir, for saying all you wish to say? Remember," was offered in placid remonstrance by what I may call my Mrs. Peters portion, "the doctor recommends nine o'clock as your regular hour for going to bed."

" I don't care," he fumed, childishly. " Let me ask you again, Mrs. Peters, to leave the room. If I want anything, I will call for it."

But he has not called me since I left him ; and during more than two hours I have been seated here in my own room, Diary, by turns thinking and telling you what has recently happened. And now, just as I finish my account, there is the sound of a carriage stopping at the street-door. She has returned. Fuller has heard the carriage stop and has gone out into the hall.

He means to burst upon her like a bomb-shell as she comes upstairs, I suppose.

## CHAPTER XLI.

AY 19.—Because my room opens into Fuller's by one door and into the hall by another, I was enabled, last night, to hear everything that passed, quite distinctly. Everything, I repeat, for the reason that Fuller evidently did not go downstairs, but remained, doubtless, as I myself had done about two hours previously, in a place where he could see those two creatures as they came upstairs.

It was not long before I heard his clear strong voice call out :

" Edith."

There was no answer. The bomb-shell had burst. If Margaret had opened the door, it was an explosion for which they were not wholly unprepared. If not, it had all the banging abruptness which I devoutly desired it to have.

Fuller's voice again, a slight while afterward :

" Edith, you hear me, do you not ? "

" Yes, Fuller ; what is it ? " The reply was just audible to me.

" I wish you to come upstairs. I wish to speak with you."

" Yes ; certainly." Again a just-audible reply.

Then I heard Fuller walk with firm even steps into

his own room. Certainly three minutes elapsed before there was a rustling in the hall as of silken garments. The rustling drew nearer to Fuller's room, and finally seemed to pass within it.

Then I heard him remark with short-toned sharpness, after a little apparent interval of silence between the two, whilst they were doubtless facing one another :

" You have taken off your bonnet."

" Yes ; " (in a nervous fluttered murmur) " I stopped a minute to take it off. Aren't you up rather later than usual ? I didn't suppose — "

He cut her short, then. " You are right. I *am* up much later than usual. I chose to sit up until you got home. I wished to ask you where you had been and why you preferred to conceal your going out by the telling of a deliberate falsehood."

" Fuller ! "

" Don't assume the reproachful, please." (He was so like the Fuller of ordinary days, now ; the quiet-speaking well Fuller, not the irascible sick one.) " You know it is quite useless to deny that you told me a false-hood this afternoon ; or rather acted it, which I regard as equally bad, if not worse. At first I could scarcely credit that you were really leaving the house. I rang the bell after your carriage had gone from the door, and Margaret appeared. The woman tried to hide from me the facts of the case by two most unblushing falsehoods ; but I finally forced her into confessing that you had really gone out and were neither in bed nor sick."

" I am not responsible for Margaret's conscience," came the low slow answer.

" No ? " (with composed bitterness). " Your own doesn't seem to involve a very heavy responsibility, either."

" Do not be too hasty in offering me insult," rippled her answer, all serenity and fluent cadences. " You may regret your haste, presently. Appearances throw dust in people's eyes to liberal amounts, now and then."

" You are certainly not going to deny that you left the house more than two hours ago."

" I have no such intention ; " (whilst a quiver, as of hurt dignity, seemed faintly to jar the words). " I merely mean that although I left the house I left it for the simple purpose of serving you."

" Serving me ! "

She seemed to speak as from a soulful of melancholy, now. She was not shedding tears, but every separate word dropped like the dropping of a tear. " Yes ; serving you. Look as skeptical as you please ; I mean it, Fuller Dobell. But how can you care to hear my defense ? And why should I " ( with a vague flash of indignation, at this point) " degrade myself by any defense, when I am wholly innocent ? "

" Innocent of what ? " I could imagine the blank amazement on his face whilst he spoke.

" Of doing anything but trying to shield you from scandalous comments," throbbed her passionate answer. (Ah, what a marvellous voice that woman has ! To hear her voice and see her face at one and the same time weakens the effect of each, I fancy, since each is such a curiosity—this of melody, that of loveliness.) " Oh, Fuller, it is because I love you so dearly, I suppose, that I take from you now what no living creature should say to me and not win my worst ill-will for saying it. Well, hear the real truth ; hear how unjustly you have attacked me. Yesterday somebody sent Flora a theatre-box for to-night. She asked me to go, and I laughed in her face, believing that she was joking.

But I learned, very soon, that she was in good earnest. ' You think it an awful thing for me to ask you,' she told me, ' whilst Fuller Dobell is sick ; but do you know that I have heard more than one person express surprise at your sudden change to this quiet shut-up life ? I suppose it's your wish that suspicions as to *where he is and why he is here*, should not begin to form in people's minds.' ' Of course that is my wish,' I made answer ; ' you know it very well, Flora.' ' Then don't make quite such a nun of yourself,' she returned, adding much more than that, and much that I could not help feeling was prudent counsel. The result has been that I have gone to-night, Fuller, and that I have deceived you about my going for just this reason and no other : I was afraid that even after hearing my explanation you would be bothered with fancies of how I had gone because I really wanted to go, and not because I only wanted people to think so."

I knew that she had gained a victory (gained at least a temporary one) some time before the mellow rhythm and richness of her voice had ended the magnificent art of its murmur. There was, indeed, hardly a second of silence after she had finished, for Fuller's answer came immediately, hot as with shame for his own gross wrong-doing.

" Edith, I take it all back, darling ! I ask your pardon. I was an infernal goose. What ! angry yet ! Don't cry ; or if you do, tell me I'm forgiven before you've actually begun."

" It is not a question of forgiveness," came the tremulous reproach. " Ah, no ; I can forgive you easily enough. But the thought of your having suspected me is so trying a one, Fuller ! Did you suspect of your own accord, by the bye, or were you made to suspect by others? John Driscoll never liked me; that Dr. Delmayne hates me, for some strange reason, I think; and Mrs. Peters—"

"No, no," he broke in, though without any deep earnestness of denial; "blame me and me only, Edith."

"But I would so much rather think that they have been trying to poison your faith! It is so much more comforting for me to think this!"

A moment or two of silence. Was he going to break faith with Mrs. Peters, and tell her the truth? I was prepared for anything after her easy victory. But no; he remembered his promise.

"Please believe that no one is to be blamed except myself," he made serious-voiced appeal. "And now let us forget all about it and talk of other things. You enjoyed the theatre? I hope so. I hope you will go again very soon. It is a shame that my illness should have kept you in-doors. You know how little I like that Flora; but her advice was good advice for once, certainly."

It was a perfect reconciliation before they parted. She had left him, and I sat with knit brows, pondering over my future course, when his steps came suddenly very near the door which led from his own room into mine. Then he knocked at the door with sharpness.

"Mrs. Peters."

"What is it?" I made instant reply.

"Are you still up and dressed?"

My next reply was to open the door.

He lifted an imperative hand, forbidding me with the gesture from crossing his threshold.

"You have heard what has just passed, I suppose."

I nodded yes.

"Very well. I have only this to say: The agree-

ment between us still remains good. I tell you in all
candor, however, that I regret having made it and that
I do not place an atom of faith in your statements. If
you desire to stay here a week longer, do so. If you
wish to go to-morrow, go, and I shall willingly release
you from the promise, the contract, or whatever it deserves to be called."

"I do not wish to go," was my firm composed answer.

"Then remain—for exactly one week." His words
breathed, through every syllable, a cold austere antipa-
thy. "I merely gave you your chance; that is all."
Then, with eyes that brightened angrily: "You are
foolish not to avail yourself of it, I can't help adding;
for perhaps, my good Mrs. Peters, you are playing a
more dangerous game than you imagine." After that
he shut the door. Shut it without insulting suddenness,
but with a certain decisive expedition.

During the whole of to-day he has spoken to me only
when speech was necessary, and then almost in monosyllables. I think that last night's developments have
had a weakening effect upon him, in a physical way.
He is so far on the road to absolute recovery, however,
that I feel my first blow to have been very well-timed.

John Driscoll and I have had another whispered con-
fab in the hall. I began by telling him everything that
happened last night and imploring his help in the work
which I began to perform.

"But how can I possibly help you," he questioned,
"even if I had all the willingness in the world?"

"*You* could think of *something*," I pleaded, flattering
him with a kind of melancholy policy.

"I can think of absolutely nothing," he made pronounced denial.

" Recollect," I persevered, " that my coming here at
all was your own brilliant idea. Do me the one more
great service of going home and thinking, thinking,
until you find *some* kind of a plan. I will tell you instantly whether it is feasible or no, just as I did before.
Anyhow, I am resolved upon one desperate course,
provided everything else fails."

" What do you mean ? " He was looking at me with
an inquisitive troubled sort of pity ; much as though he
recognized the strong probability of my telling him that
I meant to burn the house down and as though such a
startling announcement had quite lost the power of doing
more than make him feel grimly sorry.

" I mean, John Driscoll, there is a chance of Fuller's
believing Helen Dobell where he might not believe
Mrs. Peters. Should I find all other plans useless, I
could simply throw off my wig and spectacles and swear,
without them, that this abominable woman is the thing
I know her to be."

" Then you would act with much mad stupidity."

" I don't care. If you, his friend, will allow his sick-
ening deception to continue for possibly all the rest of
his days—for at least long enough to have him cast off
by mamma, ruined before the eyes of the world, driven
to Heaven knows what reckless end by the loss of position and respectability, then I, his wife, will at least
make a last desperate trial toward saving him, slight
reason though his neglect and insult have ever given me
to mix myself at all in his concerns."

" And will not save him, although you make the
trial."

" Perhaps not. But I shall have gotten a certain
amount of satisfaction from the attempt."

He gave a great shoulder-shrug and dropped his head

breastward and rambled away from me, passing downstairs. The interview had not given me a shadow of
hope. My single trump-card has been played, it is
true, as far as concerns the inducing him to devise some
plan; but I question whether that card is a very powerful one. My threats are growing an old story, doubtless
he thinks. There are such things as pushing friendship a
tittle or so too far. 'Besides,' he has perhaps been telling himself, '*I* am not likely to suffer now if Helen Dobell does behave like a fool and make exertions to publish the whole matter before the world. Let her act as
her own wild wishes dictate; it isn't my affair any longer.'

Well, perhaps I wrong him; perhaps I only put in
exaggerated colors what has really been his thought.
It is hard to tell, just yet. He may relent and help me
gloriously: who knows?

He can help me if he wishes; I am somehow possessed with the idea that he can.

A day of my stipulated week is gone already. At
present I am wholly idealess, as far as the thinking out
of any scheme is concerned. I can think of nothing; at
least nothing in any wise adequate to the dire needs of
the situation. Sometimes, when I get pondering upon
how Fuller is being befooled and hoodwinked, I feel nothing except a complete frenzy of indignation that he should
play the Merlin to that fiend's Vivien, or that I should
find myself impotent to tear the scales from his eyes.
But indignation is quite profitless. A few hours of hard
grave thought might accomplish far more sensible results.

If I wanted to revenge myself upon him how superbly
I could do it by just going away now and leaving him
in the clutches of that hypocrite, until some day when
he learned (as I believe he would learn) of her thorough
baseness. What a revenge! Why don't I take it?

Why don't I punish him as he deserves so intensely to
be punished ?

Ah, what right have I to treat myself as though I
were indeed able to prescribe punishment or dispense
with it, like any prince or satrap ?   Let me first find a
means of showing him forgiveness by saving him from
that beautiful monster : after that I can put on airs,
Diary, and talk finely to you about which of my two
powers I shall use.

*May* 20.—Another day gone.   Edith Everdell glares
at me with a curled lip whenever she can get a good
chance to do so and not be seen by Fuller.   She and
Fuller were together all the afternoon.   I believe that he
believes in her firmlier than ever, now.

John Driscoll and I did more whispering in the hall
to-day.   Mamma has sent through him a keenly urgent
message on the subject of my immediate return home.
She has recently insisted upon knowing my precise place
of residence, and on hearing it has expressed immense
horror.   It was a slight sop to Cerberus, I was told,
when she became aware that I would certainly leave
my present whereabouts in less than a week's time.

But I didn't choose to waste many words on the matter
of her virtuous disgust.   There was something else,
Diary, that I preferred infinitely to talk about.   Not so
my fellow-whisperer, however.   I am afraid that neither
threats nor persuasions will affect him.

Well, my threat was no idle subterfuge.   " Fuller
shall know the real truth concerning his nurse," I made
firm avowal, just before we separated, " unless some
other means are found of supporting my charges."

" And if you really attempt that striking little melodrama," he replied, " why feel at all confident that it
will benefit your cause ? "

" I don't feel at all confident. But any sort of action will be better than mere stagnant neutrality."

" You are wrong to think so."

" Perhaps. But I am resolved, nevertheless."

*May* 23.—Two more days remain to me after this. I take back all the unfair suspicions written against John Driscoll. More than once I have seen him looking at me with perplexed compassion that there is no misunderstanding. From his soul he pities me, I can't help believing. Dr. Delmayne made a short visit to his patient yesterday, but to-day he has not come. Doubtless he considers further visits unnecessary. My own services here are surely no longer needed, and my position has grown such a sinecure as to be right embarrassing. I feel sure that during some of their murmured conversations together (always made inaudible to my ears) Edith Everdell has advised Fuller to discharge me. Of course he yearns to do so, and is merely kept from doing so by a sullen haughty respect for our agreement.

Once or twice it has occurred to me that possibly Dr. Delmayne might be of help. But then I have remembered Fuller's ill-hidden·dislike of this man, whose untiring skill and attention beyond all doubt have saved his life ; a dislike that has only of late made itself evident and that Edith Everdell has certainly roused in him. The doctor is bold enough and is enough my friend to give me most fearless support ; but of what real profit would his support prove ? No ; in three days from now I shall have to fall back, I suppose, on what John Driscoll calls the melodrama. Well, I have the requisite courage to perform it. When the time comes I shall simply change Mrs. Peters into Helen Dobell, and with all the eloquence I can master accuse Edith

Everdell of being the most heartless mixture of wickedness and hypocrisy which nature ever devised.  Nor am I so sure that my avowal will be so free from afterresults.  I have this to aid me in the destruction of Fuller's devout faith :—he has never known me to tell him a falsehood ; and he shall have the thought of how I came to him in that awful sickness, for an evidence of how I have striven forgivingly to serve him in silent efficient deeds.  Hereafter he must think of my mad masquerade with something like gratitude and respect ; and the more he thinks of this, the more Edith Everdell's hold upon him ought imperceptibly to weaken.

Of course the melodrama will end everything between us forevermore.  I will leave the house after having performed it, and go straight home, and he will not dream of following me.  But I shall leave behind me (or at least I pray Heaven that this may be so) an influence before which Edith Everdell's shall eventually crumble.  And yet I have no right to deal so confidently in future tenses ; for I do not feel at all confident of any success, as I told John Driscoll the other day ; neither success immediate nor success sudden.  I just have a ray or two of hope and nothing more.  And when I look still further into the future, ah, how voidly dreary it is !  For weeks I have been suffering under the stress of excitement.  For years to come I must simply suffer as ordinary people suffer, dully, coldly, eventlessly !  The battle shall have ceased, the guns shall all have grown silent, and long night shall have settled on the battle-field where I lie, wounded deeply and thirsting keenly.  Yes, night without a star.  Night of such opaque blackness that the blackness of death will be like day by contrast !

## CHAPTER XLII.

MAY 25.—At the last moment John Driscoll has consented to aid me. His offer came with great suddenness, taking me intensely by surprise. He had been holding quite a long conversation with Fuller in Fuller's room. I was in my own. I daresay they were talking of private personal matters. Possibly I could have heard what they were talking about if I had chosen to eavesdrop a little. I chose not to eavesdrop at all.

Rather late in the afternoon he left Fuller's room. I softly unclosed that door of my own which leads into the hall and met him just as he was shutting Fuller's door.

"To-morrow the week expires," I plunged, in cautious whisper.

"I supposed so." After that we both kept silence for some little while. He was looking straight down into my face with those suave-colored hazel eyes. And something about his own face somehow made my cheeks flush with color, made my hand grasp his arm.

"You have an idea," I burst forth. "You're going to help me!"

He smiled nothing unless a melancholy smile, whilst nodding yes.

20

"Oh, I was sure you would," innocently fibbed I, believing, in my sudden enthusiasm, that I was speaking soundest truth.

Then he answered with as much solemnity of tone as a very low whisper can be made to accommodate:

"I was not sure of any such thing until only a little while ago. Indeed, I had made up my mind that I could do nothing." Here he gathered his brows like one through whom there shoots a most painful thought. "It takes all my nerve even to *think* of what I am going to do. And I can't help saying that I don't believe there are many Damons who would do the same for many Pythiases. Fuller Dobell would never do it for me."

"Perhaps he would if you had a wife to implore as I have implored."

He shook his head in pronounced negative. "Not if I had a regiment of wives. It is a horribly delicate matter. It may lead to a personal quarrel between him and me. Whenever I think about it at all I seem to see all my worldly wisdom in a state of personification, telling me that I am making a great fool of myself. But I mean to do it and I don't mean to back out at the last moment. Do you know that if you had not met me in the hall I should have gone and knocked at your door, running the risk of being heard by Fuller?"

"I am so glad to hear that your mind is so firmly made up. Neither Fuller nor I deserve your goodness. And now for the plan itself: you have set my curiosity aching."

He shook his head very positively. "It must ache on until to-morrow."

"You can't mean that I'm not to know anything till then?"

"No, I don't mean precisely that. There are some instructions which I must give you. And these instructions you must promise to obey."

"I promise that they shall be obeyed to the letter. I have such faith in you that I promise even before hearing them."

"They are very simple," he explained. "To-morrow, let us say at precisely eleven o'clock, A.M., you will go to Fuller and tell him that you are ready to show him the proof of your charges. Then you must ask him to follow you, making as little noise as possible. You know the small private staircase at the rear end of the house?"

"Yes."

"*I* didn't till yesterday, when my dark plotting made me search for and discover one. Well, this staircase leads into a narrow kind of butler's hall and from thence into the dining-room. The chances are decidedly in favor of you and Fuller reaching the dining-room without being heard or seen. If you are either it will be unfortunate; it may, indeed, interfere with the whole proceeding. When you reach the dining-room you will *probably* (I do not dare say ' surely ') find the folding-doors which lead from thence into the second parlor, so arranged that one may look through a slight crevice between them and run little risk of himself being seen. If the doors are so arranged, first look through the crevice yourself; you will understand instantly, from what you see, whether Fuller is to take your place. If, however, the doors should be tightly closed, then do your best to separate them ever so little without being heard. If they should be wide open, use the utmost caution in trying to find a place from which you can see without much immediate danger of being seen.

And in all cases remember to be as utterly noiseless as possible and to make Fuller the same."

"I understand. Not a word of your instructions has been lost upon me. But oh, their mystery! I shall not sleep a wink this night, I am right certain, because of trying to puzzle it out."

He smiled a dreary little smile. "I can't tell you what may happen—and simply because that word 'may,' by the bye, has to be used in speaking of the matter. Perhaps it will all prove a failure; I should not be much surprised if it did. Only, be sure that I will bring all my will and energy to bear against such a consequence. If I fail—"

"Pshaw," I broke in; "what is it Richelieu tells the young priest? I'm sure that the word isn't in the lexicon of your youth—not, at least, when you choose that it shan't be."

"The lexicon of my youth got out of print several years ago," he made soft objection. "But we have been whispering here too long already. I wonder that we haven't been interrupted, as it is. By the bye, have you a watch? Yes? Just let me see it, please; I want to compare it with mine." Then, after I had handed it to him and he had made the comparison: "There's scarcely a minute of difference between them. Good-bye; remember to begin proceedings at eleven o'clock precisely. I will make between three and five minutes of allowance for your coming."

"And you will not tell me what it is all going to be?" I questioned, pleading-voiced. "Think of my poor maddened curiosity."

"You must get your curiosity a straight-jacket," he smiled. "I should like to tell, but (to speak downright truth) I should need at least two brandys-and-soda before the necessary bluntness, bad taste and brute courage came to me."

And with these amazing words he walked away. Oh, Diary, is there any use in adding that I have been on sharpest thorns of impatience ever since? I am glad that It is going to happen at eleven o'clock. If It were to happen an hour later, I verily believe that ungratified curiosity would throw me into nervous convulsions.

## CHAPTER XLIII.

AY 28.—I sit in my own room in my own home whilst I write what follows. I am Mrs. Peters no longer.

Let me begin with the morning of the twenty-sixth; the morning when I woke up with the certainty that Fuller would make his demand.

After dressing and eating the breakfast that was brought up to me, I found that it was a little past nine o'clock. Fuller was probably ready to receive me if I chose to enter his room. Anyhow, I could knock and find out.

I knocked and found out. He pronounced a prompt but rather unpleasant "come-in," a second after the summons.

He was standing in the centre of the room when I entered. The remains of his recent breakfast stood nearby. He looked all coldness, hardness and gravity. The instant I caught sight of his face I became prepared for the words which he immediately spoke.

"Mrs. Peters, I suppose you are aware that your week has expired? Do you come to tell me that you are going to-day, or—?" Then he paused, lingeringly, fixing keen eyes on my face, as though he rather pre-

ferred than otherwise that I should interrupt him, right
here.

And then I spoke. "Mr. Dobell, I have come to
tell you that I am prepared to substantiate my charges."

He started, turned faintly paler, then smiled a quick
sneering smile that was born, I well saw, of his over-
weening confidence.

"Indeed! you are ready to substantiate them! Let
me ask how? when? and where?"

"At present," I gave calm answer, "I can only reply
to your second question. What revelation I have to
make will take place at eleven o'clock this morning."

"Eleven?" he laughed, chillingly, whilst he took out
his watch. "You are very racily mysterious, it must
be admitted. Is this all that I am to hear just yet?"

"Not quite," I returned, tranquil and even-voiced.
"I must request of you to arrange, if possible, that you
shall be alone at that time. I will then pay you a visit
and furthermore request that you will go with me somewhere."

He laughed almost good-humoredly, now. Perhaps
a vague amusing doubt crossed him, right here, on the
subject of my complete sanity. "The plot thickens, as
they say in novels and plays. Where are you to take
me? Down into a dark cellar with my eyes blindfold?"

"Not precisely. I merely want you to go a very
short distance with me—not out of the house. Will you
agree to arrange that you shall be left quite alone by the
hour at which I shall want you?"

"Certainly." His face was touched with scornful
merriment.

"And you will mention to no one, I trust, Mr. Dobell, this little fresh engagement between us?"

"Absolutely to no one;" (bowing with open mock-

ery in the movement, whilst I walked slowly doorward.)
Then I went back into my own room, shutting the
door between us, and passed there a good hour and
three-quarters in momentary dread of his receiving
either a visit from Dr. Delmayne or Edith Everdell:
from the first I knew that a visit was not strongly probable; from the last it was something that might at any
moment occur, unless she was to play some personal
part in John Driscoll's revelations.

But no one entered his room except the servant who
came to arrange it and to remove his finished breakfast.
And during that period of waiting I sat and almost
counted the minutes.

At last the time had come. It wanted only a moment or two of eleven. I rose and looked at myself in
the glass; Mrs. Peters was a trifle paler than usual.
Then I knocked at Fuller's door and was promptly told
to enter.

He sat in an arm-chair, reading. "Has the awful
moment arrived?" he wanted to know, laying down his
book as I approached. "I wish it had been eleven
o'clock and five minutes; the lady in my novel here is
just going to poison her husband."

He was nervous in spite of himself; of this I felt certain the instant that I heard his voice. He was trying
to make me—make himself, doubtless, believe that his
deep-rooted faith in Edith Everdell's constancy was not
to be shaken, how faintly soever, by the ambiguous in-
nuendoes of a rather tiresome old woman; and whilst
he so tried, the attempt was nearly pure failure. A
terrible little haunting Perhaps had perched itself on his
shoulder elfwise, very possibly, and was whispering its
little trenchant probabilities in his ear.

For myself, I felt that I was trembling a trifle and that

my cheeks had gotten to burn a trifle, also. But I was nervous not half so much because of the uncertainty regarding John Driscoll's design as because of a fear lest it might not prove practicable. Such a trifling circumstance could delay me in the keeping of that odd appointment, now. Then, too, John Driscoll had himself cast decided doubt upon the plan's feasibility. The hard shell of Fuller's bigoted faith and trust needed a tremendous telling blow to shatter it. Had we the power to "strike and strongly, and one stroke," after this annihilating fashion?

I quite ignored his humorous comment upon the homicidal lady in his novel. "I am ready to go with you, Mr. Dobell," came my placid response. "I hope that you are ready, for we wish to lose no time."

He rose. The smile that just rimmed his lips contrasted queerly with his paleness. "Where are we going?"

"Only downstairs into the dining-room. Please follow me; and I beg of you to make as little noise as possible whilst you do so." As I finished speaking I opened the door of his room which led hallward. The hall was quite empty, for which circumstance I offered Heaven my mute thanks. We walked to its further end, Fuller following me at a very short distance. We gained the private staircase and began to descend. We reached the next floor, and as yet there had been no obstacle. Only a slight while longer of untroubled descent and we should reach the dining-room threshold. Suddenly I felt myself growing weak with dread. Nothing had happened yet, but would not something happen presently? Were we fated to arrive unimpeded at the end of our little journey?

Down, down, with steps slow, stealthy, almost noise-
20*

less. We had nearly gained the narrow hall from which the dining-room opens off. Was nothing going to happen?

No, not anything in the way of molestation was going to happen, it seemed. We stood at last in the small hall adjoining the dining-room. The door was open. Whilst crossing its threshold I shot one rapid glance at the folding-doors. They had been unclosed ever so slightly. The crevice of which John Driscoll had spoken had evidently been effected.

I turned and made a sudden gesture that told Fuller to remain perfectly still, just as he was in the act of following me across the threshold. My heart had begun to pulsate wildly whilst I stole toward the crevice in the folding-doors.

With infinite caution I stole nearer, nearer. Already I heard the voice of Edith Everdell, not loudly raised and yet distinctly audible because the speaker was so near this adjoining room in which I stood.

" And pray what made you think that I never cared for you, John Driscoll? How wrong you have been ! oh, how very wrong ! "

By this time I had gained a clear view of the next room. This is what I saw there :          •

Edith Everdell, whose back was nearly opposite the crevice through which I peered. John Driscoll, whose eyes were fixed upon that crevice, plainly seeing it from where he sat, across the woman's shoulder. And upon one of his own shoulders her beautiful head had fallen, whilst one superb loose-sleeved arm had lifted itself toward the other.

I drew back then, making a rapid excited motion for Fuller to advance, whilst my face, I am right sure, wore an almost wild look of triumph.

He came hastily forward, then, though treading with much lightness. I stood pointing with nervous quickly-moving forefinger.

Oh, the intense fervor of satisfaction with which I saw him peer, as I had been peering, into the room beyond.

I was too much behind him to see his face. He stood still as stone, after that, bending forward to watch and to overhear.

The woman was speaking again, but her voice had sunk into such lowness of intonation that I could catch the mere murmur and nothing more. *He* could catch more than that, however, I felt certain. And better far, he could see clearly, indubitably, with his own eyes!

Presently her voice ceased and John Driscoll's began. Then his ceasing, hers recommenced. Then hers again; then his; then hers again for a longer time than either had yet spoken.

And at last the doors were slid violently asunder. After so sliding them Fuller rushed into the next room. I did not follow him: there was no use in my following him; I could see and hear all that passed quite perfectly, now.

And I waited to hear too much. He addressed a horrible fiery outburst toward Edith Everdell, who stood staring at him with ashen face whilst his pell-mell sentences of accusation were poured upon her. Heaven forgive him, he spoke with frightful fury! I shan't write down a word of what he said, Diary. Better that I should even, if possible, blot it out from my memory!

As the tirade was spending itself, John Driscoll, with ghastly face and the look of a man who suffers keenest shame, slipped from the room by sudden exit through a side-door. I dashed out of the dining-room, then, by the door through which Fuller and I had lately entered it, and sped through the narrow hall into the larger and longer one beyond.

He had on his hat, and his hand was on the knob of the street-door when I hurried up to him. "Oh, thanks! thanks!" I burst forth; and then the drawn sickened look upon his face froze me into instant silence.

"You see, I am running away from him," he exclaimed, with a bitter laugh. "Running away, like a coward!" And then he opened the door.

"You are not a coward, John Driscoll! Go at once, but no one except a fool could call you so." And I pushed him through the opened door, closing it sharply, just as Fuller's voice, the name of John Driscoll loud upon his lips, called from where we had left him.

And then I hurried upstairs at fleetest speed to my own room on the third floor. In the second hall I met Margaret, who stared at me amazedly as I darted past her.

Once in my own room, the first thing that I did, after closing the door, was to take off those detested spectacles. This action was the result of habit, doubtless. Ever since the first day I entered that house I have always un-spectacled myself, changed my bottle-green range of vision into something less abnormal, the instant that I have found myself alone.

After that I stood with locked hands, wondering what I had best do. There was surely no reason for me to remain in the house a moment longer, now, than I could possibly help. Let me at once make preparations to leave it. Never mind my portemanteau and the clothes; never mind if I didn't ever see these again; they would pay the price of my sweet triumph.

All that I wanted was bonnet and shawl. I hurried

to my closet, unlocked it and found these. Just as I
was laying them on the bed, steps sounded in the outside hall—steps hasty and heavy, that could belong to
nobody except Fuller. A moment later I heard him
hurry into his own room. Then I heard him walk
rapidly here and there. And then, without giving me
more than a second of warning, he opened my door and
shouted out in harsh hard tones, on discovering me :

" Do you know if my hat is here ? "

Doubtless if he had given me more warning of his
approach I should not have remembered to replace my
spectacles. As it was, his own wildly wrought-up condition prevented him from noticing their absence.

I remembered instantly that his hat was in a certain
closet of his room and hurried to get it. As I handed
it to him he did not even glance at me, just snatching it
from my hand and then rushing out of the room.

I went back to my own room. A few moments later
I heard the street-door clang loudly. And on hearing
this sound, I hurried to my already-open window and
looked pavementward through the drawn blinds. Yes ;
it was he who had just left the house. Left it, perhaps,
forever. I could not doubt, thank Heaven, that he had
left it and its vile mistress forever !

And now I myself must leave it with all available
haste. And so I began as fleet a toilette as I knew how
to make.

Very foolishly I stopped to change the light shoes I
wore for a pair of thicker walking-boots. Perhaps if it
had not been for this delay what happened would not
have happened. For after having finished this part of
my preparations I had just taken off my cap, when the
door leading from the hall was abruptly opened and in
swept Edith Everdell.

Her face was ghostlike in its severe pallor, though whether from present rage or from recent terror I was not at first sure. But after she had stood glaring at me for a moment I read in the firm straightened line of her close-shut lips and in the austere poise of her back-flung head and in the quivering curve of her nostril's pink delicacy, a *fury* that was physically sublime to look upon.

And so she glared upon me, caught capless and spectacleless, for what seemed a good minute.

Then at last she found a choked rageful voice; a voice that made me remember her in that other fierce fury at the opera-ball.

"You helped John Driscoll in his beastly plot against me. Don't dare to lie out of it and say you didn't. I saw you standing there in the next room whilst I was being stormed at." And now she lessened the distance between us by two or three quick strides. "Flora was right enough, and Margaret was right enough, when they both assured me that you were a spy. Now tell me who sent you here."

Her hot eyes were devouring my face. I expected every moment that she would lift her hand and strike me a blow. Indeed, I waited for it to come, with a kind of chilled passiveness.

"Tell me who sent you here!" she shouted, her face, in its splendid rage, almost within an inch of mine. "I *will* know the real truth about you! You're no common nurse; you're no mere paid spy. Was it Dr. Delmayne who got you to come? or John Driscoll? or was it Fuller Dobell's wi——?"

The word seemed to die on her lips. Abruptly her beautiful brows gathered themselves in a dark perplexed frown. She drew back for a second, her stare intensi-

fied and both hands lifted momentarily in a slow gesture
of amazement. And then one of those hands suddenly,
with a rapid violent force, shot out toward my forehead
and pushed back from it the grey disguise of the wig;
pushed it far enough back to let the blond hair escape
from its ambush beneath. Far enough to change Mrs.
Peters into Mrs. Dobell.

I think that nearly another good minute passed, after
that, whilst we two stood and stared at each other.

She broke the silence at last, with a shrill caustic
laugh. And straightway after this sound had left her
lips, she came quite near me again, having both hands
clinched very tightly in two white knots at either side.

She had somehow forced herself into a kind of sneering composure. "You have played a bold game, my
clever young woman, and as far as it goes a successful
one. As far as it goes;" (ending this repeated sentence
with a sharp long respiration.) "Now comes my turn."

"You mean to kill me, perhaps," I managed here,
with a faint nervous ghost of a laugh. "You are quite
capable of it, I should suppose. You are doubtless
strong enough; and wicked enough, surely. But remember, please, that the law would be apt to punish
such a little imprudent burst of temper;" (whilst I
laughed the laugh again, faintlier, more nervously.)

"No, I am not going to attempt anything half so
silly, if you've no objection. This is what I mean to
do." Her breath broke hotly against my cheek. "I
mean to make the world know where you have been—
you, Mrs. Fuller Dobell, for weeks past. I mean that
before you leave this house of mine all New York shall
ring with the story of your being here. I have power
to publish everywhere the story of your presence under
my roof, and to garnish it nicely with certain plausible

details that shall make your fine high-toned associates lift their eyebrows when they hear it. Your bonnet is on the bed yonder, but you will not need it, madam, for several days to come. We shan't separate, you and I, till I have taught you a rather wholesome lesson ; taught you that when we handle pitch so confidently we now and then run a fair chance of soiling our fingers. Do you quite understand me ? Perhaps you don't, just yet, but before long you will have done so, I fancy, to your own dear cost ! "

She was finishing this last sentence when, with all the suddenness of an inspiration, a recollection crossed my brain. Yes, it must have been sheer inspiration and nothing more that made me remember such a thing at such a time. And to remember it then was just as though someone had rushed forward with a stout weapon for my defenceless hand.

I was about to speak rapidly and excitedly, at first; but a second of thought made me control the strong impulse. Each of my words, as I pronounced it, fell measuredly tranquil.

" I learned some time ago, Mrs. Everdell, that you have a daughter whom you have seen fit to place at a most respectable school here in New York, as boarding-pupil."

Then I watched the effect of my words before I went further.

She started back as though a snake had stung her. Every gleam of anger dwindled from her face and left there a wild alarm in its stead. So far so good.

" The name by which your daughter is known, I believe, is Adèle Tremaine, and the school at which she boards is kept by a certain Madame Langlois. You will not, I suppose, presume to deny these facts ? "

She made no answer. She stood the picture of abject terror, with one hand pressed against her heart. I had not dared to expect a change like this, so sudden, so intense, so radical.

" Madame Langlois and myself are the best of friends," I progressed, with loudening voice yet with severest manner. " Indeed, I was her pupil for several years of my girlhood. A few months ago she paid me a visit and spoke of Miss Adèle Tremaine as the beauty of her school, begging as a sort of special favor that I would call and see her. I did not know, then, a word regarding.this pupil's parentage. I was as ignorant of it as was Madame herself. The truth has since reached my ears."

After that I kept silence for a little space. She had closed her eyes like one whom some great unnerving faintness overpowers. But presently, just as I was on the point of mercilessly continuing, the long gold lashes lifted themselves and one dull flash shot from the wonderful eyes.

" Well ? Admit that I admit all this."

Then I went on: " It is possibly to your interest that this daughter of yours shall continue at Madame Langlois' school : that the world at large shall remain as ignorant as it now is concerning her real name and birth ; that no mischievous tongue shall gossip about certain unpleasant truths ; that the sins of the parent shall not be visited upon the child ; that she shall grow up without knowledge or suspicion of her origin and antecedents ; that, more briefly, I shall keep silence regarding what I know. And let me add, the person who gave me my information is one from whom you have not the least reason to dread the least attempt at any exposure."

And now as I again paused she again found voice, speaking this time with a rough husky energy of tone.

"You have this knowledge and mean to use it, I suppose, at your earliest chance."

"I shall not use it if you allow me to leave your house and agree to keep a profound secret the fact of my residence here."

A look of unspeakable relief spread itself over that alarmed colorless face. And yet,

"Provided you make me such a promise," she doubted, "what reason have I for believing that you will respect it when you are once gone?"

Eying her steadfastly, I made answer:

"Silence for silence, Mrs. Everdell. Do not let us promise at all, if you discredit my trustworthiness. Let it be simply a politic armistice between you and me. Our forces are about equal, I think. If you violate the contract by discharging a gun, I shall take a like course. Meanwhile a regard for personal safety ought mutually to keep us from opening fire. Don't you think so?"

"Yes." Her face had gotten a certain hardness again. "You may go. You have conquered. You are a great woman in your way; do you know it?" (whilst every word had a sullen unwilling ring, as though it was forced from her by some extraneous influence.) "You are worth twenty Fuller Dobells. And I'm glad that such a brave strange splendid creature as you should have beaten me, rather than some namby-pamby nonentity. Do you know, it only makes me think men are greater geese and idiots than I before thought them, when I see one having his sanity about him treating you with Fuller Dobell's brutishness?"

After that she swept doorward, pausing with her hand on the door's knob. "I will have your trunk sent after you, *Mrs. Peters;*" (whilst smiling a brilliant broad ironic smile) "provided, that is, you choose to trust me. I know your address."

After I had returned a prompt "very well," she left the room without another word.

Brave strange splendid creature, indeed! Would she not have reversed her opinion if she had seen me, a little later, kneeling down by the bedside and thanking God with streaming eyes and passionate outflung arms, both for Fuller's deliverance and my own? Surely there was enough weakness about me then!

## CHAPTER THE LAST.

**B**Y about one o'clock that same day a certain female, closely veiled, rang the bell at Mrs. Jeffreys' door in Fifth Avenue.

The closely-veiled female was I. As Henry let me in I threw up my veil. I was a dreadful shock to poor Henry, but he met me superbly, after the first momentary falling of his jaw and saucerlike enlargement of his eyes. No more perfect atonement could be made for this loss of official self-possession than the grand grave bow which immediately followed, and the low-murmured "Welcome home, ma'am."

Was mamma at home? straightway I wanted to know, with as much off-handedness as I could at all master.

Yes; Mrs. Jeffreys was at present upstairs with Mr. Dobell.

"Mr. Dobell!" I iterated. "When did he arrive?"

"About three quarters of an hour ago, ma'am, I think."

I moved toward the reception-room. "Tell mamma, please, that I am here" (pointing through the open doorway) "and shall be glad to see her whenever it is convenient."

I waited perhaps a quarter of an hour before mamma

came down to see me.  There was a mutual taking of
hands ; there was also a kind of mutual kissing gone
through with, little except the extremest tips of lips
being called upon to do service during the ceremony.

Then mamma seated herself and stared at me with
much grandeur of woebegone disapproval ; decidedly
as though the plump grey puffs at her temples were justified in laying at my undutiful door several shades of
their greyness.  I also sat down.

" Helen, you have been to me for weeks past a
source of incessant anxiety," she began, in lugubrious
monotone ; " and the number of gross untruths which
you have compelled me to tell among inquiring friends
would make you shudder if you should hear it.  But I
do not positively think that I could have endured for
such a long period the knowledge of where you had
really been hiding.  It is a mercy that John Driscoll
kept me deceived until the other day."  After that there
was heaved a gigantic sigh.

" You have just been seeing Fuller," I changed the
subject, rather curtly.

" Yes.  He came into the house about an hour ago.
It was so absurd.  Here I have told people so many
brazen falsehoods about your both being out West together that I have almost gotten to believe my own fiction ; and now Fuller returns from weeks of residence
in the same house with you and asks me where you
are."

" And pray what did you tell him ? "

" The truth.  I am so tired of telling nothing but
falsehoods."

I had started up from my chair, by this, and was biting my lips in a passionate baffled way.

" What did you tell him for ? " I cried out, peevishly.

" Wasn't it enough humiliation that my love took me there, without having him know it ? "

" I thank God, Helen Dobell, that I do know it," murmured a man's deep voice behind me ; and I turned round, with a little bewildered cry, to find myself facing Fuller.

Instantly mamma rose up and slipped from the room, shutting the door after her with a noiseless expedition.

He was very pale—almost as pale as during the dangerous days of his sickness ; but his blue eyes were luminous as I had never seen the fire of fever make them.

" Your mother has told me the real truth about— about who Mrs. Peters was," his slow unsteady voice commenced. " At first I would not believe.  Then I believed her and was angry at you.  Then I felt like hating myself for being anything but very very grateful."  Here his tones grew much steadier : " You have removed from me a great curse ; you and John Driscoll."

Then I broke in, with floorward eyes.  " I am so glad that you understand the real part that John Driscoll played."

" I did not, at first.  I begin to understand it now."

At this I raised my eyes, speaking eagerly.  " I don't think any man ever had a tougher struggle with himself in the doing a service for any friend.  I used to beg him, day after day, to try and find some means of showing you what a wretch that creature was ; and at length he consented."

Whilst I spoke this last sentence his face clouded as with most bitter memories—clouded as a man's face will do when he sees, in agonizing retrospect, how he has been

" The ball of time,
Bandied by the hands of fools."

He had drooped his head and was staring down at the carpet. I walked toward the window and looked out through its half-shut blinds at the Avenue, pleasant in the balmy May weather and filled with many passers.

I had stood like this for some little time before he spoke again. "It would be simple absurdity for me to ask your pardon *now*, Helen, when I did not do so long before my knowledge of that woman's beastliness, at a time when my association with her was just the same insult to yourself as it would be at present."

"You are very right. It would be simple absurdity. I do not wish you to ask for my pardon. I saved you from that woman's further hypocrisies not because I hoped for so paltry and trifling a triumph." And then I laughed with low bitterness. "It is quite an easy thing to cry *mea culpa* after all cause of temptation has been removed."

"But you will at least take my thanks, Helen!—my heartfelt and intense thanks!" He had drawn much nearer to where I stood, by this, and his words came richly resonant. "I don't mean only for what you did in showing me the real worthlessness of that woman; I mean for your laborious and self-sacrificing hours at my bedside."

And then our eyes somehow met, though until then I had made my own stare stubbornly at a little bronze Terpsichore who was doing her perpetual metallic pirouette on a bracket against the opposite wall. Fuller's head swayed ever so faintly from side to side, as if his brain were in a mist of perplexity, whilst he went on, rapid-toned, eagerly emphatic?

"And for Heaven's sake, Helen, what made you behave as you did? How is it that you only grew the whiter angel as I grew the blacker devil?"

"Oh, Fuller! Hush!"

"It is true, and you know it right well. I gave you every reason to loathe and despise me. I married you—"

"For money," I finished, firmly, as he paused. "Don't feel afraid of wounding me by *that*s tatement; it may have had power to cut very keenly once, but the edge is a little dulled now. You married me for money; you acted toward me a most grossly deceitful part during that whole falsehood, your courtship; you did what it makes me shudder to look back upon;—and yet I am merciful and tell you with all candor that you have not been to blame. I know the rôle of temptress that mamma took in those days; I have since learned about it."

"Your mother spread snares for me, I admit," he answered, stern-voiced in his self-condemnation, "but if I hadn't chosen to be a fool and a knave as well, I need not have fallen into them. No, no," he went on, with loudening tones; "the real secret of it all was because I believed that I was marrying, when I married you, a woman who would ultimately take the matrimonial shape and color of the circles in which she moved. I thought you possessed of little character, little energy, little real womanliness. I woke up, very soon, to the fact that you were a spirited high-strung creature, with an intellect greater than my own and a sense of justice far too keen for a man in my peculiar moral position conveniently to pay it much respect. What was the result of this discovery, Helen? I did not tell myself that I owed you, in the name of common humanity, the exact reverse of what I had designed to give. I shut both ears to the eloquent appeal of your silent unmistakable love. You were the pearl cast before me, the swine ; or rather you might have been an almost holy refuge for me, placed directly in the mad path of my own selfishness, but that I chose to make you a stumbling-block, and cursed myself that I had ever married at all and tried to persuade myself that I hated you because you were not willing to live with me and be outraged by my infidelity. Please believe that these are no sudden convictions. Even before my sickness I thought as I think now ; and during my sickness I have often felt such thoughts burned into my brain by the hot iron which conscience sometimes uses for a brand."

His last sentence drove the red color to my cheeks and made my eyes sparkle.

" Remember, please, that I was Mrs. Peters all that time. I had opportunities of seeing to what extent conscience made you suffer." And here my voice gave way and the tears besieged my eyes. " Did you give that woman one kiss the less," I began to sob, " because of these fine conscientious feelings ? "

" Not one," he cried out boldly, his face almost livid. " Practical repentance is one thing ; in theory it is quite another. They say that confirmed drunkards make the best temperance-lecturers. If it had not been for what you and John Driscoll forced me to see this morning, I should have gone on believing implicitly in Edith Everdell's perfect fidelity. And whilst I so believed I should also have continued, very certainly, the same terms on which we have stood together for years past. Without the blow of to-day's discovery, or the blow of death itself, I *could* not have rid myself from her influence. I tell you this, Helen, because anything

21

like a misunderstanding between us is now horrible to me. I must have loved her and clung to her till the last, so long as I believed what I once believed."

I had sunk down upon the lounge, now, and was drying my eyes. " Do you suppose that this is any news to me ? " I asked, brokenly.

He had seated himself at my side all on a sudden and had gotten one of my hands in his. " No. I am sure it is not any news to you unless you are a little surprised that I should not be a coward and should not withhold the confession I have just made. But Helen, there is something more that I want to say."

I do not ask him what it is. I simply make my hand dead passive in his hold and fix blank eyes on the opposite wall.

" It is not much," he presently begins, his voice and words right low, right slow. " I think I have said too much already—or too little. That is always the way with talking at all, I am getting to think : one either says too much or too little. But there is something more that I must say, and it is just this : Provided you let me, I am going to devote all the rest of my life to scarcely anything else (will you overlook the mild exaggeration ?) except two stated tasks. One is the trying to absolve myself in your eyes for the shameful deeds I have committed since that day, so short a while ago, when I vowed to love, to cherish and to protect you."

I burst forth passionately here, because I cannot help it :

" Oh Fuller, there is no need of that ! I forgive you already—I didn't at first, but I do now ; " and then the tears lay their forcible veto on the utterance of another syllable.

" Hush," he murmurs, solemnly ; " I will not *let* you

forgive me yet awhile. My second task is . . . ."
He pauses here, and pauses for a long time, and at
length my swimming eyes seek his face and I just can
command voice enough to manage, in tremulous inter-
rogative :

"Well; what is the other task ?"

"That of trying to love you, Helen, as you deserve
to be loved."

And then I give a great cry and draw away my hand
from him, only that I may gird his neck with both arms
and lay my head on his shoulder. And whilst my head
is lying there, I feel his own arms stealing about me.

Then I raise my head and murmur almost fiercely :

"Fuller, you SHALL love me ! You are mine and I
*will* have it so ! You *shall* love me better, a thousandfold, than you ever loved that beautiful demon !"

He smiles whilst kissing the hungry longing lips that
I lift to him. " Is it a prophecy, Helen ?"

"No," I answer, after quite a silence, all the passion
gone from my voice and nothing but humility left there.
" It is not a prophecy. It is a prayer !"

**THE END.**

1873.    1873.

# G.W. CARLETON & CO.

# NEW BOOKS

## AND NEW EDITIONS,

RECENTLY ISSUED BY

## G. W. CARLETON & Co., Publishers,

### Madison Square, New York.

The Publishers, upon receipt of the price in advance, will send any book on this Catalogue by mail, *postage free*, to any part of the United States.

All books in this list [unless otherwise specified] are handsomely bound in cloth board binding, with gilt backs, suitable for libraries.

### Mary J. Holmes' Works.

| | | | |
|---|---|---|---|
| TEMPEST AND SUNSHINE | $1 50 | DARKNESS AND DAYLIGHT | $1 50 |
| ENGLISH ORPHANS | 1 50 | HUGH WORTHINGTON | 1 50 |
| HOMESTEAD ON THE HILLSIDE | 1 50 | CAMERON PRIDE | 1 50 |
| 'LENA RIVERS | 1 50 | ROSE MATHER | 1 50 |
| MEADOW BROOK | 1 50 | ETHELYN'S MISTAKE | 1 50 |
| DORA DEANE | 1 50 | MILLBANK | 1 50 |
| COUSIN MAUDE | 1 50 | EDNA BROWNING......(new) | 1 50 |
| MARIAN GRAY | 1 50 | | |

### Marion Harland's Works.

| | | | |
|---|---|---|---|
| ALONE | $1 50 | SUNNYBANK | $1 50 |
| HIDDEN PATH | 1 50 | HUSBANDS AND HOMES | 1 50 |
| MOSS SIDE | 1 50 | RUBY'S HUSBAND | 1 50 |
| NEMESIS | 1 50 | PHEMIE'S TEMPTATION | 1 50 |
| MIRIAM | 1 50 | THE EMPTY HEART | 1 50 |
| AT LAST | 1 50 | TRUE AS STEEL......(new) | 1 50 |
| HELEN GARDNER | 1 50 | | |

### Charles Dickens' Works.

#### "Carleton's New Illustrated Edition."

| | | | |
|---|---|---|---|
| THE PICKWICK PAPERS | $1 50 | MARTIN CHUZZLEWIT | $1 50 |
| OLIVER TWIST | 1 50 | OUR MUTUAL FRIEND | 1 50 |
| DAVID COPPERFIELD | 1 50 | TALE OF TWO CITIES | 1 50 |
| GREAT EXPECTATIONS | 1 50 | CHRISTMAS BOOKS | 1 50 |
| DOMBEY AND SON | 1 50 | SKETCHES BY "BOZ" | 1 50 |
| BARNABY RUDGE | 1 50 | HARD TIMES, etc. | 1 50 |
| NICHOLAS NICKLEBY | 1 50 | PICTURES OF ITALY, etc. | 1 50 |
| OLD CURIOSITY SHOP | 1 50 | UNCOMMERCIAL TRAVELLER | 1 50 |
| BLEAK HOUSE | 1 50 | EDWIN DROOD, etc. | 1 50 |
| LITTLE DORRIT | 1 50 | MISCELLANIES | 1 50 |

### Augusta J. Evans' Novels.

| | | | |
|---|---|---|---|
| BEULAH | $1 75 | ST. ELMO | $2 00 |
| MACARIA | 1 75 | VASHTI......(new) | 2 00 |
| INEZ | 1 75 | | |

## Captain Mayne Reid—Illustrated.

| | | | |
|---|---|---|---|
| SCALP HUNTERS | $1 50 | WHITE CHIEF | $1 50 |
| WAR TRAIL | 1 50 | HEADLESS HORSEMAN | 1 50 |
| HUNTER'S FEAST | 1 50 | LOST LENORE | 1 50 |
| TIGER HUNTER | 1 50 | WOOD RANGERS | 1 50 |
| OSCEOLA, THE SEMINOLE | 1 50 | WILD HUNTRESS | 1 50 |
| THE QUADROON | 1 50 | THE MAROON | 1 50 |
| RANGERS AND REGULATORS | 1 50 | RIFLE RANGERS | 1 50 |
| WHITE GAUNTLET | 1 50 | WILD LIFE | 1 50 |

## A. S. Roe's Works.

| | | | |
|---|---|---|---|
| A LONG LOOK AHEAD | $1 50 | TRUE TO THE LAST | $1 50 |
| TO LOVE AND TO BE LOVED | 1 50 | LIKE AND UNLIKE | 1 50 |
| TIME AND TIDE | 1 50 | LOOKING AROUND | 1 50 |
| I'VE BEEN THINKING | 1 50 | WOMAN OUR ANGEL | 1 50 |
| THE STAR AND THE CLOUD | 1 50 | THE CLOUD ON THE HEART | 1 50 |
| HOW COULD HE HELP IT | 1 50 | RESOLUTION ...... (new) | 1 50 |

## Hand-Books of Society.

THE HABITS OF GOOD SOCIETY.   The nice points of taste and good manners, and the art of making oneself agreeable.....  $1 75
THE ART OF CONVERSATION.—A sensible work, for every one who wishes to be either an agreeable talker or listener.....  1 50
THE ARTS OF WRITING, READING, AND SPEAKING.—An excellent book for self-instruction and improvement.....  1 50
A NEW DIAMOND EDITION of the above three popular books.—Small size, elegantly bound, and put in a box.....  3 00

## Mrs. Hill's Cook Book.

MRS. A. P. HILL'S NEW COOKERY BOOK, and family domestic receipts.....  $2 00

## Miss Muloch's Novels.

JOHN HALIFAX, GENTLEMAN..... $1 75 | A LIFE FOR A LIFE ..... $1 75

## Charlotte Bronte [Currer Bell].

JANE EYRE—a novel..... $1 75 | SHIRLEY—a novel..... $1 75

## Louisa M. Alcott.

MORNING GLORIES—A beautiful juvenile, by the author of "Little Women".....1 50

## The Crusoe Books—Famous "Star Edition."

ROBINSON CRUSOE.—New illustrated edition.....  $1 50
SWISS FAMILY ROBINSON.   Do.   Do .....  1 50
THE ARABIAN NIGHTS.   Do.   Do .....  1 50

## Julie P. Smith's Novels.

| | | | |
|---|---|---|---|
| WIDOW GOLDSMITH'S DAUGHTER | $1 75 | THE WIDOWER | $1 75 |
| CHRIS AND OTHO | 1 75 | THE MARRIED BELLE | 1 75 |
| TEN OLD MAIDS......[in press] | 1 75 | | |

## Artemus Ward's Comic Works.

| | | | |
|---|---|---|---|
| ARTEMUS WARD—HIS BOOK | $1 50 | ARTEMUS WARD—IN LONDON | $1 50 |
| ARTEMUS WARD—HIS TRAVELS | 1 50 | ARTEMUS WARD—HIS PANORAMA | 1 50 |

## Fanny Fern's Works.

| | | | |
|---|---|---|---|
| FOLLY AS IT FLIES | $1 50 | CAPER-SAUCE ......(new) | $1 50 |
| GINGERSNAPS | 1 50 | | |

## Josh Billings' Comic Works.

JOSH BILLINGS' PROVERBS..... $1 50 | JOSH BILLINGS FARMER'S ALMINAX, 25 cts.
JOSH BILLINGS ON ICE..... 1 50 | (In paper covers.)

## Verdant Green.

A racy English college story—with numerous comic illustrations.....  $1 50

## Popular Italian Novels.

DOCTOR ANTONIO.—A love story of Italy.  By Ruffini.....  $1 75
BEATRICE CENCI.—By Guerrazzi.  With a steel Portrait.....  1 75

## M. Michelet's Remarkable Works.

LOVE (L'AMOUR).—English translation from the original French.....  $1 50
WOMAN (LA FEMME).   Do.   Do.   Do.  .....  1 50

## Ernest Renan's French Works.

THE LIFE OF JESUS ..............$1 75 | LIFE OF SAINT PAUL.............$1 75
LIVES OF THE APOSTLES...........1 75 | BIBLE IN INDIA. By Jacolliot.....2 00

## Geo. W. Carleton.

OUR ARTIST IN CUBA.—With 50 comic illustrations of life and customs......$1 50
OUR ARTIST IN PERU.   Do.    Do.    Do.   ........1 50
OUR ARTIST IN AFRICA. (In press)   Do.    Do.   ........1 50

## May Agnes Fleming's Novels.

GUY EARLESCOURT'S WIFE........$1 75 | A WONDERFUL WOMAN. (In press).$1 75

## Maria J. Westmoreland's Novels.

HEART HUNGRY.................$1 75 | CLIFFORD TROUP   (new)......$1 75

## Sallie A. Brock's Novels.

KENNETH, MY KING.............$1 75 | A NEW BOOK......(in press)......

## Author of "Rutledge."

RUTLEDGE.—A novel...........$1 50 | LOUIE.—A novel................$1 50

## Victor Hugo.

LES MISERABLES.—English translation from the French. Octavo...........$2 50
LES MISERABLES.—In the Spanish language.........................5 00

## Algernon Charles Swinburne.

LAUS VENERIS, AND OTHER POEMS.—An elegant new edition....... ........$1 50
FRENCH LOVE-SONGS.—Selected from the best French authors...... ........1 50

## Robert Dale Owen.

THE DEBATABLE LAND BETWEEN THIS WORLD AND THE NEXT.............$2 00

## Guide for New York City.

WOOD'S ILLUSTRATED HAND-BOOK.—A beautiful pocket volume...............

## The Game of Whist.

POLE ON WHIST.—The late English standard work.........................$1 00

## Mansfield T. Walworth's Novels.

WARWICK.....................$1 75 | STORMCLIFF...................$1 75
LULU.........................1 75 | DELAPLAINE...................1 75
HOTSPUR......................1 75 | BEVERLY......(new)............1 75
A NEW NOVEL......(in press)

## Mother Goose Set to Music.

MOTHER GOOSE MELODIES.—With music for singing, and illustrations.........$1 30

## Tales from the Operas.

THE PLOTS OF POPULAR OPERAS in the form of stories...............$1 50

## M. M. Pomeroy "Brick."

SENSE—(a serious book).........$1 50 | NONSENSE—(a comic book).......$1 50
GOLD-DUST   do.  ..........1 50 | BRICK-DUST   do. ................1 50
OUR SATURDAY NIGHTS..........1 50 | LIFE OF M. M POMEROY.........1 50

## John Esten Cooke's Works.

FAIRFAX......................$1 50 | HAMMER AND RAPIER...........$1 50
HILT TO HILT..................1 50 | OUT OF THE FOAM..............1 50
A NEW BOOK......(in press)........

## Joseph Rodman Drake.

THE CULPRIT FAY.—The well-known faery poem, with 100 illustrations........$2 00
THE CULPRIT FAY.    Do.    superbly bound in turkey morocco.. 5 00

## Richard B. Kimball's Works.

WAS HE SUCCESSFUL?.. ..........$1 75 | LIFE IN SAN DOMINGO ..........$1 50
UNDERCURRENTS OF WALL STREET. 1 75 | HENRY POWERS, BANKER ..........1 75
SAINT LEGER ...................1 75 | TO-DAY........................1 75
ROMANCE OF STUDENT LIFE.......1 75 | EMILIE......(in press)............

## Author "New Gospel of Peace."

CHRONICLES OF GOTHAM.—A rich modern satire (paper covers).........25 cts.
THE FALL OF MAN.—A satire on the Darwin theory   do.  ..............50 cts.

## Celia E. Gardner's Novels.

STOLEN WATERS.................$1 50 | BROKEN DREAMS.. ...............$1 50

## Edmund Kirke's Works.

| | | | |
|---|---|---|---|
| AMONG THE PINES | $1 50 | ADRIFT IN DIXIE | $1 50 |
| MY SOUTHERN FRIENDS | 1 50 | AMONG THE GUERILLAS | 1 50 |
| DOWN IN TENNESSEE | 1 50 | | |

## Dr. Cumming's Works.

| | | | |
|---|---|---|---|
| THE GREAT TRIBULATION | $2 00 | TEACH US TO PRAY | $2 00 |
| THE GREAT PREPARATION | 2 00 | LAST WARNING CRY | 2 00 |
| THE GREAT CONSUMMATION | 2 00 | THE SEVENTH VIAL | 2 00 |

## Stephe Smith.

ROMANCE AND HUMOR OF THE RAILROAD.—Illustrated.................... $1 50

## Plymouth Church,—Brooklyn.

A HISTORY OF THIS CHURCH ; from 1847 to 1873.—Illustrated................ $2 00

## Orpheus C. Kerr.

| | | | |
|---|---|---|---|
| O. C. KERR PAPERS.—4 vols. in 1 | $2 00 | THE CLOVEN FOOT.—A novel | $1 50 |
| AVERY GLIBUN.—A novel | 2 00 | SMOKED GLASS.    Do. | 1 50 |

## Miscellaneous Works.

| | | | |
|---|---|---|---|
| BRAZEN GATES.—A juvenile | $1 50 | CHRISTMAS HOLLY.—Marion Harland | $1 50 |
| ANTIDOTE TO GATES AJAR | 25 cts | DREAM MUSIC.—F. R. Marvin | 1 50 |
| THE RUSSIAN BALL (paper) | 25 cts | POEMS.—By L. G. Thomas | 1 50 |
| THE SNOBLACK BALL   do | 25 cts | VICTOR HUGO.—His life | 2 00 |
| DEAFNESS.—Dr. E. B. Lighthill. | 1 00 | BEAUTY IS POWER | 1 50 |
| A BOOK ABOUT LAWYERS | 2 00 | PASTIMES, with little friends | 1 50 |
| A BOOK ABOUT DOCTORS | 2 00 | WOMAN, LOVE, AND MARRIAGE | 1 50 |
| GOLDEN CROSS.—Irving Van Wart. | 1 50 | WILL'O-THE-WISP.—A juvenile | 1 50 |
| PRISON-LIFE OF JEFFERSON DAVIS | 2 00 | WICKEDEST WOMAN in New York | 25 cts |
| RAMBLES IN CUBA | 1 50 | COUNSEL FOR GIRLS | 1 50 |
| SQUIBOB PAPERS.—John Phoenix | 1 50 | SANDWICHES.—ArtemusWard (pa'r) | 25 cts |
| WIDOW SPRIGGINS.—Widow Bedott. | 1 75 | | |

## Miscellaneous Novels.

| | | | |
|---|---|---|---|
| MARK GILDERSLEEVE.—J. S. Sauzade | $1 75 | FAUSTINA.—From the German | $1 50 |
| FERNANDO DE LEMOS | 2 00 | MAURICE.—From the French | 1 50 |
| CROWN JEWELS.—Mrs. Moffatt | 1 75 | GUSTAVE ADOLF.—From the Swedish | 1 50 |
| A LOST LIFE.—Emily Moore | 1 50 | ADRIFT WITH A VENGRANCE | 1 50 |
| ROBERT GREATHOUSE.—J. F. Swift. | 2 00 | UP BROADWAY.—Eleanor Kirk | 1 50 |
| ATHALIAH.—J. H. Greene, Jr | 1 75 | MONTALBAN | 1 75 |
| FOUR OAKS.—Kamba Thorpe | 1 75 | LIFE AND DEATH | 1 50 |
| PROMETHEUS IN ATLANTIS | 2 00 | JARGAL.—By Victor Hugo | 1 50 |
| TITAN | 2 00 | CLAUDE GNEUX.—By Victor Hugo | 1 50 |
| COUSIN PAUL | 1 75 | THE HONEYMOON.—A love story | 1 50 |
| VANQUISHED.—Agnes Leonard | 1 75 | MARY BRANDEGEE.—Cuyler Pine | 1 75 |
| MERQUEM.—George Sand | 1 75 | RENSHAWE.—Cuyler Pine | 1 75 |

## Miscellaneous Works.

A BOOK OF EPITAPHS.—Amusing, quaint, and curious....(new)............ $1 50
WOMEN AND THEATRES.—A sketchy book by Olive Logan................... 1 50
SOUVENIRS OF TRAVEL.—By Madame Octavia Walton LeVert................ 2 00
THE ART OF AMUSING.—A book of home amusements, with numerous illustrations, 1 50
HOW TO MAKE MONEY ; and how to keep it.—T. A. Davies................... 1 50
ITALIAN LIFE ; and Legend.—Anna Cora Mowatt. Illustrated.............. 1 50
BALLAD OF LORD BATEMAN.—Illustrations by Cruikshank (paper)............ 25 cts
ANGELINA GUSHINGTON.—Thoughts on men and things.................... 1 50
BEHIND THE SCENES ; at the "White House."—By Elizabeth Keckley........ 2 00
THE YACHTMAN'S PRIMER. —For amateur sailors. T. R. Warren (paper)..... 50 cts
RURAL ARCHITECTURE.—By M. Field. With plans and illustrations......... 2 00
LIFE OF HORACE GREELEY.—By L. U. Reavis. With Portrait............... 2 00
WHAT I KNOW OF FARMING.—By Horace Greeley......................... 1 50
THE FRANCO-PRUSSIAN WAR IN 1870.—By M. D. Landon. With maps........ 2 00
PRACTICAL TREATISE ON LABOR.—By Hendrick B. Wright.................. 2 00
TWELVE VIEWS OF HEAVEN.—By Distinguished Divines.................... 1 50
HOUSES NOT MADE WITH HANDS.—An illustrated juvenile, illustrated by Hoppin 1 00
LIVING WRITERS OF THE SOUTH.—By Professor J. W. Davidson........ ... 2 00
CRUISE OF THE ALABAMA AND SUMTER.—By Captain Semmes ........... 1 50
NOJOQUE.— A question for a continent. By H. R. Helper. ...... 2 00
IMPENDING CRISIS OF THE SOUTH.     Do.      .... .............. 2 00
NEGROES IN NEGROLAND.          Do.      (paper)............. 1 00